Also by Lynsay Sands from Gollancz:

A Quick Bite
Love Bites
Single White Vampire
Tall, Dark and Hungry
A Bite to Remember
Bite Me If You Can
The Accidental Vampire
Vampires are Forever
Vampire, Interrupted
The Rogue Hunter
The Immortal Hunter
The Renegade Hunter
Born to Bite
Hungry For You
The Reluctant Vampire
Under a Vampire Moon
The Lady is a Vamp
Immortal Ever After
One Lucky Vampire
Vampire Most Wanted
The Immortal Who Loved Me
About a Vampire
Runaway Vampire
Immortal Nights
Immortal Unchained
Immortally Yours

Twice Bitten

LYNSAY SANDS

First published in Great Britain in 2018 by Gollancz
an imprint of the Orion Publishing Group Ltd
Carmelite House, 50 Victoria Embankment
London EC4Y 0DZ

An Hachette UK Company

1 3 5 7 9 10 8 6 4 2

A CIP catalogue record for this book is
available from the British Library.

ISBN 978 1 473 22157 4
eBook ISBN 978 1 473 22158 1

Printed in Great Britain by
Clays Ltd, St Ives plc

MIX
Paper from
responsible sources
FSC® C104740

www.lynsaysands.net
www.orionbooks.co.uk
www.gollancz.co.uk

One

Elspeth stumbled into her apartment, pushed the door closed, and leaned against it with relief. Normally she didn't mind living on the second floor, and wasn't bothered by the steep, narrow stairs leading up to it. Today was not normal. Today those stairs had been hell, and the pain of mounting them had left her shaky and sweaty.

Eager to reach her bed and collapse on it, Elspeth pushed away from the door and staggered up the hall. She dropped her keys and purse on the entry table in passing, and then shed her coat and tossed it over the couch as she crossed the living room. The apartment was dark and silent except for the soft shuffle of her feet on the hardwood floor as she made her way to the bedroom. Once there, she didn't bother to remove her clothes or even her boots, but simply stumbled to the bed and dropped to lie across the bottom. A cry of startled pain slid from her lips when her face slammed into something much harder and lumpier than her memory foam mattress should have been. When there was an answering shriek, and the bed moved under her, Elspeth instinctively rolled away.

Tumbling off the bed, she hit the floor with a hard jolt and squeezed her eyes closed as agony shot through her. She was aware of noise around her, a rustling from the bed and the patter of footsteps from the hall, but was too busy taking deep breaths to try to manage her pain, and didn't bother to look around until she heard, "What on earth is going on? Elspeth? What are you doing on the floor?"

Elspeth forced her eyes open. The lights were now on, and Martine Argeneau Pimms stood in the open bedroom door. Dressed in a long red silk nightgown, the tall blonde was peering at her as if *she* was the one out of place in her own apartment.

"Mother?" Elspeth said with bewilderment. "What are you doing here?"

"Your sisters and I decided to surprise you with a visit." She gestured to the bed, and Elspeth turned her head to see the twins, Julianna and Victoria, kneeling at the end of her bed in matching pink babydolls that did nothing to hide their voluptuous figures. They looked like the stars of a porn film, the Boobsy Twins, waiting for the pizza delivery guy.

"Surprise," they said together with a distinct lack of enthusiasm.

Elspeth just let her head fall back wearily to the floor and asked, "How did you get in?"

"Your landlord. He let us in after I explained we were family," Martine said with a shrug.

Elspeth sat up abruptly, alarm replacing the exhaustion of a moment ago. Her landlord was a lovely elderly lady named Meredith MacKay. "*He* let you in?"

"Yes, and he's a cutie," Julianna announced.

Victoria nodded. "A super cutie."

"Girls," Martine growled with irritation. "Enough of this nonsense. It's late, nearly dawn, and—Where are you going?" she interrupted herself to ask when Elspeth suddenly lunged to her feet and hurried past her.

Elspeth didn't respond. It would mean she'd have to stop grinding her teeth, and if she did that she wouldn't be able to prevent the moans and groans of pain she was desperately suppressing. Crossing back through her apartment, she grabbed her keys off the table where she'd just left them, and rushed out into the hall.

Much to Elspeth's relief, going down the stairs was much easier on her wounded leg and back than going up had been. Still, she was trembling by the time she got to her landlord's door. Elspeth knocked sharply and then began to rifle through her keys in search of the one to Meredith's apartment.

"Elspeth Pimms! What are you doing?" her mother hissed, coming down the staircase after her.

"It's fine, Mother. Go back upstairs," she whispered.

"No. Get back here! I want to talk to you. What are you doing getting home so late? And why aren't you obeying me? You . . ." Her words trailed off as Elspeth finally found the right key and quickly unlocked her landlady's door.

Pushing it open, Elspeth hurried into the apartment, nearly crashing into a large, burly man. Catching herself at the last minute, she stumbled to a halt and then gaped at the blond hunk in front of her. Her knock had obviously roused him from sleep. The man was sporting some serious bedhead, his short blond hair standing up in all directions above wide, startled baby-blue eyes in a chiseled face. He had pulled on jeans that, while zipped, were not buttoned, and he was shirtless, his wide, muscular chest bare . . . and damn, he smelled good, Elspeth thought as she stared at his beautiful chest and inhaled the deep, spicy aroma of him. A scent that was oddly familiar.

"El? How—? What are you doing here?"

That question in a bewildered tone drew Elspeth's attention away from the man's chest, and back to his handsome face. Frowning when she saw the combination of recognition and confusion on his face, she asked, "Who are *you*? And what are *you* doing in Merry's apartment?"

For some reason her questions made his head jerk back as if she'd surprised him. Before she could ponder that too long, footsteps sounded behind him.

"Good morning, Ellie dear. Perfect timing as always. The kettle just came to a boil."

Elspeth leaned to the side to peer around the large man, and smiled with relief when she spotted the white-haired woman standing in the kitchen doorway further down the hall. Noting that she looked fine and healthy, Elspeth said uncertainly, "Morning, Merry. Is everything okay?"

"Oh, yes, wonderful." The woman smiled at her brightly, skin wrinkling around twinkling blue eyes much like those of the man between them. "That young buck in front of you is my grandson, Wyatt MacKay. He came to visit . . . as a surprise," she added, her tone as dry as dust.

Elspeth's eyebrows rose a bit, and then understanding and sympathy covered her face. Meredith's son worked for a large insurance company. He'd started here in Toronto, but twenty years ago had been offered a promotion that had meant moving to British Columbia. Despite having to leave family and friends behind, he'd accepted and

moved there with his wife and their young son, Wyatt ...
who was obviously the now grown-up hunk standing in
front of her. That explained how Wyatt had known her
name, she supposed. No doubt Merry had mentioned her.
The question now was, why the "surprise" visit?

"Elspeth, come here, please."

Elspeth glanced over her shoulder, a little startled to
see her mother standing in the open doorway in her silk
robe. She'd quite forgotten she had her own visitors to
deal with.

"Is that one of your sisters, dear?" Meredith asked. "I
was a little surprised when Wyatt told me that your sisters had arrived and he'd let them into your apartment last
evening while I was having my bath. You didn't mention
they were coming."

Hearing the concern in the woman's voice, Elspeth
turned back and leaned to the side again to give her a re-
assuring smile around Wyatt's wide shoulders. "Because
I didn't know. My mother and sisters decided to *surprise*
me with a visit, too." Grimacing, she added, "It must be a
full moon or something."

"Yes," Meredith said with a conspiratorial grin.

"*Mother* and sisters?" Wyatt asked with surprise and
Elspeth realized her mistake. Her mother didn't look
a day over twenty-five, which was why she usually introduced her as a sister. Not doing so now had been a
slip-up. Before she could decide how to deal with that
slip-up, her mother spoke again.

"Well, we had to surprise you, Elspeth." Martine's
voice was grim. "If we waited for an invitation or for
you to come to us, we would never see you. You have not
come home once since taking that job at the university
and moving here."

"It's only been two months, mother," Elspeth ground out, turning back to the beautiful blonde. Her eyes narrowed when she saw that she'd entered the apartment and was moving toward her. Elspeth took a nervous step back, knowing that if her mother touched her she'd take control of her and make her leave. Actually, Elspeth was a little surprised that her mother hadn't already taken control of her, but then she recalled her mother's surprise that she wasn't obeying her and wondered if the pain she was experiencing was somehow interfering and making her able to resist.

"No dear, you moved in six weeks ago today," Meredith corrected her gently.

"Right," Elspeth said, turning to offer the woman a grateful smile before swinging back to her mother. "Not even two months, just six weeks without a visit. I don't know what I was thinking. I mean, I had just moved to a different continent, and I was getting settled into my new apartment, and preparing for the summer classes, as well as helping out Mortimer, but really I should have made time to fly back and forth from England every weekend to visit."

Martine narrowed her eyes and took another step closer. "Helping Mortimer?"

Eyes widening with alarm as she realized what she'd given away, Elspeth moved back and opened her mouth to try to fast-talk her way out of the corner she'd painted herself into. But all that came out was a weak "Uh" as she bumped up against the man still standing behind her.

Frankly, considering the alarm bells screeching in her head and the sudden cold sweats coursing up and down her body, even that pitiful response was impressive.

"Elspeth?" Martine's eyes were narrow and cold, Elspeth noted vaguely as she felt Wyatt's hands settle on her shoulders to balance her. Distracted by his touch, she barely heard her mother ask, "What have you—?"

"Oh, there's the kettle!" Meredith interrupted cheerfully as a whistling sound came from the kitchen. "Come along, dears, and we'll have a nice cup of tea. Do you like tea, Mrs. Pimms? If not, I can make some coffee."

There was silence for a moment as her mother kept Elspeth pinned with her gaze, but then she released her and offered Meredith a sweet smile. "Tea sounds lovely."

"Oh, good. I still have some cookies too. Wyatt made a good effort, but didn't quite manage to eat them all. They're homemade peanut butter chocolate chip," Meredith told her mother. "Elspeth just loves my cookies."

"I am sure she does," Martine said stiffly, and Elspeth bit her lip. Her mother was not the cookie baking type. Actually, her mother hadn't cooked a day in her life that Elspeth knew of.

"Come along then, girls, Wyatt," Meredith said firmly, turning back into the kitchen. "Let's have some tea and cookies."

Much to Elspeth's relief, her mother nodded and moved forward, but as she slid by her, Martine growled, "We shall talk about what you are doing for Mortimer when we return upstairs."

Elspeth grimaced, but nodded. "Of course, Mother."

"She's your mother?" Wyatt asked with obvious disbelief as her mother followed Merry into the kitchen. "She doesn't look old enough to be your mother."

"She's older than she looks," Elspeth said wearily, and when Wyatt just arched one eyebrow in question, she glanced toward the kitchen door and added spitefully, "It's amazing what a little dermabrasion and Botox can do."

"Botox!" The squawk was followed by her mother's head poking around the kitchen doorway to scowl at her. "I would never stoop to that poison." Turning her gaze to Wyatt, she added, "I just happen to have excellent genes."

Rolling her eyes, Elspeth limped around Wyatt, heading for the kitchen.

"Why are you limping?" Martine asked sharply as Elspeth moved past her into the room.

"It's nothing. I'm fine," Elspeth muttered, and then forced a smile as she walked toward Meredith. "What can I do to help, Merry?"

"Everything is pretty much ready, dear," her friend assured her with a smile as she set the kettle back on the stove with one hand, and dropped the lid on the steaming teapot with the other. "I had it all prepared and was just waiting on the water to boil. But you can take the plate of cookies to the table if you like. I'll get out another cup. I thought it would be just you, me, and Wyatt when I set them out."

"You were expecting her?" Wyatt asked, moving to take the tray holding the teapot, sugar, cream, plates, and spoons. He carried it to the table where Elspeth was setting down the cookies. Three cups already sat waiting on the table, she noted as she straightened.

"Oh my, yes. Ellie often stops in for tea when she gets home from work in the morning. It's a nice start to the day for me, and a chance to unwind before bed for her," Meredith said with a complacent smile.

Feeling his gaze on her, Elspeth glanced Wyatt's way, noting the various expressions crossing his face as he watched her. In the end, his expression settled into a combination of perplexity and suspicion. Elspeth supposed he was worrying that she was trying to worm her way into his grandmother's will or something. To be honest, after what had happened with Madeleine Cartwright, Meredith's previous tenant in the basement apartment, Elspeth supposed she couldn't blame him . . .

Which was probably why Wyatt was here, she thought suddenly. Elspeth knew Merry's son had been trying to convince the woman to move into assisted living ever since her husband's death five years ago. When Merry had confided that to her, Elspeth had thought it was to ease his guilt about not being here for her, but between Madeleine Cartwright's efforts to swindle her and an incident with a phone scam recently, Elspeth suspected the son, Wyatt's father, was concerned she might give away his inheritance. No doubt Wyatt had been sent to either convince her to move to an old folks' home, or find the evidence needed to prove she was incapable of caring for herself and force her into one.

Well, Elspeth thought now, if that was the case, she'd do whatever was necessary to prevent it. Merry loved her home and was perfectly capable of taking care of herself in it. She merely disliked driving now and needed a little help getting to the bank and the grocery store. There were services to help with that. As for Madeleine . . . well, Merry had trusted the wrong person there. However, that wasn't due to senility or any other age-related issue. It was just her sweet nature.

"Ellie is working nights?"

Groaning inwardly at her mother's sharp question, and knowing that gaining this kind of information was exactly why her mother had decided that tea sounded "lovely," Elspeth busied herself removing plates from the tray and setting one by each of the fancy and delicate china teacups with their beautiful hand-painted flowers.

She then walked back to the cupboards to fetch a fourth plate. Her mother wouldn't eat, but Elspeth knew that if she didn't fetch a plate, Merry would, so she saved her the trouble.

"Oh my, yes. Of course, as you know, she won't be once summer courses start up," Merry said, and Elspeth had to bite her lip. Unfortunately, her mother didn't know. At least, she hadn't known that Elspeth was working nights right now for the rogue hunters. And Elspeth had rather been hoping she never would. But Merry continued chattily, "Until then, though, she's been helping out that special division of the police and working nights to do it. You must be proud of her."

"Hmm." Her mother turned a sharp scowl on Elspeth.

"You work for the police?" Wyatt asked, and Elspeth was relieved to turn her attention away from her mother until she saw that Merry's grandson was looking like he wasn't sure what to make of that, or if he should even believe it.

"Yes, she does, dear. Ellie's a criminal behaviorist," Merry said, not hiding that she was impressed. "She'll be teaching criminology courses at the university once summer classes start. In the meantime, she's working for the police. In fact, Ellie's the one who realized what my former tenant, Madeleine, was doing and got her to confess and give back the money she'd stolen."

Not all of it, unfortunately. Madeleine had spent most of the money, but Elspeth had made her give back what remained and had then made up the difference herself. She hadn't told Merry that. She'd known the woman wouldn't accept her money. She'd also known Meredith needed it. The dear lady had a bit of a nest egg, and the rent she earned on the apartments covered her mortgage, utilities, and heat, but she still needed to eat and pay for the various medications she took for arthritis, high blood pressure, and other ailments.

Elspeth noted the way Martine's narrowed gaze shifted from her to Wyatt to Merry, and was quite sure her mother was reading their minds to find out what they were talking about. Whatever she learned, she pretended she hadn't and asked, "Who is Madeleine and what did she confess to?"

"Oh." Merry clucked and shook her head as she settled in a seat at the table. "She was my tenant in the basement apartment. She lived here for nearly a year before Elspeth moved into the upstairs apartment, and she . . ." Merry paused, her mouth tightening before she admitted unhappily, "I'm afraid my arthritis was acting up this winter past. I was having a little trouble getting around and Madeleine was sweet enough to offer to help with little chores, like shopping and banking and such. I thought she was so lovely for helping me like that, but shortly after Elspeth moved in, she realized Madeleine was doing more than helping me. She was helping herself to my accounts."

Meredith shook her head. "I was so surprised and disappointed when Elspeth made Madeleine confess what she'd been up to. I just don't know why she'd do that. I guess I was an old fool for trusting her, but she seemed so nice."

Elspeth reached out to pat Meredith's hand sympathetically. "She seemed nice to me too, Merry."

"Yes, but you saw through her act," Merry pointed out.

Aware that Wyatt was staring at her, Elspeth forced

a smile and lied glibly, "Actually, I just recognized her name from a report that crossed my desk on a previous case she was involved with."

Elspeth was quite used to lying. She'd been trained to it from birth . . . as all immortals were. Lying was a necessity to ensure the survival of their kind. Mortals would not take well to learning that they shared the world with immortals. Most would call them vampires, but that was a title her kind didn't care for. Besides, it didn't really fit them. Immortals were not dead and soulless as vampires were purported to be.

"This Madeleine woman had done this before?" Wyatt asked, his voice sharp.

"Apparently," Elspeth said with a shrug.

"Then why wasn't she charged in this instance?" he asked at once.

"Because I didn't want her charged," Meredith said firmly. "At least not on my behalf. I got my money back and I didn't want to go through all the trouble of a court case and the embarrassment of admitting to being conned like that. Besides," she added solemnly as she took the tea bags out of the pot, "Madeleine already has other charges to deal with. With or without my charging her, she is going to jail."

Elspeth merely nodded and murmured, "Thank you" when Meredith poured tea into her cup.

After ascertaining that Meredith didn't want to charge Madeleine, Elspeth had taken the woman to the police station and ensured she confessed to the other illegal activities she'd been involved with. Meredith hadn't been the first victim. In fact, Madeleine Cartwright hadn't even been her real name. Her birth name was Nina Albrecht. She'd taken on the Madeleine alias because she was already wanted by the police for several similar cases in Alberta, as well as fraud, shoplifting, and writing bad checks. Madeleine/Nina had been arrested on the spot, and since she'd already tried to evade the previous charges by fleeing to Ontario and changing her name, she wouldn't be let out of jail until the court case, and then she wasn't likely to get out for some years.

"What branch of the police department do you work for?" Wyatt asked Elspeth as his grandmother poured tea into his cup.

When Elspeth hesitated, it was Merry who answered.

"She works with a special division that goes over information and tips and decides which are most likely to need investigation, and which are bogus. She also sorts out the threat level involved with the ones that they deem are real," Merry told him, excited color in her cheeks.

Wyatt's eyebrows rose and he eyed Elspeth speculatively. "Something to do with Crime Stoppers?"

"Oh, no, it's far more extensive than Crime Stoppers," Meredith said at once. "They get tips and leads about things from all over North America; the US and Canada both. And it isn't just called-in tips. They track large purchases of certain items and such. It's a new initiative," she told him proudly, repeating Elspeth's own explanation a month earlier. "And very exciting."

"I didn't realize that any of our branches of the police worked directly with the US," Wyatt said, the suspicion in his eyes growing. "Except perhaps the Royal Canadian Mounted Police or the Canadian Security Intelligence Service."

Elspeth hesitated, and then just shrugged. Now that the adrenaline was dissipating, her earlier exhaustion and pain were returning and she simply couldn't be bothered to make up more lies or defend herself. She considered slipping into his mind to remove his suspicions, but was too tired even to do that. Meredith's grandson could think what he liked for now. She'd deal with him later if he became a problem. Her gaze slid over his hard eyes and grim expression. Wyatt was a very attractive man, or would be if he smiled, she thought.

"Elspeth?"

She glanced to her mother, eyebrows rising as she took in her concerned expression.

"You are swaying in your seat and you have got blood on Meredith's chair," she announced, getting to her feet.

Frowning, Elspeth looked down to see there was a smudge of blood on the pale gray, faux leather chair she was perched on . . . and she was indeed swaying, she noted with a little concern of her own. More worrisome than that, though, she was starting to have trouble focusing her eyes. She really should have grabbed blood when she got home this morning rather than stumbling to her room. She'd intended to but by the time she'd pulled into the driveway, her only objective had been to get to her bed.

"Can you stand?"

Elspeth refocused on her mother to see that she'd grabbed one of the napkins from the holder in the center of the table and was waiting to clean up after her. Nodding, Elspeth forced herself to her feet, but had to grab the table to steady herself as the room began to revolve around her.

Wow, I'm not in good shape, Elspeth acknowledged with surprise as she noted the way her legs were trembling. She was also sweating like crazy . . . and now the pain was becoming unbearable. *Oh jeez, this isn't good*, she thought with dismay.

"Not good at all," her mother agreed in a grim voice as she quickly wiped the blood off the chair. Crumpling the napkin in her hand, she then scooped Elspeth up as if she were still a child.

Elspeth gasped with surprise and glanced wildly around.

"I took control of them," Martine said even as Elspeth noted that both Meredith and Wyatt had blank expressions on their faces. Carrying her out of the kitchen, her mother added, "I've given them both a memory that you were weary and we left them to reminisce so that you could retire."

"Oh," Elspeth breathed and allowed herself to sag in her mother's arms.

"Do not fall asleep," her mother growled as she carried her out of Merry's apartment and upstairs to Elspeth's. "You have got some explaining to do."

Two

Two

"What happened?"

Elspeth jerked awake at her mother's question, and glanced around to see that they were entering her apartment. She'd obviously dozed off for a few seconds there, she thought as her mother kicked her apartment door closed behind them and continued, "How were you injured?"

"It's nothing," Elspeth muttered, and then frowned when her mother carried her into the living room, heading for her white sofa. "Not the couch! The blood will ruin it. Take me to my room. My bed has a protector to keep blood off the mattress."

Her mother paused, and pointed out, "The girls are sleeping in there."

"The girls can move," Elspeth said abruptly. "It's *my* bed."

"But where will they sleep?"

"A hotel?" Elspeth suggested dryly. She hadn't invited them here and wasn't at all pleased at this "surprise visit." She wasn't giving up her bed.

Her mother stiffened.

Suspecting she'd read her thoughts, Elspeth relented enough to say, "There's an air mattress in the linen closet. They can blow it up and sleep in the living room."

Nodding stiffly, Martine carried her into the hall leading to the bedrooms. Of course, Elspeth's bedroom door was closed. Her younger sisters must have closed it behind them and gone right back to sleep. Too bad. She wanted her bed. Elspeth leaned down to turn the doorknob when her mother paused.

"Wake up, girls," Martine caroled as she approached the bed. "Up and out of bed, please."

Neither girl obeyed, but Julianna did groan and pull her pillow over her head to muffle their mother's voice.

"Julianna and Victoria Argeneau Pimms, get up this instant!" Martine snapped.

That did the trick. Both girls opened their eyes and sat up at once.

"What's going on?" Julianna asked, peering at them bleary-eyed.

"Why are you carrying Elspeth?" Victoria asked on a yawn.

"Because she is bleeding and obviously injured," Martine snapped. "Now, both of you up and out of that bed at once. Julianna, pull the blankets back so I can lay Elspeth down, and Victoria, go fetch some blood from the kitchen."

The twins scrambled to do as they were told, Victoria bounding up to run across the bed in her pink babydoll and leaping off to race from the room. Meanwhile, Julianna crawled out to stand next to the bed so that she could fold the sheet and duvet back.

"Why are you putting her here?" Julianna asked suspiciously.

"Because it's my bed," Elspeth said dryly as her mother set her down and she sank into the soft, still-warm sheets.

"But we're sleeping here," Julianna pointed out with a scowl as their mother straightened and hurried out of the room.

"No, you're not," Elspeth countered. "You and Victoria can sleep in the living room on the blow-up mattress. It's in the linen closet."

"You're a terrible hostess," Julianna complained, stamping her foot. "You should be the one on the air mattress."

"I'm not a hostess at all. You weren't invited," Elspeth pointed out in a sharp voice. "And stop stamping on the damned floor. I have neighbors."

"So?" she asked with irritation. "If they come up to complain, we'll take control and send them on their way."

"You will do no such thing," Elspeth growled. "You'll be kind and courteous and apologize nicely and then leave Meredith and her grandson alone."

When Julianna merely glowered, Elspeth narrowed her eyes on her sister and asked, "Whose idea was this visit?"

She shrugged unhappily. "Mother was driving us crazy. Without you there to deflect some of her attention, she is beyond unbearable. So I suggested a visit to see if I wouldn't like to move here too, and then, of course, Victoria wasn't staying behind without me. Unfortunately, now Mother's decided that we should all move here," she ended with misery.

"Seriously?" Elspeth asked with dismay.

"Yeah, I know. Nightmare city, huh?"

"The nightmare is that I put up with that crap for over a hundred years before the pair of you were even born, and then I waited until you were both done with school before I finally moved to another continent to escape it, and you two couldn't last even two months before you came chasing after me, dragging her along with you?"

"You don't know what it's like," Julianna complained as Victoria returned carrying several bags of blood. "She won't let us go anywhere alone. Not even to the bathroom when we're out at restaurants, for God's sake. She makes us go together. And if we take more than a couple minutes, she follows to check on us."

"At least you have a twin to go with you," Elspeth pointed out. "Mother insisted on walking me to the bathroom like a two-year-old until I was over fifty."

"See! So you know how bad it is," Julianna said at once.

Victoria nodded as she dumped the bags of blood on the side of the bed. "It's cray cray."

Elspeth narrowed her eyes, refusing to feel sympathy for her sisters. She'd been the sole focus of their mother's vulture-like hovering for one hundred eleven years before the twins were born, and then she'd stuck around until now before making her great escape. She'd known her sisters wouldn't last as long as she had, but *six weeks*?

"Not even two months," she repeated grimly.

"It's easier with you around," Victoria said pleadingly. "Mother's focus is spread around a bit more, rather than lasering in on us."

Elspeth laughed without humor. "Well, I have news for you two. You aren't living here with me. Mother will no doubt buy a house somewhere on the outskirts of the city and move the two of you in there with her, and you're still not going to have me around to take some of the flak. At least, not in the house."

"No," Julianna groaned with dismay.

Victoria, however, predicted, "She'll make you move there too."

Elspeth shook her head firmly. "I'm out, and staying out."

"Yeah. Until she takes control of you and makes you move," Julianna said dryly.

Elspeth stiffened at the suggestion. She'd thought she'd escaped that sort of thing when she'd moved to Canada, but there was no reason her mother couldn't do that again just because they were no longer in England. This was exactly why Elspeth had arranged everything for the move ahead of time without telling her mother. She'd even waited until Martine was out of the country with her father and the twins before calling to tell her she was moving. She'd made that call from the taxi on the ride to the airport. It hadn't prevented Martine giving her hell over the phone, but at least she hadn't been able to stop her. Now, thanks to her sisters, all that effort had been for nothing.

"Julianna, Victoria, fetch the air mattress out of the linen closet and get it ready. You two should be in bed," Martine said firmly as she returned carrying a bowl of steaming water, a washcloth, and a towel. "And Elspeth, you get started on consuming that blood," her mother ordered as she set the bowl of water on the bedside table.

Elspeth promptly picked up one of the bags Victoria had dumped on the bed and slapped it to her fangs. So long as she had a bag in her mouth, she couldn't be made to talk. Of course, she couldn't prevent her mother from reading her mind and talking to her, she realized as her mother caught her arms to pull her into a sitting position and then set to tugging her jacket off as she accused, "You lied to me."

"Uh-uh," Elspeth muttered around the bag in her mouth.

"You said you were coming here for a teaching position. That you could not continue to teach in England because everyone knew everyone else in the industry and it would soon become obvious that you were not aging. That it was smarter for you to move out of country and you preferred Canada because we have so much family here." She tossed the jacket aside and set to work on the long-sleeved black cotton shirt she wore as Elspeth nodded vigorously to indicate that had been the truth.

Her mother ignored the gesture and continued, "And yet here you are, not teaching, but working as an Enforcer, hunting down rogues."

Much to her relief, the bag at her mouth was just finishing at that point. Ripping it from her mouth, Elspeth said quickly, "I will be teaching at the university as soon as the summer classes start. I just thought since I had some time on my hands I'd help out at the Enforcer House until then. You know how shorthanded they are what with more than half their force down in Venezuela. They need help. And I'm not hunting down rogues. I'm mostly analyzing the tips and deciding which are soft calls and which are more dangerous."

The last few words came out muffled as her mother had forced her other arm out of her shirt and chose that moment to tug it off over her head. Tossing it aside, Martine turned to survey her blood-covered side and back. Her mouth tightened. "How does analyzing tips get you stabbed?"

Elspeth twisted around, just barely managing to get

a look at the large wound in her lower back. The sight made her wince. It was much nastier than the slice she'd taken to the leg. Unfortunately, her assailant hadn't just stabbed her in the back. He'd twisted the knife, carving a two-inch hole that was taking much longer to heal than a normal knife wound would. Grimacing, she met her mother's gaze and said, "It was—"

"Do not lie to me and tell me you have not been going on calls," Martine snapped, cutting her off. "I read your mind and already know you checked out a tip tonight on your way home."

Heaving a sigh, Elspeth shook her head. Honestly, having a mother who could read your mind was a real pain. It made for extremely well-behaved and miserable children.

"Fine," she said, the word short. "I sometimes go on soft calls on my way home if they're on my route. Mortimer doesn't know," she added quickly. "And I only ever check out the soft calls, or what the hunters call joke jobs. They are the ones I assess as not being dangerous."

"Well, you got it wrong this time," her mother said, her expression tight. "This was not a soft call. It was dangerous."

"It *was* a soft call," Elspeth assured her. "There was no rogue immortal involved, just a mortal with mental health issues. He was delusional and certain his neighbor was a vampire." Scowling, she added, "Unfortunately, once I realized that, I let my guard down. I followed his wife into the kitchen to talk to her about getting him put in the hospital. He must have been listening outside the door. He decided I must be a vampire too, and the minute I left, he stabbed his wife for colluding with vampires. I heard her scream and rushed back inside, but he was waiting behind the door. He stepped out and stabbed me from behind when I entered."

Pausing, she sighed wearily and then shook her head. "I was too startled to react until he'd twisted the knife, and then he got in a slash on my leg as I turned to confront him. But then I knocked him out and called the mortal police to tend to the woman and take the husband into custody. But," she added firmly, "it *was* just a mortal. A soft call."

"Hmm." Mouth tight, Martine urged Elspeth to turn onto her uninjured side on the bed so that she could wash away the blood on her back.

Much to Elspeth's relief, when her mother finished cleaning the area, no more blood bubbled to the surface. The bleeding had stopped and the wound itself was smaller. Healing.

"If he was mentally disturbed, you couldn't wipe his memory alone," her mother said with a frown. "Did you call Mortimer so that he could arrange it?"

Elspeth lifted her gaze from her wound to meet her mother's eyes. Grimacing, she admitted, "No. I planned to tell Mortimer all about it when I go in tonight. I thought it could wait since the man is mad and no one would take him seriously anyway."

"Not good enough," Martine said sternly. "I will call Mortimer immediately and have him take care of it." Martine set the bloodied cloth in the water and stood up. "What is the man's name and where was he taken?"

Elspeth rattled off the information, relieved to have the woman turn her attention to something else. Otherwise, she had no doubt her mother would be even now continuing to strip her to get to her leg. It was the kind of thing she'd fled England to escape, being controlled and treated like a child. And she'd done it. She'd got away and lived like a real grown-up woman for six whole weeks.

"I presume you at least took control of the police and ensured they didn't remember you?" Martine asked as she picked up the wireless phone on Elspeth's bedside table and punched in numbers.

"Of course, Mother," Elspeth said with exasperation.

"Do not 'of course, Mother' me. You did not ensure the madman was handled. How am I to know you did not leave the police with their memories too?" she asked sharply.

"Because I'm not an idiot," Elspeth said resentfully, but her mother wasn't listening. Mortimer had apparently answered.

After gesturing sternly at the blood bags on the mattress next to her, Martine moved away to explain the situation to Mortimer.

Elspeth grabbed another bag and popped it to her fangs with relief. She should have headed to the refrigerator and taken in blood the minute she arrived home the first time. In fact, seeking out her bed instead had been incredibly stupid. If her sisters hadn't already been occupying it, and she'd simply have flopped on the bed and passed out . . . Well, she wouldn't have died, but she would have woken up in horrible pain later.

Elspeth could only think that shock from her injuries was the reason she hadn't gone for the fridge when she first got home.

But it had been anxiety and a shot of adrenaline that'd had her racing down to her landlady's door the moment she heard that a man had let her mother and sisters into her apartment, she acknowledged as she tugged the empty bag off her fangs and slapped a fresh one to it. She'd feared the worst for Meredith. That either the woman had suffered a heart attack or stroke and a friend or family member had been in the apartment gathering things for her, or that someone had broken in and, having tied up Meredith, had pretended to be the landlord when her mother and sisters had knocked.

Finding Meredith's grandson there had been something of a surprise, but not as surprising as how ridiculously attractive the man was. The pictures Meredith had of Wyatt and his parents were somewhat old. In them, Wyatt hadn't been any older than fourteen or fifteen. He'd been attractive even then, but in more of a cute way, rather than the sexy-virile-well-built-stud way he was now.

"I realize you did not know, Mortimer," Martine growled as Elspeth switched the now empty bag at her mouth for another full one. "That is not the point. She cannot be allowed to go out on calls. She is not a hunter."

Elspeth rolled her eyes. She was one hundred forty-two years old and her mother still felt she had the right to interfere in her life.

"What do you mean, how are you supposed to stop her when you did not know she was doing it in the first place? Order her not to."

Elspeth snorted at the suggestion. That wasn't going to work. She was a volunteer. Mortimer wasn't her boss. Besides, compared to her mother, he was a pussycat. She wasn't the least afraid of him. She'd still check out soft calls if they were near enough. She just wouldn't get caught the next time. What were the chances she'd get stabbed again?

No, Elspeth thought as she switched out for the last bag, her mistake here had been letting her guard down once she was assured she was dealing with mortals. She'd know better next time . . . and there would be a next time, because she had every intention of continuing to help out by checking nearby soft calls on the way home.

Feeling a slight ruffling in her thoughts, Elspeth stiffened, her gaze shooting to her mother. As she'd feared, the woman was staring at her, eyes narrowed, a look of concentration on her face. Dammit! She was reading her mind, Elspeth realized, and immediately began reciting "Mary Had a Little Lamb" in her head.

"Too late," Martine growled, and turned her attention to the phone again, saying, "Fine. Mortimer, since Elspeth won't listen to you or me, you have yourself one more hunter. I shall be working with Elspeth from now on. Wherever she goes, I go."

Ah, crap, Elspeth thought and dropped back on the bed.

"**W**hat do you think, dear?"

Wyatt nodded absently at his grandmother's question, but his attention was already split between the dishes he was rinsing and his thoughts, and he didn't really catch what she'd said. He couldn't seem to stop thinking about Elspeth. He couldn't believe he'd found her again. Even more amazing was the fact that she didn't seem to even remember him. Had their encounter four years ago meant so little to her? It had been life-altering for him. He'd searched for her for months after that first meeting, and while he hadn't been able to find her, he'd never been able to forget her either.

"Wyatt?"

His grandmother's sharp voice pulled him from his thoughts and he glanced around in question.

"I said, I'm thinking of inviting Ellie and her family to dinner tonight," she told him, her voice a touch dry. "What do you think?"

"Sounds good," he said at once and turned back to the dishes, his eyebrows drawing together as he tried to recall when Elspeth and her mother had left. He had a vague recollection that El had been tired and they'd left to allow him and his grandmother to visit. But that's all. He had no memory of walking them out, which he definitely would have done. He'd been raised to perform such niceties, but it also would have allowed him to ensure the door was locked behind them.

That thought made him pause. After the barest hesitation, he set the teacup he'd been rinsing into the sink and turned off the tap. Drying his hands on the dish towel slung over his shoulder, he headed out of the kitchen.

"Where are you going?" his grandmother asked with surprise.

"I just want to be sure the door is locked," Wyatt explained as he started up the hall.

"Oh, I'm sure it is," Meredith said, following him. "Ellie is always fretting about that, insisting I lock the door behind her, or locking it herself. She—Oh," she ended weakly as he reached the door, saw it was unlocked, and locked it. "How strange. She always fusses about that. She really must have been tired. I hope she isn't coming down with something. She was very pale this morning."

Wyatt turned back to see that his grandmother was frowning as she turned into the kitchen. Swinging back to the door, he tried the knob just to be sure the lock had caught, and then followed her, a thoughtful expression on his face.

"Gran?" Wyatt moved up next to where she was finishing up the teacups. She'd insisted they were too delicate for the dishwasher and had to be hand-washed.

"Yes, dear?" she murmured, concentrating on what she was doing.

"El knocked and then let herself in before I could get to the door," he said slowly.

"Yes. She has a key," his grandmother said easily.

"A key?" he asked.

"Yes, dear. It's a little metal thing that opens locks," she explained lightly.

"I know what a key is," Wyatt said with exasperation. "But why does she have one?"

"Why, so that she can unlock the door, of course," she said with amusement.

"But Gran, you barely know her. You said yourself she's lived here less than two months."

"I may not have known her long, but I know her well. She's a dear girl. Completely dependable. I trust her."

"You trusted Madeleine too," he pointed out, and immediately felt bad when he saw her flinch at the reminder. It wasn't that he didn't trust El. At least, Wyatt wanted to trust her. But she had promised to meet him and then hadn't, and now he found her ensconced in one of his grandmother's apartments, yet acting as if she'd never even met him.

"Madeleine fooled me," Meredith acknowledged now. "But Ellie is not Madeleine."

"No, I'm sure she's not," he said soothingly, even though he wasn't at all sure that was true. "Still, don't you think that you should take what you learned from

Madeleine and perhaps be a little more cautious with people?"

His grandmother was silent for so long, Wyatt began to think she wasn't going to respond, but then she turned and peered at him solemnly. "Wyatt, if you go through life suspecting everyone, you will never know who might be trustworthy."

"And if you go through life trusting everyone, you're going to be robbed blind," he countered at once.

Meredith's mouth tightened with displeasure. "I don't trust *everyone*."

"Gran, you made a mistake trusting Madeleine and now have given Ellie a key after—How long has she had a key?"

"Two weeks," Meredith said stiffly.

"One month, then. You gave her a key after knowing her only a month. Don't you think that's a bit risky?"

"No, I don't," she said resentfully.

"Next you'll be giving her your banking information like you did Madeleine," he said with a frown, worried now that his father might be right and his grandmother had reached that age when she needed help taking care of herself. Maybe a seniors' home was a good idea.

"I'm not an old fool, Wyatt," Meredith snapped impatiently. "I knew Madeleine for eight months before I trusted her with my accounts and such, and she gave me no reason to worry about what she might do. Yes, I was wrong," she added quickly when he opened his mouth to comment, "but I know I'm not wrong this time. Ellie works with the police. She is also the one who discovered what Madeleine was doing, put an end to it, and made her pay me back. Ellie's a very trustworthy and responsible young woman, and she's my friend." Eyeing him sternly, she added, "And you will be nice to her while you are here, or you will be invited to leave."

Wyatt's jaw dropped and his eyes widened incredulously. He was her grandson, for God's sake, and Ellie was nearly a stranger . . . at least, to her. Really, Elspeth was a stranger to him now too, though he'd thought once that he knew her well.

"And I will not be moving into an old folks' home."

Wyatt snapped his jaw shut, and avoided her eyes guiltily. "Who said anything about an old folks' home?"

"Didn't I mention that I'm not an old fool?" she asked with some asperity. "I haven't seen you for years. Ever since joining the army, you've been too busy to visit, and then this Madeleine business happens and suddenly you arrive as a surprise to see me?" She snorted. "Not likely. Your father sent you to make sure I wasn't giving away his inheritance and to see if you couldn't shuffle me into a home."

"Now, Gran—"

"Who told him about Madeleine?" she asked abruptly. "Oscar?"

Wyatt grimaced. It *had* been Uncle Oscar. Wyatt didn't say so. At least not verbally, but apparently his expression said it for him.

"I knew it," she said with disgust. "I told Violet, and she would have run right home and told him. True to form, he then tattled to your father." She turned back to the sink, muttering, "I don't know why my sister ever married that man. Or why she has to tell him every damned thing I say."

"Oscar's just worried about you, Gran," Wyatt said wearily. "First you got caught up in that iTunes scam, and then—"

"I didn't get caught up in it," she countered quickly.

"When Uncle Oscar and Aunt Violet arrived, you were on your way out the door with the phone to your ear, heading to the bank to get out money to—"

"I wasn't going to get out money," she insisted. "I was going to go to the bank and ask them first if the iTunes cards that fellow was talking about were real and if the government did take them in lieu of payment as he suggested. If they said no I would have hung up. I just didn't know. I don't use the computer. I have no idea what newfangled things they have out there nowadays, and that man was yelling at me!" she cried, growing increasingly agitated.

"All right, Gran. It's all right," Wyatt said soothingly.

"No, it's not. Oscar's doing his damnedest to convince your father that I'm an incompetent old fool, and it's working. But it just isn't so. I don't need to go into a home. I still have my faculties," she finished, her face flushed with hectic color and her lips trembling.

"Okay. I'm sorry. It's okay." Wyatt crossed the space between them and hugged her gently. "Everything will be okay."

His grandmother sniffled into his chest and shook her head. "No, it won't. Oscar's a spiteful old bastard. He wants to get back at me for telling Violet to leave him, and he won't stop until he succeeds in seeing me into a home."

Wyatt's eyebrows rose. "You told Aunt Violet to leave Uncle Oscar?"

"Repeatedly," she said angrily. "The bastard was always cheating on her, but now he's violent as well and hitting her. I've been telling her to leave him for years."

Frowning at this news, Wyatt patted her back, but was

thinking he'd have to look into Uncle Oscar and Aunt Violet while he was here.

"Ask Ellie," his grandmother said suddenly. "She'll tell you I'm not going senile."

"She hardly knows you, Gran," he said solemnly.

"She does so," she insisted. "She has tea with me every morning, and quite often has dinner with me before leaving for work each night too. We spend a lot of time together."

Wyatt's mouth tightened at this news. It just didn't seem right. What the hell was a young woman like Ellie doing hanging around with an old woman all the time? What was she after?

"The poor girl has been lonely since moving here. She will make friends eventually, but right now she's missing her family and her home in England. Well, she was. Now they're here and I don't suppose she misses them as much." A soft chuckle slipping from her lips, she added, "In fact, I suspect she's probably wishing they'd never come."

"Why?" he asked with curiosity.

"Because her mother is apparently a bit overbearing and tends to interfere in her daughters' lives. That's why Ellie moved here from England in the first place, to get away from her. But despite that she, of course, missed her."

"Isn't that kind of contradictory?" he asked, wondering about El's mother. Elspeth hadn't said anything to him about that the first time they'd met, but then, she hadn't talked about her family at all.

"No," Meredith said, surprising him. "It's like any bad relationship. A girl can leave, and know she made the right decision, but still miss parts of that relationship. Nothing is bad twenty-four hours a day. But when the bad outweighs the good, it's time to go. That doesn't mean you won't miss that little bit of good afterward." Shrugging, she backed out of his hold, and said, "Of course, Elspeth missed the good parts of having a mother, and distance makes the bad stuff fade somewhat, but about now she's remembering exactly why she moved to another continent."

"Hmm," Wyatt murmured. El's mother had seemed nice enough to him. Well, except maybe for the fact that she'd come wandering in wearing nothing but a nightgown and robe. That had seemed a little . . . odd.

"Oh!"

"What?" Wyatt glanced to his grandmother anxiously at that cry. "What's wrong?"

"I'm missing my game shows," she exclaimed and hurried out of the kitchen.

Wyatt watched her go and then shook his head and sat down at the kitchen table. He was in a hell of a spot here. His grandmother was right. Uncle Oscar did have his father convinced that she needed to be in a home, and he *had* asked Wyatt to come out, expecting him to arrange that.

The problem was, Wyatt wasn't so sure she needed to be in one. Meredith had seemed fine when he'd arrived here yesterday afternoon. They'd had tea and talked, and then he'd taken her out to dinner, and they'd talked some more. Actually, they'd talked most of the evening, and she'd seemed as sharp as ever. Until he'd learned she'd given El a key to her apartment and such. Her trusting a virtual stranger so much so quickly seemed a little iffy.

And then there was that business of the iTunes scammer. Apparently, several older people had been convinced to buy thousands of dollars in iTunes cards, then read out the code numbers over the phone to people claiming to be tax collectors. They called suggesting that they owed thousands in unpaid taxes, and threatening to repossess their homes and such if they didn't comply. He'd thought it a ridiculous scheme when he'd heard about it, and that anyone taken in by it must be incompetent, but his grandmother's words had made him think again. She didn't even own a computer, probably had no idea what iTunes was, and if the man had been yelling and frightening her, she would have been flustered and upset and more likely to at least find out what the bank thought.

Her claim that Uncle Oscar was just out to get her back for suggesting Aunt Violet leave him troubled Wyatt. He didn't know the couple well. He hadn't seen them since his parents had moved him to British Columbia. Actually, he hadn't seen them much before that. Aunt Violet was his Gran's sister and they were actually a great-aunt and -uncle, so he'd never been close with them. But from what he recalled, he'd never thought much of Uncle Oscar the few times he *had* encountered him.

Standing up, he placed one hand on the back of the chair next to where he'd been sitting. The seat El had occupied when she and her mother were here. He ran his hand along the seat back, his memory drawing up her image again. It had been four years since he'd last seen her, and she'd looked exactly the same today as she had that day in the café. And his feelings on seeing her?

Wyatt blew out a breath. It hadn't just been his mind that had recognized her. His body had too, and had responded just as it had all those years ago. If he hadn't been so shocked to see her standing there, he would have pulled her into his arms and held her hard and tight and never let her go. But shock had stopped him just long enough for her to ask who he was, and then he hadn't known what to do or how to act with her. He still didn't. How could she not remember him? Or perhaps the question was, why was she pretending not to remember him? He needed to bide his time and find that out. So, he now had two projects here—settle the business with his grandmother, and find out whether El remembered him or not and why she would claim not to if it was all an act.

Three

"Mother's right, Juli. Ellie's going to be more than just upset when she finds out what we've done. She's going to wake up in pain and needing blood and will be royally pissed when she learns we drank it all."

Elspeth's footsteps slowed midway across the living room as she heard Victoria's comment coming from the kitchen. Her sister was right. She had woken up in pain and needing blood. The healing had begun in earnest the moment she'd finished the last bag of blood that morning, and had quickly become agonizing. It had been noon before the worst of it was over and she'd fallen into an exhausted sleep. Elspeth had only managed four hours of sleep before the terribly painful cramping of her body's need for blood had forced her back to consciousness.

She'd woken up half an hour ago, dragged herself from bed and headed for the bathroom for a quick shower to rinse the dried blood away before examining her wounds in the mirror. They were healed, at least on the surface.

But the cramps of hunger weren't the only pain Elspeth was suffering. The deep throbbing ache in her lower back told her there was still healing going on inside, muscle being reknit together and deep tissue being repaired.

Taking long, slow breaths to fight the pain, Elspeth had quickly dried herself off, scraped her wet hair back into a ponytail, and dressed in a pair of black jeans and a T-shirt. She'd then left her room, eager to get to the kitchen and down five or six more bags of blood to ease her pain . . . at least the cramping. The pain of healing itself wouldn't stop until the nanos were done their work, but she could stand that, so long as the sensation of acid pouring through her veins and attacking her organs was abated. Only consuming more blood would do that.

Except, if what she'd just heard was true? It sounded like there was no blood, and no relief from this pain. Elspeth's hands curled into fists at her sides. Victoria was right. She was royally pissed that they'd drank all her blood.

"Serves her right for making us sleep on the air mattress," Julianna said without sympathy. "She could have let us have the bed and slept on the couch. It's comfortable enough. Or she could have shared the bed in the guest room with Mother. But no, she had to have her bed all to herself and stick us on that godawful air mattress. I didn't sleep at all. I don't know how you did."

"I didn't," Victoria admitted. "I just pretended to sleep so I wouldn't have to listen to you rant and rave."

"Nice," Julianna said with disgust.

"Sorry," Victoria said, actually sounding remorseful, and then added defensively, "But Juli, you've been going on about Elspeth's moving to Canada for six weeks now."

"Well, she did. She just packed up and snuck off while

we were in Italy. No warning, not even a hint until that phone call."

"She's one hundred forty-two years old, Juli. It was past time she moved out on her own," Victoria said solemnly.

"Yeah, but she could have at least taken us with her."

"And how could she have done that?" Victoria asked with exasperation. "The only reason she managed to move out this time was because Mother was out of the country. If we'd been in England, Mother would have been too, and she would have taken control of Elspeth and stopped her again as she has every other time Ellie's even brought up the idea of moving out."

Mouth tightening, Elspeth closed her eyes. She'd wanted to move out on her own since her fifties, when it began to become acceptable for women to work and live independently. That was early on in the twentieth century. Women had got the vote in the 1920s and had soon started to go for higher education and degrees. More and more women had joined the working force, and started living alone. Elspeth had wanted to be one of those women, but every time she'd brought it up, her mother had talked her out of it.

Elspeth had always suspected her mother had used some mind control to help "convince" her. But those suspicions had always faded almost as soon as she had them, and only cropped up again when her mother wasn't around. Noticing that, Elspeth had, this time, kept her plans to herself, refusing to even think of them in her mother's presence. It was also why she'd planned leaving for when she knew her mother wouldn't be home, or even in England.

And it had worked. She'd had six full weeks of blissful independence, and had loved every moment of it. But that was now over. Her mother had followed her here to Canada, and it looked like she planned to stay.

Thanks to Julianna and Victoria, Elspeth thought with irritation. Honestly! She'd put up with their mother's smothering helicopter parenting for nearly a century and a half, and her sisters couldn't give her more than six weeks before dragging their mother over here after her?

Scowling now, Elspeth continued on into the kitchen and speared her sisters with a glare as she took in the empty blood bags on the table between them. There were ten in all, she saw at a glance. Every last bag she'd had . . . and two more than they'd normally consume in a twenty-four-hour period.

"Oh, good afternoon, Elspeth. How are you feeling?" Julianna asked sweetly.

"Like I should kick your ass," she said grimly. "You couldn't even leave me *one* bag of my own blood? You knew I was healing and would wake up in pain and needing it."

"Oh, I'm sorry, sister. We didn't expect you up so early. Although we've been up for hours ourselves, *it being so uncomfortable on that air mattress*," she finished sharply.

"Get used to it," Elspeth responded coldly. "Or better yet, go check into a hotel."

"Girls!" Martine hurried into the kitchen, silencing them with a look, before saying impatiently, "It is beyond me why the three of you cannot get along."

Elspeth scowled, but merely said, "I gather you didn't bring blood with you?"

"No," Martine admitted on a sigh. "But I called Argeneau Enterprises and ordered some. I gather they're busy and weren't going to deliver any until tomorrow, but—" she added quickly when Elspeth gasped in dismay and opened her mouth on a protest "—I called your cousin Bastien. He's having someone deliver a shipment later tonight. Thank goodness he runs the place," she added in a mutter.

Elspeth merely grunted and then turned to scowl at her sisters.

"Your sisters are sorry they thoughtlessly consumed every last bag of your blood," her mother added, glaring at the twins. "They were not thinking."

"Right, and the fact that they glutted themselves on five bags each in a couple of hours when they normally have only three or four bags each in a twenty-four-hour period supports that theory," Elspeth growled and spun on her heel to stride angrily from the kitchen. Fuming, she marched to the hall table, grabbed her keys and purse, and turned to open the door.

"Stop!"

Elspeth stopped so abruptly she almost overbalanced. Throwing out one hand, she caught at the hall table to save herself and then found herself turning to face her mother.

"What is it, Mother?" she asked wearily.

"Come back to the kitchen and have some juice or something. You can hold out until the blood gets here, I'm sure."

Elspeth took a step toward her before the pain cramping her body made her stop and shake her head. She noted the startled look on her mother's face, but simply turned and moved back to the door, muttering, "I'm in pain and need blood now."

She made it out onto the landing before her mother hurried after her.

"You cannot leave."

Her mother sounded shocked, Elspeth noted, and suspected Martine was trying to control her again, but wasn't able to. Apparently, her pain was helping her fight the iron-like control her mother had always had over her thoughts and actions. *Interesting*, she thought grimly, but merely picked up her pace, afraid her resistance might not last long.

"Elspeth."

She heard the tap of Martine's heels as her mother hurried after her, but didn't even dare look back as she started down the stairs.

"Where are you going?"

"To The Night Club," she answered shortly.

"You cannot," her mother protested at once. "Your friend Meredith invited us to dinner tonight. You do not have time to go out for blood first."

Elspeth stopped again and turned on the step to peer up at where she stood on the landing. "Dinner?"

"Yes."

"And you agreed?" she asked with surprise.

"The girls were hungry and there was no food here," Martine said, taking a step down.

Elspeth scowled. "There is plenty of food here. There are fruits and vegetables, yogurt, eggs, bread, and meat in the freezer."

"Yes, but there is nothing here that your sisters will eat," Martine said with frustration.

"Because you don't cook, and they haven't bothered to learn how to," Elspeth said with irritation, then rubbed her throbbing forehead and said, "You'll have to go to dinner without me."

"What?" Martine gasped with dismay. "Don't be ridiculous."

"I'm not being ridiculous, mother," Elspeth said quietly. "I need blood. It's just good sense that I go and take care of that rather than risk being around mortals in this state."

"Or you could snack on Meredith's grandson," Martine suggested, and when Elspeth's eyes lifted to her with shock, she added, "Just a little to tide you over until the delivery arrives. This is an emergency, after all."

"It's not an emergency," Elspeth growled. "An emergency is when you need blood desperately and cannot get it readily anywhere else *but* from a mortal donor. I can go to The Night Club and get it."

"Well, then, I will go with you," Martine said at once, moving down another step toward her. "After all, the girls did not leave me any blood either."

Elspeth scowled at the suggestion and shook her head. "You're not—"

Her words died as her mother took another step down, bringing her close enough to reach out and take her by the wrist. The moment Martine's fingers closed around her skin, Elspeth's mind went blank and she forgot what they were arguing about.

She peered at her mother with bewilderment and then heard the outer door opening in the entryway below and the murmur of voices. Turning her head, Elspeth glanced over her shoulder to see Wyatt ushering an older couple into the entry. They brought with them a rush of cool air and a bevy of delicious scents, she noted as her mouth tightened at the sight of the couple.

Elspeth recognized Meredith's sister, Violet, at once. The two women were very similar in looks with trim figures, short white hair, and large blue eyes. Although

Merry's eyes always seemed to be twinkling with mirth and joy. That was not true of Violet, she noted. No doubt thanks to her husband, Oscar, Elspeth thought as her gaze slid over the tall, stick-thin, and mean-faced man.

"Oh, hello," Wyatt said as he noticed them on the stairs. He stared at Elspeth thoughtfully for a heartbeat, and then his gaze dropped to where her mother held her wrist. One eyebrow rose, but he merely said, "Perfect timing. Dinner's ready."

Elspeth's gaze shifted to the paper bags he held up. They bore the logo from a fried chicken franchise, but while they were emitting delicious scents, they weren't the source of the smell that had her stomach cramping.

"Lovely," Martine said behind her. "The girls are starved."

"Well now, Wyatt, you didn't mention we'd have two such sexy broads to dine with," Oscar said, leering up at them. "I wouldn't have given Vi such a hard time about coming if I'd known."

Elspeth saw the way Wyatt's expression tightened, and then the sound of rushing feet drew her gaze over her shoulder as Julianna and Victoria hurried out onto the landing above with excited faces.

"I told you I smelled food," Julianna said with satisfaction as she started down the stairs.

"Fried chicken," Victoria moaned, following her.

Wyatt turned to unlock Meredith's door and then stepped aside to allow Violet and Oscar to enter. When he then shifted his gaze expectantly to them, Martine moved to the side to allow Julianna and Victoria to pass, and then started down the stairs after them, using her hold on Elspeth's wrist to pull her along.

"Thank you," Julianna said as she snatched one of the bags of food in passing. Smiling cheerfully, she said, "We'll take this for you so you can get your coat off."

"Thanks," Wyatt said dryly as Victoria took the other bag. Shaking his head, he waited for Martine and Elspeth to follow the girls in, and then stepped inside and closed and locked the door.

Martine immediately ushered Elspeth and her sisters up the hall toward the kitchen, getting them out of the way for Violet, Oscar, and Wyatt to maneuver in the narrow entry.

"There you are." Meredith smiled in greeting around the open refrigerator door. "Everyone arrived at the same time, I see. What would you girls like to drink? I'm afraid I only have ginger ale or cola when it comes to soft drinks. But I have iced tea, juice, milk, and water or tea and coffee too."

"I'll have water, please, Meredith," Martine announced as Julianna and Victoria set the bagged food on the table and then rushed to join Meredith at the refrigerator. "And so will Elspeth. The twins will have milk."

"Milk with fried chicken?" Julianna squawked with dismay.

"It's good for you," Martine said firmly, ushering Elspeth to the table.

"Yes. It's good for us," Julianna agreed, her expression going blank.

"Milk would be delicious," Victoria added, her own face devoid of emotion.

Meredith's eyebrows rose at the abrupt about-face, but shrugged and retrieved the milk, saying, "Whatever you like."

"Take off your jacket," her mother ordered.

Elspeth automatically obeyed, slipping her jacket off one arm and then pausing until her mother let her go so that she could finish the task. However, the moment her mother released her, Elspeth's mind began to clear. Unfortunately, before it could clear enough for her to think to move out of reach, Martine took her other wrist in hand, silencing her thoughts once more. When her mother murmured, "Hang your jacket over the chair," Elspeth did so without hesitation. She draped it over the back of the chair, and then settled in it.

Martine promptly dropped into the seat next to her, still holding her wrist.

"Here we are then. All present and ready for the grub," Oscar said in a pompous voice as he entered the kitchen. "Thank God it's takeout and not some sad little attempt of yours to cook, Meredith. This should be edible at least."

Elspeth would have scowled at the man if she could have, but instead merely eyed him silently before glancing to Meredith to see the way she had stiffened, her mouth tightening. It was obvious she hadn't invited him to dinner, which Elspeth supposed meant Wyatt had. She had no idea why. Elspeth had encountered the man three or four times since taking up residence in the apartment upstairs. Meredith loved her sister and invited her over for tea weekly. Unfortunately, Violet didn't like driving any more than Meredith nowadays and Oscar had to drop her off and collect her. He didn't bother to get out of the car when he dropped Violet off, but he did come to the door to collect her when she was ready to go home and had invited himself in when he saw Elspeth there. Oscar was an odious creature who bounced between crude jokes and insulting everyone in his presence. He'd also made rather base passes at her. At least, he had the first time. She'd been too startled to do anything about it then, but when he'd started in on that nonsense on the visits since, she'd quickly taken control of his mind and shut him down. From what she could tell, the man was a pig who had made his wife, Violet, miserable for years and now seemed set on making Meredith's life as difficult as possible as well.

Elspeth's gaze shifted to Meredith's sister. Pale and almost shamefaced, Violet cast a quick glance to Merry before looking unhappily away. It didn't take mind reading, or even much thought, to know the woman was feeling guilty for what she'd told her husband and more so for what he'd done with the information. It was also pretty obvious Meredith hadn't yet forgiven her sister for it. Her face was set in a scowl, and the usually polite and generous woman didn't ask what Violet, Oscar, or even Wyatt wanted to drink. She merely pushed the two glasses of milk she'd poured along the counter toward the waiting Julianna and Victoria, and then quickly carried the three glasses of water she'd also gathered to the table. She set one in front of Martine, another in front of Elspeth, and then settled in the chair next to Elspeth with the third glass as Julianna and Victoria followed with their drinks.

"Well," Wyatt said after a brief pause. "Sit down, Aunt Violet, Oscar. What would you like to drink?"

Elspeth was vaguely aware of the couple's answering and Wyatt's puttering around, fetching drinks for them, but most of her attention was on Meredith. With the eight of them squeezed around the round table made for six, it was a bit cramped and Merry was close enough that they bumped arms on occasion. She could also hear her heartbeat—slightly elevated thanks to her agitation—as it pumped the sweet elixir of life through her veins. Blood. Elspeth fancied she could smell it there under Merry's thin, crepey skin. Deep, red, luscious blood that would ease her pain and sate her hunger.

"Elspeth."

Blinking at that sharp voice, Elspeth realized she had leaned toward Meredith and quickly straightened and turned to her mother. She noted her concerned frown, but then glanced around as Oscar said, "Shove over, Vi, and make room so the twins can sit on either side of me. I've always fancied being with twins."

"Stay put, Violet," Meredith growled, her body stiff. "The twins can sit between us."

"Always out to ruin my fun, aren't you, Meredith?" Oscar said, sounding churlish. "What's wrong with the girls sitting with me?" Shifting his gaze to Victoria and Julianna, he offered a lecherous smile and said, "I could be the thorn between two roses."

"You might prick them," Meredith snapped.

"That's the hope," he admitted with a laugh.

Meredith gaped at him with disgust. "Have you no shame? Your wife is sitting right beside you."

"So?" he asked with indifference.

"So?" she echoed with dismay and then glanced at her sister as if expecting her to speak up for herself. When Violet lowered her head, avoiding her eyes, Meredith's mouth tightened. Shifting hard eyes back to Oscar, she growled, "These girls are my guests. Stop acting like an old lecher and let them eat in peace."

Oscar's eyes narrowed and his mouth opened, and then just as suddenly snapped shut, his expression going blank. Elspeth knew at once that her mother had taken control of the man and shut him down before he could behave too badly. She wasn't sure that was a good thing. She thought Wyatt should probably see just what the man was truly like. At least then he'd know just who was carrying tales to Merry's son. Unfortunately, her mother had nixed that, and before Oscar had even said anything really bad. Still it had been enough to make Wyatt's mouth thin out with anger. He apparently didn't think much of his comments, Elspeth decided as she watched Wyatt carry the drinks he'd collected for himself and his aunt and uncle to the table and distribute them before taking his seat.

"Eat your food, Elspeth," Martine said suddenly, and Elspeth glanced down to see with some surprise that her plate was full of food. Somehow a piece of chicken, cole-slaw, macaroni salad, and fries with gravy had all landed on her plate. Her mother must have placed it there, Elspeth supposed. Certainly she hadn't put it there herself.

"Eat," Martine insisted quietly. "You will feel better."

Elspeth raised her hand to pick up the piece of chicken, but paused when her mother's hand followed, still attached to her wrist. She stared at it blankly, and then, aware of a sudden silence around the table, raised her head to peer from person to person. The twins were busy piling food on their plate, and Oscar was too preoccupied ogling the twins to notice anything else, but Meredith, Wyatt, and Violet were all peering at Martine's hold on her.

A moment passed in silence when she imagined her mother debated controlling everyone at once, and then Martine's mouth tightened and she released her wrist. The moment she was no longer in her hold, Elspeth's mind began to clear. She almost leapt to her feet at once, but realizing her mother was watching her tensely and would simply grab her again and take control once more, Elspeth forced herself to pick up the piece of chicken and take a bite. It was delicious, but while she was hungry for food, she positively *needed* blood. Her body was cramping painfully with that need. Trying to ignore it, Elspeth forced herself to eat, vaguely aware of, but paying little attention to, the conversation taking place around her until she felt Meredith stiffen at her side. She tuned in to the conversation just as Oscar said, "Yes, well, as I said, your grandmother's just got to that age where she can't be trusted to handle money anymore."

Elspeth narrowed her eyes on the man, slipped into his thoughts, and had him add what he was really thinking.

"Besides, the old bitch is always interfering. She never liked me. Thought Vi was too good for the likes of me just because I catted around a bit. What man doesn't bang all the bimbos he can, eh?" he asked, and when Wyatt simply stared at him with amazement, he added, "If that wasn't bad enough, now the old bitch has taken umbrage at my hitting Vi once in a while. Like it's my fault the woman's become a dried-up nag in her old age and needs correcting."

Oscar had been waving a chicken leg around as he spoke, but now bit into it, and chewed with satisfaction as everyone else stared in shock. Well, everyone but Elspeth and Meredith. This wasn't the first time they'd heard his opinions, and it seemed obvious Meredith was no more impressed than her to hear them again. But while Meredith looked furious, and Elspeth was angry on her behalf, it was Wyatt who responded. Setting down his fork, he sat back, took a deep breath and briefly contemplated his grandmother's angry face before turning to Violet to ask, "Do you really want to be with this man?"

"Of course she does," Oscar snapped, dropping the now gnawed chicken leg and reaching for the bucket to retrieve another. "Violet knows how lucky she is to have me. Who else would put up with her lousy cooking and nagging ways?"

"I asked Aunt Violet," Wyatt growled, and then peered at her expectantly.

When Violet hesitated, Elspeth shifted her gaze to the woman and slipped into her mind to read her thoughts. Much to her surprise, Violet didn't know what she wanted. She loathed her husband and the way he treated everyone, including herself. She always had. But she was afraid to be alone, and to her mind, she'd invested so much time in the man, she felt she had to stick it out.

Releasing her breath on a sigh, Violet shrugged unhappily. "I married him for better or worse."

Nodding, Wyatt stood and moved to grab his phone off the kitchen counter. After some tapping on the screen, he finally held the phone to his ear and then said, "Good evening. I'd like a taxi at—"

"Taxi?" Oscar interrupted, scowling at his nephew. "What the hell do you need a taxi for?"

Wyatt ignored him until he'd finished his call, and then hung up and said, "For you and Aunt Vi, Oscar. I assumed, since you obviously think so little of Grandmother, you'd want to leave her home. Immediately."

"Well, you thought wrong," the old man snapped. "I'm not done eating yet. Besides, you were supposed to drive us home. I'm not paying for any damned taxi."

"I'll pay," Wyatt said firmly as he set his phone back on the counter.

"Fine." Oscar shrugged indifferently, and then pulled

the bucket of chicken closer. "But the taxi will have to wait until I'm done eating."

Wyatt narrowed his eyes, and then began to search through the cupboards until he found his grandmother's plastic food wrap. Bringing it to the table, he tore off a sheet and wrapped it over Oscar's paper plate, announcing, "You can take your meal to go . . . and consider yourself lucky that I'm making that offer. You've insulted my grandmother and Aunt Vi both, and while Aunt Vi seems willing to put up with it, I won't have you insulting Gran in her own home. You aren't welcome here, Oscar."

The old man scowled briefly, and then stood and snatched away his plate. "Mouthy little shit. I'm going to tell your father about the shabby way you treat your elders. Don't think I won't."

"That's fine, because I plan to tell him about how disrespectful you are to *his mother*," Wyatt said coldly.

Grunting at that, Oscar turned and shambled out of the kitchen with his plate. "Come on, Violet. We'll wait for the taxi on the porch."

"You don't have to go," Wyatt said quietly when Violet stood to follow her husband.

Pausing, she offered him a pained smile. "Oscar and I have caused your grandmother enough trouble." She turned to Meredith then and said, "I'm sorry, Merry. I never should have told him about Madeleine. I was just so outraged at what she'd done, and I didn't think he could use it against you. I'm sorry."

Violet didn't wait for Meredith to respond, but hurried out of the room after Oscar.

Wyatt followed, presumably to pay the driver when he

arrived, and then Meredith stood and quickly wrapped up Violet's still full paper plate of food with more plastic wrap before rushing after them. The moment she'd gone, Elspeth sat back with a sigh. She'd needed to let Wyatt see what Oscar was really up to, but hated the idea that Meredith might have been hurt by Oscar yet again.

On the bright side, though, it looked like Meredith would never have to deal with the man again. Wyatt would see to that. And she was quite sure the odious man would never influence Wyatt's father again either. Meredith was, hopefully, now safe from the threat of being put in a home. On top of that, Elspeth had been given a break from the scent of mortals for a few minutes. Dear God, she needed blood, and if she didn't get some soon, she was definitely going to be a threat to Meredith and Wyatt.

That thought uppermost in her mind, Elspeth stood abruptly.

"Where are you going?" her mother asked sharply, reaching toward her.

Avoiding her hand, Elspeth stepped to the side so that her chair was between herself and her mother. Mouth tight, she said, "I'm going to go up and see if the blood was delivered while we were eating."

"Oh, that's not coming until midnight," Julianna said cheerfully.

"Midnight?" Elspeth asked sharply, her gaze shooting to her mother. Noting the way she was scowling at Julianna for spilling the beans, Elspeth growled and spun away to leave the room.

"Where are you going, Elspeth?"

Elspeth stopped in the hall the moment she spotted Meredith and the others beyond the open apartment door. Not wanting to risk running amuck and attacking one of them in her need for blood, Elspeth swung to the left to head toward the back of the apartment.

"Elspeth, where do you think you are going?" Martine demanded, hard on her heels.

"For some fresh air," Elspeth ground out, picking up speed to avoid being touched and controlled again.

Crossing Meredith's living room, Elspeth opened the sliding glass door and stepped out onto the porch. She then turned back and pulled the door firmly closed, scowling at her mother in warning as she did. Elspeth really didn't have the patience to deal with her just now and if Martine insisted on following and trying to touch her again, she was likely to hop over the porch rail and head straight for her car.

Elspeth suspected her mother was reading her and caught that last thought, for Martine stopped abruptly and then headed away, leaving her alone.

Releasing her breath on a sigh, Elspeth turned and paced to the rail. Fingers clenching the cold wood, she leaned against it and stared out at the garden. It was April, and the weather had been doing a crazy dance, one day warm enough that a jacket was unnecessary, the next cool enough that a winter coat was needed. Today it was somewhere in the middle. A light jacket would have been more comfortable and being without one left her chilled. Not that she really noticed. The pain eating her up inside was a tad distracting. All Elspeth could think of was the quickest way to get blood. She was not waiting until midnight, and she didn't want to rush out to the Enforcer House while Mortimer and Sam were trying to eat dinner. It was the only point in the day when the pair got any private time to themselves. Mortimer set it up that way, sending hunters out on their evening calls before the meal, and refusing to answer the phone during dinner. That was why Elspeth didn't start her shift until eight or nine o'clock at night. She liked to give the couple as much alone time as possible before showing up. It couldn't be easy living there, with hunters coming and going all day and night, and people often staying at the house with them for days or even weeks on end.

No, she wasn't heading out to the house early. The Night Club was the answer, and she intended to head there the minute Oscar and Violet had left in their taxi and Wyatt and Meredith had returned to the kitchen. She didn't want to run an obstacle course of blood-filled mortals to get out of here. Not the way she was feeling.

Lowering her head, Elspeth closed her eyes and breathed slowly in and out, trying to focus on that rather than her pain. It wasn't working at all, so she was almost relieved when she heard the sliding door open behind her. Expecting it to be her mother, Elspeth straightened and turned abruptly, ready to battle with her, only to find herself staring at Wyatt.

"Your mother asked me to bring you your coat," he said and held up her lightweight black leather jacket.

"Oh," Elspeth breathed, but her mind was racing. Her mother had obviously sent him out here for her to "snack on," and that just infuriated her. She needed to get the heck out of there right now and go to The Night Club.

"Are Oscar and Violet gone?" she asked abruptly.

"Yes," he said, his mouth thinning, and then he sighed and said, "I'm sorry about them."

"It's not me you should be apologizing to. Meredith—"

"I know," he interrupted solemnly. "She told me why he was doing what he was doing, but instead of taking her word for it, I put us all through this . . ." He waved vaguely back toward the sliding glass doors and grimaced. "I should have believed her. I guess I should trust her more."

"You should," Elspeth said firmly. "Your grandmother is not a doddering old fool. She's smart, and funny, and very kind."

Wyatt considered her solemnly for a moment and then said, "She says you spend a lot of time together."

Elspeth sighed wearily. He might have come to recognize that Oscar was just out to hurt Meredith, but he obviously still had his suspicions about her. Unfortunately, she was desperate for blood, and didn't have the patience to reassure him properly. The best she could do was say, "I know you're just looking out for your grandmother, and I appreciate that. I'm glad she has people who care about her but, believe it or not, I'm not interested in her money. Now if you'll just give me my coat, I really need to get out of here."

"Get out of here?" he echoed, his eyebrows rising.

"Yes," she said firmly, holding her hand out. "It's actually an emergency. So, please . . ."

Wyatt was silent for a moment and then held up her leather jacket by the collar, but without really moving it closer to her. She'd have to step nearer to claim it.

Elspeth hesitated, not wanting to reduce the distance between them. She could smell him from where she stood, and his scent made her think of both food and sex. The food part wasn't surprising. At the moment, he was looking like a blood bag on legs. The sex, though, *that* caught her by surprise. Although Elspeth supposed it shouldn't. He was one hell of an attractive specimen, and it wasn't just his pretty face, and well-built body. She also liked the way he carried himself. Wyatt moved with the confidence and grace of a man who knew how to handle himself. She found that incredibly attractive.

Pressing her lips tight together, Elspeth reached for her jacket, but rather than hand it over, Wyatt opened it and slid the arm hole over her hand and partway up her arm before walking around behind her to help her don the other sleeve as well.

Elspeth stiffened and closed her eyes. Of course he'd be a gentleman. That just figured, didn't it? Grinding her teeth together, she held her other hand back behind her so that he could slide the jacket up onto her shoulders and draw it around in front. The action brought him close up behind her. But he wasn't done. Next, he caught her long hair and lifted it out from under the collar for her. Elspeth bit her lip as his scent enveloped her, but feeling the sharp fangs pressing into her upper lip, she pressed her mouth tightly closed and struggled to force her fangs back up and out of sight.

"What kind of emergency?"

Elspeth shuddered as he whispered those words by her ear, but not because of what he said. She barely took note of the words. Her focus was centered wholly on his mouthwatering scent, the feel of his breath brushing her ear, and the heat of his body at her back.

"You're trembling."

Elspeth blinked her eyes open at that soft rumble by her ear, and then tried to step away from him, but he caught her hand to stop her and then gave a tug that drew her around to face him. She could have freed herself easily, but didn't have the wherewithal to do it. She didn't want to. Instead, Elspeth wanted to move closer to him and run her hands up his arms as she buried her nose in his neck and inhaled the enticing aroma wafting to her. His scent was spicy and sweet at the same time with a tinny hint of the blood rushing through his veins. It was positively delicious to Elspeth, heady even, and she wanted to press her body against his. She wanted to feel his chest against her breasts as she moved her hands up to clasp his head and then turn and tilt it slightly so that she could sink her teeth into—

"Your eyes."

Elspeth blinked away the image in her mind and focused on his face at those words.

"I thought I'd imagined how beautiful they are," he breathed with wonder. "That bright blue, with little sparks of silver that—" His words died suddenly and she caught a glimpse of the blank look that slid over his face. Then he pulled her closer, one hand sliding to the back of her head to urge her face toward the side of his neck. Elspeth knew at once that this was her mother. That Martine had taken control of him and was trying to make it impossible for her *not* to feed on him. And it almost worked. Elspeth nearly gave in and bit him, but then her gaze moved past his shoulder and she spotted her mother through the glass doors. Martine stood in Meredith's living room, her gaze concentrated, but it was Merry entering the room behind her mother that snapped her out of it, and stopped her from biting Wyatt.

A soft curse slipping from her lips, Elspeth abruptly jerked her head to the side and away from his neck.

She should have turned to the right, away from his face. Instead Elspeth turned to the left and her lips brushed the corner of his mouth. Martine must have released the control she'd taken of Wyatt then. Merry had no doubt startled her and broken her concentration, Elspeth thought, but whatever the case, Wyatt's embrace eased and confusion flashed briefly on his face as she glanced up to him. Before she could slip out of his arms, though, he inhaled deeply, his pupils dilating, and then his head lowered toward hers.

Elspeth froze with surprise as his lips brushed soft and warm across hers, shocked by the tingle that started on contact, and then slithered through her body, raising another hunger to clamor next to the bloodlust. When his tongue slid along the seam between her lips, she opened to him without thinking. His tongue swept in and the tingle turned into an explosion of hunger and need that left her in chaos, both mind and body.

Truly, Elspeth had never experienced such raw need and desire. Not that she'd had a lot of experience. Life with her mother had stifled her in a lot of ways, but she had been kissed before. Just never like this, never with such hunger and command. Now Elspeth's heart was racing, her body warming and melting into his, her hands clutching at the front of his shirt, and her lips clinging as his mouth moved over hers, drawing a deep, needy moan from her throat that he answered with a groan of his own.

When he urged her upper body back and tugged her jacket open so that he could cup her breasts through the cloth of her shirt, Elspeth broke their kiss on a gasp and let her head fall back. He pushed her jacket and shirt off her shoulder and began to nibble his way down her throat to press kisses along her collarbone while he continued to caress her breasts, and Elspeth murmured excitedly and lifted her head. She then opened her eyes to find the left side of his neck exposed, the vein visible and throbbing with the blood rushing through it.

Elspeth felt her fangs drop down and ran her tongue

over them, her gaze shifting to the living room again. Her mother was still there, her expression concentrated again, but Meredith was still there too . . . only now her expression was blank. Martine was controlling her as well now. She was controlling all of them, Elspeth thought with a frown. Playing them like puppets, making her and Wyatt do this, no doubt infusing their minds with this incredible passion. It wasn't real, none of it, except her hunger for blood.

That thought infuriated her. Elspeth snapped her mouth closed and pushed herself backward out of Wyatt's arms. She bumped up against the porch railing.

"El?" he asked softly when she began to slide to the side along the rail.

Unable to open her mouth for fear of revealing the fangs she hadn't yet managed to force back up, Elspeth just shook her head and turned away to walk quickly to the end of the porch.

"Elspeth? Just tell me . . ." Wyatt's words died abruptly when she hopped over the porch rail to the muddy ground below and moved quickly to the gate that opened to the side yard.

Wyatt stared after Elspeth with amazement until she slipped through the gate and disappeared, and then he hopped the rail and hurried after her. He was terribly confused. He hadn't planned on kissing her when he'd come outside. In fact, he didn't really recall deciding to even come out and bring her the jacket. He remembered Martine Pimms saying Elspeth had stepped out for some air, and had some vague recollection of her suggesting he should take the jacket out to her. And then he'd found himself taking the jacket off the chair and heading out to the porch without consciously deciding he would.

The weirdness didn't stop there. When Elspeth had held her hand out to take the coat, he'd started to hand it over and then instead was suddenly helping her into it, and moving up close behind her to lift her hair out from beneath the collar. He remembered tugging her around, and pressing her against his chest, urging her face into the curve of his throat, but had no idea why he'd done it. It had felt like he was just a passenger in his body, watching it do things he hadn't decided on doing.

Kissing her, though, that had been him, Wyatt acknowledged to himself as he reached the gate. She'd been in his arms, her scent filling his nostrils, her body warm against his. He'd looked down into her beautiful eyes and his mind had filled with the memory of other times he'd held her in his arms. He hadn't been able to resist kissing her. He should have, Wyatt supposed. He had all sorts of questions when it came to this woman. How she could have forgotten him, if she really had? Why she was pretending to have forgotten if she hadn't? What her game was, and why she was insinuating herself so deeply in his grandmother's life? But none of that had seemed to matter in that moment, and then their mouths had met and . . . dear God, he'd managed to convince himself over the years that he'd imagined the depth of their passion, just as he'd been sure he'd imagined the silver tint to her eyes. But he hadn't imagined anything. Like he remembered, passion had exploded between them as hard and fast as an IED. Or maybe a firebomb was a better description, because he'd immediately been on fire for her.

Wyatt had pulled her closer, eager to fully explore that passion. But instead, he'd found himself breaking the kiss he was so enjoying and turning to nibble at her collarbone. That had not been what he'd wanted to do. What he'd wanted was to press her against the wooden rail, and grind himself up against her as he thrust his tongue into her mouth. If he'd broken the kiss at all, it would have been to work her shirt open and claim those full, soft breasts that had been pressing against him, nudging his memories of other times he'd enjoyed them, not to nibble at her collarbone like some weirdo. Where the hell had that come from?

Bewildered at his own incomprehensible behavior, Wyatt pushed through the gate into the side yard just in time to see Elspeth disappear around the front of the house. Mouth tightening, he picked up his pace, determined to reach her and . . .

Well, frankly, Wyatt didn't know what he wanted. He knew he wanted to kiss her again. He'd kissed and bedded a lot of women in his life but not one had affected him like Elspeth Pimms had with just a kiss. That was something special, something crazy hot. How the hell had she found it within herself to break the kiss and walk away? And not just this time. What about the first time they met? Did she really not remember? Had he been that forgettable to her? Did she not experience the same need and passion he did?

"Don't come near me."

Those sharp words from Elspeth made Wyatt slow and glance around as he reached the corner of the house. He thought they were meant for him, until he saw that Elspeth was rushing down the steps of the front porch with her mother on her heels.

Wyatt narrowed his eyes on the pair. Neither of them even seemed to realize he was there, and the way Elspeth scowled over her shoulder at her mother told him that Martine was the one she was warning off. That was interesting.

Damn, the woman was fast if she'd rushed inside and upstairs to get her purse and got back down before he'd caught up to her, Wyatt thought with amazement as he noted that she was now carrying one. And then Martine stopped on the stairs and growled, "Just stop and listen to me, Elspeth."

When Elspeth halted at the sidewalk and turned to glare at her mother, curiosity made Wyatt stop walking to watch the pair. This was looking almost like a stand-off, or pistols at dawn. Martine appeared determined, and Elspeth seemed ready to run.

"You are being ridiculous," Martine said after a pause. "You should have used him while you had the chance. Your pain would be considerably eased now and you could wait on the delivery from Bastien rather than rush out to get—"

"I am not breaking the Council's laws and I don't know why you're trying to make me. If I used him like that, it would be—"

"This is an emergency," Martine interrupted firmly.

"No, it's not. Not really," Elspeth argued. "It might be close enough to one that the Council might not execute me. But they'd probably at least ban me from ever living here or—Oh," she said with sudden understanding. "That's what you're trying to do. You're trying to get me to bite Wyatt so that Uncle Lucian would be forced to ban me from North America."

Wyatt's eyes widened incredulously. He was having

a little difficulty following this conversation. What had Martine meant when she'd said Elspeth should have "used him" while she had the chance? Used who? Him? As far as he knew he was the only "him" around. But used him how? And how would it ease pain? And what delivery? None of this was making any sense to him.

"So, you'd rather see me executed than out from under your control?" Elspeth sounded bitter.

"Stop being melodramatic. Lucian wouldn't execute you," Martine said, her expression tight. "You are his niece and this is close enough to an emergency that he'd choose the lesser punishment and ban you."

"Probably," Elspeth agreed gloomily. "Unless enough people raised a fuss and suggested he was playing favorites. They might point to what happened with Uncle Jean Claude, and suggest Uncle Lucian shouldn't be allowed to decide my case, and then whoever was given the decision might have me executed to prevent anyone thinking *they* play favorites with Argeneaus too," she pointed out. "But you're willing to risk that just to keep control of me, aren't you?"

"That will not happen," Martine insisted, looking angry.

"No, it won't. Because I don't intend to break any Council laws," Elspeth said in a cold voice and turned to hurry toward the driveway, widening the distance between her and her mother.

Wyatt didn't hesitate, but immediately chased after her. He cast a wary glance toward the woman on the porch as he did, but her focus was wholly on her daughter, her expression strained and concentrated in a way that kind of gave him the heebie-jeebies as he followed Elspeth down the driveway. She was heading for a white Mazda, a cute little two-door sports car, he noted and frowned at the hunted look Elspeth cast over her shoulder toward the house.

Eyebrows rising, Wyatt glanced over his shoulder as well and saw that Martine had given up her concentrated expression for one that was . . . vexed. That was the only description he could think that fit. The woman looked vexed, and for some reason, in that moment, she made him think of the thwarted evil stepmother from a Disney film.

Almost embarrassed by the thought, Wyatt slowed as he neared Elspeth. She had reached the driver's side door, but paused as she spotted him approaching. Expression wary, she withdrew keys from her coat pocket and murmured, "Thank you for bringing me my jacket."

"No problem," Wyatt said easily, and then debated what to say next. He was quite sure that straight-out asking what the women had been talking about was not going to get him the answers he sought. It also wouldn't get him another one of those amazing kisses they'd shared, which he probably shouldn't be worrying about right now, but—

Well, hell, he was a guy, and kissing, along with everything that might follow, was pretty much taking up ninety percent of his mind at the moment. It was purely Elspeth's fault. Just standing close and looking at her was making him want to experience that kiss again.

Christ, he'd always been offended when he heard women claim men thought with their dicks, but that was what he was doing right now, Wyatt acknowledged with self-disgust.

"Did you want something?"

Wyatt shifted his gaze back to Elspeth at her tense question, and then simply asked, "Are you all right?"

"Yes, I'm just . . . I have to go to work," she muttered, avoiding his gaze.

Elspeth was a terrible liar, he decided with amusement. "I'm sure Gran said you start work around eight or nine at night and it's barely even six thirty yet."

"Yes, well, I have to . . . pick up something first, so I'm leaving a little early tonight," she muttered.

This time she didn't avoid his eyes and he was quite sure she was telling the truth. She planned to go straight to work from wherever she was headed now. But she wasn't comfortable even discussing whatever she was doing first. She looked half-guilty, as if she was giving away something she shouldn't, and he suddenly recalled her mentioning an emergency earlier. He was pretty sure she wouldn't explain if he asked her about it, so he let that go for now and simply said, "Right. Well, I was just going to run out and pick up some flowers or something for Gran as an apology for forcing Oscar on her tonight. I could pick up whatever you need while I'm at it and save you a trip."

"Flowers?" she said dubiously. "At this hour? Most flower shops close at five or six and—as you said—it's almost six thirty now."

"I stopped at a gas station on my way in from the airport yesterday and they had flowers there. I was just going to go grab some of those for her," he said, making it up quickly.

"Oh, yeah, gas station flowers are really going to make up for Oscar," Elspeth said, rolling her eyes.

"Maybe not, but it's a start," he said defensively. "I'll get her something nicer tomorrow."

"All you need to give her is love and support. That's

what she truly wants from you," Elspeth said softly. "Your grandmother is a wonderful woman. She's perfectly capable of looking after herself, and she needs you to believe that."

"I do," he said gruffly. "At least, I'm starting to believe it."

"Well, good," she muttered, and opened her car door.

A dark, rust-colored stain on the white leather of the driver's seat immediately caught Wyatt's eye and he stiffened. It looked like dried blood to him, but he only got a quick look before she slid into the vehicle and sat on it.

"I have to go."

Wyatt shifted his gaze to her face to see that she was eyeing him a little anxiously.

When he didn't respond, she added, "But thank you for the offer to pick up what I need. It was kind. I'll see you soon."

"Yeah, soon," Wyatt said and then, realizing that he was holding the top of her door, he released it. She immediately pulled it closed. Wyatt eyed her briefly through the window as she started the engine, and then he turned to continue down the driveway. He'd parked on the road rather than block the parking spots allotted to the renters when he'd arrived the day before. But now that he knew the basement apartment hadn't yet been rented out again, he'd park in the spot meant for that apartment's tenant when he returned later . . . after following Elspeth to wherever she was going. The woman had secrets, and he planned to find out what they were before he kissed her again . . . and hopefully bedded her. Maybe.

Wyatt grimaced at that last word, but knew it was true. He wanted to know whether she really didn't remember him or not, and what the hell she and her mother had been talking about with the using him and execution talk, but he wasn't fooling himself. If Elspeth got back out of the car right now and offered herself to him, he'd probably be hard-pressed to recall the questions he wanted answered. His mind would no doubt shift to lizard brain and his concentration would all be on the quickest way to get her clothes off, and whether he dared just do her right there on the front lawn, or whether he could find it in himself to take the time to try to find somewhere to do it that wasn't the spare bedroom in his grandmother's apartment, or her bedroom in her apartment with her mother and sisters there.

He might be able to make it to the backyard, Wyatt supposed, glancing around the quiet street. It would give them a small semblance of privacy for him to rip her clothes off and revel in her body.

The sound of the Mazda's engine drew Wyatt from his thoughts as he reached the SUV he'd rented. He saw Elspeth bring it to a halt at the foot of the driveway and look both ways as he slid into his own vehicle and started the engine. Spotting him in the SUV, she tossed him an anxious smile and wave, and then pulled onto the road, headed in the direction his vehicle was pointed.

Wyatt glanced back at the house to see Martine's shoulders sag as she turned to reenter the house. His gaze slid from the despondent woman to Elspeth's Mazda, and then he shifted into gear and pulled out to head up the street behind the little car, but his mind was replaying the entire encounter in his head. The shared kiss, the argument he'd overheard, the stain on Elspeth's car seat.

Wondering if that stain really had been the dried blood it looked like, Wyatt made sure to keep a safe distance between their vehicles. He was determined to find out where the woman was going, and was happy to play detective to do it.

Twenty minutes later Wyatt found himself in downtown Toronto. It was nearly another ten minutes, though, before Elspeth pulled into a multilevel parking lot.

Wyatt didn't pull in behind her. Instead, he glanced around at the businesses nearby as he continued up the road. He turned at the first cross street, circled around, and turned back onto the road just as she hurried out of the parking garage. He'd barely noticed her rushing toward the street when the car in front of him stopped abruptly. Slamming on his brakes to avoid hitting the white sedan, Wyatt watched Elspeth rush across the road in front of the stopped vehicle. Traffic coming in the opposite direction had stopped as well, he noted with surprise. Toronto drivers weren't usually this polite or accommodating, he was sure. At least, cars stopping to let jaywalkers pass wasn't something they did in Vancouver as a rule.

As he watched, Elspeth gained the opposite curb and hurried through a bloodred door fronting an otherwise nondescript building. Wyatt's eyes ran over the small unassuming sign above the door and he frowned as he read, The Night Club.

A loud honk behind him drew Wyatt back to the fact that traffic was moving again. Removing his foot from the brake, he let the rental ease forward, but cast another glance at the door Elspeth had slipped through as he went. What the hell could Elspeth be "picking up" in a nightclub? Besides booze and men, that is. Surely the emergency hadn't been her nipping out for a drink or a quickie before work?

Scowling over the possibility, Wyatt took another spin around the block.

Four

Elspeth blinked her eyes rapidly, trying to adjust to the much dimmer interior of The Night Club as she stumbled to the bar along the back. Her eyes weren't adjusting as quickly as they should, a result of her being low on blood, so she switched to rubbing her eyes in an effort to move the process along. She sensed, rather than saw, the bartender approach.

"A Virgin Bloody Mary without the Worcestershire, Tabasco, or lemon," she requested quietly.

"So . . . blood?" the bartender asked, his deep voice full of amusement.

Elspeth nodded with a sigh and breathed, "Yes, please," as she gave up on her eyes and sank onto the nearest barstool. She was staring wearily at the black stone countertop of the bar when a tall, blue-tinted glass of red liquid was set in front of her. Elspeth pounced on it like a starving person on food and quickly gulped it down.

"Another?" the bartender asked as she lowered the now empty glass.

Nodding, Elspeth braced her hands on the bar top as the blood hit her system. She was struck with a brief light-headedness and a sense of being off-kilter. It was like standing on a listing ship and trying to keep your balance, an effect of her system rushing to collect the blood in her stomach and redistribute it.

"Here you are, El," the bartender said, setting a fresh glass in front of her.

She glanced up with surprise on hearing her name and then stilled, her eyes widening incredulously as she gaped at the giant on the other side of the bar. Six-foot-seven with a twelve-inch green Mohawk that took him to seven-foot-seven, the man was as wide as a linebacker with his padding on, and awash in tattoos and piercings. G.G. She'd encountered him many times at The Night Club back in London, an establishment that, like this one, was geared toward immortals and had a doorman who usually steered mortals away. It was a place for her kind to relax and enjoy blood-based mixed drinks in the company of other immortals. Her parents had taken her and her sisters to The Night Club in London to celebrate special occasions like birthdays, graduation, etc., but Elspeth had also been there many times on her own while at university. G.G. had always manned the door, and had always been very nice to her. He'd often even joined her inside and chatted with her about life and such on her visits.

"G.G.," she breathed with amazement. "What are you doing here?"

"I own the place now," he said with pride.

"Really? How? Why?" she asked with amazement. "Did you sell The Night Club in London?"

G.G. shook his head. "I still own it, and I've done well there. So when Lucern called up saying he was interested in selling The Night Club here, I jumped at it."

"Wait a minute. Lucern owned this place?" she asked with confusion. "My cousin, Lucern Argeneau?"

G.G. chuckled at her expression, but nodded.

"I had no idea," Elspeth admitted, her eyes wide.

"I guess no one knew," G.G. said with a shrug. "I gather he was afraid certain relatives might take advantage if they knew he was the owner."

Amusement curved Elspeth's lips. "I can see that. Thomas probably would have before he met Inez. If for no other reason than that it would have annoyed Lucern."

"I suspect he was more concerned about Jean Claude than anyone else," G.G. said quietly.

"Oh, yes," Elspeth said, frowning as she thought of her now dead uncle. There was nothing more unpleasant than an immortal with a drinking problem, unless it was one with a drinking problem who was mean as a snake after consuming a drunk's blood. Although, to be fair, Jean Claude had been mean as a snake when sober too. Pushing thoughts of that unpleasant man away, she forced a smile and said, "So you bought it, but still own The Night Club in London too?"

G.G. nodded again. "I like London. But this is a good investment. Besides, my parents will soon have to move out of London again for that whole 'decade thing' you immortals got going on, to keep mortals from noticing you aren't aging, and they were talking about Canada as a possible destination for the next ten years, so this seemed fortuitous. I can travel back and forth between England and Canada, keep an eye on both places, and visit my parents while doing it whether they're there or here. It's all good."

"Yes," Elspeth agreed with a nod, and then shook her head and said, "I can't believe Lucern owned it. He isn't The Night Club type."

"It was one of his investments," G.G. said with a shrug. "But now that he and Kate are going to start a family, he's decided to divest himself of some of his businesses. This is one he felt needed more time than he might have in the near future."

"He and Kate are pregnant?" she asked with amazement. Good Lord, the man knew more about her family than she did.

"Not yet," he said at once. "But Kate is retiring from Roundhouse Publishing later this year and they're going to start trying for a baby then."

"Oh." Elspeth nodded, not surprised to hear Kate was retiring. She'd worked at Roundhouse when she'd met Lucern and been turned, and it had been more than the usual ten years since then. It was time for her to move on. Otherwise she risked someone picking up on the fact that she wasn't aging.

"So, I'd heard you'd moved here to Canada," G.G. said with a grin. "Good for you. I think getting away from your mother will be good for you."

"You heard?" Elspeth asked with amazement. She hadn't told him. She hadn't been to The Night Club in London the last four years. Not since the family had moved out of London for the family home in York. But she supposed she shouldn't be surprised he knew about her move. The immortal grapevine was faster and more efficient than the mortal grape vine. Everyone seemed to know everyone's business.

"Yes, Lissianna and Jeanne Louise came in a few weeks ago for a girls' night and invited me to sit with them to catch up on things. They mentioned it, and were planning to drag you out with them on their next girls' night. They said you were busy getting settled in and they'd bring you next time."

"Oh," Elspeth smiled. Lissianna had invited her out about three weeks ago, but she'd been expecting her furniture to be delivered, and after three weeks living in a mostly empty apartment, she hadn't wanted to reschedule. Lissianna had offered to change the outing date but Elspeth hadn't wanted to disrupt her plans and had said no. She'd join them next time. And she would . . . if her mother didn't try to prevent it, she thought unhappily, and then glanced to her purse with a frown as her phone began to ring. Sliding the leather bag off her shoulder, she set it on the bar and quickly dug out her phone. She wasn't surprised to see Mother listed as the caller. She'd been out of Martine's sight for half an hour. Of course she'd call.

Elspeth hit Decline, then dropped her phone back in her purse and glanced up to see G.G.'s raised eyebrows. He'd obviously noted who the caller was. Forcing a smile, she tried to steer his thoughts away from the call.

"So," she said brightly, "you work the bar here instead of the door?"

G.G. shook his head. "No, I work the door here too . . . when we're open."

Elspeth blinked at him with confusion, and then turned to peer around the club. She was the only person there. The Night Club had other rooms, of course, but she suddenly suspected they were probably empty too as she realized it was just a little after seven. The sun was still up and would be for at least another hour. The Night Club was only for immortals, and so was run differently than your average bar or nightclub. For one thing, it was only open from sunset to sunrise. Everyone knew that.

"Oh, crap," she muttered and turned back to G.G. with dismay. "I'm so sorry."

"It's fine," G.G. said with good humor. "My own fault. The phone was ringing when I came in and I rushed to answer it and forgot to go back and lock the door."

"Yes, but I know the club's hours. I can't believe I didn't think of that when I headed here." She began scrambling through her purse for her wallet. "You should have just sent me on my way. I just—Why on earth did you give me my drinks?"

"Because you were pale as death and looked like you needed the blood," he said quietly. "And you don't look much better after just the one glass, so stop fussing with your wallet and drink. You can pay me after."

"Thank you," she said with a sigh, and set her wallet down so that she could pick up the glass of blood and take a long swallow.

"Rough day?" G.G. asked, leaning his arms on the counter and offering her a sympathetic smile.

"The worst," Elspeth admitted with a grimace. "I got home this morning to find Mother and my sisters had decided on a surprise visit. They were already in bed. Mom in the guest room and the twins in *my* bed," she added with disgust.

"Pretty presumptuous of them," G.G. commented.

"I know, right?" she said, glad to have the support.

"Did you kick them out of your apartment?" he asked.

"No, but I kicked the twins out of my bed. Made them sleep on the air mattress in the living room. They weren't too happy about it, though, and drank me out of blood before I got up."

"Punishing you," he said with a nod.

"Yeah, but hell, I don't know what they have to be angry about. They're the selfish twits who couldn't last two months alone with Mother and dragged her over here. Now they all might be moving here. Plus Dad," she added as an afterthought. "Although I don't mind Dad. He's great, and Mother behaves a little better when he's around. Problem is, he's always off running his 'empire.'"

"Hmm," G.G. murmured. "So, you moved here to get away from your mother, and now she's moving here."

"Worse than that, Mother told Mortimer this morning that she was going to be a hunter and work with me. I'll have her hovering over me all damned night every night."

"Wait, wait, wait," G.G. said with confusion. "Lissianna said you got a position at the university, teaching criminology."

"I did," she said on a sigh. "But it doesn't start until the summer, and even then, it's a part-time gig. I've been volunteering at the Enforcer House, helping to sort through all the tips they get to see what might be real threats and what aren't. I wanted to see if I like it, and if I do, maybe I can work there officially in the future. At least part-time. And I do like it. At least, I did, but now . . ."

"But now if you do work for the enforcers, you'll have your mother working with you," he said with understanding.

"Yeah." Elspeth sighed the word and then shook her head. "It's my own fault. I should have headed back to the Enforcer House when I got stabbed this morning rather than go home. She never would have known I was working for them if I had," she said, and then frowned and argued her own point. "But it's not like I knew they were at the apartment, so why would I?"

"Wait, wait, wait," G.G. said with amazement. "You got *stabbed* this morning?"

Grimacing, Elspeth nodded. "I stopped to check out a soft call on my way home and a mortal stabbed me in the back and slashed my leg."

Much to her surprise, that made him throw back his head and laugh loudly.

Elspeth stared at him wide-eyed, noting a little absently how the green strands of his Mohawk caught the bar lights as his head bobbed with laughter. Finally she scowled and asked, "What's so funny about my getting stabbed?"

"Oh," he gasped, and shook his head. Making an obvious effort to control his amusement, he waved his hand and finally got out, "No, not your getting stabbed. That's not funny at all, but the fact that you got stabbed this morning and didn't include it as part of why today was your worst day ever is."

Elspeth blinked, and then sagged where she sat as she understood. He was right. She hadn't even considered the stabbing as part of her rough day. In comparison to the appearance of her mother in her new home, getting stabbed was like a pesky paper cut. Frankly, she'd rather be stabbed every day of her life than have her mother back ruling her.

"I knew that was blood on your car seat."

Elspeth swiveled sharply and gaped at the man standing beside her. Wyatt. How the heck had he snuck up on them like that? They should have heard the door open at the very least. Well, unless he entered while G.G. was laughing so uproariously at her misadventures. He must have, she realized and asked, "What are you doing here?"

"Forget that," he said, waving his hand impatiently. "You were stabbed this morning?"

Elspeth gaped at him briefly, and then sighed and narrowed her gaze as she concentrated on sending her thoughts out to search his mind, take control and— Whoa! What the hell? Her thoughts were crashing up against a black wall of nothing. Mouth tightening, she redoubled her efforts with the same results.

"Elspeth?" Wyatt said, frowning now as well. "Answer me. Were you stabbed this morning?"

"It was nothing," she muttered and slipped off her stool. Mortals weren't really welcome at The Night Club. She had to get him out of there. Casting a regretful glance at her drink, she picked up her wallet and quickly pulled out money, saying, "Thanks, G.G. We'll go now."

"Finish your drink," both men said at once, and Elspeth glanced from one to the other with surprise. G.G. was looking stern and insistent. He knew she needed the blood and felt she should drink it before she left. Wyatt just looked kind of annoyed. She had no idea why.

"Finish it," Wyatt repeated. "You had to rush off to have it, so finish it. In fact, I'll have a drink too. A beer," he decided, settling on the neighboring stool. "Because I want to hear about this getting stabbed business where Gran can't overhear and be upset."

Elspeth hesitated, but then said, "Fine. But we'll have to go somewhere else. The club isn't open yet. Besides, they don't serve alcohol here."

"What? A nightclub that doesn't serve alcohol?" he asked with open disbelief.

"The Night Club is just the name," she said on a sigh. "It's not a real nightclub. At least, not like your normal nightclub. It's more like a coffee shop. A place where people can gather, relax, and drink . . ."

"Power drinks," G.G. said when she floundered.

"Power drinks," Wyatt echoed with disbelief and shook his head. "A nightclub that serves power drinks instead of alcohol."

"Yes," Elspeth said, casting G.G. a grateful look.

"Damn hipsters are ruining everything," Wyatt muttered, and then glanced at her glass. "What's that, then? I thought it must be a Bloody Mary, but the color isn't quite right, and if they only serve power drinks, it—"

"It's beet juice, tomatoes, kale, spinach, kelp, and a bunch of other disgusting things I wouldn't drink if you paid me," G.G. lied glibly, interrupting him.

"You just sling the drinks and don't consume them yourself, huh?" Wyatt asked with amusement, his mood suddenly lightening . . . although, she wasn't sure why. Had he worried his grandmother had rented to a lush?

"Pretty much," G.G. said solemnly. "Elspeth's right, we aren't open yet, but she needs a few more power drinks to help her heal, so I'll mix you up a power drink too if you like. Or I keep some soft drinks here for myself. Some Coke, ginger ale, maybe some root beer. What'll it be? A power drink or—?"

"A Coke," Wyatt said firmly. "Thanks."

Nodding, G.G. grabbed a glass, threw some ice in it and then retrieved a can of Coke from the refrigerator under the counter and poured it as he carried it back to them. He set it in front of Wyatt, and then nodded at Elspeth's drink.

"Knock it back and I'll get you another, Elspeth. You obviously lost a lot of blood this morning and need it," he said, his tone brooking no argument.

Grimacing, she did as he instructed. The moment she set the empty glass down, G.G. whisked it away and moved off to prepare another . . . at the other end of the bar. He was being careful that Wyatt not see what he was working with, she realized, and glanced nervously toward the windows to see that the day was waning, but slowly. Still, other immortals would start arriving the moment the sun was gone and then Wyatt's presence would be a problem.

"Who stabbed you and where?"

Wyatt's question drew her attention back to him and she grimaced. "It was during work. I was checking out a tip and encountered a mentally ill man. He attacked his wife and then stabbed me when I rushed to help her."

"I meant where on your person were you stabbed?" he said grimly. "There was blood on your car seat."

"Oh." She grimaced, but admitted, "He stabbed me in the lower left side of my back, and slashed my left leg."

His gaze immediately slid to her side, but of course he couldn't see anything through her clothes and jacket. Even if she'd been sitting there naked there wouldn't have been much to see. When she'd got up that evening the wound had healed to the point that it was a large, dark, ugly scar. She'd needed more blood for the healing to continue. Elspeth could feel it happening again now that she'd had more blood. It was like someone was repeatedly jabbing her with a handful of needles in the spot. Most unpleasant, and she was holding herself very still to try to keep from flinching or otherwise give away that she was in pain.

"And you aren't in the hospital because . . . ?" he asked dryly.

"Because it was just a flesh wound, a scratch, really," she lied. Actually, it had been pretty bad. Were she mortal she would have bled out within minutes. Fortunately, she wasn't mortal.

Elspeth glanced at Wyatt and saw that he was shaking his head. Scowling, she asked, "What?"

"I didn't realize your job was so dangerous," he admitted, his gaze on his glass as he turned it on the countertop. "Gran made it sound like your position was mostly analytical. A desk job."

"It is," Elspeth said, and glanced toward G.G., wishing he'd hurry. The sooner she finished this next drink, the sooner she could get Wyatt out of there. It would have been easier if she could have slipped into his thoughts, rearranged them, and sent him back to his grandmother's without recalling any of this, though. That idea made her turn to peer at him again to try to do just that. Nothing. She just kept coming up against a black wall of nothing. Either the man was brain dead, or—

Elspeth shied away from the "or" and smiled in gratitude at G.G. as he returned with her blood. Aware of the man beside her and the time crunch, Elspeth downed half of it at once, careful not to come away with a blood mustache afterward.

"But you got stabbed," Wyatt pointed out. "How did you get stabbed working a desk job?"

"There are some days when stuff happens and I end up going out on calls. This morning was one of those days," Elspeth said vaguely, and cast a pleading glance G.G.'s way, hoping he'd change the subject. He did. Just not to a subject she liked any better.

"So, what are you going to do about your mother?" he asked abruptly.

"Her mother?" Wyatt asked G.G. with interest and then turned to Elspeth. "What about your mother?"

"Nothing. She's just a little overprotective," she said firmly, and scowled at G.G. as she picked up her drink.

"Martine is more than a little overprotective," G.G. told Wyatt as Elspeth drank. Apparently, he hadn't got the silent message behind the scowl, she decided as he went on, "She's a control freak and almost obsessive-compulsive about keeping her daughters near her. They've all led very sheltered lives."

"She's not that bad," Elspeth countered, which was an absolute lie. Martine Argeneau Pimms wasn't *almost* obsessive-compulsive about keeping her daughters near her. She was full-on, certifiably obsessive-compulsive about it.

"Really?" Wyatt asked G.G., apparently believing him over her, which was kind of ironic when you thought about it. He trusted the big tattooed bartender with a Mohawk over a clean-cut woman he believed worked for the police. Go figure.

Maybe he had trust issues with women, Elspeth thought.

"Oh, yeah," G.G. told him. "Martine wouldn't let them out of her sight for a minute as kids. All three girls were homeschooled until university. Never let out of the house. Never allowed friends."

"We had our cousins," Elspeth argued stiffly.

"Whom you saw once every couple of years or so," G.G. said dryly.

"How do you know that?" Elspeth asked with surprise.

"Julianna," G.G. said at once and then grinned and

added, "Did you think you were the only member of your family to skip uni classes at least once a week and slip away to The Night Club to hang out with other im— club members?" he finished, catching his own slip with a grimace.

"Damn," Elspeth breathed. It had never even occurred to her that her sisters might skip classes. It should have, she supposed. Elspeth had made a practice of signing up for an extra class every term. She'd show her mother her schedule once she got it, and then cancel the extra class. Her mother would think she was in university during that time, while she was actually at The Night Club chatting with G.G., or at a movie, or just shopping, taking time for herself. However, when G.G. had asked how she'd managed to slip away from her mother the first time they'd chatted, she'd simply said she was supposed to be in class.

She didn't explain it now, either, but set her empty glass on the bar top and glanced to Wyatt as she slid off her stool. "We should go. You have to pick up flowers for Meredith."

"He can go, but you're not going anywhere, Elspeth," G.G. said firmly, and then, picking up her empty glass, he added, "You're looking better, but you need at least two more of these before you go anywhere."

"Fine," she snapped, a bit irritated at all this bossing about. It was like being with her mother. That thought made her scowl at Wyatt as she said, "I'll have two more. But you should go before Meredith worries."

"I called and explained things before I came in here." He smiled like the cat that caught the canary and said, "I can keep you company while you have your power drinks."

That brought a soft chuckle from G.G. as he moved to the other end of the bar to fetch her another "drink."

Elspeth hesitated, wanting to just walk out and leave, but in the end, she sank back onto her stool. G.G. was right. She was feeling better, but still cramping and achy. Two more of the twenty-ounce glasses should see her right.

"Those power drinks really seem to be working," Wyatt commented now, peering at her face. "You are looking a little better. You have more color in your cheeks. Maybe I should try one of those drinks myself."

Elspeth's eyes widened with alarm, and then she asked abruptly, "What are you doing here? Did you follow me?"

"Yes," he admitted without hesitation. When she gaped at him, Wyatt shrugged and said, "Look, Gran's already been burned once by a tenant who was supposed to be a friend, and she nearly fell for that iTunes scam too. Now there's you, who already have a key to her apartment." Scowling, he added, "And then . . ." He paused briefly, several expressions flashing across his face, and simply said, "Once I saw the blood on your car seat I was suspicious, and followed you to make sure you weren't up to no good."

Elspeth stared at him. Between the expressions that had crossed his face and the way he'd hesitated, she suspected he was leaving out something. Had he overheard the argument she'd had with her mother in front of the house?

"Elspeth up to no good?" G.G. asked with amusement as he returned to place two tall blue glasses in front of her this time.

"He thinks I'm after his grandmother's money," Elspeth explained quietly as she picked up one of the drinks.

G.G. snorted at the suggestion. "Elspeth's family has money. Loads of it. Besides, like I said, she's led a pretty sheltered life. I think your grandmother's money is safe."

Wyatt considered G.G. briefly and said, "So, a beautiful young creature like Elspeth is really just friends with my very sweet but very old grandmother because . . . ?"

Elspeth blinked and blushed. Did he really think she was beautiful? Aware that G.G. was grinning at her reaction with amusement, she raised her glass and hid her red face by chugging down the blood he'd just brought her. Chugging was better. Elspeth wasn't especially keen on the taste of blood. She preferred consuming it from the bag where you just popped it on your fangs and let them do the work of sucking in the red liquid. That way you didn't have to taste it at all.

"I'd imagine she's more comfortable around older people," G.G. said as she drank. "She's spent very little time around young people. Instead, most of her life has been spent around the very old."

Elspeth almost snorted at G.G.'s words. He wasn't kidding. Most everyone in her life was well over two or three hundred years old. Heck, she herself was twice as old as Wyatt's grandmother. In comparison, Merry was a youngster. Setting down the now empty glass, Elspeth slid it toward G.G. and wrapped her hand around the other glass he'd brought her.

"Hmm," Wyatt murmured, and then, before she could lift the second glass, asked, "Is that why you rented from her? Because she was older and you were comfortable around her? No other reason?"

Elspeth rolled her eyes at the question. "I didn't know your grandmother was the landlady when I rented the apartment. I didn't know who owned it at all. I found and applied for it online while still in England. I've always loved old Victorian houses, and there were pictures of the front of your grandmother's house with the listing on a rental website. It . . ." Elspeth grimaced. It had looked familiar to her, like home. But she couldn't even explain that to herself, so merely said, "It looked charming and homey."

"She advertised on the internet?" Wyatt asked with surprise. "Gran doesn't have a computer."

"Meredith uses a management company to rent the apartments," she explained. "They posted the pictures and a description on a rental website. They're who I dealt with."

"So you didn't pick my grandmother?" he asked slowly. "That was just a coincidence?"

Elspeth had no idea what he meant by coincidence, but assured him, "I didn't know about Merry owning or living there until the day I arrived, when she introduced herself and offered me a plate of cookies as a welcome gift." Glancing to G.G., she added, "Merry makes some killer cookies."

"Yeah, she does," Wyatt said with a faint grin.

"You're making me jealous," G.G. said with a sigh. "Mom used to make great cookies too, but she and Alfred travel so much now . . ." He shrugged, and then commented, "I was wondering why you hadn't bought instead of rented, but if you had to arrange it all from England . . ."

Elspeth nodded. "I would never buy a house or condo without seeing it first. I planned to rent for a year or so while I checked out the city and where I might want to live, and then buy later," she said, which was true. But she also hadn't bought because she hadn't been at all sure her escape plan would work. There had always been the chance that her mother might have caught a stray thought of hers, realized what she was doing, and put an end to it.

Fortunately, she hadn't. But now Martine was here, in her apartment, and planning to move to Toronto as well. There was a good possibility that Victoria was right and her mother would try to make her move into whatever house she and Father bought here.

Elspeth lowered her glass and bit her lip at the thought, but then recalled how she'd been able to resist her mother's mind control efforts today. Martine had managed to make her stop, briefly, in her apartment, but hadn't been able to make her stay until she'd got close enough to touch her on the stairs, and then she hadn't been able to stop her at all during her second attempt to leave. The pain she'd been suffering had helped her to push past her mother's efforts to take control. At least, Elspeth thought that must be how she'd managed to escape. If it was, she might have to stab herself once a day to make sure she could have a life not controlled by her mother.

Elspeth considered that as she downed the last of the blood. She'd have to keep a knife on her at all times, and maybe stab herself each morning before she left her room. That way, her mother couldn't sink her hooks into her mind and control her life. It didn't sound pleasant, but hopefully she wouldn't have to do it long before her mother gave up and stopped trying to control her.

"Right. I'll just hit the bathroom and then I'll walk you to your car," Wyatt said when she finished and set down her glass. Glancing to G.G., he asked, "Where are the washrooms?"

G.G. pointed toward the back, and Wyatt nodded and murmured "Thank you" before following the silent instructions.

"Well?" G.G. said the minute Wyatt was out of hearing. "What are you going to do?"

"I don't know. I understand why Mother acts the way she does, and I've tried to be patient, but . . ." Elspeth closed her eyes with frustration. "She doesn't realize what she's doing to us. And tonight I think she was actually trying to get me to break Council law so that I'd be banished and sent back to England."

"That sounds whacked," G.G. said, his eyebrows climbing his forehead, and then he grimaced and added, "But I meant, what are you going to do about your friend?"

"Wyatt?" she asked with surprise.

"Is that his name?" G.G. asked innocently, and then pointed out, "You never introduced us."

"Oh! I'm sorry, you're right," she said with amazement. She'd been so befuddled by her inability to read and control him that she'd—

"You couldn't control him," G.G. said as if reading her mind.

"How do you know that?" Elspeth asked with surprise.

"Because you didn't control him and make him leave," G.G. said dryly. "Besides, I saw you look at him like you were trying to fry him with your eyes. I assume you were trying then to read or control him?"

"Yes," she admitted solemnly.

"And couldn't," he said with certainty and, when she nodded, added, "So . . . life mates?"

Elspeth grimaced, but shook her head. "If we were life mates, we would have had shared dreams today while I slept. He's staying with his grandmother on the floor below my apartment," she pointed out. "We should have had shared dreams and didn't. Ergo, we are not life mates."

"Or maybe he wasn't sleeping. He is mortal, after all, and was probably awake all day while you slept," G.G. pointed out. When Elspeth sighed, her shoulders sagging in defeat, he smiled and said, "So, Wyatt *is* your life mate."

Elspeth glanced away unhappily. This was not something she wanted to have to deal with just now. She had enough on her plate. Taking a deep breath to calm herself, she shrugged and said, "A possible life mate."

G.G. tilted his head. "You don't want him for a life mate?"

Elspeth avoided his gaze, her mind returning to that incredible kiss on Meredith's back porch. Finally, she said, "It's not that I don't want him. I just . . ." Closing her eyes briefly, she sighed and then admitted, "I want to have a life, G.G. You were right when you said I've led a sheltered life. I haven't been able to do *anything*. I've never dated, never been kissed properly until today, never had a girls' night—unless you count the pajama party we had for Lissianna's birthday when she met Greg. And even then our parents were all there," she added with a grimace. "I want to experience at least *some* stuff before I settle down to a life mate. I want to go on dates, go dancing, eat popcorn in movie theaters, have fun girls' nights, and . . ." She shook her head unhappily and then noticed the crooked smile on G.G.'s face and raised her eyebrows. "What?"

"I was just thinking God must have an ironic sense of humor," he admitted with mild amusement.

"How's that?" she asked with curiosity.

"Well, most immortals are pining for their life mate, and probably on their knees praying every night to find them, but they don't," he said solemnly. "While you, who isn't at all interested in finding her life mate, and who just wants some freedom to experience life for a change, have your life mate thrown at you right out of the gates." He shook his head. "I sometimes think God, or the Fates, or whoever it is he puts in charge of this stuff, really needs a good slap up the side of the head."

Elspeth smiled wryly, thinking he might be right. After all, she wasn't the only example of God's sense of humor. There was G.G. himself, a mortal whose mother had been widowed while he was still a boy, and then found herself a life mate to an immortal. She'd allowed the immortal to turn her, and then, when G.G. was eighteen, had offered to use her one turn to turn her son. But whereas most mortals would give a lot for such an opportunity, G.G. wasn't interested. Of course, that had crushed his mother. She didn't want to have to watch her son grow old and die. So his stepfather had bought The Night Club and given it to G.G. on his eighteenth birthday with the hope that one day, an immortal would walk in that G.G. might be a life mate for, and he might yet agree to be turned.

"Wow, this place is something special."

Elspeth turned at that comment as Wyatt returned from the washroom.

"The bathrooms are first class, and I spotted a room through a glass door on my way there that looks like a high-class New York dance club."

"If this place is anything like The Night Club in London, there will be other rooms too, all with different themes," Elspeth said with a faint smile and then glanced to G.G. "Are there?"

He nodded. "Lucern had it set up pretty good, but I did redecorate a couple of rooms to my own taste when I bought it."

"You own this place?" Wyatt asked with amazement.

G.G. nodded.

"Wow," he breathed, and then said solemnly, "Well, you have a real classy place here. Nice job."

"Thank you," G.G. said with dignity.

"We should get going," Elspeth said, standing up. "My mother and sisters are probably still with Merry, and I wouldn't want to inflict them on your grandmother for any longer than necessary. Besides, I do have to get to work eventually."

"Yeah." Wyatt got up and pulled out his wallet. "I've got our drinks."

Elspeth exchanged a glance with G.G. and then quickly rolled up the money she'd taken out earlier and passed it to G.G. in a handshake as she murmured, "Thank you."

"My pleasure," G.G. said solemnly, but held on to her hand. "You're going to have to confront her, Elspeth. I know there's a reason for her behavior, but this isn't healthy for any of you. Not only is she making you and your sisters' lives miserable, she's hampering your development. The twins are like a couple of sixteen-year-olds, and you . . ." He shook his head. "This has to end. You have to find a way to end it."

"Yes," she said on a sigh, and withdrew her hand when he released it. Noting the curiosity on Wyatt's face, she forced a smile. "Shall we go?"

Nodding, Wyatt held a fifty out toward G.G. for what he thought were a Coke and four power drinks. "Will this cover it?"

"It's all good," G.G said, waving the money away and

walking around the bar. "I'll see you guys out and lock the door."

Wyatt tried to protest, but fell silent, his eyes widening incredulously when the man reached them. Wyatt was probably an inch over six feet tall and well built, but G.G. was a giant in comparison, and twice as wide.

Grinning, Elspeth took Wyatt's arm and urged him toward the door. "Come on. Let's get moving and let G.G. finish prepping for the rush."

Five

the door."

"Jesus, that guy's huge," Wyatt breathed as they stepped out onto the sidewalk and heard the door lock behind them.

"That's why he's called G.G.," Elspeth said with amusement, and then explained, "It's short for Green Giant."

"Green Giant?" Wyatt asked with surprise. "You were calling him G.G.? The whole time we were in there I thought you were saying Gigi, like the girl's name, and couldn't figure out who would be stupid enough to name him that."

Elspeth chuckled as they wound their way toward the curb, maneuvering around the pedestrians walking past. "His real name is Joshua. But someone nicknamed him Green Giant because of the green Mohawk and his size, and then it was shortened to G.G. and it stuck."

"Hmm," Wyatt murmured and then grinned and asked, "Did he kill the guy who called him Green Giant?"

"Not that I know of," she said with a laugh as they reached the curb.

Wyatt smiled. He liked her laugh. He'd forgotten how musical and sweet it was. He was glad he'd followed her this evening. He still hadn't got the answers to a lot of his questions, but at least he knew she hadn't rushed off to drink or pick up men at The Night Club tonight. Also, he believed what she'd said. Her renting from his grandmother was nothing more than coincidence, and—

A startled yelp and Elspeth suddenly falling out into the road in front of him brought Wyatt's thoughts to an abrupt halt, and then horror crashed through him as she disappeared under the wheels of a car. It all happened so fast he was left gaping briefly, his heart and lungs coming to a full stop, and then slamming back to work as the car skidded to a halt and alarmed shouts and concerned cries rose up around him.

Wyatt hurried to the back end of the car, but Elspeth wasn't there. Dropping to his knees, he peered under the vehicle, his heart stuttering in his chest when he saw her pinned under the back tires.

"I'll lift the car. You're going to have to pull her out."

Wyatt glanced around with a start and found G.G. kneeling beside him. Obviously, he'd seen what had happened and come out of the club to help, Wyatt thought as the man got to his feet and bent to grab the back bumper.

"I won't be able to hold it up long, so you have to be quick," G.G. warned. "Are you ready?"

Shaking off his shock, Wyatt nodded and dropped onto his stomach on the pavement. He then reached for Elspeth's hand. She was lying on her back with the car tire on her lower leg, but her arms were free and the one on this side was lying thrown out toward him, as if she were reaching for him. Her eyes, though, were closed, and her face . . .

Wyatt ground his teeth together, and turned his gaze determinedly away from her battered face. He didn't know if it was road burn, or from the bottom of the car, but Elspeth would never be the same. Reaching for her hand, he clasped it firmly, and then glanced up at G.G. and said, "I've got her. Go ahead."

Nodding, the huge man took a deep breath, bent to the job, and began to pull up with all his might. For a moment, Wyatt was afraid G.G. wouldn't be able to manage it, but then the car began to rise. Still, he was relieved when a couple of passersby rushed to help hold the vehicle up. It made Wyatt a lot less nervous about the possibility of the car dropping on Elspeth while he worked to retrieve her, which he did now, pulling her toward him as far as he could, and then releasing her hand to catch her further up the arm, and then by the belt buckle to drag her out.

The moment she was clear, the men released the car. It slammed down with a crash and Wyatt was glad they'd waited until he had Elspeth completely out. He was quite sure the rear end had bounced off the pavement when it landed.

"Has someone called an ambulance?" he asked, peering over Elspeth's bloodied body with concern. Dear God, he'd seen a lot while in the army, but he'd never seen anything like this. She looked like she'd been chewed up and spat out.

"I'm sure they have," G.G. said, but didn't sound happy at the thought.

"G.G.? What's going on?"

Wyatt glanced up to see a young woman pushing her way through the surrounding crowd to reach them. She had long white hair that was scraped back into a pony-tail, but her face was youthful, as was her figure in the jeans and T-shirt she wore.

"Sofia," G.G. said with relief. "We need some help here."

The woman's gaze shifted speculatively to Elspeth. "Is she an imm—?"

"An Argeneau," G.G. interrupted and stood up. Nodding to Wyatt, he added, "And he's her LM. Can you deal with the crowd while we take care of her?"

"Of course," she said at once.

"Thank you," G.G. said and then turned back to Wyatt. "Can you carry her? Or do you want me to?"

Wyatt frowned. "Should we be moving her? I mean, we had to get her out from under the vehicle, but they say you shouldn't move—Hey!" Wyatt protested when G.G. suddenly bent and scooped Elspeth out of his arms.

Leaping to his feet, Wyatt stepped in front of the big man, about to demand he put her back down until the EMTs arrived and could examine her. Elspeth might have a broken back or something else that movement could worsen.

"Sofia," G.G. said, and Wyatt suddenly found himself stepping aside and letting the huge man by. He didn't want to, or he hadn't. Now he was a little muddled as to what he did want, but he was following G.G. through the gathered crowd to the entrance of The Night Club like a puppy following its owner. Again he was feeling like a passenger in his own body, as if it were under someone else's control.

"Get the door," G.G. ordered.

Wyatt didn't hesitate. He opened the door for the larger man to carry Elspeth in and then continued to follow him. He expected G.G. to carry her to the nearest booth or table and lay her there so that they could see if there was anything they could do while they waited for the ambulance. Instead, he headed for the hallway at the back of the bar, and Wyatt followed silently.

"Door," G.G. said a moment later as he paused in front of one that said Employees Only.

Wyatt moved around him to push through the door and then held it open for the big man to enter. They were in a midsized kitchen full of stainless steel. It wasn't as large as he would have expected in an establishment of this size, but Wyatt supposed most people came for the power drinks. That thought was supported by the fact that the actual cooking area was small with a range, an oven, a microwave, and a long metal prep table. The rest of the room appeared to be taken up with huge industrial-size refrigerators.

G.G. carried Elspeth to the stainless steel prep table and laid her gently on it. The moment he moved away, Wyatt stepped up to look her over. His heart sank as he got a good view of her under the bright lights of the kitchen. Elspeth really did look as if she'd been chewed up by the car and the road. There didn't appear to be a part of her that had got away unscathed. Her clothing was torn, as was the skin under it, nearly everywhere.

"Step aside."

Wyatt glanced around at that order. G.G. was back and was carrying half a dozen bags of what looked like blood.

"What—?" Wyatt began with bewilderment as he was nudged out of the way.

G.G. set the bags on the table next to Elspeth, but then

turned to peer at him solemnly. "What you're about to see is going to freak you out. Do not panic. Everything is fine. You are in no danger. Elspeth's a lovely woman, and I'll explain everything, but I need to see to her first. All right?"

Wyatt's eyebrows rose high on his forehead, but he nodded once.

G.G. hesitated briefly, his expression suggesting he wasn't entirely convinced Wyatt would remain calm, but then he sighed and turned to Elspeth. Wyatt immediately moved closer to the table again and leaned over Elspeth's legs to see what G.G. was doing.

At first the big man didn't do anything but pick up one of the bags and hold it over her face. After a moment, he clucked with agitation and muttered, "She's unconscious. I need to get her to—"

Leaving the comment unfinished, he set the bag back on the table, and then turned to retrieve the smallest knife from a collection in a holder on the wall.

"What are you going to do with that?" Wyatt asked when G.G. turned back with the wickedly sharp-looking paring knife.

G.G. didn't respond. He simply held his hand over Elspeth's face and sliced the end of one finger with the knife so the blood quickly bubbled to the surface.

While Wyatt gaped at him, G.G. set the knife aside, and then shifted the bleeding finger back and forth in front of Elspeth's nose a couple times. After the third pass, her mouth opened slightly on a soft moan and they were able to see her upper canines shift and slide out of her jaw, looking remarkably like fangs.

Wyatt was still struggling to accept what he'd just seen when G.G. suddenly picked up one of the bags of blood he'd collected and slapped it to her mouth. The big man waited a moment and then sighed with relief when it stuck and turned to peer at Wyatt, his eyes narrowing warily.

"How are you doing?" he asked after a pause. "Feeling a little panicky, maybe? Ready to stab me and run screaming from the room?"

"Stab you?" Wyatt asked with surprise, shocked out of his silence at the suggestion.

"Well, you're gripping that knife pretty tightly, and looking like you might want to stab someone," he pointed out dryly.

Wyatt glanced down and stared with confusion at the paring knife in his hand. He must have picked it up after G.G. set it down, though he didn't recall doing it. He was, however, gripping it like he was ready to use it, he noted. Wyatt raised his hand to set it on the table, but then hesitated, reluctant to release it. He'd been trained to respond automatically to combat situations, and the adrenaline shooting through his body was suggesting this was just such a situation.

"Hang on to the knife if it makes you feel better," G.G. suggested. "Just don't stab me with it. I don't mean you any harm, and *I* am mortal. It would be a shame for you to go to jail. On top of that, I don't particularly want to die."

"You're mortal?" Wyatt snatched at the words.

"Born and bred, just like you," G.G. assured him solemnly, and then smiled wryly and added, "My piercings and tattoos should tell you that. The holes would seal up and the tattoos would slough off like a bad tan if I were immortal."

"Immortal?" Wyatt glanced to Elspeth. "Is that what

she is? Immortal, not a . . . vampire?" He winced even as he asked the question. What he was seeing now suggested vampire, but that was so ridiculous. There was no such thing as vampires. Right?

"Not a vampire," G.G. assured him solemnly. "Vampires are dead and cursed. Elspeth is immortal born, an entirely different beast."

"Immortal born," Wyatt murmured, noting that the bag at her mouth was quickly shrinking as if the blood was being syphoned from it. When G.G. grunted in the affirmative, he asked, "So her mother's one too? That's why Martine looks so young?"

"Yes," G.G. agreed. "They don't age past about twenty-five or thirty. That's when a human is at their peak condition. Fully grown and fully developed. After that it's all downhill. For mortals anyway."

"Is she human?" he asked at once.

"Oh, yes," G.G. assured him as he removed the now empty blood bag from Elspeth's mouth.

"How is she doing?"

Both men glanced toward the door at that question. It was the woman who had approached them outside. G.G. had called her Sofia.

"Good, I think," G.G. said, tossing aside the empty bag of blood he'd just removed and reaching for a fresh one. "Did you take care of everything out front?"

"Yes. The ambulance arrived just as I finished with the driver and witnesses. It's all handled," she announced and joined them at the table, but frowned when she saw Elspeth. "Why haven't you tied her down?"

"Tied her down?" G.G. and Wyatt asked together.

"Yes. Once she starts to heal, she'll—Shit!" They all jumped back in surprise when Elspeth suddenly sucked in a sharp breath and sat up on the prep table, her arms pinwheeling, and then she released a long, drawn-out, pain-filled shriek and started to claw at her mutilated face. It was like she was trying to tear away the abraded and cut skin, Wyatt thought as Sofia leapt forward to catch at Elspeth's hands and try to prevent her harming herself further.

"Help me!" Sofia snapped as she struggled with Elspeth.

Wyatt and G.G. hurried forward, but Elspeth was incredibly strong. She was also writhing and thrashing violently about, arms and legs flailing, body twisting. Even with the three of them, they couldn't hold her down or stop her struggles. They were all three just half lying on her, doing their best to hold her still, and then Sofia, who had been trying to restrain Elspeth's hands, suddenly went flying. Wyatt had just registered that when the giant man followed Sofia, soaring through the air to crash against the front of one of the refrigerators with a thud before dropping to the ground with a groan. The next thing Wyatt knew, Elspeth had launched herself at him.

Shouting in surprise, he fell back. She rode him to the floor, where Wyatt landed hard on his back. The wind was knocked out of him, but it could have been worse if she hadn't grabbed his head in both hands. Elspeth had saved him from what would no doubt have been a concussion, but it was just blind good luck for him. That hadn't been her intention. At least, Wyatt didn't think it was when she used her hold to turn his head to the side and bent to sink her teeth into his neck. This explained the earlier bit he'd heard about biting, he supposed as he felt her sharp fangs scrape against his throat. Unable to free himself, Wyatt closed his eyes, bracing against the coming pain as they started to pierce his skin, and then her weight and teeth were suddenly gone.

Blinking his eyes open in surprise, Wyatt glanced around to see two men dressed in black leather dragging Elspeth away from him. One was a tall, dark-haired man with golden-brown eyes. The other was blond, with piercing silver-blue eyes like Elspeth's. Both were straining to hold the woman between them and not succeeding very well. They were barely managing to hold on to her arms. She was jerking them about like they were a couple of toddlers.

"Thank Christ."

Wyatt glanced around at that relieved growl to see G.G. dragging himself to his feet with help from Sofia. The man was holding his ribs with one hand as he straightened.

"We need chains," the dark-haired man snapped, struggling to hold onto a thrashing Elspeth.

"This is a nightclub, not a bondage shop," G.G. growled.

"There are some in our SUV. Key's in my pocket," the blond said urgently. "There are padlocks there too. We'll need a couple of them."

Leaving G.G. leaning against the wall, Sofia rushed to the men, reached into the blond man's pocket, and retrieved his keys and disappeared. She moved so fast, Wyatt couldn't even track her. One minute she was there and then she became a blur of motion and was gone.

Giving his head a shake, Wyatt got to his feet. He briefly watched Elspeth struggle and writhe in the arms of the two newcomers, and then moved over to G.G.

"You okay?" he asked, looking him over quickly. He didn't see blood anywhere, but judging by the way G.G. was holding his ribs, he'd guess one or two were broken.

"Fine," G.G. sighed.

Wyatt didn't believe him, but didn't argue. Instead, he asked, "Who are these guys?"

"The blond one is Valerian. The other is Tybo," he answered through gritted teeth. "They're good guys. They work with Elspeth. They'll take care of her."

"They're with the police?" Wyatt asked with surprise. Dressed all in black as both men were, he'd been thinking mafia or motorcycle gang, not cops.

"Police," G.G. echoed and smiled wryly. "Yeah, the immortal version. They're Enforcers, or rogue hunters. They hunt rogue immortals. Criminals mortal police wouldn't be able to handle."

"Oh," Wyatt said blankly. He supposed that was a special division as Elspeth had told him. Probably one the mortal police didn't know about, but she hadn't exactly lied.

"What happened to her?" Tybo asked.

Wyatt glanced toward the men, and frowned when he saw that Elspeth appeared to have passed out. She was sagging in their hold as they carried her to the stainless steel table she'd escaped just moments ago.

"She was run over by a car," Wyatt said, helping G.G. when the big man started to limp toward the immortal police.

"Out front," Tybo said with a nod. "Mortimer heard about an accident on the police frequency, recognized the address, and suggested we stop in and check that it had nothing to do with The Night Club."

"She'd just left here," G.G. muttered. "I'd just finished locking the door behind them and was watching from the window when some guy pushed her in front of a car."

"Someone pushed her?" Wyatt turned on the man with

surprise. He hadn't realized. One minute they'd been talking, and then she'd flown out into the road and—

"Yeah," G.G. said, his expression grim. Turning back to the men then he continued, "By the time I got the door unlocked and got out, he was gone and the car was stopped on top of Elspeth. I figured it was more important to get her inside before the ambulance came than to chase after the guy."

"You did right," Valerian assured him.

The clank of chains announced Sofia's return as she hurried to join the men around Elspeth.

"Why did she go crazy like that?" Wyatt asked as Tybo took the chains and the two men began to wrap them around Elspeth and the table.

"The healing," Sofia explained quietly. "She should have been chained down before you gave her blood. The minute it hit her system the nanos would have started the healing and . . ." She grimaced. "It's painful. The worse the injury, the more painful the healing is, and she was hurt pretty bad."

Wyatt thought that was one hell of an understatement. Elspeth was a mangled mess, basically hamburger in torn clothes. If she were human, she'd be dead for sure. Or if she were mortal, he supposed, since G.G. claimed she was still human. Hard to believe, though, after seeing her fangs and how strong she was. But Sofia had said once the blood hit her system the nanos would have started the healing. What the hell were nanos?

Before he could ask, G.G. said quietly, "Sorry. I didn't know she needed to be chained. This is my first time dealing with an injured immortal."

"Not your fault," Tybo assured him, sliding a padlock through the ends of the chain and snapping it closed.

Tugging on the chain to test their handiwork, he added, "Someone should have thought to tell you things like that. With immortals for customers, we should have figured you'd run into something like this eventually. Truthfully, it's lucky you haven't encountered it before this."

"Yeah, maybe," G.G. said wryly as they watched Tybo grab a bag and slap it to Elspeth's mouth.

Turning away from Elspeth, Valerian eyed G.G. with concern. "You need a hospital."

"Nah," G.G. said with a grimace. "It's just a couple of cracked ribs. I've had them before. I'll survive. Just tape me up. It's all they'd do."

Valerian and Tybo exchanged a glance, and then Tybo pulled out a phone and turned to walk to the other end of the kitchen, punching in numbers as he went.

"What are nanos?" Wyatt asked finally and found all four people looking at him. Even Tybo paused and turned, the phone pressed to his ear.

"Mortal," Valerian grunted, his gaze narrowed on Wyatt.

Wyatt eyed him warily back, vaguely aware of a small ruffling sensation in his head.

"Yes, he's mortal. He's Elspeth's friend," G.G. said, and then added solemnly, "She couldn't read or control him."

Valerian's head went back slightly and his eyebrows rose. "Well, hell, that makes things more complicated."

"Why?" Wyatt asked sharply, and then glanced to G.G. and asked, "And what do you mean she couldn't read or control me? They can read and control us?"

"Elspeth didn't tell him a damned thing about us," Valerian said with exasperation.

G.G. shook his head, a permanent wince on his face now. "I think she only realized today while here that she couldn't control him and he was her LM."

"What is an LM?" Wyatt asked now, recalling G.G. mentioning that earlier.

The four of them glanced at each other as if each hoped one of the others might volunteer the answer.

"What the hell was Elspeth doing bringing an uninitiated mortal to The Night Club? She knows better than that," Tybo groused, slipping his phone back into his pocket as he returned to the group.

"She didn't bring him. He followed her," G.G. explained wearily, and then muttered, "I need to sit down."

Tybo and Valerian exchanged another glance and then Tybo nodded. "Let's move this conversation to your office so you can sit while we figure out what to do."

"What about Elspeth?" Wyatt asked at once, his gaze sliding to where she lay. She was still silent and unmoving, he noted, and the blood bag at her mouth was now a dehydrated and wrinkled wad of plastic.

Valerian ripped the plastic away, then slapped another bag on. Turning to them then, he shrugged. "She'll be fine."

When Wyatt scowled at him, he asked, "Do you want to know what's going on here or not?" He paused briefly and then added, "We'll leave the door open and check on her frequently."

"Fine." He sighed and moved back to G.G. to ask, "Are you okay to walk?"

G.G. arched one eyebrow. Tone dry, he asked, "Why? You planning to carry me if I'm not?"

"Hell no," Wyatt said at once. "I make it a rule never to carry cars, tanks, or giants."

A bark of startled laughter erupted from the big man. It was quickly followed by a pained wince and a groan.

"I got this," Sofia announced and stepped up to scoop

the man off his feet as if he weighed little more than a toddler. When G.G. immediately roared in protest, she rolled her eyes and moved quickly toward a door at the other side of the room, muttering, "Oh, stifle it, you big baby. I'll put you down in a minute."

Realizing that the door she was headed for was closed, Wyatt rushed ahead and opened it for her, then watched with amusement as she carried the huge man in. Sofia was perhaps five-feet-four-inches and didn't look like she would weigh more than a hundred pounds soaking wet, but she was carrying the giant like *he* was the pipsqueak.

Shaking his head, Wyatt moved into the office and glanced around. It was a good size, with one wall painted dark brown, and the other three painted beige. The floor was hardwood. There was a large desk, a couch, a chair, and a television on one side, while several large filing cabinets, a printer/copier/fax combo, and a shredder took up part of the other side, with a small bar in the far corner. Sofia carried G.G. around the large, solid oak desk and set him in the cushioned leather chair behind it. She then moved over to the bar to pull ice out of the freezer. She dumped some in a glass and then grabbed a bottle of pop and began to pour it over the ice.

"Tahiti Treat?" Wyatt said with a grin. "Man, I love that stuff. Haven't seen it in the stores in ages, though."

"It's called Tahitian Treat now," G.G. told him.

"He orders it from the States at a ridiculous price," Sofia said dryly as she replaced the pop container and closed the refrigerator.

"Hey, I don't comment on what you drink," G.G. muttered and then added a surly, "Thank you," when she handed him his drink.

Sofia nodded and headed out of the room. "I'm going to open up."

"Thanks, Sofia," G.G. repeated, and then turned to Tybo and Valerian. "So, are one of you guys going to tape up my ribs, or what?"

"No," Tybo said at once. "Dr. Rachel's on her way to do it for you."

"What?" G.G. asked with alarm.

"I'm not going to risk being responsible for one of your ribs puncturing your lungs or heart or something," Tybo told him firmly. "I will not be known as the immortal who killed the Green Giant."

"Neither will I," Valerian added.

"Cowards," G.G. muttered.

"Rachel should be here soon. She and Sam were already downtown shopping when I called," Tybo announced as Wyatt moved back to the open door to peer out at Elspeth. She was still lying silent and unmoving on the tabletop, he noted with a frown.

"What's the matter? The bag's not empty already, is it?" Valerian asked, moving up beside him to look at Elspeth as well.

"Nearly," Wyatt said, but asked, "Why isn't she screaming and thrashing again? Isn't she healing anymore? You said that's why she reacted that way after the first bag, but she's not reacting at all now and that's her third bag."

"She will," Valerian assured him solemnly. "She just wore herself out with her first round. She'll start up again. Soon," he added darkly as they heard a soft moan. "I'm going to change out the blood bag. Tybo, why don't you start explaining about immortals to Wyatt while I do?"

"Yeah, yeah," Tybo said and then eyed Wyatt speculatively. "So . . . Elspeth hasn't told you anything at all about us?"

Wyatt shook his head and glanced out to the kitchen as Valerian tugged the empty bag from Elspeth's mouth and slapped another on.

"Great," Tybo said lightly. "So, okay, here's the deal. Our ancestors come from Olympus."

Wyatt swung around to blink at him. "Olympus?"

"Yeah, we're the children of Gods and nymphs, so we're super strong and also super sexy."

A burst of laughter slipped from G.G. that was quickly followed by a gasped curse. "Damn, Tybo, cut that out. It hurts to laugh."

"Sorry, buddy," Tybo said with a grin, and then taunted, "But if you'd let your mother turn you, you wouldn't have to worry about stuff like broken ribs. You'd already be healed."

"Oh, just shut up about that and tell him the truth," G.G. growled with irritation.

"All right. Jeez, you're turning into a grumpy sod in your old age, G.G.," Tybo accused.

"I'm thirty-six," G.G. muttered, rolling his eyes. "A damned sight younger than you. Now start again, and the truth this time."

Six

Wyatt waited patiently as Tybo gathered his thoughts. It seemed to take a while, but finally the man settled on the corner of G.G.'s desk, crossed his arms, and began.

"So, there was this doctor fellow. Kind of a mad scientist type. He wanted to find a way to heal injuries and fight illnesses such as cancer and stuff without having to perform surgeries, or administer chemo or radiation. He felt those things just caused more damage. He wanted something that worked from inside the body. Understand?"

Wyatt nodded. So far the man was making sense. Raising his eyebrows, he suggested, "And the nanos Sofia mentioned are what he came up with?"

"Yes," Tybo said. "But they aren't your typical tiny machines. He managed to bioengineer nanos that travel in blood, and use blood to propel themselves and perform their work as well as to replicate themselves. That way they could be injected into the body without fear of the body's immune system attacking them. They could also make more of themselves if higher numbers were needed for more serious wounds."

"Okay," Wyatt murmured when he paused. "Sounds brilliant."

"Yeah," Tybo agreed. "But after working to get his idea to that point, our scientist got lazy. Rather than develop nanos programmed for each different injury, or illness, he made one program with a map of the male and female body at their peak condition and the executive order for the nanos to ensure their host was at that peak condition. Once they'd accomplished that, they were supposed to self-destruct."

"What went wrong?" Wyatt asked, knowing something must have. There was no other explanation for these immortals who apparently had the nanos living inside them.

"Our mad scientist didn't consider that the body is always under attack. There's pollution, sunlight, airborne germs, bacteria on every surface . . ." He shrugged. "Even the simple passage of time. The nanos never finish their assigned task of getting their host at their peak. They never self-destruct, so just continue to work inside their host, keeping them from aging, getting ill, or—hell, even getting cavities. They just stay, toiling away and keeping their host forever healthy and forever young."

"What about the fangs?" Wyatt asked when he fell silent. "And the superhuman strength? I mean, Sofia carried G.G. around like a baby, and Elspeth was throwing everyone around like some crazy strong bull."

"Yeah," Tybo said with wry amusement. "They weren't part of the programming. The nanos apparently came up with that stuff themselves."

"What?" Wyatt asked with disbelief, but Tybo nodded.

"See, this mad scientist developed this stuff way back before Jesus Christ."

Wyatt stiffened, the first grains of disbelief slipping into his mind, and he said sarcastically, "Right. In Olympus."

"No. Atlantis," Tybo responded.

Wyatt snorted with disbelief.

"He's telling the truth this time," G.G. said a little breathlessly. "Atlantis did exist and it was more developed technologically than the rest of the world."

"They were isolated from the rest of the world by mountains and the sea and advanced much more quickly than everyone else," Tybo explained. "But then Atlantis fell. A series of earthquakes sent it sliding into the sea. The only survivors were the Atlanteans who had the nanos. But these nanos use a lot of blood to accomplish their work, more than the human body can produce. They handled that in Atlantis with blood transfusions, but when the survivors crawled out of the ruins of a collapsing Atlantis and joined the rest of the world, it was to find that world barely past the caveman stage.

"There were no doctors or scientists to help them, and no blood transfusions to supply the blood they needed to survive. Some killed themselves rather than suffer the agony the lack of blood caused. Some went crazy with blood hunger and were so desperate to get the blood they needed, they attacked the primitive people they encountered. But the nanos in another portion of them lived up to their programing. Their directive was to keep their host at their peak condition. They needed blood to accomplish that, so the nanos forced a sort of evolution on their hosts to get the blood they needed—the fangs, increased strength, night vision, mind reading, and the ability to control their prey."

"So the nanos turned you into vampires," Wyatt said quietly.

"The correct term would be immortals," Valerian said dryly, returning to the room. "Do not call us vampires."

"Told you," G.G. said with amusement.

Wyatt nodded an acknowledgment, but asked, "Why? It's what you are, isn't it?"

"No," Valerian snapped. "Vampires are dead, soulless corpses that crawl out of their graves at night to drink the blood of the living. We are neither dead nor soulless and do not have graves to crawl out of. We are merely mortals made nearly immortal by scientific advances."

"If you'd read one of the gazillion vampire romances out there, Valerian, you wouldn't mind being called a vampire."

Wyatt turned with a start at that amused comment and stared at the lovely redhead with silver-green eyes who stood behind him in the doorway.

"Vampires are considered sexy nowadays," she continued. "While immortals . . ." Wrinkling her nose, she shrugged. "No one's even heard of immortals."

"Which is just the way we like it," Valerian assured her.

"Let Rachel in, Wyatt," G.G. said, sounding relieved at her arrival.

"You're the doctor," Wyatt said, his gaze sliding past her to Elspeth even as he moved to the side.

"I looked at Elspeth on the way in. She's doing fine," Rachel told him gently as she entered the room.

Wyatt nodded, and then glanced at the woman following Rachel. He recalled Tybo saying the doctor had been shopping with someone named Sam. This woman appeared to be Sam. She was slender with long, wavy dark hair framing a face with large eyes, a slightly crooked nose, and a full mouth that all somehow worked together to make a very attractive face.

"Hi," she murmured, offering him her hand. "You must be Elspeth's life mate."

"Her what?" he asked with surprise.

"Er . . . Sam?" Tybo said with amusement. "We hadn't got around to explaining to him about LMs yet."

"Oh." Grimacing apologetically, she slipped past Wyatt to join Rachel as she walked around the desk to the injured giant.

Wyatt frowned after her and then shifted his gaze to Tybo in question as he recalled G.G. saying he was Elspeth's LM to Sofia. "So, an LM is a life mate?"

"It's what G.G. calls them," Valerian explained.

"Okay." Wyatt nodded. "So, what the hell is a life mate, then?"

Tybo opened his mouth to respond, but Elspeth chose that moment to start shrieking and thrashing about in the next room.

"So . . . life mates!"

Wyatt dragged his gaze away from the closed office door to gape at Tybo with disbelief when he shouted that. Cupping a hand to his ear, he yelled, "I'm sorry. Did you say something? I couldn't hear you over the headbanger music from the bar, and the *screaming* coming from the kitchen. You know, where Elspeth's suffering the agonies of hell?"

The moment Elspeth had begun to shriek, loud music had started thumping in the bar. Apparently, Sofia was trying to drown out the screaming so The Night Club's customers wouldn't be troubled by it. Wyatt had no idea if it was working in the bar area, but it wasn't back here. Elspeth's piercing cries seemed to drown everything else out for him. Turning to Rachel, he asked with frustration, "Can't you give her something to help with the pain?"

"I did," Rachel reminded him as she finished taping up G.G.'s ribs. "But at this point it will barely touch the pain. She'll just have to fight through it. If it makes you feel better, I can tell you she won't remember this when she wakes up. While the drugs can't do much for her pain when it's this bad, they will at least ensure she doesn't remember her suffering."

It didn't make him feel better. *He* would remember this. Wyatt suspected Elspeth's mangled face twisted in a rictus of pain and her frenzied shrieks and struggles against the chains would haunt his nightmares for years to come. He'd never seen such suffering before, and hoped to God he never did again. As ashamed as he was to admit it, he'd been relieved when Rachel and Tybo had forced him back into the office once Rachel had done all she could for her. He wanted to be there for Elspeth, but this was unbearable.

"So . . . life mates!" Tybo shouted again.

Wyatt released his breath on a sigh. "Fine! What the hell is a life mate?"

Now that he had his attention, Tybo paused briefly, as if considering how best to explain. Finally he said, "You know how wolves mate for life?"

"What?" Wyatt asked with bewilderment, not following what wolves had to do with immortal life mates, and then, horror claiming him, he said, "Please tell me immortals aren't werewolves too."

"No, of course not," Tybo snapped, sounding annoyed.

"Look, there are animals that mate for life, like wolves, coyotes, beavers—"

"Termites," Wyatt added dryly. "So what's that got to do with life mates?"

"Immortals mate for life too, and that's what a life mate is," he explained with exasperation. "An immortal's mate . . . for life."

"Well, at least until one of them dies," Valerian put in. "Then, if they're lucky, the survivor might find another life mate."

"And you guys think I'm that for Elspeth?"

All five of them nodded, and then G.G. said, "But Elspeth will fight it. As I mentioned, she's led a very sheltered life. She hoped to enjoy a little taste of freedom before she settles down with a life mate. Finding you right away wasn't in her plan."

Wyatt supposed he could understand that, but let it go for now and asked, "Why do you think we're life mates?"

"She couldn't read or control you," G.G. said solemnly.

Wyatt recalled him saying something about that before, and frowned. "Well, surely you all encounter a person once in a while you can't read?"

"The only mortals an immortal can't read are either insane, or life mates," Valerian assured him.

"And we know you aren't insane because the rest of us can all read you," Rachel assured him.

"Except me," G.G. added with wry amusement and said, "Mortal here, remember? Can't read anyone."

Wyatt nodded and turned back to peer at the immortals. They could read him? That was alarming. Had they been reading him all this time?

"Of course we have," Rachel said with amusement as she put away the items she'd been using to tend to G.G.'s ribs. "Aside from the fact that you're shrieking your thoughts at us, the way you've been gripping that knife would be rather alarming if we didn't read your mind to reassure ourselves that you weren't planning to use it on someone and were just holding it as a security blanket."

Wyatt glanced down at the knife in his hand. He'd forgot he still had it. Now he felt like a fool. A security blanket? The description made him think of Linus from Charlie Brown with his blanket against his face and his thumb in his mouth. Grimacing, he set the paring knife on the corner of G.G.'s desk and then paced back to the door, before swinging back to ask, "But Elspeth can't control me? You're sure about that?"

"She tried when you first came into The Night Club," G.G. told him. "Mortals aren't really welcome here. At least, not if they do not know about immortals. She tried to take control of you and send you out of the club, but couldn't. She admitted that while you were in the men's room."

"Oh," Wyatt frowned at this news. For a moment, he'd thought he found the explanation for that strange disassociated feeling he'd experienced when he'd found himself on the porch with her jacket in hand, and then when he'd pressed her face to his throat. He'd thought perhaps she'd controlled him, but if G.G. was right, it couldn't have been her.

Martine, he thought suddenly as he recalled Elspeth's words to her mother in front of the house. The using him business had obviously been about Elspeth's literally biting him. From what he could sort out, Martine had wanted her daughter to bite him to get the blood she'd been in need of. Probably because of her getting stabbed, he guessed. As for the Council and execution part of the conversation, he suspected biting wasn't allowed and might be punishable by death or something. He supposed he'd have to ask if that were the case.

"It is."

Wyatt glanced to Tybo uncertainly. "What is?"

"Biting mortals is against Council law here in North America except in cases of an emergency," Tybo explained. "And it *is* punishable by death. Martine should not have been trying to talk Elspeth into doing it."

"I'm thinking we should tell Mortimer about that," Valerian said quietly. "From what I'm reading from Wyatt's memory, she didn't just try to talk Elspeth into it. She took control of them both and tried to force it."

Wyatt glanced at him sharply as he wondered what else she'd controlled. Had she made them kiss? It was possible, he supposed, but he didn't think she'd controlled their response to the kiss.

"Why would she do something like that?" Rachel asked with dismay, distracting him. "It could have got Elspeth executed."

"Elspeth seemed to think Martine was trying to get her thrown out of the country and sent back to England," Wyatt told them solemnly as he recalled the argument he'd overheard.

"Really?" Rachel asked with amazement, and then shook her head. "I'd heard Martine had some control issues, but that's seriously messed up."

"Yeah, but that business about her getting stabbed might have pushed Martine over the edge," G.G. commented quietly, and when all eyes turned to him, he explained, "Elspeth was apparently stabbed this morning. And Martine is pretty overprotective. That would have freaked her out."

Tybo's phone rang just as the screaming died abruptly in the next room.

Spinning on his heel, Wyatt hurried to the door, yanked it open and rushed across the kitchen to peer down at Elspeth with concern. Much to his surprise, most of her injuries appeared to have healed. The shallower gashes and abrasions that had covered her were gone, while the deeper, more serious ones had healed into scabs and some even to scars. Even her face was healing, her features beginning to look like hers again. At least, she was recognizable as herself now. But she was also dead still and silent.

"Is she all right?" he asked fretfully when Rachel appeared beside him and began to examine Elspeth.

"Yes," Rachel said with a smile. "She's still healing, but the worst of it is over now. She should sleep through the rest."

"Good," Tybo said, putting his phone away as he joined them. "Because we have to get Elspeth home."

"What?" Wyatt asked with surprise.

"Martine is going ballistic. She's been calling Elspeth for hours and not gotten a response."

Wyatt's eyes widened. "I don't even know where her phone is. Or her purse."

"Probably strewn all over the road," G.G. said with a frown. "I doubt anything in her purse survived."

"The point is, Martine couldn't reach Elspeth," Tybo said, and then glanced to Wyatt and added, "And when she found out your grandmother couldn't get ahold of you either, she called Mortimer in a panic."

Cursing, Wyatt pulled out his phone and saw that he had twelve missed calls. He hadn't heard it ring, but then, between the loud music and Elspeth's screaming . . .

"I wouldn't bother calling your grandmother," Rachel said soothingly when he started to punch buttons to do just that. "Martine has probably taken control and soothed her already. She wouldn't have wanted her to call the police about the two of you going missing. Immortals avoid getting the authorities involved in anything."

"Did Mortimer tell Martine what happened and where Elspeth is?" G.G. asked with concern.

Tybo nodded. "She was going to head straight here, but Mortimer assured her we'd take her home at once."

"Elspeth's car's in the parking lot across the street," Wyatt told them.

"But her keys were probably in her purse," Tybo pointed out.

"Nope," Rachel said, pulling them from Elspeth's jacket pocket. "Unfortunately, they're as wrecked as she was," she added, grimacing as she looked through the broken bits of plastic and bent keys.

"We'll take her home in our SUV and arrange for her car to be picked up and new keys to be made tomorrow," Valerian said, taking the mess from her. Glancing to Elspeth, he asked, "You're sure she's through the pain part and won't suddenly come to screaming life in the car on the way to her place?"

Rachel hesitated and then sighed. "You know these things aren't always predictable. She should be done, but . . ." She shrugged helplessly.

"We'll keep her chained for the ride," Tybo decided. "And I'll sit with her in the back to be sure she doesn't wake up and cause problems."

Valerian nodded and then glanced at Wyatt. "Are you okay to drive?"

"Of course," he said at once. "I wasn't the one hurt."

"Yeah, but it's after 1 A.M. and it's been a long day for you," Tybo pointed out.

Wyatt's eyes widened incredulously. But he checked his phone again and saw that it *was* nearly one thirty in the morning. He had no idea where the last six and a half hours had gone. It hadn't seemed like he'd been here that long.

"I'll drive him," Rachel offered. "It's on our way home anyway." She glanced to Sam then and added, "If that's okay with you?"

"Sure. I'll follow and take you home from there," Sam said easily.

"It's all settled then," G.G. commented, and Wyatt noted the amusement on the man's face. The giant obviously thought it was funny how the immortals were settling his life for him, but Wyatt didn't care in that moment and allowed himself to be ushered from The Night Club.

It wasn't until he was in the passenger seat of his rental, following Tybo and Valerian's dark SUV home, that it occurred to him to wonder if he really wasn't upset at having his life decided for him, or if someone had taken control and ensured he would go along with their plans without causing a fuss. Wyatt had barely had the thought when he suddenly found himself growing weary, closing his eyes, and drifting off to sleep.

Seven

Elspeth was smiling when she opened her eyes, the remnants of sleep clinging and leaving her feeling sated and drowsy. She couldn't remember her dreams, but despite that was reluctant to wake up fully and abandon them, so let her eyes drift closed again. Only to have them pop open once more when a loud laugh disturbed her peaceful dozing.

Recalled to her unwanted guests, Elspeth groaned and dragged her pillow over her head, but when she felt a tug and pinch at her inner elbow, immediately pushed it away again to look at her arm. She stared with confusion at the catheter taped just below the bend of her arm and then followed the tube up to an empty IV bag that hung from a stand next to the bed. More disturbing than that, though, were the dried streaks of blood on her arm . . . and hand and fingers, she saw with a frown. On both arms and hands and sets of fingers, Elspeth realized as she reached to pull the catheter out of her arm.

Confused, Elspeth hurriedly tossed the sheets and duvet aside, leapt from bed and rushed into her bathroom. She skidded to a halt on the cold tile floor, though, when she spotted herself in the mirror over the sink.

"Dear God," she breathed, her gaze sliding over her reflection. She was completely naked, which was odd. She usually wore a nightgown to bed, or at least a T-shirt and underwear, but that wasn't what had her gaping. It was the dried blood covering her body. It seemed to be everywhere, in her hair, on her face, her neck, her chest and stomach, arms and legs.

Elspeth ran her hands lightly over the streaks and clumps of dry blood and shook her head with bewilderment.

"What the hell?" The words were barely a breath of sound, but it startled her out of her inactivity. Giving her head a shake, she forced herself away from the mirror and to the shower. Obviously, she couldn't do without one, she thought, struggling with her confusion.

Elspeth turned on the taps, and then stepped back as the water sprayed out. As she waited for it to reach the desired temperature, she tried to sort out how she'd ended up so bloodied. She wound up having to run through the last two days, from being stabbed on the soft call, to her visit to The Night Club, which was the last thing she remembered clearly. She recalled leaving The Night Club with Wyatt, chatting on the curb with him as she surveyed the traffic. She'd been considering whether to control the drivers or wait for a natural opening and then—

Elspeth closed her eyes as she recalled tumbling into the road, reaching out with her hands to break her fall, and then being slammed from the left, knocked to the pavement, and then rolling as a dark and hot monster rode over her, repeatedly catching at her, spinning her and crushing her as it passed until she knew no more. Literally. She didn't remember anything after that until she woke up here in her bed.

"Right," Elspeth breathed. She'd been hit by a car. Sighing, she reached out to test the water. Finding it just the right temperature, she stepped under the spray and tugged the curtain shut. At first, she just stood there with her head bowed, allowing the water to pour down over her as she thought.

Elspeth couldn't recall how she'd got home, but presumed G.G. had got her back here. Although, she thought, reaching for the soap and beginning to run it over her body, the mortal bartender couldn't have done it without help. It would have taken an immortal to keep her from being taken away by an ambulance, she was sure. And to control Wyatt, who would probably have insisted on that ambulance.

Wyatt. Where was he and how had he been handled? Elspeth wondered about that as she ran the soap over her breasts. She then stilled at a sudden flash of memory of someone else's hands gliding over her body. It was more like a remnant of a dream. A warm body at her back, whispering by her ear, followed by kisses along her neck that sent shivers through her entire body before arms slid around her and hands claimed and caressed her breasts, holding, squeezing, and lifting them eagerly until she moaned and leaned her head back against a strong shoulder. And then she turned her head to the side and a mouth claimed hers, a talented tongue invading to explore as one hand slid away and drifted down over her stomach to slide between her legs.

Gasping, Elspeth blinked her eyes open and then

shifted quickly out from under the spray as both eyes were hit with water. Leaning against the shower wall, she hugged herself briefly and tried to sort out what had just happened. Where had that come from? Because it certainly hadn't been a real memory from something she'd experienced in life. Her mother had seen to that. During the short bouts of time she'd managed to steal for herself away from her mother, all Elspeth had managed to experience were a dozen stolen kisses and a groping session or two.

Realizing she was almost panting, Elspeth closed her eyes and forced herself to relax. She then set the soap back on the holder, and stepped determinedly under the water to let it sluice away the soap and the remaining blood. It took longer than it would have had she used soap and her hands to help with the effort, but the fragment of memory she'd experienced had been disconcerting. Elspeth wasn't ready for more, so took the time and concentrated on how she would get out of the apartment without her mother knowing. Because she was quite sure that her little car accident would just increase her mother's protectiveness and make her more determined to stick to Elspeth like glue.

By the time she stepped out of the shower and began to dry herself off, Elspeth had an idea. She dressed quickly, pulled her hair back into a ponytail and then took a minute to rearrange the pillows in her bed, and cover them with the duvet in hopes it would look like she was still asleep. Once finished, Elspeth slid out of her room through the French doors leading to her balcony. It was situated on the flat roof of the open porch that ran the length of the back of the house. Meredith, or perhaps her husband when they'd had the whole house to themselves, had put a deck floor on the roof and a railing around it, turning it into a large, lovely balcony that overlooked the backyard.

Elspeth glanced to her right as she slipped out onto the balcony, relieved to find that, as expected, the curtains were drawn over the French doors off the living room. The only time Elspeth opened the curtains was at night to enjoy the moon and what stars were visible. As an immortal, the sun was something to be avoided, and curtains remained closed unless you had a UV filtering film on the windows. Elspeth didn't have that . . . yet. She planned to get it eventually, but hadn't got around to it yet. A good thing, since it ensured her mother and sisters wouldn't open the curtains and spot her escaping.

Easing the French door closed, Elspeth tiptoed quietly to the balcony rail and peered down at the grass below and the edge of the back porch just visible from where she stood. Meredith had told her she loved to sit out on the back porch in the summer with iced tea and a book. But it wasn't summer yet. It was only a few weeks into spring. Though with the way the weather had bounced between warm and cool, the plants appeared to be a bit confused and some were beginning to bud. Even the grass had been fooled into thinking winter was over and was sending out bright green shoots to mingle with the remnants of grass from last year that the snow and cold had turned brown.

Elspeth was quite sure Meredith wouldn't be sitting out on her porch this evening, but there was a possibility that her blinds were open and she would be seen. Grimacing, Elspeth started to climb over the rail. She'd have to risk it, and really, Merry knew about the issues she had with her mother and probably wouldn't be surprised to see her exiting the house this way to avoid dealing with her.

That thought made Elspeth smile faintly as she grasped the rail and began to lower herself toward the grass below. She was acting like a rebellious teenager rather than a dignified hundred-forty-two-year-old.

Elspeth's legs were dangling in the air between the upper and lower balcony when she heard the telltale swish of Merry's sliding glass door opening. She'd obviously had her curtains open and spotted her, Elspeth thought with a grimace, but continued to lower herself, only pausing when her hips were suddenly clasped in firm hands. Freezing, she peered down just as Wyatt leaned out to peer up at her.

"Good evening," he said with amusement. "Need a hand?"

Groaning inwardly, she shook her head and quickly lowered herself until she hung from the lip of her balcony. She dangled there briefly, with her breasts directly in front of Wyatt's face, and was about to let go and drop to the grass below the lower porch when Wyatt simply gave her a little tug, dragging her down and forward so that she slid his length to land on the porch in front of him.

"Good evening," he repeated, his voice deep this time, with a sexy huskiness that reminded her of both their kiss last night right here on this porch, as well as the dream remnant she'd recalled in the shower. Shivering at the recollection, she bit her lip, her eyes focusing in on his full, sexy lips as they lowered toward her.

"Good evening, Ellie dear. Do you have time for tea? Or are you rushing to work?"

Elspeth and Wyatt both froze, and then he released his

hold on her and smiled wryly as he stepped to the side so that she could see Merry standing in her open sliding glass door.

"Evening, Merry," Elspeth greeted her. "No tea for me today. I'm afraid I'm running late."

"You need a coat, dear. It's warmer than one would expect for this time of year, but it's cooling quickly as night approaches. Wyatt, grab her one of my jackets out of the coat closet," Merry ordered.

Nodding, Wyatt led the way into the house and to the hall closet by the apartment door. As he sorted through the available coats, he asked, "Do you need a ride to work?"

Elspeth accepted the dark, midthigh trench coat he handed her, but folded it over her arm as she glanced at him with surprise. "No. Why would I need—"

"We left your car in the parking garage across from . . . downtown the night before last," he finished, his gaze sliding to his Gran and back. "I'm sure the mechanic has picked it up by now and will drop it off when he's done with it, but in the meantime, you're without a vehicle."

"Oh." Elspeth blinked and then asked, "Mechanic? What's wrong with my car? And what do you mean the night before last?"

Wyatt cast a glance toward his grandmother, but then simply pulled out a black leather jacket for himself and announced, "I'll drive you to work."

"Wyatt parked in the spot closest to the house," Merry told them from the living room door. "So you should be able to avoid Martine spotting you leaving. Though I'm sure she'll notice you're missing soon enough."

"Yes, I'm sure she will," Elspeth agreed solemnly. "But hopefully it won't be for a while yet."

Nodding, Merry smiled faintly. "Well, I'm glad you're

recovering from your flu. Have a good night, dear. And do stop in for tea when you get back in the morning."

"I will," Elspeth murmured, thinking that the flu must have been the cover story they were using to explain her being bed bound. They could hardly tell Meredith the truth, she thought, as Wyatt opened the front door and quickly ushered her into the entry and then out of the house.

They were both silent as they hurried to the car. In fact, neither of them spoke until they had pulled out onto the street and Wyatt said, "You'll have to direct me. I'm not sure where the Enforcer office is."

Elspeth glanced at him sharply, her eyes wide.

"Left or right?" he prodded, glancing in the rearview mirror at the house behind them.

"Right," Elspeth said, and then cleared her throat before asking, "How long was I—?"

"We were at The Night Club two nights ago," Wyatt said solemnly. "You've been sleeping nearly forty-eight hours. But Rachel said that was normal."

"Rachel?" she asked uncertainly.

"Rachel Argeneau," he explained. "The doctor who's been looking after you. She's been stopping by to check on your progress several times a day, and dropped in to let me know how you were doing afterward each time. She didn't think your mother would keep me informed."

"No. She probably wouldn't have," Elspeth admitted quietly, wondering just how much he knew or understood.

"I'm surprised they expect you to work today after everything that happened the other night," Wyatt murmured once they'd started up the street. "Did you call Mortimer to see if you were expected in the office?"

Elspeth's head whipped around at that. His knowing

about the Enforcer House was startling enough, but his mentioning Mortimer's name was shocking. "How do you know about the Enforcer House and Mortimer?"

"Valerian and Tybo," he answered as he brought the SUV to a halt at a stop sign. "Which way?"

"Right. You want to head to the highway," she said, and then asked, "You met Valerian and Tybo? What happened that night? I know I got hit by a car, but I don't recall anything after that."

Wyatt was silent as he made the turn, but then said, "G.G. came out and lifted the car off of you with the help of some others. I pulled you out. We got you inside and gave you blood to heal. Valerian and Tybo showed up and called in Dr. Rachel. She gave you some drugs that didn't seem to help much at first, and then wrapped G.G.'s ribs."

"Wrapped his ribs?" she asked with surprise. "What happened to G.G.?"

"You threw him across the kitchen at The Night Club. He hit a wall pretty hard and has a couple of cracked ribs."

"Oh no," Elspeth breathed with dismay, guilt rushing through her.

"Anyway, once you were through the worst of your healing, Valerian and Tybo took you home in their SUV, and Dr. Rachel drove me home in mine with Sam following behind to take her home."

"Sam? Mortimer's wife?" Elspeth asked. That was the only Sam she knew, so she wasn't surprised when Wyatt nodded.

"She and Dr. Rachel were shopping when Valerian called her. Or was it Tybo?" he pondered and then shook his head. "One of them called her."

"I see," she said softly, but was peering at him worriedly now. He obviously knew something about what she was, but how much?

Elspeth was fretting over that when he said, "Tybo explained about immortals to me."

"Oh," she said weakly, and then cleared her throat and asked, "Are you okay?"

"Yes. I wasn't hit by the car. It was just you," he said at once.

"No, I mean about . . . us. About what you learned? You're not freaked out or . . . ?" She shrugged helplessly, unsure how most mortals would react to what he'd been told.

"Yeah," he said, but she could hear a note of uncertainty in his voice, and then he sighed, and admitted, "I'm a little alarmed at the mind reading and control business though."

"Yes. That is a bit distressing," she murmured. Elspeth hated it when her mother or other immortals read or controlled her.

"And the drinking blood part is kind of—I mean no one likes to hear they're little more than cattle to another group of people. That's just—"

"You aren't cattle to immortals," she said with exasperation. "Any more than you would be for hemophiliacs or people who have been in accidents, need blood, and source it from blood banks." Elspeth paused briefly, and then admitted, "It used to be different before blood banks, of course. I mean, we needed blood, and there was only one way to get it. But now that there *are* blood banks, a lot of immortals stopped feeding off the hoof and reverted to bagged blood as a much safer source."

"Off the hoof?" he asked with a wince.

"Oh. Yes, sorry. That's just . . ." She shrugged help-lessly, and then went on, "Anyway, in some countries it's even against our laws to take blood directly from a mortal except in an emergency, or . . . in certain other instances."

"Some countries?" Wyatt queried dryly. "So it's legal in other countries?"

Elspeth shrugged. "Every country has their own Coun-cil and their own laws. Here in North America, feeding off a mortal when it isn't an emergency is punishable by death."

"In case of emergency or certain other instances, you said," he reminded her and when she nodded, he asked, "What other instances?"

Elspeth hesitated and then admitted, "As a part of love play."

"Biting as part of love play, huh?" he asked with a small smile.

Trying not to blush, she shifted uncomfortably and muttered, "I gather partners can become overexcited and get nippy in the heat of the moment."

"Yeah?" he asked with interest and what she suspected was amusement at her discomfort. "Do life mates bite each other?"

Elspeth stiffened. Just how much had Tybo told him? Apparently, a lot. But he couldn't have told him that he was a possible life mate for her. Tybo didn't know. Unless G.G. told him, she thought with concern.

"Do they?" Wyatt prodded.

"It's not recommended between two immortals," she said finally. "Taking another's nanos that way causes an imbalance in both partners and means a need for more blood for both. The donor has to replenish the lost blood and rebuild the lost nanos, and in the one who takes the blood, the extra nanos use up more blood until the body can rid itself of them. They need to consume extra blood to make up for it. We all try to avoid anything that will make it necessary to consume more blood. Blood banks have enough trouble getting in the blood they need for emergencies. It's frowned upon to waste it that way."

"I see," Wyatt murmured with a nod. "But what about between an immortal and their mortal lover? It's allowed then as part of . . . love play?" Smiling suddenly, he added, "I like that term. Love play."

Elspeth just stared at him, her cheeks heating up. Although she wasn't sure if it was embarrassment causing it, or the images his words suddenly had sliding through her mind. An immortal and her mortal lover. Like them. Except they weren't lovers, she told herself quickly, but then recalled their shared kiss and the images that had flashed into her mind in the shower.

"Which exit do I take?"

Elspeth glanced around to see they were approaching the entrance ramps leading to the highway and quickly directed him to the right one.

"Did you call Mortimer to see if he expected you in today?" Wyatt asked again once they'd traversed the on-ramp and merged with traffic.

"No," Elspeth admitted wearily. "I was so busy figuring out a way to get out of the apartment without encountering Mother that I didn't even think of it. Actually, I didn't even think to grab my purse and phone before leaving," she admitted now as she realized that.

"Your cell phone was destroyed when you were run over the other night," he said solemnly. "Most everything in your purse was. We thought it was probably strewn all over the road at one point, but it turned out Sofia had collected it after we took you inside, and brought it in with her. She gave it to us as we were leaving. Most of the contents were crushed, or in pieces, including your wallet. It was pretty battered, but the contents were fine. Everything else in the purse, though, was a write-off. Actually," he added suddenly, glancing toward her side of the car, "I think it's all in that bag at your feet. At least, it looks like the bag Sofia handed over as we left, and I know Rachel brought it along, intending to give it to your mother."

Leaning forward, Elspeth picked up the white garbage bag. She set it in her lap and opened the top to look inside. She immediately recognized her squashed and torn purse. She pulled it out, she retrieved her wallet, and looked it over. As he'd said, it was pretty battered, the metal clasp bent and twisted, but the money, driver's license, and credit cards inside were fine.

"I wonder why she didn't give it to your mother," he said thoughtfully.

"Perhaps she forgot," Elspeth said with a shrug, setting the wallet back in the bag and closing it, but keeping the bag on her lap.

"Like I forgot entering Gran's apartment and going to bed that night?" he asked dryly, and when she glanced at him with surprise, he said, "I remember getting into the passenger seat of this SUV and Rachel getting in behind the wheel, and then I was suddenly very tired. The next thing I recall is waking up midmorning yesterday, on top of the covers of my bed in the guest room at Gran's."

"Rachel probably carried you in and put you to bed rather than wake you," Elspeth said, and didn't mention that the woman would have had to slip into his mind to make sure he didn't wake up during the maneuver. She did wonder, though, why Rachel had done that.

Probably to avoid his being a party to whatever her mother might have said when they'd brought her and Wyatt home, Elspeth decided. Martine would have raised a ruckus, she was sure, which made her glad neither of them had been awake for it. She'd have to thank Rachel the next time she saw her for keeping Wyatt from witnessing that. And apologize to her for having to suffer it herself. Although Rachel was married to Elspeth's cousin, Etienne, and as family she would have known what to expect from Martine. Still, she really needed to apologize to her, Elspeth thought on a sigh. But she would probably get the chance soon. Etienne was one of Marguerite's sons, and if she knew her aunt Marguerite, the woman would have them all together for a gathering once she knew Mother and the twins were here.

Noting their surroundings, Elspeth said, "The next exit is the one we want."

"Right." Wyatt put the blinker on and maneuvered into the outside lane.

They had taken the off-ramp and were driving up the road leading to the street where the Enforcer House was when Wyatt suddenly announced, "Valerian and Tybo were surprised to hear about your getting stabbed."

"I haven't seen them since before I was stabbed and hadn't told them. I guess Mortimer hadn't either," Elspeth said absently as she took note of the rural routes they were passing. "You want to take a right onto that next crossroad."

Wyatt slowed down and put his blinker on.

"So, who tattled?" she asked as he took the turn. "You or G.G.?"

"G.G. told them while Rachel was wrapping his ribs," Wyatt said quietly.

Elspeth winced, guilt assailing her again at the thought of her hurting the dear man. She'd always liked G.G. and wouldn't purposely have hurt him for the world.

"I don't think he meant to tattle. Neither of us realized it was supposed to be a secret."

"It wasn't," she said at once, and then added, "I just wish I'd been able to tell them myself so they didn't get the wrong idea. It's not a big deal and nothing they need worry about." Gesturing to the gated driveway ahead on their left, she added, "That's where we're going. Just pull up to the gate and roll down your window. One of the guys will come out."

Wyatt slowed again, and then said, "I think you're probably the only one who doesn't think it was a big deal. At least, Tybo and Valerian seemed concerned about you."

"Of course they did," she muttered as he put on the turn signal.

"I don't blame them. I'm worried too," he added solemnly.

Eyebrows rising, Elspeth glanced to him with surprise as he turned into the driveway. "Why?"

"Why?" he asked with disbelief. "Are you kidding?"

"Roll down your window," she reminded him as he drew the car to a halt. "And no, I'm not kidding. There's nothing to worry about."

"Of course there's something to worry about," he countered impatiently as he hit the button to roll down the window. "You were stabbed in the morning two days ago, and pushed under a car that same evening. I'd say that's reason to worry."

"Sounds worrisome to me too."

Elspeth had been staring at Wyatt with stunned disbelief at the news that she'd been pushed into traffic that night, but now glanced past him to the man who had come out to greet them. With dark hair, and deep brown eyes with bronze flecks in them, the man was peering through the car window, his gaze sliding from her to Wyatt with displeasure.

"Hi, Uncle Francis," she greeted him with a forced smile. "How are you?"

"Worried about you, now," he said dryly and then raised his eyebrows and asked, "Who is it you pissed off?"

Elspeth rolled her eyes, and then a wry smile caught her lips and she said, "The only person who comes to mind is my mother."

"Ohhh." Wincing, he wrinkled his nose. "She's a scary woman, but she's more likely to smother you to death than stab you."

"Tell me about it," Elspeth said on a sigh.

Francis smiled and then glanced to Wyatt with interest. "So, is this the life mate Tybo and Valerian were talking about?"

Elspeth's eyes widened with dismay. "He—I—"

"Yes," Wyatt said over her stammering, and when she turned on him with shock, he shrugged. "G.G. said you couldn't read or control me. Apparently, that means we're life mates."

"Damn," Elspeth breathed, suddenly feeling a little less guilty about hurting the giant while she was insensate. How could G.G. tell Wyatt that he was her life mate when he knew she wasn't even sure she wanted one?

"Trust me, Elspeth. It is something you want. A life mate is a gift from God, and finding them is a blessing."

Elspeth stared at Francis. He'd been sending her his

thoughts. She'd heard the words, but his lips hadn't moved. Aloud he added, "Besides, Wyatt here has some hot little thoughts about you floating around in that head of his. They're delicious. If I were you I'd take him right up to one of the bedrooms and let him show you the benefits of having a life mate."

"Oh, God," Elspeth muttered and flopped back in her seat, her eyes closing.

"Isn't she adorable? One hundred forty-one years old and she still blushes like a teenager," Francis said with amusement, and then, in a suddenly serious tone full of warning, added, "And that should tell you something, so go slow and gentle with our little Ellie. Her mother hasn't let her out much."

Elspeth groaned, but refused to open her eyes or respond to the incorrigible man's comments, until she heard his laughter fade as if he was moving away. Squinting one eye open, she saw with relief that he had and opened the other eye as well, but she refused to look at Wyatt. Family could be so embarrassing at times.

"Interesting guy, your uncle," Wyatt commented as he steered the car slowly forward through the first gate. "Doesn't look anything like you."

"He's my uncle's wife," she said. "I mean his husband. Whatever, he's my uncle by marriage."

"Okay," Wyatt said easily, and then paused in front of the second gate to wait, and cleared his throat before asking, "Did he say you were one hundred forty-one years old?"

"I'm not one hundred forty-one," she informed him.

"Oh," he breathed.

Noting his relief, she added, "I'm one hundred forty-two."

Wyatt's eyes widened incredulously. He swallowed and then said weakly, "Oh."

"Wyatt, about this life mate business, I—"

"It's all right," he interrupted, his voice gaining strength again. "G.G. said you weren't ready for one, that you left your mother intending to enjoy a taste of freedom."

"Yes," she breathed with relief.

"I understand." Wyatt smiled at her reassuringly and then asked, "So, who is this guy?"

Elspeth turned to peer at the blond man who had approached the SUV and was now running a mirror on a long stick under the car. "That's my uncle Russell, Uncle Francis's husband."

"What's he checking for under the SUV?" Wyatt asked with a frown.

"Bombs, trackers, or rogues hanging underneath the car. Anything that might be a problem," she explained, smiling at her uncle when he glanced her way.

"You're kidding," Wyatt said with amazement. "Just what goes on out here?"

"It's just a precaution," she assured him as Russell finished and walked back to the gatehouse. "They've had some trouble in the past."

"Right. Trouble," Wyatt muttered, easing his foot off the brake as the second gate began to open.

"They won't make you go through that on the way out. They only check incoming vehicles. Usually," she added to be honest, and then told him, "Just follow the lane that curves up in front of the house."

"Where does the other lane go?" Wyatt asked, his gaze sliding over what he could see of the buildings behind the house.

"To the dog kennels, the cells, and the garage where

the Enforcers' SUVs are," she responded absently as she saw Valerian and Tybo coming out of the house.

"Cells? Like for prisoners?" Wyatt asked with surprise as he pulled to a halt in front of the house.

"Sure. We have to put the rogues somewhere," she pointed out, collecting the bag holding her ruined purse and its contents. Reaching for the door, she smiled at him and offered, "Thank you for understanding. And thank you very much for driving me out here. I appreciate it. Will you be okay finding your way back home?"

"Sure. The car has GPS," he said easily.

"Right. Thanks again." She pushed her door open and smiled when Tybo held it for her.

"Elspeth! Feeling better today I hope?" the hunter said, offering her a hand out.

"Yes. Thank you," she murmured as she stepped out.

"Good, good," Tybo said cheerfully, and then urged her to the side so that he could look inside the SUV. "Hey Wyatt! How's it hanging?"

It seemed Wyatt had made new friends, Elspeth noted. Nodding a greeting to Valerian, she left the men talking and hurried into the house.

Eight

"Wait. What?" Elspeth stared at Mortimer with disbelief. "You're putting bodyguards on me?"

"It's just until we sort out who's behind these attempts on your life," Mortimer said soothingly.

"The stabbing wasn't an attempt on my life," Elspeth snapped impatiently. When he arched one eyebrow, she grimaced and said, "Yes, all right, it was. But it was a one-time thing. The guy was mortal. He was also psychotic or something. He was off his meds and delusional, and the police took him away. He's in jail or a hospital now. The two incidents weren't connected. In fact, the second incident was probably just an accident. Someone in a hurry just bumped me and accidentally knocked me into the road," Elspeth assured him.

"You were pushed. It wasn't an accident," Mortimer said firmly.

Shaking her head with frustration, Elspeth paced away from his desk. This had been the last thing she'd expected to be greeted with when she'd entered Mortimer's office. This was just crazy, and so freaking *unfair*!

Spinning around, Elspeth marched back to his desk and slammed her bag on its wooden surface. "Mortimer, I moved to Canada so that I wouldn't have to live with my mother hovering over me all the time. Now she's here, *and* you want to stick a couple of men on me to boot? Unbelievable!"

"Yes, well . . ." Mortimer shifted his stapler on the desk, and then his mouse, and grimaced. "Unfortunately, I don't have any men to spare to guard you at the moment. As you know, we're stretched pretty thin just now."

"Thank God," she said with relief, thinking it meant she would avoid guards after all.

"However, Sam, Rachel, Lissianna, and Alex have volunteered to take turns guarding you in pairs until we figure out who is behind these attacks and put an end to them."

"Attack," she snapped. "Singular. And we don't even know if it was a serious attack on me. Maybe it was just another mentally ill individual running around randomly pushing people into the road."

"Fine. Attack in the singular," he agreed. "But it does not matter. One attack or two, you will still have a guard with you until we know what is happening."

Elspeth dropped into the chair in front of Mortimer's desk with a sigh. It seemed she hadn't escaped a guard after all. Sam, Rachel, Lissianna, and Alex were going to—

"Alex who?" she asked suddenly.

"Sam's sister," Mortimer admitted apologetically.

"You mean my brother Cale's wife?" she asked with a frown.

"Oh, yeah." He smiled faintly. "I always forget he's your brother."

Elspeth nodded, and then arched her eyebrows. "Alex is going to guard me?"

"She's very good with a knife," he assured her.

"Yeah, at chopping and dicing onions! She's a chef, Mortimer," Elspeth said with exasperation. "And Lissianna is a housewife now, Rachel a doctor, and Sam a lawyer. They aren't bodyguards, Mortimer."

"Have I mentioned that we're shorthanded?" he growled. "Just think of it as a girls' night that's going to last days . . . or weeks. However long it takes," he ended with a grimace. "Just go get your nails done, have facials, or hit The Night Club, drink Wino Reds, and giggle about how stupid and pathetic we men are or something, but do it with the women accompanying you."

Elspeth sat back and eyed him with sudden understanding. "Mother wanted the bodyguards."

"She wanted me to put six men on you around the clock," he said unhappily. "But I just don't have the manpower. Hopefully, having the women with you will prevent future attacks and appease your mother."

"Hmm," Elspeth said on a sigh. She didn't think it was likely. Her mother would not be appeased. She'd insist on guarding her as well and would end up herding them all around like they were a gaggle of grade-schoolers on a field trip. But then, Martine would have done the same thing had her guards been six strong and able Enforcers armed to the teeth. Her mother had issues with the safety of her children. She was also an original Atlantean, born there before the fall, owned a home in New York where she went when they had to leave England to handle the not-aging business, and as such had a seat on both the North American and British Councils of Immortals. On top of that, she was a member of the board of directors for Argeneau Enterprises, which paid Mortimer and the hunters for their work. With all of that weight behind her, Mortimer couldn't really afford *not* to do as she wished . . . unless Uncle Lucian trumped her demands. Unfortunately, Uncle Lucian wasn't here to intervene.

"Do you have any idea who might have pushed you in front of the car?" Mortimer asked suddenly, pulling her from her thoughts.

Elspeth shook her head unhappily. "I had no idea I was even pushed until Wyatt told me on the way here, and I didn't get the chance to ask him about it," she admitted, and then said, "Are we sure I was pushed? Who were the witnesses? Maybe I just stumbled off the curb or something."

Mortimer was shaking his head before she finished the suggestion. "G.G. was one witness. He was watching out the window and saw someone push you and run off."

Damn, Elspeth thought. Someone was trying to kill her. That was hard to believe. Good Lord, she'd only lived in Canada six weeks and hadn't pissed off anyone that she knew of. Well, aside from Madeleine/Nina, she supposed. But Meredith's thieving tenant was in jail. Now, if this was England . . . Actually, she couldn't think of anyone in England who might want her dead either. She hadn't got out much there thanks to her mother's—

"Maybe it's someone trying to hurt my mother by hurting me," she suggested suddenly.

"Maybe," Mortimer allowed, and added, "She's old and difficult enough to have made enemies," he said dryly. "Which makes it more likely than someone wanting to hurt you."

"Exactly," Elspeth said with satisfaction. It was always good to hear that she was more likeable than her mother.

"I'll look into that possibility too, then," he decided, jotting a note on a yellow pad on his desk. "But in the meantime, Alex is on her way here and she and Sam will watch you until dawn, when Lissianna and Rachel will take over." After a hesitation, he added, "Greg might be bringing Lucy to join you as well. Lissianna says little Lucy has trouble sleeping without her there, and Greg says he does too," he added with a roll of the eyes.

Elspeth's eyebrows rose with disbelief.

"And if Etienne catches wind that Greg and Lucy are with Lissianna, he'll probably wander over too to be with Rachel," he finished with disgust.

"Mortimer, if it's so dangerous I need guards, do you really think it's a good idea to have a baby around?" She didn't wait for an answer, but added, "Besides, my apartment only has two bedrooms, and it already has four people in it thanks to my mother and sisters deciding to visit. I don't have room for five more people."

"We can use the basement apartment."

Elspeth swiveled in her seat to see Wyatt standing in the open doorway. While his comment had startled her, his presence surprised her more. "What are you doing here? I thought you'd left."

Nodding politely at Mortimer, he entered the room and moved to stand beside her chair. "Valerian and Tybo mentioned that Mortimer planned to have you guarded, so I thought I'd come in and see if there was anything I could do." Turning to Mortimer, he offered his hand, "Hi. I'm Wyatt MacKay."

"Garrett Mortimer." The head of the Enforcers stood up to take Wyatt's hand. His gaze narrowed on the mortal's forehead as they shook, and then he nodded and released his hand. "We'll pay the rent for the basement apartment. I'll arrange to have furniture delivered later today."

"You don't have to rent it. It's free right now anyway," Wyatt said solemnly.

"We'll rent it," Mortimer said firmly, and then smiled and added, "Martine and the twins can move down there to make room for Elspeth's protection to stay in her apartment."

Elspeth perked up. "Really?"

"It's the smartest move," he said with a shrug.

She grinned briefly, but then deflated and shook her head. "Mother won't do it."

"She will," he assured her. "Sam will make her. She's had a lot of practice dealing with powerful immortals since marrying me. The woman has no fear. She essentially lawyers them to death."

Elspeth wondered how exactly that was done.

"I'd be happy to help guard Elspeth," Wyatt announced a little stiffly.

Probably because he knew Mortimer would refuse, Elspeth thought. Wyatt was mortal, after all, easy to kill in comparison to an immortal, and—

"I'll get you suited up with guns and whatnot then," Mortimer said.

"What?" Elspeth gasped with amazement. "Mortimer, he's mortal!"

"He's also a former member of the JTF2," Mortimer informed her as if that should mean something to her.

"I'll never get used to this mind reading business," Wyatt muttered, but Elspeth and Mortimer paid him no attention.

Elspeth was staring at Mortimer with bewilderment, mentally running through the possible meanings behind the initials JTF. Jazz Tune Fans, Just The Facts, Justice Truth Freedom, Junior Twinkie Finders, Jolly T—

"Dear God, stop!" Mortimer barked suddenly, and then, shaking his head, he asked with disbelief, "Jolly Titty Fondlers?"

Flushing with embarrassment that he'd caught that one even as he'd interrupted her, Elspeth shrugged helplessly. "Well, I don't know what it stands for."

"Joint Task Force," he said abruptly.

"Oh." Elspeth shifted on her feet and then sighed. "Some kind of think tank?"

"No, Elspeth. They're like navy SEALs in the States," Mortimer said wearily, and then frowned when she continued to look bewildered, and said, "Like the British SAS, but made up of Canadian soldiers."

"Oh," she said with understanding. She knew the British SAS were super soldiers who handled the more dangerous things that cropped up in the world, like coups, hostage situations, and so on. The idea that he belonged to the Canadian version of the same thing was more than a little surprising, though. Wyatt seemed like just your average nice guy. Although he did have a pretty awesome physique, and that air of command, she thought, eyeing him.

"Elspeth, Sam is in the kitchen," Mortimer said, moving around his desk, headed for the door. "Why don't you go see if Alex has arrived yet while I take Wyatt to the outbuilding to look at weapons?"

Nodding, Elspeth watched the men leave the room, and then sighed and turned back to the desk. She'd come expecting to work, but Mortimer thought she should take a day or two off to "recover" . . . under the watchful eye of his wife and her sister, apparently. At least until dawn, and then Lissianna and Rachel would take over. Her mother, however, would be there around the clock, she was sure. Elspeth didn't think for a minute that Sam was going to be able to make Martine move down to the basement apartment. It was more likely her mother would make Sam, Alex, Lissianna, and Rachel stay there . . . without her.

Picking up the bag holding her ruined purse and its contents, Elspeth headed out of the office and along the hall to the front of the house, where the kitchen was situated.

"Good evening, Elspeth," Sam greeted her cheerfully. "Looks like we'll be hanging out for a while."

"Looks like," Elspeth agreed with a smile, her eyes widening slightly as she looked her over. Sam was dressed in black jeans, a black T-shirt, and black boots. She had a gun holstered on one hip, a TASER on the other, and a knife strapped to her leg on top of her jeans. "Looks like you're armed for bear."

"So is Alex," Sam announced with a grin. "She's in the bathroom. Should be out in a minute."

"I'm back."

Elspeth turned to see Alex entering the room, also dressed all in black and prickly with weapons. The woman had large eyes and a full mouth like Sam, but Alex wore her shiny brown hair in a bob while Sam's darker hair was long and wavy.

"Cale says, 'Hello, little sister,'" Alex told her with a smile.

"He doesn't mind you playing babysitter to me?" Elspeth asked with a faint smile.

"Nope. He'd be here with us, but he's helping Mortimer with a job," Alex explained.

Elspeth nodded solemnly. "A lot of nonhunters are helping out right now."

"And those who aren't are freaking out and going rogue," Sam said dryly. "Honestly, I've never seen it this bad. It's like going rogue is contagious and we're having an outbreak."

"And yet Mortimer benched me," Elspeth pointed out with irritation, dropping her garbage bag of possessions on the marble top of the island that took up the center of the kitchen.

"Your lunch?" Alex asked.

"My purse," she said dryly. "It got destroyed during my accident."

"Being pushed in front of a moving vehicle is not an accident," Sam said solemnly. "And you've only been benched until you've finished healing . . . or maybe until this mess is cleared up," she added, looking uncertain. "I'm not sure."

"So, you need a new purse?" Alex asked, moving to her side to open the plastic bag and look inside. Eyes widening, she murmured, "Ooooh. You need a new phone too. And a wallet . . . was that a compact? I'm pretty sure that pink goop was lipstick, and the loose powder looks like . . . blush?"

"Yes, blush," Elspeth said on a sigh. "I don't bother with face powder, but will put on a little blush when I'm without blood and a bit pale."

"Ah." Alex lifted her face from the bag and grinned. "You need to go shopping."

"Well, I guess I know what you're doing today, Wyatt,"

Mortimer said almost sympathetically, drawing their attention to the men's arrival.

Elspeth glanced over her shoulder at them, and then did an about-face to gape at Wyatt. His jacket and the dress shirt he'd been wearing earlier were off and over his arm, leaving him in a tight T-shirt that clung to an extremely muscular chest . . . that presently sported a shoulder holster with two guns, one on either side. He also had a gun strapped to his hip. He too was loaded for bear, but Elspeth was a bit distracted by this glimpse of his chest. He dressed to hide it, but as she'd noted before, the man was in impressive shape.

"Wyatt's coming with us?" Sam asked with surprise.

Mortimer nodded. "He has some special skills that may come in handy. He was a soldier, and has worked as a bodyguard for the last four years since leaving the army."

"You have?" Elspeth asked, turning to Wyatt with surprise.

He nodded abruptly, looking uncomfortable with the attention he was receiving.

"So," Mortimer said, turning away. "I'll leave you to your shopping and go back to work."

Elspeth watched him leave with a wry smile. The man seemed more than eager to escape and she couldn't blame him. With everything else going on, this situation was the last thing Mortimer needed added to his plate. Her mother could be a difficult woman at the best of times, but with one of her children under threat, she was no doubt unbearable.

"Well, where do you want to go shopping?" Sam asked once her husband was gone.

Elspeth considered the question and then said, "I don't know. I need to hit an Apple store, I guess. I can get a new phone there, and then maybe Walmart? There has to be one between here and the apartment."

Alex's eyebrows rose. "I was expecting you to want to go to somewhere a little more . . ."

"She was thinking a designer store," Sam said with amusement when Alex's voice trailed off.

"Like I could afford that," Elspeth said with a snort. "No. Walmart is good."

Alex's eyebrows rose, but she shrugged. "Sensible. Nice to know you aren't blowing the money your parents gave you."

"What money?" she asked with amusement, and when Alex looked confused, Elspeth explained, "Yes. Mom and Dad have a lot of money. And they have given stocks to my brothers, but my sisters and me . . ." Grimacing, she shrugged. "Mother wouldn't even consider doing the same for us. We might use it to run away. Not that I mind," she added quickly. "I can make my own way."

"So," Wyatt said into the silence that followed. "Phone or purse first?"

"Walmart is closer," Sam said at once.

He nodded. "And Mortimer said we would be taking one of the SUVs from here?"

"Yeah. Donny prepped and moved one to the house garage earlier today," Sam explained.

"Prepped?" Wyatt asked.

"Gassed it up and stuff." When Wyatt's eyebrows rose with curiosity, she explained, "The SUVs have UV film on the windows, as well as a blood cooler and weapons chest. Donny made sure the film was in good shape, that the vehicle was full of gas, and that the cooler and chest were stocked."

"Everything a vampire could need," Wyatt said wryly, and then grimaced. "Sorry. Immortal."

"No problem," Sam said lightly, coming around the island. "Just don't slip up in front of the old ones. They get testy about it." Pausing in front of him, she pulled out a set of keys and raised her eyebrows. "I was going to drive, but now that you'll be with us, I suppose you'd prefer—"

"No. I'm good with you driving," Wyatt interrupted, waving away the keys.

"Wow. A man who doesn't have to be at the wheel. Impressive," Alex teased lightly.

"I haven't lived in Ontario since I was a teenager. I don't know where anything is," he said with a shrug. "Besides, not driving leaves my hands free to handle defense if necessary."

"All righty, then," Sam said lightly, turning to lead the way to the door to the garage. "Let's go."

"Do you want the front seat, Elspeth?" Alex asked as they followed Sam out into the garage.

"No," Wyatt said before Elspeth could answer. "The front seat exposes her from two sides, the front and side window. The back only exposes her to the window on her side of the vehicle. She'll be more protected in the back seat."

"Oh, I never thought of that," Alex admitted, her eyes wide.

Wyatt shrugged. "Like Mortimer said, I'm a bodyguard by trade. It's my job to think of these things."

"So, you're the brains on this job," Sam said with a smile.

Alex raised her eyebrows. "What's that make us? The muscle?"

"I guess it does," Sam agreed with amusement.

"Yeah, well, I know it does," Wyatt assured them with amusement, and when they glanced to him with curiosity, he explained, "Sofia picked up G.G. and carted him around like he was a toddler the other night. If you two are as strong as her, you're definitely the muscle, and I'm content to be the brains."

"Wow," Alex said again. "Doesn't have to drive, and doesn't feel his manhood is threatened by being around women stronger than him. I think I'm impressed."

Elspeth didn't say so, but she was rather impressed herself. She was quite sure Wyatt wasn't used to thinking of himself as the physically weaker one in the group. Especially when that group consisted of women . . . but he was handling it well.

"So, exactly how strong do these nanos make you?" Wyatt asked with interest once they were in the SUV and had pulled out of the garage. "Is someone G.G.'s size the limit, or could you pick up two guys his size? Three? Could you pick up a car?"

Elspeth noted the blank look Sam and Alex exchanged in the front seat, and said, "I don't know. I've never tried to pick up two big guys like G.G. Or one, for that matter, let alone a car."

"Neither have I," Alex admitted, turning slightly in her seat. "I've picked up a stove to move it once, but have never had reason to pick up two or three guys or a car." Shifting her gaze to her sister, she asked, "Sam?"

Sam shook her head. "The heaviest thing I've had to carry was Mortimer once when he got injured. I'm not sure what I can lift."

"We should test it out sometime," Alex suggested as the gate began to open.

"Yeah, we should," Sam agreed, waving at Frances and Russell as she drove through the gates. "How?"

"I don't know. Maybe hit a gym with weights, pile on a ton, and see if we can lift them," Alex suggested.

Sam snorted at the suggestion. "Oh yeah, like that wouldn't raise any eyebrows."

"Yeah, I guess," Alex agreed with a grimace and then shrugged. "I'll think of another way."

Silence fell briefly in the car, and then Alex twisted around to peer at Wyatt and said, "So, you're a bodyguard by trade?"

Wyatt nodded.

"Have you ever guarded anyone interesting?" she asked with curiosity.

Wyatt shrugged. "Depends on who you think is interesting. I've worked with actors, actresses, musicians, politicians, and the wealthy."

Alex looked impressed, and then asked, "Who was the most interesting?"

"Elspeth," he said at once. When Elspeth turned to him with surprise, he smiled wryly and pointed out, "The others were all mortal. You guys are the most interesting people I've ever met."

"Ah," Alex said with a grin. "What a sweet talker."

Wyatt smiled faintly, but asked, "So Elspeth is one hundred forty-two. How old are you girls?"

"Okay, so not such a sweet talker," Alex said on a laugh, turning forward in her seat.

When Wyatt frowned slightly and glanced to her, Elspeth reminded him gently, "It's rude to ask a lady her age."

"Even an immortal?" he asked with surprise. "I mean,

since you guys all look young and hot, I didn't think it would be an issue."

"Nice attempt at a save," Sam said, smiling at him in the rearview mirror. "And while that may be true for Elspeth and others born immortal, those of us who were turned still tend to be a little self-conscious about our age. Give us a century or two and that might change, but right now . . ." She shrugged and returned her attention to the road.

When Wyatt glanced to Elspeth, his eyes wide, she raised her eyebrows. "You look surprised. You thought Alex and Sam were born immortal?"

"They're sisters. I just assumed . . ."

Elspeth nodded. "Sam was turned first. She met Mortimer while at their family cottage up north. Mortimer and a couple of other hunters were in the cottage next door. They were on the job at the time looking for a rogue immortal in the area."

"And then I spent ages trying to find life mates for my sisters," Sam told him with a wry shake of the head.

"Sisters?" Wyatt asked at once. "There are more of you?"

"One more," Alex told him. "Our youngest sister, Jo. She found her life mate next."

"Yeah, and that nearly gave me a heart attack," Sam muttered.

"Why?" Wyatt asked with curiosity.

"Jo's life mate is my cousin, Nicholas Argeneau," Elspeth told him with a smile and then explained, "He was kind of considered rogue at the time."

"Fortunately, that was all cleared up," Alex told him lightly. "And then I met my life mate, Cale."

"My brother," Elspeth told him, and when his eyebrows rose, she shrugged. "I have a lot of family."

Sam snorted at the claim, and said, "The Argeneaus were one of the original Atlantean families. They've been making babies for millennia. You can't turn around without tripping over one."

When Wyatt turned to her with curiosity, Elspeth shrugged and admitted, "I have relatives I've never even met yet." Noting his shock at the comment, she quickly added, "But then, until recently, I didn't get out much."

"That's an understatement," Sam said dryly. "And in point of fact, you haven't really got out much since moving to Canada either."

"What?" Elspeth met Sam's gaze in the rearview mirror with surprise.

"Well, you haven't," she pointed out. "You've mostly worked, shopped for furniture for your apartment, and spent your downtime relaxing with Meredith."

Elspeth frowned. What Sam said was true, but—"I've only been here six weeks," she pointed out defensively. "And I had to buy the furniture. Besides, once I'm done with work and shopping, I'm usually tired and Meredith is soothing and . . ."

"I wasn't criticizing you," Sam said gently. "There's nothing wrong with being a homebody. It's probably why you were able to withstand your mother's overprotectiveness and controlling for so long without going crazy."

Elspeth turned to peer out the window as she considered Sam's words. She wasn't a homebody. Was she? She wanted to go out and party with the girls. She wanted to go to movies, and shop, and . . . well, do whatever it was normal people did when they didn't have a mother hovering over them and restricting their every move. Didn't she?

"Here we are."

Elspeth glanced up at that announcement from Sam to see that they were pulling into the Walmart parking lot.

"So," Wyatt said, glancing out the window as Sam found a spot near the back of the lot. "The sun's still peeking over the horizon. I thought since you were out a little earlier than this when I followed you to The Night Club that the sun wasn't a problem for you. But Sam mentioned the sun-filtering film on the SUV." Raising his eyebrows, he asked, "Is the sun a problem? Is having to walk so far in it going to be an issue?"

"No. We're fine," Elspeth assured him solemnly. "It's not like we burst into flame when sunlight touches us. It just does the same kind of damage it does to mortals, only a little more of it. At least, for those of us who were born immortal," she said and explained, "We're trained from childhood to avoid the sun, so having had minimal exposure to it, our skin tends to be more sensitive."

"Then why do you avoid the sun?" he asked as he pulled on his jacket. "I mean, if your skin reacts the same way as ours—"

"Because unlike mortals, the nanos immediately repair the damage," she explained.

"And they use blood to do it," he said with understanding.

"Exactly. We try to avoid anything that will force the use of more blood."

"Cold has the same effect," Alex announced now. "The body tries to keep the body temperature regulated and uses more blood to do it."

Sam added, "A lot of things do that. The heat in the

summer means more blood is used to cool the body. Exposing ourselves to lots of people and the germs they carry means the nanos work to remove those before they can make us sick, and so on and so forth. Basically, pretty much everything forces the nanos to work harder and use more blood."

"Then we'll make this shopping trip a quick one," Wyatt announced, opening his door, and letting the cool air in.

They didn't just walk quickly through the parking lot; they were quick in the store too. Elspeth had never been a browser, meandering the aisles and looking at all the things she didn't need or couldn't afford. She knew what she wanted, and found them fast—a purse, a wallet, new lipstick and another blush, hairbrush and perfume. They were headed for the till when she saw the pocketknives. Pausing, she looked them over quickly and then selected one with a black blade and handle.

Wyatt was at her side the entire time, always with one hand on her arm or at her back. But she didn't mistake that hand as anything but all business. She knew it was so he could move her where he wanted if something happened, because his other hand hovered constantly by the front of his coat, ready to slip in and whip out one of his guns. This man wasn't the Wyatt she had met in Meredith's hall and kissed on the back porch. This Wyatt was a soldier—straight, stiff, and braced for action. His gaze was narrowed, examining each passing shopper and searching the surrounding area for trouble. Actually, it was kind of disturbing, causing her tension level to ratchet up several degrees. Elspeth was glad to be done and head to the checkout.

The Apple store followed, but was an equally quick trip. Elspeth was able to get a new phone, but left it turned off until she could charge it properly.

They were just leaving the store to head for the car when Sam's phone rang.

"It's Mortimer," she announced after glancing at the screen. Pressing the button to accept the call, she said, "Hello," and then her eyebrows rose as she listened . . . and listened . . . and listened. Finally she said, "Okay. I love you too, honey," and put her phone away.

"Everything okay?" Alex asked.

"Yes," Sam said, and then explained, "Mortimer just wanted to let us know that Martine discovered that Elspeth wasn't in her bed and called him to bawl him out for not having guards on her before this, and to see if she was at the Enforcer House. Mortimer told her where we'd gone, but that we'd no doubt head back to the apartment once done shopping."

"Oh dear. I'm sorry," Elspeth said with a wince, and then added, "She probably blamed him for my climbing over the balcony to avoid her too. Everything would be his fault, of course, and not hers."

"Damn, girl!" Alex peered at her with amazement. "Cale said your mother could be controlling, but climbing over the balcony to leave your own apartment?"

"Yeah." She shrugged helplessly. "Climbing down from the balcony was the only way to get out of the apartment without her attaching herself to me like a conjoined twin."

Alex shook her head. "Why on earth did you invite her to visit if she's this difficult?"

"I didn't invite her. She and the twins just showed up. To surprise me," she added with disgust.

Sam grimaced with sympathy and reached out to pat

her arm. "I suspected as much when I heard she was here. I mean, her control issues are the reason you left England and moved here. Besides, you hadn't mentioned that they were coming."

Elspeth nodded solemnly. She'd become friends with Mortimer's wife since she'd started helping out at the Enforcer House. She enjoyed talking to her and had shared things about her life.

"Gran mentioned that you moved here because your mother is controlling," Wyatt admitted. "But isn't moving out of the country a bit extreme?"

"Mother's control issues are extreme," Elspeth assured him.

"It took Elspeth almost a century to get to move out on her own," Sam told him. "And she had to sneak around to do it."

His eyebrows drew together with uncertainty. "I don't understand. Are you saying—"

"She's been trying to move out on her own since she was fifty years old," Sam explained.

Eyebrows rising, Wyatt turned to Elspeth. "Why would that be a problem? I mean, once you were eighteen she couldn't stop you from leaving."

"Have you met Martine?" Alex asked with amusement. "She's pretty intimidating."

"But it wasn't intimidation that kept Elspeth from moving out," Sam said with a scowl. "Any time she said she wanted to move out, or get a job, Martine just took control of her and changed her mind for her."

"You're kidding!" Alex said with dismay, and then turned to Elspeth. "She didn't, did she?"

"She did," Elspeth assured her. "Fortunately, Dad stepped in when it came to an education and a job, but he let her have her way about the other. I think he felt we should fight for our independence ourselves."

"Wait," Wyatt said with a frown. "Are you saying immortals can control each other too?"

"Older immortals can read and control younger ones," Elspeth explained quietly.

"Wow," Alex breathed now, her gaze on Elspeth. "Your mother controlling you like that . . . That's pretty messed up. What's her deal?"

Elspeth's eyebrows rose at the question. "Did Cale never explain the reason she's like this?"

"There's a reason?" Wyatt asked.

Elspeth nodded, but then glanced to Sam when her phone rang again.

The other woman pulled her phone back out, peered at the screen and groaned. "It's your mother. Mortimer must have given her my number."

"Decline it," Alex suggested.

"No. She'd just call Mortimer and harass him and he has enough on his plate what with the Russians in town and Beth and Scotty getting themselves burnt to a cinder." Hitting the button to accept the call, she turned to walk away.

Elspeth stared after her and then turned to Alex. "What did she mean when she said Beth and Scotty got burnt to a cinder?"

"Oh, right, you don't know yet," Alex said and then grimaced. "Well, you know that joke job you sent Beth and the Russians on the night your mother arrived?"

"Joke job?" Wyatt asked.

"A soft call. The hunters call them joke jobs," Elspeth explained, and then turned back to Alex and asked, "You mean the call about a coffin in a barn?"

"Yes." Alex nodded. "Well, it turns out the barn was booby trapped with wires and explosives. Beth was supposed to lead her team in there, get beheaded by wires, be trapped inside when other wires pulled the barn doors closed, and then be finished off with a firebomb."

"What?" Elspeth gasped with shock.

Alex nodded.

"Is she all right?" Elspeth asked with a frown. "And how did Scotty get burned? He wasn't working with Beth and the Russians."

"No, he wasn't," Alex agreed, and then explained, "Scotty was among the backup, but before he got there Beth and one of the women with her went in to collect the pieces of the first Russian, it set off the firebomb. Beth came running out in flames, as Scotty got there. He threw himself on top of her to try to put out the flames and *whoosh*!" She gestured an explosive action with her hands. "He went up in flames too."

"Damn," Elspeth breathed.

"How?" Wyatt asked, his eyes narrowing. "Was some kind of accelerant splashed on everyone?"

"It wouldn't be needed," Elspeth said quietly. "We're extremely flammable. In fact, it's the only real way to kill an immortal."

"And beheading," Alex put in.

"Yeah," Elspeth agreed, but added, "Although, even that can heal if the head's put back on the neck quickly enough."

"Seriously?" Wyatt asked with amazement.

Elspeth nodded, but asked Alex, "Do they know who the trap was for and who set it?"

"They're pretty sure it was meant for Beth, but they have no idea who's behind it."

"Jeez," Elspeth breathed. "Poor Mortimer. His plate is overflowing just now."

"Yeah. Sam's worried about him. She says the stress is really starting to pile up. I mean first they drag off more than half his hunters to Venezuela, and then everybody and their brother hops on the rogue bandwagon up here. Now Beth and Scotty got themselves toasted." She shook her head. "I guess they brought them to the Enforcer House and the pair were screaming all that first day and part of the second too. Sam and Mortimer haven't had much sleep lately."

"No, I don't imagine they have," Elspeth said solemnly.

"Yes, and—"

"Grrrrr! Argh!"

Elspeth glanced to the side even as Alex did and they watched Sam drop her phone in her purse as she returned to them.

"Your mother wanted us back right away," she said dryly as she reached them. "But I told her we were still at Apple and would be another half hour." Glancing to the store behind them, she smiled and added, "Which wasn't a lie. We are still at the Apple store. Or at least in front of it."

"So why are we going to be another half an hour?" Alex asked.

"I thought since we're in the neighborhood, I'd take you all to my favorite restaurant for burgers and the most amazing shakes ever."

"Sounds good," Wyatt said.

"It does," Elspeth agreed and then arched her eyebrows and asked with amusement, "Trying to delay going back to my apartment?"

"No. Your apartment is fine. In fact, I'd be happy to

see it. I was hoping to delay having to deal with your mother," Sam admitted bluntly.

"Hmm," Elspeth smiled crookedly. "And here Mortimer told me you weren't afraid of anyone."

"He's right," Sam assured her. "I'm not afraid, but that doesn't mean I'm looking forward to it."

"So? Milkshakes?" Alex asked.

"And burgers," Wyatt added. "El didn't have anything to eat when she got up."

Elspeth glanced at him with surprise. "How did you know?"

"You crept out of your bedroom and climbed down off the balcony," he pointed out, ushering her toward the SUV. "I hardly think you made a quick trip to the kitchen first if you wanted your mother to think you were still sleeping."

"No," she admitted. "You're right. I didn't have anything to eat."

"Wait a minute," Alex said, drawing them all to a halt as they were about to get in the SUV. Once they'd all turned to peer at where she stood by the back of the vehicle, she asked Elspeth, "Does that mean you didn't have anything to *drink* either?"

The way she emphasized the word "drink," told Elspeth that Alex meant blood. It also drew Elspeth's attention to the mild cramping she was experiencing and had been trying to ignore. Grimacing, she shrugged and simply said, "I can wait till we get back to the apartment."

"Oh, hells, no," Alex said at once, and opened the back of the SUV. "Why would you when there's no need?"

Eyebrows rising, Elspeth moved to join her, aware that Wyatt was following.

"Hide them under your coat until you get back in the SUV," Alex said, handing her two bags. "I'll bring the other two."

"Thanks." Elspeth tucked both bags inside her jacket, and turned to move around to the back door on the driver's side. Wyatt opened it for her, closed it and then walked around to get in the other side as Alex slid into the front passenger seat and passed two more bags back to her.

"Suck 'em back," Alex said lightly before turning to put on her seat belt.

Nodding, Elspeth slapped the first bag to her fangs. Holding it in place, she then tried to do up her seat belt one-handed. A difficult task, so she was grateful when Wyatt brushed her hand out of the way. At least, she was until he bent his head and leaned in to take over the task for her. His nearness and his hands moving against her waist as he worked the seat belt were more than a little unsettling, and she stared down at the top of his head as her body responded to both.

Once done with the task Wyatt sat back and watched her solemnly and then suddenly asked, "So is our being life mates the reason my body responds the way it does to touching you in even the most casual way? I mean I've never got a semi boner just helping a woman with her seat belt before."

Elspeth found her gaze dropping automatically to his lap and felt herself flush when she saw the expanding bulge there. She wasn't sure if that was the reason for the heat that suddenly filled her cheeks, or his bluntness. The man certainly didn't seem to be shy about discussing this stuff. Although, he had kept his voice low, probably in an effort to keep this conversation between them. He failed miserably, of course. Immortals' hearing was as advanced as the rest of their skills and abilities and Elspeth noticed the way Alex turned around to peer at the man wide-eyed.

With the bag at her mouth still a quarter full, all Elspeth could do to answer was nod, silently. But Sam decided to help her out. Or perhaps she did so to let Wyatt know they could hear him no matter how low he pitched his voice. "Life mates are very," she hesitated and then finished, "responsive to each other."

"Life mates are horny dogs around each other," Alex countered, her voice full of dry amusement. "Horny dogs in heat. They can't resist each other. They can try, but in the end, if they don't deal with their attraction and the needs it stirs in them, they can lose it and go at each other at the most inopportune times and in the most unfortunate places." Grimacing, she added, "Actually, even after they give in to it, they can lose it at the most inopportune times and in the most unfortunate places."

"Yeah, like you and Cale in the restaurant kitchen when you had Thanksgiving dinner for the family there, the first year you and Cale were together," Sam said with a grin. Glancing in the rearview mirror at Wyatt and Elspeth, she added, "Dinner was delayed until they regained consciousness and we could fetch the food. Of course, it was a dried-out mess by then."

"Christmas at Nicholas and Jo's was no better thanks to you and Mortimer," Alex countered. Turning sideways in the front seat as far as her seat belt would allow, she told them, "Jo asked Mortimer to carry the turkey out, and gave Sam the potatoes. I followed a couple of minutes later with the gravy, but stopped when I saw what they'd got up to and backed up into the kitchen to wait."

"That was Mortimer's fault," Sam said in self-defense. "I put the potatoes on the table, turned to leave and he was there. He gave me a kiss, and . . . Honestly, I think he meant it to be just a quick peck, but it's never just a quick peck with new life mates," Sam said on a sigh.

"No, it's not," Alex agreed, and then burst out laughing, before adding, "I wasn't too worried at first. I thought, so okay, dinner's going to be a little late and cold. Right?" she asked and when Elspeth and Wyatt nodded, wide-eyed, she continued, "But, no! We ended up having to order in because it wound up all over the floor when the table broke under Sam and Mortimer's weight. Or perhaps the activity was just too vigorous, but whatever the case, it just collapsed with a crash."

"I was washing cranberry sauce and mashed potato out of my hair for days after that," Sam said with a grimace, and then pointed out, "But at least we didn't end up with fourth stage frostbite like Jo and Nicholas did after that New Year party Marguerite held."

"Oh, God! The New Year party," Alex said with a groan. "That was a bloody mess."

Wide-eyed, Elspeth ripped the empty bag from her mouth and asked, "What happened at New Year?"

"Marguerite had a big party for everyone on New Year a couple years back," Sam explained. "There were dozens of us there. Too many to sit at a table, so she had a buffet so we could grab a plate, fill it up and eat while we circulated. It was really nice, actually, getting to see everyone and visit."

"Yeah," Alex grinned. "And then midnight struck."

"What happened at midnight?" Wyatt asked with curiosity when she paused briefly.

"All the couples gave each other their New Year kisses,"

she said dryly. "We have a lot of new life mate couples recently. Marguerite's been acing it in that department. Well, the minute they kissed . . ." She shook her head. "Marguerite has a lot of rooms in her house, but not *that* many."

"I swear every closet, bathroom, and just room, period, in that house had an unconscious couple in it fifteen minutes after midnight," Sam said with something like awe.

"Yeah, but there were also others who couldn't find rooms and took it outside," Alex said with a grimace. "They passed out in the snow and woke up later with frostbite and whatnot. Jo and Nicholas were among them and would have lost their toes and fingers at least if they were mortal."

Wyatt's eyes narrowed. "So it's normal for life mates to pass out after sex?"

Something about the way he phrased the question made Elspeth glance to him with a frown. It sounded almost like he had experience of that and had thought that passing out was something unusual. But they hadn't had sex yet. Her gaze slid to Alex and she noted that the other woman was peering at Wyatt with concentration, and surprise. She was obviously reading his mind, but whatever she was reading was apparently unexpected.

Elspeth was about to ask what that was, when Sam announced, "Here we are. The finest diner in the GTA."

"What's the GTA?" Wyatt asked, glancing out at the restaurant Sam was parking in front of.

"Greater Toronto Area," Alex explained, and then glanced to Elspeth and scowled. "You've only had one bag of blood."

"Oh." She peered down at the three bags she still held

and grimaced. She'd got distracted with the tales of life mate hijinks.

"Suck 'em back now before we go in," Alex ordered.

"Wait!" Sam interrupted as Elspeth started to raise another bag. "Tell me what you want first and I'll go in, get us a table and order while you finish up out here. We only have a half hour. I don't want Martine bothering Mortimer again because we're late."

Elspeth asked for a cheeseburger, fries and a chocolate shake before popping the bag to her mouth. Sam then took Alex and Wyatt's orders before slipping out of the SUV.

Alex asked Wyatt questions about British Columbia while they waited for Elspeth to get through the three bags of blood, and then the trio exited the car to join Sam in the restaurant. The food was just being delivered as they arrived, and as Sam had claimed it was really good, and yes, the shakes were amazing. Sam had ordered dessert for everyone as well, but all but Wyatt were too full to eat it, so they had theirs boxed up while Wyatt devoured his, and then he ordered one to go too before they paid and left.

"Here we go," Sam said grimly as she started the SUV engine. "Time to meet momma bear."

Nine

"No. The girls and I are staying right here." Martine's voice and eyes dripped ice as she peered down her nose at Sam. "You, Wyatt, and Alex can stay in the basement apartment."

Sam opened her mouth to respond, but Elspeth stepped up next to her and intervened. "That's fine, Mother. The basement apartment has two bedrooms too, and is newly furnished thanks to Mortimer. I'll stay down there with them."

"You will not," Martine said firmly. "You'll stay right here with us."

"I . . . will stay right here with you," she agreed, her anger slipping away. In fact, she suddenly couldn't remember what she'd been upset about . . . or why Sam, Alex, and Wyatt were all narrowing their eyes on her, their expressions turning grim.

"That's fine," Sam said after a moment, her voice cheerful. Pulling her overlarge purse around in front of her, she dragged out a stack of papers stapled together. It looked like a contract. "You just need to sign this release form and we'll get out of your hair."

"What? Release of what?" Martine asked, her eyes narrowing.

"It's just a form stating that you've refused protection for Elspeth and release us from any liability when she's killed," Sam explained pleasantly. "Just sign here on the bottom line and—"

"I'm not signing that," Martine said with dismay. "And I'm not refusing protection. I want you to guard her. Just not from here. She's fine here. Go down and stay in the basement apartment and you can guard her when we leave the apart—"

"Now, Martine," Sam interrupted gently. "Either we're guarding her or we're not, and you know we can't guard her from two floors away. If you insist on staying here and making us leave, then you are essentially refusing her protection." Holding out the papers, she said, "So, just sign this form acknowledging responsibility for her life, and refusal of our help, to ensure there can be no problem with the Council when Elspeth is killed."

"Did Elspeth say there were two bedrooms downstairs?" Julianna asked, pushing the kitchen door open to peer in at them.

Obviously, she'd been listening from the living room, but that was no surprise, Elspeth thought.

"Yes, she did," Alex said with a smile. "We stopped to see it on the way up here. One of the bedrooms has twin beds, and Mortimer had a big flat-screen television, and a computer put in it too."

"Really?" Julianna's eyes widened and she turned to their mother. "Come on, Mom. We can stay down there.

That way Victoria and I will have an actual bed instead of having to sleep on the air mattress on the floor."

"Please, Mom," Victoria begged. "You were the one who insisted Mortimer put guards on her, and like Sam says, they can't guard her from another apartment. Let's just stay down there. You can always come up and visit all you want."

Martine had opened her mouth on what no doubt would have been a refusal, but paused at Victoria's last words. She was silent for a moment, her expression considering, and then she nodded. "Very well. We will sleep in the other apartment and visit up here."

"Well, all right, then," Sam said just as cheerfully, slipping the sheaf of papers back into her purse. "If you go pack, we'll help you move your luggage when you're done."

Martine pursed her lips, and Elspeth was quite sure she was considering ordering the trio to pack and move her luggage for her, but then she apparently thought better of it and turned to leave the room. The moment she was gone, Elspeth felt herself again and knew her mother had released her. And for some reason Martine hadn't taken the trouble to erase the moments since taking control of her from her mind. She remembered her mother's comment about visiting, and she knew exactly what that meant. Her mother would move her luggage down to the lower apartment and spend all her time up here anyway.

"Well done, Sam. You actually won out over Martine," Alex congratulated her sister.

"To be honest, I'm not sure I did win," Sam responded thoughtfully. "She gave in way too easy."

"But she gave in," Alex pointed out. "She's moving to the basement apartment."

"Yeah," Sam nodded, but then turned to Elspeth and asked, "She's going to move her luggage down there and then come right back up until dawn, isn't she?"

"Yes," Elspeth said on a sigh and walked over to grab the coffee carafe. She turned to carry it to the sink, her gaze landing on the radio/CD player on the counter behind Alex. Pausing, she smiled suddenly. "Although, if you turn the CD player on, she won't stay long. She hates the CD I have in it and simply refused to allow me to play it at home."

"Really?" Alex turned to the CD player and opened it to retrieve the disc inside. Turning it in her hand, she raised her eyebrows. "Queen's *Greatest Hits*?"

Elspeth noted the way Wyatt stiffened, his expression stilling, and it raised her curiosity, but she said, "Yes. She hates it."

"You're a Queen fan?" Sam asked.

"I guess I am," she said with a faint smile. "At least, I love this CD. Other than that, though, I don't listen to modern music."

"Then why Queen? Where did you get this CD?" Wyatt asked quietly, walking over to peer at it above Alex's shoulder.

Elspeth glanced to him and shrugged. "It just showed up in my player one day and I listened to it and loved it. It always makes me happy," Elspeth admitted.

"It just showed up in your player?" Wyatt asked solemnly.

Elspeth nodded. "At the time, I assumed it was Julianna or Victoria's, but they both claimed it wasn't. So, I'm guessing it belongs to one of my cousins and they left it when they visited."

"You didn't get it when you went to the play?" he asked carefully.

Elspeth raised her eyebrows. "What play?"

"*We Will Rock You*," he said. "It played at the Dominion Theatre in London for something like twelve years."

Elspeth raised her eyebrows. "No. I've never seen it."

Wyatt speared her with his eyes. "Are you sure?"

"Quite sure," she said with amusement. "I've never been to any play. Mother doesn't care for them, and she certainly wouldn't let my sisters and me go without her. We were lucky to be allowed to go to university without her there holding our hands."

"You really don't remember," Wyatt said with quiet amazement.

"Remember what?" she asked with confusion.

"Going to see *We Will Rock You*," he said solemnly.

Her eyebrows rose slightly. "I told you I've never been."

"You have," he assured her.

"No, I haven't," she countered.

"Elspeth," he said, his voice gentle, "I was there. I saw you attend. *I took you*. You loved it."

"No, I—You've been to England?" she asked with surprise.

"Yes. Four years ago. I took you to that play."

"What?" she asked with bewilderment, unconsciously shaking her head no. She'd remember if that had happened. She'd remember him.

"I did," he said solemnly and reached into his pocket to pull out his wallet. Opening it, he retrieved a collection of three or four small photos. The first one was of she and Wyatt in front of the Dominion Theatre. *We Will Rock You* was on the billboard out front.

They looked so happy, she thought and took the picture to look closer, but paused when she saw the photo underneath. It was of a much younger Wyatt and Merry, in front of Merry's house. Elspeth suddenly suspected she knew why the house had looked so familiar to her when she'd seen it online. She'd seen it before. Wyatt must have shown her that picture when they met years ago, and while her mother had erased her memories, her subconscious had recognized the house. Her renting from his grandmother hadn't been chance.

Feeling sick over what her mother had done, Elspeth handed back the photo of them in front of the theatre.

Wyatt took it, but didn't put it away at once. Instead, he peered at it for a moment and said, "This was just after I finished my last enlistment. I took a couple weeks to travel and decide if I should enlist again, and if so, for how long. I was going to tour several European countries while I thought about it. I started in England. France was supposed to follow, but I never got there."

"Why?" she asked, but already knew the answer.

"Because I met you. I stopped to have lunch in a café the first day after I arrived. You were at a neighboring table. I asked to borrow your vinegar and we started talking. You were playing hooky, you said. You had called in sick to work because it was your birthday." A smile curved his lips. "We ended up sitting there for a couple of hours, and only left when the workers started giving us dirty looks. I was booked for a tour of the Tower of London and was going to cancel, but you said you'd come with me. In the taxi on the way we briefly got held up in traffic in front of a theater that had *We Will Rock You* playing. The Dominion Theatre. I mentioned I was kind of interested in seeing it and you said, then we should. We'd go on the tour, have dinner, and then go to the play. And that's what we did. We went on the tour and spent the entire time talking and laughing, annoying the heck out of our tour guide."

He grinned at the memory and Elspeth grinned back. She could almost picture what he was describing. In fact, she could see a ginger-haired Yeoman Warder scowling at them for laughing while he was trying to talk to the group.

"Afterward, we went to dinner, and then we went to the theater to see if we could get tickets to *We Will Rock You* for that night. I didn't think we would, but apparently it had been showing for years at the time, six or eight I think the guy said. There were seats available." Peering at her solemnly, he said, "You told me it was the first play you'd been to and I believed it, because you sat there wide-eyed with wonder throughout . . . and I just sat and watched you. I couldn't take my eyes off you."

"I don't . . ." She shook her head helplessly.

"Do you remember what you did on your birthday four years ago?" Sam asked quietly when Elspeth continued to just shake her head.

Elspeth paused and tried to think back. "We always go away for my birthday. Last year we went to Spain. The year before that it was Greece. The year before that was Germany, and the year before that . . ." She thought briefly, and then remembered and was oddly disappointed to say, "Italy. I was in Italy for my birthday four years ago."

"That's not true. It can't be," Wyatt said with a frown.

"It isn't," Victoria announced, drawing their attention to her presence in the open kitchen door.

Elspeth raised her eyebrows as the twins entered. "Yes,

Victoria, it is. I remember we stayed with Raffael, and he took us to a little trattoria for my birthday dinner."

"We did stay with Raffael that year, and he did take us to a trattoria for your birthday dinner, but it was the day *after* your birthday," she assured her solemnly.

When Elspeth frowned, Julianna told her, "It's true. You went missing on your birthday and didn't show up until the day after. Mom freaked. She went into full-on panic mode. Even Dad couldn't calm her down. She must have called the head of the UK Enforcers a hundred times, demanding he take every one of his hunters off any jobs they were on and send them out to search for you."

"Yeah. I think she nearly drove Scotty over the edge. At least, it looked that way when he came to the house," Victoria said with a grimace.

"Scotty came out to the house?" Elspeth asked with amazement. Scotty, whose true name was Cullen Mac-Donald, had been helping out Mortimer the last several weeks. She'd spoken to him several times since moving to Canada and he hadn't mentioned anything like this. Which was probably a good thing since she wouldn't have known what he was talking about, she supposed.

"Oh, yeah, although at the time I wasn't sure if he was there to try to calm her or kill her," Victoria said dryly.

"I was sure it was kill," Julianna put in with amusement. "Mom was constantly on the phone to him, shrieking her head off, freaking all over him, calling him an idiot and useless and whatnot. After twenty-four hours of that, I'd want to kill her."

Elspeth turned to Wyatt with wide eyes. "Twenty-four hours?"

Wyatt nodded. "After the play we went back to my hotel room."

"Really?" Alex drawled the word out and leaned forward, her gaze on Wyatt becoming concentrated briefly before her eyes widened. "Not quite after, though. You left early," she said with a grin.

"Yes," he acknowledged, looking somewhat embarrassed.

"Why?" Elspeth asked with surprise. "Why would we leave early?"

"Actually, we were asked to leave," Wyatt admitted almost apologetically.

"We were?" Elspeth gasped with shock. She'd never been kicked out of anywhere. Ever. "Why?"

Wyatt blew out a sigh. "I kissed you."

Alex snorted at the claim.

Wyatt scowled at her, and then admitted, "It was *supposed* to be a quick, gentle kiss, but . . ." He shook his head. "It was like an explosion happened. My lips brushed lightly over yours and the next thing I knew, we were tearing at each other's clothes and . . ." He shrugged helplessly.

"Yeah, that life mate sex is a killer. I mean, none of us intended to ruin the holidays we told you guys about. You just intend to give your loved one a quick kiss in passing and *kapow*!" Sam said on a sigh.

Alex nodded. "A kiss, a touch—heck, even a look—and it can happen. *Kapow* and you're gonzo."

Elspeth glanced from Alex to Sam. Noting the secret smiles they both wore made her wish she'd experienced what they were talking about. It sounded . . . interesting. And then she recalled that she supposedly had experienced it and simply didn't remember it and heaved a sigh. Another memory and moment stolen by her mother, she thought bitterly, and turned to Wyatt to ask,

"So we left early that night, but I didn't show up at home until the next day?"

"We stayed in bed until midafternoon the next day," Wyatt explained quietly. "And we only got up then because we were hungry. We went to a café. I went to the bathroom and when I came back you were talking to some guy. You said he was a family friend and he and a lot of other people had been looking for you since the night before. You said your mother was freaking out. You should have called her, and you had to go home and calm her down. You'd meet me in that café the next day, at the same time."

Wyatt frowned as he recalled it. "The guy was pulling you away as you talked. Afterward, I didn't understand why I didn't intervene. Now I suppose the fellow was controlling me and making me accept what was happening. But I didn't even get a chance to ask your phone number. I tried to follow you, but I had to pay for our meal, and by the time I got out you were both gone."

"I'm guessing she didn't show up the next day?" Alex asked quietly.

"I waited for hours for her, but no, she never showed," Wyatt admitted and then turned back to Elspeth. "So then I tried to look you up. I started looking for an Elspeth Pimms in the phone book, and on the internet, but there was nothing. No phone number listing, no Facebook, not even a Google search of your name turned up anything. It was like you didn't exist."

Elspeth turned to her sisters. "What happened? Why didn't I go back the next day?"

Victoria exchanged a glance with Julianna and then both turned back to her and shook their heads helplessly before Victoria said, "Mother got a call from Scotty saying one of his men found you and he was bringing you home. Then she sent us out with Father. She said she wanted to talk to you."

"Dad took us out to lunch and shopping," Julianna put in. "And then Mother called Dad. When he got off the phone, he said you and Mother were meeting us at the airport. We were flying to Italy to stay with Raffael for a belated birthday celebration for you, and it was probably better not to bring up your disappearing act as it would just upset Mother. So that's what happened. We flew to Italy, visited Raffael, and celebrated your birthday."

"Your disappearing was never brought up again," Victoria finished.

"Not even to Elspeth?" Sam asked with surprise. "I mean, I understand your not bringing it up around your mother, but why did you never say anything to Elspeth about it? Weren't you curious about where she'd been or what she'd done?"

"Yes," Victoria admitted. "But Mother kept Elspeth pretty close after that, at least for the next couple of months."

"She watched her like a hawk," Julianna put in. "I mean, she rarely left her side. She wouldn't even let her go to work."

"What?" Elspeth asked with shock. She didn't remember any of this either. "I didn't go to work? For how long?"

"At least two months. Right?" Julianna asked Victoria.

"Yeah," the twin agreed. "The first day back from Italy she insisted on driving you in to work, but came back a little later with you still in tow and said you had been given a short sabbatical. She'd arranged it with the head of your department."

"Then she kept you by her side that whole two months," Julianna continued. "By the time she eased up . . ." She shrugged. "Life had moved on."

"And so had we," Victoria said with a frown and then glanced at her twin and pointed out, "That's about when Mother insisted we move back to York. Isn't it?"

"Yeah." Julianna nodded slowly, and then said, "By the end of the two months we'd moved back to the family estate there and Mother had arranged a new position for you at the University of York."

"She arranged my position there?" Elspeth asked with shock. She had some vague recollection of doing that herself. The very vagueness of the memory told her it wasn't true.

"I'm sorry, Elspeth," Julianna said quietly. "Really. If we'd known you'd met your life mate, and what Mother was doing, we would have said something. Truly. I know I can be a PITA, but I would have told you about that."

"I know," Elspeth said on a sigh, and reached out to catch Julianna's hand and squeeze it affectionately.

"Me too," Victoria assured her and then added with anger, "I can't believe she would take that from you. I mean, it's one thing to make us miserable with her overprotective and controlling ways, but to get between you and your life mate? That's just not on."

"Wait, wait, wait. How could she make you forget like that?" Alex asked with a frown. "Wouldn't that take a three-on-one mind wipe? I mean, Jean Claude had to arrange a three-on-one to erase Julius from Marguerite's mind."

"Jean Claude wanted to erase something like twenty years from Marguerite's mind, though," Elspeth pointed out solemnly. "He wanted to erase her meeting and loving her true life mate, having his child, and . . . basically he had to erase a whole life from Marguerite—every memory from every one of the days in those twenty years so that nothing would spark a return of them. He couldn't do that without performing a three-on-one," she explained. "But for me, Mother merely had to remove one twenty-four-hour-long first date."

"And then move you out of London to make sure nothing sparked those memories and brought them back to you," Sam said quietly. "I gather that's why she moved you to York?"

"And made sure we celebrated my birthday in foreign countries," Elspeth added grimly. "It ensured we didn't accidentally go anywhere Wyatt and I had gone, and that nothing around me would be likely to remind me of whatever Wyatt and I did on my birthday and bring those memories back."

"Wow," Alex breathed. "That's . . ."

"Evil?" Sam suggested when her sister seemed at a loss as to what to say.

"I'd like to say no," Alex said apologetically to Elspeth. "But frankly, I can't think of another description that would fit. I mean, she got between you and your *life mate*. What if she had done that to Cale and me?" she asked with horror. "What kind of person does that? What kind of *mother* does that?"

"An evil one," Sam muttered with disgust.

"Yes," Elspeth agreed with regret. She'd always given her mother excuses for her behavior, but now—Turning, she raised the carafe she still held. "Victoria, will you make the coffee for me? I need to have a word with Mother."

"Of course," Victoria took the carafe and carried it to the sink at once.

"I'll help," Julianna added, moving to collect the coffee out of the cupboard.

"Thank you," Elspeth said solemnly and moved to the bags they'd set on the counter when they'd entered. Opening the first bag, she began sifting through the contents until she found the pocketknife she'd bought.

"What are you going to do?" Alex asked, her eyes narrowing on the knife as Elspeth flicked it open.

"Just going to have a little talk with my mother," Elspeth assured her, slipping the open knife into her jacket pocket. "I'll be right back."

"Ellie, talk, don't kill," Alex called out worriedly as Elspeth left the kitchen.

Elspeth moved at a quick clip, not slowing until she reached the closed door of the guest room. Pausing then, she slipped the knife out of her pocket, peered at it silently and considered her options. Pain had helped her resist her mother taking control of her that first night. Hopefully pain would help her resist her control again now, because G.G. was right—she needed to confront her mother. She'd gone way too far intervening between her and Wyatt. Way too far.

Mouth compressing, Elspeth tightened her grip on the knife, took a deep breath, and then quickly plunged it into her upper leg and promptly cursed a blue streak.

Cripes, that hurt! Like big-time hurt! Like a what-the-hell-had-she-been-thinking-doing-that-to-herself kind of pain.

"What the hell have you done?"

Elspeth glanced around sharply, her eyes widening when she found Wyatt at her side.

"What were you thinking?" he asked, bending to peer at the knife sticking out of her leg. "Good God, woman, I'm here to protect you from some mad stalker trying to kill you. I didn't realize I'd have to protect you from yourself too." Straightening, he scowled at her. "Are you a self-abuser? One of those people who cut themselves and—"

"No," she interrupted quickly, glancing anxiously toward the guest bedroom door. Grabbing his arm, she started to drag him away up the hall, but gasped in a sharp breath as pain shot through her leg with the first step. Cursing under her breath, she stopped and clung to his arm briefly as she waited for the pain to subside.

"Are you all right?" he asked with a frown.

"No," she said at once. Elspeth took a deep breath, held it briefly and then let it out as she reached down to yank the knife back out of her leg . . . and damned if it didn't hurt more than putting it in had. Another string of curses followed, and then she paused and took deep breaths again.

"Better?" Wyatt asked sympathetically when she finally reopened her eyes.

Elspeth nodded and said a little shakily, "Yes, thank you."

"Good," he said solemnly, and then snapped, "Now, would you care to tell me why the hell you stabbed yourself?"

Elspeth opened her mouth, and then snapped it closed with surprise when he suddenly knelt beside her and clasped her thigh in his hands so he could examine her wound.

"Jesus. You really got yourself good," he muttered, tugging his T-shirt out of his jeans.

"Don't—Oh, shoot," Elspeth sighed when she was too late to stop him from tearing off a strip along the bottom of the T-shirt. It was a waste of a good shirt since her bleeding would probably stop before he finished wrapping the makeshift bandage around her leg, Elspeth thought as she watched him arrange it over the wound. She groaned in pain and grabbed for his shoulder to keep her balance when he tied it off tightly with a sharp tug.

Finished with his field dressing, Wyatt straightened and growled, "Well?"

"Well, what?" she asked uncertainly.

"Why did you stab yourself?" he asked with disbelief.

"Oh, right," she muttered. Sighing, she limped several feet away, and then glanced nervously back toward the door and explained, "My mother usually has no trouble controlling me."

"Yeah, I got that from the conversation in the kitchen," he said tightly. "But you didn't seem to have a problem getting away from her the night we went to The Night Club."

"Yes. I was able to keep from being controlled then, but I was in pain at the time. My injuries were still healing and I needed blood, and my stomach was on fire, my body cramping and aching . . . I think that's why she wasn't able to control me."

"So you stabbed yourself so you could confront her without her taking control of you again," he reasoned quietly, a lot of his anger slipping away.

Elspeth nodded.

Wyatt shook his head. "There's got to be a better way, El. You can't stab yourself every time you talk to your mother."

"I know," she said on a sigh. "And I will try to come up with another way, but later."

"Another way?" he asked with a frown.

"To be in pain without stabbing myself," she explained. "This way uses up blood unnecessarily, and I know I shouldn't be wasting blood like this. But I—"

"I don't give a damn about the blood," Wyatt said with amazement. "I'll give you blood if you need it, but Elspeth, I don't want you to be in pain. There has to be a better way to deal with your mother than that."

Elspeth glanced down and ran a finger over the cloth around her wound. "Or maybe I shouldn't deal with her at all after this." When he didn't comment, she raised her head and said, "I've tried to be understanding. I know she went through a lot when my brothers died, and it's made her paranoid and overprotective. I tried to remember that when she hovered, or treated me like a child, or when I suspected she controlled me. But she stepped over the line when she removed meeting you from my mind."

"When your brothers died?" he asked quietly.

Elspeth nodded, but then waved the question away. "I'll tell you about that later. Right now I need to confront my mother."

"All right." He took a step back, but that was all.

Elspeth narrowed her eyes. "You're not going back to the kitchen, are you?"

"Hard to guard you from the kitchen," he pointed out dryly.

"Right," she muttered. "Well, do me a favor and at least wait in the hall. I didn't stab myself just so she could control you and use you against me."

Wyatt stiffened at once. "How could she use me against you?"

"In any number of ways," Elspeth assured him, and

moved past him to the door. She raised her hand to knock, but then noticed the door was cracked open and simply pushed it wider instead. Knocking was requesting entrance. It wasn't a strong approach and Elspeth needed to come on as strong as she could for this confrontation. Besides, this was her home, and her mother was packing, not changing into a peignoir or something.

Actually, she wasn't even packing, Elspeth realized as the door swung open on an empty room.

Ten

"**S**he's not here," Wyatt said quietly behind her as Elspeth walked into the empty guest room. "Neither are her clothes or her luggage."

She glanced over her shoulder to see that he was standing by the door, his gaze moving around the room, including the empty closet visible through the open bifold doors.

"She must have finished packing and headed down to the basement apartment while we were in the kitchen," Elspeth said thoughtfully.

"Doesn't seem like her. I'd have expected her to at least make us carry her luggage down," Wyatt commented, moving up beside her.

"At least," Elspeth agreed.

"She went down after your sisters joined us in the kitchen, or they would have mentioned she'd left," he pointed out.

Elspeth merely nodded, and then gasped in surprise

when he scooped her up in his arms. Grabbing for his shoulders, she protested, "I can walk."

"It'll be faster if I carry you, and I need to be sure she didn't leave the door unlocked," he explained as he hurried out of the room and up the hall.

"Of course she didn't," Elspeth said calmly. "She's the one who's overprotective and . . ."

Her words died as they reached the front entry hall and saw that the door was unlocked.

"She came out and overheard the conversation in the kitchen and now knows you know," Wyatt said with certainty.

"What makes you say that?" she asked curiously, reaching out for the wall to balance herself when he set her on her feet and moved over to lock the door.

"It's the only reason she'd leave and not think to lock the door when she knows someone is trying to kill you," he reasoned.

"Maybe. Or maybe she was just using the attack as an excuse to regain control of me and doesn't really think I'm in much danger," she murmured, and when he glanced to her in question, she pointed out, "Well, whoever pushed me in front of that car couldn't have been an immortal. Any immortal would know that wouldn't kill me, so it had to have been a mortal, which means they aren't much of a threat."

"You don't consider mere mortals a threat?" he asked, his gaze narrowing as he walked back to her.

Elspeth got the distinct impression he felt insulted by the idea that she might not think him dangerous, so said honestly, "You would be. You know how to kill us. Most mortals don't though. Most don't even know we exist."

Appearing somewhat mollified, he nodded and scooped her up to carry her into the kitchen.

"Ellie!"

"Elspeth!"

"What happened?"

"Nothing. I'm fine," Elspeth said quickly as Sam, Alex, and the twins rushed forward to crowd around Wyatt as he carried her to a chair.

"Do you have any bandages here?" Wyatt asked as he straightened.

"Bandages are a waste of money," Alex assured him as she retrieved a bag of blood from the refrigerator. "It will close quickly. It's already stopped bleeding."

"Thank you," Elspeth murmured as she took the bag and slapped it to her mouth.

"Mother didn't do this, did she?" Julianna asked with a frown.

"No," Wyatt answered for her. "Elspeth stabbed herself."

"What?" Alex asked with amazement. "Why would you do that?"

Elspeth rolled her eyes above the bag at her mouth and again it was Wyatt who answered.

"She was able to resist Martine's control the other night because she was in pain, so she thought if she stabbed herself . . ."

"Martine couldn't control her," Sam finished for him on a sigh, and then raised one eyebrow. "So? Did it work?"

"She wasn't there," Wyatt said quietly. "The room was empty and she and her belongings were gone."

"Really?" Julianna asked with surprise. "She hadn't come out before we came into the kitchen."

"Yeah, and she isn't likely to leave without us," Victoria said dryly. "She usually doesn't let us out of her sight for more than a couple minutes."

Elspeth shifted her gaze to Wyatt and gave him a meaningful look.

"You're thinking she overheard the conversation we were having and knows we know about her controlling you and getting between you and Wyatt," Alex said quietly.

"It makes sense," Victoria commented. "Something made her leave."

They were all silent until the bag emptied, but as Elspeth pulled it from her teeth, Julianna asked, "You don't think Dad knows what she did, do you?"

"No way," Victoria said at once. "But I do wonder what she told him about what was going on when Elspeth was missing."

"Hmm," Elspeth murmured. She wondered about that herself.

"You don't think she's the one behind the attacks, do you?" Alex asked suddenly, and when everyone turned to peer at her blankly, she said, "Well, the attacks started the night your mother got here, and they're pretty weak attempts. I mean, neither attack would have killed you. And it was the perfect excuse for her to track you and even get guards put on you so that if you escape her, she can track you through us. All she has to do now is call Mortimer to find out where you are. Right?"

Elspeth stared at her silently. The suggestion wasn't actually that crazy. If her mother would get between her and her life mate to maintain her control over her, who was to say she wouldn't feign attacks on her to regain that control? Except—"The stabbing was a mortal with a mental illness, and the tip that came in about him was two or three days old when I went to check him out. Mother and the girls weren't here two days earlier."

"Then maybe that wasn't part of it," Sam suggested. "Maybe it just gave her the idea and she arranged the second attempt to give her ammunition to convince you to return to England, where you'd be safer."

"Oh come on," Victoria said with a frown. "I know Mother is . . ." She shrugged helplessly, and then said, "But having you attacked and hurt that badly? I don't think so. There are just lines you don't cross."

"And getting between me and my life mate isn't crossing those lines?" Elspeth asked dryly, and then added, "I'm not sure she has any limits. Mother tried to make me bite Wyatt for blood at Meredith's when we had dinner there. She controlled him to get him on the porch, and then tried to make me bite him."

"What?" Julianna asked, obviously shocked.

Elspeth nodded, but then said, "Still, I don't think she was behind my being pushed into traffic. G.G. said it was a man."

"She could have controlled someone and made them push you," Sam pointed out.

Elspeth shook her head. "She wasn't there. She was back at the house with Meredith and the girls."

"With Meredith," Julianna corrected her, and then explained, "She sent Victoria and me upstairs with our chicken after you and Wyatt left, and she stayed downstairs with Meredith alone for a while."

Elspeth stiffened. "How long?"

Julianna and Victoria looked at each other and then Victoria shrugged and said, "An hour. Maybe more."

"That's long enough for her to have got downtown

and back," Wyatt pointed out quietly. He took the empty bag she held, walked over to throw it out in the garbage next to the refrigerator, and then retrieved another bag of blood before returning.

"But we were inside The Night Club for a good fifteen or twenty minutes, maybe even half an hour, and I was in there alone for five or ten minutes before that," she pointed out as he walked back. "It would have taken her at least an hour and a half to get there, make someone push me, and get back. I don't think it was her."

"Okay." Wyatt nodded and held out the bag to her.

"Thank you," Elspeth murmured, taking the blood bag.

"You're welcome," Wyatt assured her and then said, "If it's not your mother then we need a pen and some paper. Do you have any?"

"In that drawer next to the sink," Elspeth told him, gesturing with the blood bag. "Why?"

"Because," he said, opening the drawer and retrieving the items. "You can write down the names of every mortal you know in Toronto while you feed on the blood."

"There's no need for a pen and pad, then," Elspeth assured him with amusement as he set both before her. "It's a short list."

"How short?" he asked.

Elspeth picked up the pen, quickly wrote three names and handed it to him.

"Wyatt, G.G., and Meredith," he read and then lowered the pad to stare at her. "That's it?"

"I've only been here six weeks," she pointed out defensively. "And most of that time I've either been unpacking, working, or visiting with your grandmother. It's not like I've been joining social clubs or visiting the bar scene or anything. Not that I would anyway."

"Why do you want to know what mortals she knows?" Sam asked curiously.

"Because if it's not Martine, then it's a mortal. As Elspeth pointed out to me earlier, an immortal would know pushing her into traffic wouldn't kill her."

"Oh!" Alex said with surprise, and then grinned and congratulated her, "Good one, Elspeth. None of the Enforcers picked up on that. Not even Mortimer."

"If you're looking for a mortal who might want to kill her, you might consider Violet and Oscar," Victoria suggested solemnly.

Elspeth's eyes widened in surprise. "You read their minds and got that they want to kill me?"

"No," Victoria wrinkled her nose. "I would never willingly put myself in his perverted mind. But while Violet seems all-right-ish, Oscar's creepy and I wouldn't put it past him to push you into traffic if you rebuffed one of his pervy advances."

"What about that woman who was originally in the downstairs apartment?" Julianna asked. "You got her arrested. Maybe she got out on bail and wants revenge."

Elspeth shook her head. "Madeleine-Nina wasn't going to be let out on bail. They said she had already proven herself a flight risk," she assured them. "As for Oscar and Violet, I'd only ever met them a couple times in passing before the night we had dinner together. Besides, Wyatt sent them both home in a taxi before we left for The Night Club, and I'm quite sure G.G. would have mentioned if the pusher was a geriatric who shuffled off like Oscar would."

"He said they ran off," Wyatt announced.

"Oh," Victoria said with disappointment.

"But you didn't list Oscar and Violet, or even Madeleine when you listed the mortals you know," Julianna pointed out. "Maybe there are other mortals you're not thinking of."

"Julianna's right." Wyatt sat down at the table next to her, drew the pad in front of him, and then picked up the pen. "So maybe we should go through this logically."

"What does that mean?" Alex asked.

"Go through it day by day," Wyatt explained, and then asked Elspeth, "You flew here, right?"

She nodded.

"Did you take a taxi from the airport to here?" he asked.

Elspeth shook her head. "I rented a car. I knew I'd need a vehicle to get around until I bought myself one."

"So you talked to someone at the car rental agency," Sam said in an *ah-ha!* voice.

"I did," Elspeth admitted and Wyatt scribbled *car rental agent* on the pad. "But it was a woman, and G.G. said a guy pushed me into traffic."

"Yeah," Wyatt agreed, and then gestured to the blood bag she still held. "Get busy with that and we'll ask yes and no questions until you're done."

Elspeth grimaced, but popped the bag to her fangs.

"Okay, the car rental person is out," Wyatt said, crossing out the entry. "So you drove the rental here, met my grandmother, got your keys, and came up to your apartment?"

Elspeth nodded.

"And then what did you do?" Wyatt asked, turning the pen in his hands.

"She went food shopping," Alex answered for her, obviously reading her thoughts now. "Write down *grocery cashier*, Wyatt."

"Okay," Wyatt wrote, and then raised his head and asked, "What happened next?"

"She went to bed," Alex answered for her.

"So the next day, did you do anything before going to the Enforcer House?" Wyatt asked.

Elspeth pulled the now empty bag away with relief. "Yes, I did. I went furniture shopping and met a very nice salesman. But other than cashiers and salesmen, the only other mortals I have encountered since coming here were the moving men and the wife of the mentally ill patient who stabbed me. But she's female, and no doubt still in the hospital from her husband's stabbing her, so it can't be her." She crumpled the empty bag in her hand, walked to the garbage, and tossed it in, adding, "This is a waste of time. I hardly think I managed to piss off a cashier, salesman, or even the moving men to the point that they'd start stalking me, trail me downtown, and push me into traffic."

"Probably not, but that only leaves your mother controlling someone and making them do it," Wyatt pointed out, and then frowned when she headed for the door rather than the table. "Where are you going?"

"To change my clothes before the bloodstained side of my pants dries and glues itself to my skin," she muttered, pushing though the swinging kitchen door.

"Elspeth, wait!" Julianna cried.

Pausing halfway through the door, she swung back wearily and raised her eyebrows at her sister. "What?"

Much to her surprise, the twin hesitated, looking anxious, and then swallowed and begged, "Please, can we stay here? We'll sleep in the guest room, or on the air mattress in the dining room to be out of the way, and I promise we'll behave. No attitude, no drinking or eating anything without asking first. Just please don't make us go down there with her."

"Please," Victoria added.

Elspeth didn't even hesitate. She simply nodded, then let the door swing closed and continued on her way. She hadn't even taken two steps before the door swung open again and she was suddenly in a sister sandwich, Julianna and Victoria forcing her to a halt as they each hugged her from either side.

"Thank you," Julianna whispered, squeezing her tightly. "I'm sorry for being such a brat since we got here. Mother just makes me so crazy."

"Me too," Victoria said.

"She makes us all crazy," Elspeth murmured, hugging them back. "Now, go grab your suitcases and take them into the guest bedroom."

"Thank you," Julianna and Victoria repeated, each kissing a cheek and giving her another squeeze before releasing her and slipping away.

Elspeth turned to watch them slip back into the kitchen, and stiffened slightly when she saw Wyatt standing silent and still next to the door.

"I'll see you to your room," Wyatt murmured, moving up beside her now and taking her arm as he had while escorting her through the different stores.

"It's not that big an apartment," Elspeth said with weary amusement. "I'm sure I can get there on my own."

"I'll walk you to your room," he repeated firmly, but this time added, "You'll wait just inside the door while I check to be sure the windows and doors are closed and locked and that there's no one inside."

The words were said in a tone of voice she could only

describe as businesslike. He wasn't being chivalrous or polite. He was being the professional bodyguard, she realized, and merely nodded.

Elspeth expected to have to wait in the doorway. Instead, he ushered her into the room, closed the door, and urged her up against the wall next to the hinges.

"Stay right here," he instructed, his gaze shifting around the room. "If there's trouble in the room, leave and run back to the kitchen with the others. If the door starts to open unexpectedly, stay here behind the door and out of sight until you know if it's friend or foe. If it's a foe, let them come after me and then slip out and return to the kitchen while they're distracted, but make sure they're far enough away not to be able to grab you before you move. Understand?"

Elspeth stared at him wide-eyed, but nodded.

Apparently satisfied, he turned away and moved directly to the French doors. She'd left them unlocked when she'd left earlier, and he opened one to peer outside, then quickly closed and locked it.

"I expected you to make me wait in the hall," she admitted as he closed the blackout curtains.

"I can't watch you in the hall if I'm in here," he pointed out, moving to her closet next.

"Yes, but I should have been safe in the hall," she pointed out as he opened her closet door and poked around briefly before shutting it.

Much to her surprise, Wyatt shook his head. He didn't explain, however, but moved to the bathroom and pushed the door open to look around. He disappeared inside, and she heard the screech of the metal hooks of the shower curtain being opened before he called out, "Someone could have broken in through the guest bedroom window and be in there right now. They could have snuck up and snatched or attacked you without my knowing it if I'd left you in the hall while I searched your room."

Elspeth gaped at the empty bathroom door, shocked at the thought that someone could break into her home and attack her as he was suggesting. She'd thought of her apartment as her safe haven since moving here, but it was quickly proving less than safe. First her mother and sisters showed up and gained entrance, and now he was suggesting whoever had pushed her into traffic could break in?

"All clear."

Elspeth glanced up at that announcement to see Wyatt coming out of the bathroom. Letting her breath out, she nodded and moved to her closet to gather a clean pair of black jeans and a red shirt. Carrying them with her, she stopped at her dresser to collect a bra and panties and then headed for the bathroom.

"Leave the door cracked open so I can hear if you have any trouble," Wyatt ordered as he stepped aside for her to enter the bathroom.

Pausing, Elspeth turned to him with surprise. "What?"

"The lock on the window in there is iffy," he explained gently. "I promise I won't look, but leave the door open just a crack so I can hear if you have a problem."

"Oh," she breathed and then nodded, and muttered, "Right," as she turned to continue into the room. She almost closed the door all the way behind her by habit alone, but caught herself at the last moment and made sure it was open an inch or two. She then placed her clothes on the hook on the top of the door and set her underwear on the counter before moving to the shower and turning on the water.

The shower was in the corner of the bathroom on the hinge side of the door. Wyatt would have had to open the door further and stuck his head in to see anything. Still, she was self-conscious about stripping with the door open even the little bit it was. Turning her back to it, she quickly stripped off her bloodstained pants and the rest of her clothes and then pretty much leapt into the shower, yanking the curtain closed as she went. Big mistake. She should have checked the water first, Elspeth realized as ice-cold water poured over her.

Gasping in shock, she tried to back quickly out of the water, forgot about the need to step over the lip of the shower base, and tumbled backward through the shower curtain. Elspeth instinctively caught at the sheet of vinyl, trying to save herself, and heard the *plink, plink, plink* of the curtain holders snapping up to hit the shower rod as the vinyl tore free. The next thing Elspeth knew, she was crashing to the bathroom floor with the vinyl shower curtain as her only cushion. It didn't do much to protect her head when it hit the tile floor.

"El!"

Groaning, Elspeth reached up to cover the back of her head and rolled onto her side into a fetal position as she tried to ride out the pain. It felt like her head was splitting in two, and she was positive the dampness under her fingers must be blood. God, it hurt!

She was vaguely aware of Wyatt's concerned voice, and then her hands were forced away so that he could examine her head. It couldn't be as bad as she'd feared, Elspeth decided when he released a relieved sigh and slid one arm under her legs and the other around her back.

"How is it?" she asked with a frown. The pain was beginning to recede now, surprisingly quickly, Elspeth noted. Still, it had been terrible just a moment ago, so she kept her eyes closed as he lifted her up off the ground.

"You're already developing a goose egg, but you didn't break the skin, at least, and your skull seems intact," Wyatt said solemnly as he set her on the bathroom counter.

"But it felt damp," she protested, lifting her head and opening her eyes with surprise.

"Water," he explained with a crooked smile.

"Oh," Elspeth grimaced. Sighing, she shifted her attention to Wyatt and then froze when she saw where his gaze had gone. His eyes were roving hungrily over her body, and she could almost feel his gaze like a touch as it burned its way over her breasts, and then down her stomach and between her legs.

"Wyatt?" she said gently, surprised at how breathless her voice was. She was panting, Elspeth realized with amazement. The man hadn't even touched her and she was panting like an overheated dog . . . or a horny one, she thought, recalling Alex's description.

"I'm sorry," Wyatt growled, and turned away to quickly search the room. He spotted the bath towel over the towel rack, grabbed it, and turned back to offer it to her.

Elspeth automatically reached for it, but froze when their hands touched. For a minute, they just remained like that, both silent and still as shockwaves rolled through them from where they touched, and then Wyatt cleared his throat. His voice a husky rasp of sound, he said, "I know you're not ready for a life mate, and I—"

That was as far as he got before Elspeth finished taking the towel from him, let it drop to the floor, and reached for him instead.

"Oh thank God," he growled and bent his head to kiss her.

Kapow didn't describe the passion that suddenly exploded inside Elspeth as his mouth covered hers. Shocked at the extent of the response her body had to such a simple caress, Elspeth slid her arms around his shoulders and held on in a dazed way as his tongue slid along the seam of her lips. When she opened her mouth and his tongue slid in to explore, she groaned in welcome and instinctively wiggled forward on the countertop, trying to get closer.

The moment she did that, Wyatt's hands dropped to her thighs, urging them apart. Elspeth obeyed the silent demand, and spread her legs for him. He immediately stepped between them, moving as close as he could.

Elspeth gasped, and jerked back a bit, though, when her naked breasts brushed across the cold metal of the guns in his double chest holster.

"Sorry," he muttered, and pulled back enough to unsnap and remove the gear.

Elspeth let her hands glide over his T-shirt—covered chest as he set the gun holster in the sink next to her. When he then turned his attention to the holster at his hip, she let her hands drop to grab the material of his T-shirt just above his belt and began to tug it upward. Dragging the cloth out of his jeans, she pushed it up until she could run her hands over the skin she'd bared.

Now it was Wyatt's turn to groan as her fingers skimmed lightly over the rippling muscles of his stomach and up to explore and caress his pecs. The man had some muscle on him, Elspeth noted with appreciation as she squeezed and caressed him, and then she moaned in protest when he broke their kiss.

"Be careful not to accidentally turn on the taps," he warned, his voice a sexy growl as he set the hip holster with its gun in the sink as well. He then began to remove his T-shirt. Elspeth helped eagerly, taking over tugging it up over his head. She then let it drop to the floor and covered his hands with an encouraging moan as they suddenly closed over her breasts.

"God, I thought surely it couldn't have been as good as I remembered," he growled, watching her face as he caressed her breasts and rolled her nipples. "I thought I'd built it up in my head, or just gone briefly mad or something, but dear God, just touching you is . . ."

Rather than finish, he bent to kiss her again. This time the kiss didn't start softly or as a sweet caress. It was a hungry, almost violent taking on both their parts, a violent battle of tongues as his body urged hers back until she was at a fifty-degree angle to the counter. Giving up her hold on his hands, Elspeth clutched at his shoulders to keep from falling, and then he broke the kiss again, this time to lower his mouth and claim one breast.

"Oh God," Elspeth gasped, her hips jumping and then sliding forward on the counter until his body stopped her. They both groaned then as their groins met, pressing against each other through his jeans, and then Elspeth wrapped her legs around his hips and used her hold to urge him tighter still. He began to grind against her as he suckled at her breast.

It wasn't long before they both wanted more, though. At least, Elspeth wanted more, and reached for his face with one hand, trying to urge him back up for a kiss. Wyatt responded to the silent request, but not before nipping at the nipple he'd been laving. He let it slip from his mouth then, and raised his head to kiss her again. The moment he did, Elspeth reached for his belt buckle and began feeling around blindly, trying to undo it, a difficult task when she couldn't see it. Fortunately, Wyatt urged her hands away after a moment of fumbling and quickly undid the belt, and then the button and zipper of his jeans as well. He reached for the material on each side to push his jeans down, but jerked to a halt, even his mouth freezing midkiss as she reached into the open jeans, found him, and carefully pulled him out.

When Elspeth had him out and was finally able to close her hand around his hard erection, he gasped into her mouth, a sound she echoed as the excitement she'd caused in him reverberated through her own body.

Once that first shock had slid through her and begun to fade, Elspeth moved her hand, groaning along with him as his pleasure rang through her, making her wiggle on the countertop with excitement and need. She knew he was about to find his satisfaction, because she was too, when Wyatt suddenly caught her hand and jerked it away from him.

Panting heavily, he leaned his forehead against hers briefly to catch his breath. He then kissed her hard and quick, before dropping to his knees in front of her and burying his face between her legs. When he began to rasp his tongue across her soaking and sensitive skin, Elspeth cried out and grabbed for his head, trying to get him to stop, but it was too late. She was too excited. They both were, and she'd barely touched his head when she felt something press into her. Elspeth froze, her body arching so far back now she was sure it would snap, and then something did snap, something deep inside, a fine gossamer string that had been holding back her release. Without it, she screamed and began to thrash on the countertop, vaguely aware that Wyatt was doing the same between her legs as her release poured over him, pushing him into his own, and then she slid away into the unconsciousness new life mates experienced.

Eleven

Wyatt shifted sleepily, and grimaced as his body complained at the hard, cold bed he'd chosen to sleep on. He was getting too old for the rough living necessitated by being in the JTF2, he thought wearily, shifting again and barely restraining a moan when his hip began to throb.

"Elspeth! Wyatt!"

Frowning, he opened his eyes and peered with confusion around the smoky room . . . until his brain woke up enough to realize that the smoke in the air was a bad thing and that the room he was in was Elspeth's bathroom. Cursing, Wyatt sat up abruptly, bumping his shoulder against something as he did. He looked to see what it was and paused, his eyes widening as he saw that it was Elspeth's knee. She was still seated on the counter; her upper body slumped against the mirror.

"Wyatt! Elspeth!"

He turned his head and peered out into the bedroom to

find the source of the shouting. He didn't see anyone, but he did see flames filling the next room. Cursing, Wyatt lunged to his feet and moved to the door, doing up his pants as he went.

"Thank God!"

That cry drew his gaze to the door, where Sam and Alex were looking in from the hall. Their faces were riddled with anxiety as they peered at him across the burning room, he saw, coughing in reaction to the smoke he was inhaling now that he was off the floor.

"Where's Elspeth?" Sam asked anxiously. "You have to get her out of here."

"I've got it!" he assured them, an icy calm settling over him as it always did in a crisis. "You get the twins and my grandmother out, and make sure Martine is out of the basement apartment as well. Go!" he barked when they didn't move at once. "Get everyone else. I'll see to Elspeth."

The women left then, disappearing away up the hall. Wyatt turned back into the bathroom and quickly turned on the shower taps, allowing the water to pour down over him before he stepped out and grabbed the hand towel off the rack beside the sink. He tied the hand towel around his head so that it covered his mouth and nose, offering some protection from the smoke. He grabbed the bath towels off the rack, and tossed them under the spray to soak up the water pouring down, again taking extra time to stick his legs under the spray while there—first one and then the other. Wyatt then grabbed his T-shirt off the floor and stepped under the water with it to let the spray soak the shirt as well as his body and jeans before he stepped out and moved to Elspeth.

"El, love, wake up," he murmured, catching her by the

shoulders and pulling her upright so that he could put his wet T-shirt on her.

"Wyatt?" she said sleepily, and then blinked her eyes open with shock as the cold, wet material touched her skin. Wyatt pulled the shirt over her head. Her eyes were closed when he tugged it down to her neck, but opened again as he began to urge one of her arms into a sleeve.

"What's happening?" she asked with confusion. "I smell smoke. Do you smoke? I didn't know you smoked."

"Not me, sugar," he said with a crooked smile as she helped him get her other arm into its sleeve. "The house is smoking. It's on fire."

"What?" That brought her awake in a hurry, a sudden rush of adrenaline no doubt helping as she sat up straight and peered around. When she looked out into the bedroom and saw the fire licking across the floors and up the one wall they could see, she issued a foul curse that made him smile. Damn . . . beautiful, smart, sweet, sexy as hell, mind-blowing in bed—or on the bathroom counter, to be more accurate—*and* she had a potty mouth. He could love this woman, Wyatt thought with a smile.

"What happened?" Elspeth growled, slipping off the counter. She was not smiling, he noted, and he couldn't blame her. His grandmother's house was going up in smoke, taking Elspeth's home and belongings with it. It was nothing to smile about, and yet he'd found his El again. After four years of searching, and long after he'd given up on ever having her back, here she was. Nothing was going to take her from him again, not her mother, and not even this fire. He wasn't letting her go.

Pulling her away from the door, Wyatt moved back to the shower and retrieved the towels. They were sopping wet and heavy as he quickly wrapped them around her, leaving only a small hole for her to breathe through. He then scooped her up and carried her to the bedroom door. The fire was following a starburst pattern from the middle of the room outward, and he was pretty sure he could smell gas. A Molotov cocktail, then. *Nice*, he thought with disgust. Definitely not an accident.

Mouth compressing, Wyatt tightened his hold on Elspeth and launched himself into hell. That's what it felt like. The air was so hot it was painful to breathe, so Wyatt held his breath. But there was nothing he could do about the fire that licked at his feet and lower legs as he ran through the flames to the bed. When he reached it, Wyatt simply leapt on top and ran across the soft mattress. He pushed off hard, and leapt high when he reached the side nearest the French doors. Still, he came down several feet short of them, his feet disappearing in the flames as he landed, but Wyatt simply continued forward, charging through the broken glass from the shattered door to get out onto the balcony where cool night air greeted them.

Wyatt didn't stop until he reached the railing. Pausing then, he set Elspeth down and quickly unwound the towel from around her legs. She needed mobility for him to lower her down to his grandmother's porch.

Wyatt straightened from the task to find Elspeth had removed the upper towel as well and was now peering sadly back into her burning bedroom.

"El?" he said gently. "We have to go."

Nodding, she turned back to him and then frowned as she looked him over. "You got burned."

"I'm fine," he assured her and urged her closer to the rail. "I'm going to lower you to Gran's porch and—"

"I can climb," she interrupted. "Do you want me to help you?"

Wyatt smiled crookedly at the offer, but shook his head. "I'm good. Let's get moving. The fire hasn't spread to the porch yet, but it still could."

Elspeth nodded and began to climb over the rail. Wyatt followed suit, throwing one leg over the rail and then quickly lowering himself even as Elspeth did. When she swung out and dropped to the grass in front of his grandmother's porch, he did as well, and then he caught her arm to urge her away.

"Oh thank God!"

Wyatt glanced down with surprise as he was suddenly caught up in a ridiculously tight hug by Alex, he saw. She'd approached so quickly he hadn't even seen her coming, and now she lifted him off his feet briefly, and then set him back down and clasped his face, pulling him down to buss his cheek. "You saved her. And yourself. We're so glad you're both okay."

Alex had barely finished saying that before she released him and switched places with Sam, whom he now saw releasing Elspeth. Alex caught El up in a hug now even as Sam rushed around her to hug him as well. "Thank you, thank you, thank you! And thank God you were here! We never could have got to her."

Wyatt chuckled and patted the woman's back, his gaze now moving around the backyard just in time to see Julianna and Victoria rush around the corner of the burning house and hurry toward them. His grandmother and Martine followed, the two women moving at almost a jog, which was as good as a full-on run for his elderly grandmother. She looked fine, though, he noted with relief. They all did.

"How are you?" Sam asked, pulling back to look up at him with concern.

"I'm good," he assured her, stepping back. "I—" The word ended on a grunt as the twins reached them and both threw themselves at him at once, nearly knocking him over before he managed to regain his balance.

"Thank you for saving Elspeth, Wyatt," Julianna said, hugging him tightly. "And thank goodness you're all right too."

"How do you know *she* didn't save *me*?" he asked with amusement.

"I read it from your mind as we rushed up," she said easily, and then gave him another squeeze, and slid away to hug Elspeth.

"Thank you," Victoria said simply and gave him another squeeze as well before following Julianna.

"Wyatt?"

Turning back at that anxious cry, Wyatt hurried toward his grandmother, intent on making sure she was okay too.

"**Y**ou're good?"

Elspeth smiled at that question from Julianna. "Yes. Perfect. Not a blister or splinter."

"Good, good." Julianna hugged her again and then said, "But Wyatt was hurt."

"Yes, I saw that he had a bit of scorching on one arm," Elspeth admitted, her worried gaze sliding to the man as he greeted his grandmother. She noticed her mother standing next to the pair, talking on the phone, but then glanced back to Julianna as she continued speaking.

"Not his arms, although he has more than a bit of scorching there," she said solemnly. "His feet and lower legs are badly burned from running through the fire, and his feet are cut up pretty bad too . . . from the broken glass from the French door."

Cursing, Elspeth turned and rushed over to where Wyatt was talking quietly with Meredith.

"I'm fine, Gran, really," he was saying as she reached them.

Elspeth slowed to a stop and looked him over with concern. Julianna was right. He was more than a little scorched on the arms. There were a couple of good burns on the bottoms of his lower arms, but there were a lot of larger, deeper scorch marks on his legs and feet. Elspeth closed her eyes briefly. He'd run through the fire. She hadn't been able to see that. She'd thought he'd found a way around the flames or something. She'd never imagined he'd run right through it. She couldn't imagine what the bottoms of his feet must look like.

"We are going to Marguerite's. Rachel is meeting us there. She will look after Wyatt," Martine announced as if she thought she could still order them all around.

Elspeth turned slowly to stare at her mother, a dozen different thoughts racing through her head. Trust and appreciation for her thinking ahead and making the necessary phone calls for these arrangements were not among those thoughts. For one moment, Elspeth even considered telling her mother to go to hell, that they'd go check into a hotel. All of them . . . except Martine. Unfortunately, she couldn't really afford it herself, and knew Meredith couldn't either.

No, it was better for them to stay at Aunt Marguerite's until they could get ahold of the insurance companies, both hers and Meredith's, and see if there was any kind of housing allowance in a situation like this. Until then, Aunt Marguerite's would do. Elspeth was very fond of her aunt, and knew she'd be kind and understanding with Meredith.

"So, I talked to Mortimer," Sam announced, leading Alex and the twins to join them. "He says we're going to Marguerite's?" She looked at Elspeth in question, and when she nodded, relaxed and smiled. "Okay then. Mortimer is sending Donny to collect Martine and the twins, and I thought Wyatt would rather Meredith ride with us?"

When everyone looked his way, Wyatt nodded solemnly, but his gaze was shifting around the dark yard, searching the shadows and corners. No doubt looking for their arsonist, Elspeth supposed and started looking as well.

"I think we'd do better to wait in the front yard where the streetlights offer more illumination," he said now.

"Good thinking," Sam said with a nod and began to usher the group around the house.

Elspeth couldn't help noticing that Wyatt positioned himself between her and his grandmother, one hand holding each of them by the elbow, ready to move them where he wanted if trouble hit. Usually he would have had one hand hovering near his weapon as he escorted them, she knew. Unfortunately, he didn't presently have his guns. Those were sitting in the bathroom sink in her burning apartment.

"Is Mortimer sending someone to deal with the police and the firemen?" Alex asked Sam as they reached the front of the house and found both departments in evidence. There were two police cars, a large fire truck, and uniformed men running everywhere, Elspeth noted as they made their way across the front yard. One of the neighbors must have called 911 relatively quickly for them to already be here.

"Yes. Magnus and Rickart are going to come handle the police and firemen," Sam assured her, mentioning two of the men from the UK Enforcers who had come to assist while the North American hunters were short on Enforcers. "They were the closest crew and should be here—right now," Sam finished with a wry smile as they saw an SUV glide into view on the street.

"Not a moment too soon," Elspeth said dryly as she noted that they'd been spotted and several of the uniformed mortals were making a beeline for them.

"Which one of you is the homeowner?"

"Did everyone get out?"

"Is there anyone still in the house?"

"Is anyone hurt?"

"Do you know how the fire started?"

The questions came rapid-fire as half a dozen men converged on them.

Elspeth saw Meredith open her mouth to explain that she was the homeowner, but the woman never got the chance to say it. The men had already turned away as one and were walking back across the yard.

"Well, that was . . . What on earth . . . ?" Meredith said a little shakily. Elspeth slid into her thoughts to calm her and then watched as the officers and firemen made their way straight to Magnus and Rickart as they got out of the SUV. The two men had obviously taken control of them from their vehicle when they saw them converging on the group. She'd have to thank them later, Elspeth thought on a sigh. She was just too tired to deal with things like that at the moment.

"It's all right, Merry," Sam said soothingly as Elspeth retreated from the woman's thoughts. "That's Magnus and Rickart. They work with Elspeth and me. They'll take care of everything."

"Oh, how nice," Merry said with a weary smile.

"That's impressive," Wyatt said solemnly next to her, his gaze on the two immortals facing the half circle of men in uniform. "And one hell of a handy trick."

Elspeth smiled faintly, and then spotted a second SUV pulling up behind the first, and breathed a sigh of relief.

"There's Donny," Sam said now. "Martine—"

"Yes," her mother interrupted. "Come along, girls. Our ride is here."

She sailed across the yard then, simply expecting the girls to obey, but for one of the few times in their lives, Julianna and Victoria did not obey at once. Instead, they simply watched her until she was several feet away and then turned to Sam and begged in unison, "Can't we ride with you?"

Sam eyed them sympathetically, but shook her head. "I'm sorry. There isn't enough room for all of us in our SUV."

"We could ride in the back with the cooler and the gun chest," Julianna said desperately.

Sam hesitated, but then pointed out, "It wouldn't be comfortable and there are no seat belts back there."

"We'd be safe enough," Victoria assured her. "So long as we aren't beheaded we're good, and that can happen as easily with seat belts as without."

"And a little discomfort is fine," Julianna added firmly, "so long as we don't have to ride with . . ."

They all turned to watch Martine crossing the yard and Elspeth could see the struggle taking place on Sam's face. It was obvious she didn't want to say no. Finally, Elspeth said, "If you're going to allow it, you better say so now and get them in the SUV before Mother notices they aren't with her and takes control of them."

"Yes, yes, all right. Get in the back quickly, girls," Sam said, and then shook her head as they watched the twins run for the SUV parked in the driveway. As the rest of the group followed at a quick clip, Sam elbowed her sister and muttered, "Your mother-in-law is so going to hate me."

"But my sisters-in-law won't," Alex pointed out. "Besides, the more I see of my mother-in-law, the less I like her, so what do I care what she thinks?"

The driveway was much closer than the road, and their group reached Sam's SUV faster than Martine reached the one Donny was in.

"Uh-oh. I think you'd best get this puppy in gear and get us out of here, Sam," Alex said suddenly in warning as they were doing up their seat belts. "Martine just noticed the girls aren't with her and doesn't look pleased."

Elspeth glanced toward her mother to see that she'd stopped in front of Donny's SUV and was looking back to where they'd been standing when she started off. No one was there anymore. Of course, when she didn't spot them at once, Martine glanced around until she did spot them. But Sam already had the SUV started and was maneuvering around the police cars in the driveway to get to the road.

"Call Donny and let him know the twins are with us and he only needs to transport Martine," Sam ordered once they were accelerating away up the road.

"You don't think he'll figure that out for himself?" Alex asked dryly, even as she pulled her phone out of her pocket.

"He might not. The girls ducked out of sight in the back the minute they got in," Sam explained, glancing in the rearview mirror as both girls popped up now in the back.

"She has to see you to . . . do her thing," Julianna finished with a glance at Meredith.

Victoria nodded, and added, "We thought ducking might be for the best. If she'd try to make Elspeth . . ." She paused briefly, and when Elspeth noted the concentrated look on her face as she peered at Meredith, she realized she was taking control of the woman, and understood why when she finished, "If she was willing to make Elspeth bite Wyatt, she might not be above making us jump out of a moving vehicle."

"Yes," Julianna agreed unhappily. "She appears to be less concerned about our well-being than controlling us."

Elspeth would have liked to argue the point, and say that their mother loved them all and certainly wouldn't have made them jump out of the vehicle, but she wasn't at all sure that was true. In fact, she was rather surprised her mother hadn't taken control of Sam and made her stop the car. The only thing she could think was that Alex must have been in the way, preventing her seeing Sam to do that. Or perhaps she'd just been so shocked at being disobeyed so openly that she hadn't thought to do it.

Whatever the case, they'd got away and were en route to Aunt Marguerite's. Unfortunately, it was only a brief escape. Martine would follow them there and they'd still have to contend with her.

Wyatt's hand covering hers drew Elspeth's attention, and she glanced to him in question, but he wasn't looking at her. His concerned gaze was on his grandmother. Turning to the woman on her other side, Elspeth noted that Meredith appeared to be sleeping.

"Julianna, did you put Merry to sleep?" she asked, turning her head to peer over her shoulder.

"Yes," she admitted apologetically. "I'm sorry, but Merry was pretty upset, Elspeth. She lost everything. Including every picture she had of her dead husband. She was panicking as she thought about that, so I decided it was better if she slept."

"Thank you," Wyatt said solemnly before Elspeth could respond, and then he sighed wearily, and shook his head. "She and Gramps were neighbors growing up, and started dating at fifteen. They truly loved each other." Peering at the older woman, he added, "I remember how crushed she was when Gramps died. She still gets teary-eyed when he comes up in conversation. Now she's even lost her pictures of him. This will be like losing him all over again."

"I'm sorry," Elspeth murmured quietly.

"What for?" Wyatt asked with surprise.

"This is all my fault," she pointed out. "That wasn't a natural fire. Even with the towel you wrapped around me I could smell the gasoline in the room. Someone threw a firebomb in."

"Molotov cocktails," Alex said grimly. "We were still in the kitchen when it happened. We heard breaking glass and ran to the door just as a flaming bottle came flying through a hole in the French doors and crashed in the living room."

"It landed right next to a large rock that must have been

thrown through first to break the door," Sam told them. "And then we heard the glass breaking in the bedroom too. We sent Julianna and Victoria down to get Meredith and your mother out, and then ran up the hall to make sure you guys were okay."

"The room was an inferno," Alex said with remembered dismay. "We couldn't see you, but we couldn't go in to try to find you either. All we could do was stand there and scream for you, but it took forever for you to respond."

"We were asleep," Wyatt explained.

"In the bathroom?" Alex asked with disbelief. "What on earth—Oh. Oh! You two had life mate sex and passed out!" she said with sudden realization, and Elspeth was very glad that Merry was asleep.

"Awesome!" Julianna squealed suddenly, and shifted to her knees to crawl forward in the back to half hug Wyatt over the car seat. "Welcome to the family, bro!"

"Yeah, Wyatt, welcome to the family!" Victoria said with excitement, moving up beside Julianna to half hug him over the seat as well.

"Sit down, girls," Elspeth growled. "You'll have a police officer pulling us over for no seat belts."

"Sam would just control him and send him on his way," Julianna said with unconcern, but the twins did settle back to a sitting position in the back of the SUV. They also shut up, which was even better, since Elspeth felt like she was about to hyperventilate. What the heck was that all about? *"Welcome to the family"*? Dear God, they'd had sex, not got married, for heaven's sake.

"Here we are," Sam announced suddenly as she turned into Marguerite's treed driveway.

"Lissianna's car is here," Alex pointed out. "And I think that's Rachel's car next to it."

"Yes," Sam said, and explained, "That fire made Mortimer think it might be better if the four of us were onsite at all times." She glanced at her sister worriedly. "If that's okay with you?"

Alex shrugged. "That's fine. Cale is out of town on that job for Mortimer anyway."

"Thanks," Sam said with a smile, but Elspeth frowned. Meredith's home and all her belongings were gone, Wyatt had been injured, and now Sam, Alex, Lissianna, and Rachel were going to have to spend twenty-four hours a day babysitting her? Everyone's lives were being disrupted because of her and whoever it was who appeared to be out to kill her. She had to sort out who was behind all of this, Elspeth thought as she watched the front door of Marguerite's house open. Several people hurried out, heading for the SUV as Sam parked it.

"Will Gran stay asleep if I pick her up?"

Elspeth glanced around at that question from Wyatt, but it was Julianna who answered.

"I can keep her asleep if you like," she offered.

"Yes, please. I think it's probably for the best if she just sleeps right through until morning," he said quietly.

"Okay," Julianna said easily. "I'll follow you to whatever room Aunt Marguerite has for her, and make sure she's well under before we leave. I can't guarantee she'll sleep through the night, but . . ." She shrugged.

Wyatt nodded, and then glanced to Elspeth as he undid his seat belt. "I'm going to walk around to the other door to get her out. I think it's better if you follow her out that door. This one faces the road and if we were followed . . ." He didn't bother to finish his sentence, but opened his door and got out.

Elspeth turned her attention to her seat belt then and didn't realize anything was wrong until she heard a grunt. She turned back toward Wyatt just in time to see him crash to the ground outside the SUV.

Twelve

"What is it? What's wrong with him?" Elspeth asked anxiously as Rachel turned Wyatt onto his back on the paved driveway and began to look him over. Everyone had rushed around the car when Wyatt had collapsed. The group reached him almost as quickly as Elspeth had scrambled out to kneel next to him.

"I'm not sure," Rachel admitted, her narrowed gaze sliding over his bare chest. "I don't see a gunshot or any other kind of wound."

"Could it be his feet?" Sam asked, getting out of the SUV now that she'd shut off the engine.

"His feet?" Rachel glanced down toward his feet, and then stood to move down and kneel behind them for a better look.

The way the woman drew air in on an alarmed hiss didn't bode well, Elspeth decided with concern. "Are they very bad?"

"I'd say so," Rachel said grimly. "I'm not surprised he passed out if he tried to walk on that."

"He walked to the SUV okay," Elspeth said with a frown. "He limped a little, but seemed fine."

"Adrenaline," Rachel guessed. "Or shock. We'd better get him inside."

Nodding, Elspeth bent and scooped him up. She was carrying him around the SUV when she remembered Meredith. Pausing, she turned toward the back passenger door.

"I'll get her," Julianna said at once, seeming to recognize the problem.

Elspeth waited until her sister had opened the door and leaned in to pick up Wyatt's grandmother, before turning to carry Wyatt inside.

"Mom's on the phone putting in an order for extra blood. Follow me and I'll show you which room to put him in," Lissianna said, slipping past her to lead the way.

Elspeth followed silently, her attention shifting between Wyatt's face and the stairs she was mounting. He was awfully pale, and even unconscious his face showed signs of pain. It made Elspeth wonder just how bad his feet were.

"Do you want me to show the others to rooms, Liss?"

Elspeth glanced back at the people crowded into the entry, her gaze sliding over them briefly. Aside from Sam, Alex, Victoria, and Julianna carrying Meredith, she recognized her cousin Christian's wife, Carolyn, Lissianna's husband, Greg, Rachel's husband, Etienne, and Marguerite's husband, Julius. It was Carolyn who had asked the question, and Lissianna nodded. "Yes, please, Caro. Thanks."

They reached the top of the stairs then and moved much more quickly up the hall, leaving the others behind.

"We didn't know whether to put you and Wyatt in the same room or not, so gave you connecting rooms," Lissianna said as she opened a door halfway up the hall and stepped aside for her to enter.

"Thanks," Elspeth murmured, slipping past her to carry Wyatt to the bed. She had no idea what else to say. She didn't know herself if they should have been given one room or two. She didn't know much of anything at that point except that Wyatt needed tending.

"Do you have anything for pain?" Elspeth asked as she watched Rachel hurry ahead of her to pull back the sheet and duvet for her to lay Wyatt down.

"Not for mortals," Rachel admitted with a frown as she watched Elspeth set him gently down and straighten.

"I'll call Bastien and see if he can have something sent over," Lissianna said, heading for the door.

"You'd better ask for antiseptic, antibiotics, and bandages while you're at it," Rachel called after her.

"Will do," Lissianna responded, but Elspeth barely heard her. She'd moved to the foot of the bed to look at Wyatt's feet, and the sight of them shocked the breath right out of her.

"You looked worse after you were run over," Rachel said as she bent to lift one of his feet and look it over. Setting it back to pick up the other, she grimaced and said, "Or at least as bad."

"I'm immortal. Wyatt's not," Elspeth pointed out and then leaned closer. "Is that glass?"

"Yes, it's ground into the burns and . . ." She shifted his foot, and frowned. "It looks like he was burned, ran through glass, and then was burned again. Some of the blisters formed around the glass." Turning to Elspeth, she asked, "He ran through fire?"

She nodded solemnly. "Carrying me. I suppose the glass would have come from the French doors. It had to have been broken for the Molotov cocktail to be thrown through, or would have been broken by the firebomb itself, I suppose."

Nodding, Rachel set Wyatt's foot down and straightened. "I'm going to go see if Aunt Marguerite has something to help me clean his feet. If not, I'll have Bastien arrange for that to be sent over as well."

"Will they have things like that at Argeneau Enterprises?" Elspeth asked dubiously.

"If not, he'll send someone to fetch them," Rachel assured her. "And it's better than harassing Mortimer to look into it. He has enough on his plate."

Elspeth nodded, but didn't take her eyes off Wyatt's feet, very aware that he'd got injured saving her. She'd come out without a scratch while his feet had been butchered. And it wasn't just the bottoms of his feet that had suffered for his heroism. The tops of his feet, his ankles and his lower legs were black and blistered from the flames as well.

Wyatt's body jerked and Elspeth glanced to his face to see that his eyes were open. He'd woken up. Judging by his expression, it wasn't a pleasant awakening. He hid that quickly behind a crooked smile, though, and managed to croak, "Hi."

"Hi yourself," Elspeth murmured, moving up to the head of the bed as he frowned at the weak sound to his own voice and cleared his throat. "How bad is the pain?"

"I've had worse," he said with a shrug.

Elspeth didn't question that. She could see a thin line on his stomach, an old scar, and she'd felt more on his back as she'd carried him in. There had been a large swath of ridges and puckered skin that suggested he'd suffered a serious injury at some time.

"A knife wound," Wyatt said, noting that she was looking at the scar on his stomach. "I got it as a bodyguard, not as a soldier."

"And the scar on your back?" she asked.

"Which one?" he countered with wry humor and then shrugged and said, "One's a gunshot wound. One's from an explosion. All of my scars are from my work as a bodyguard. It might seem ironic that I managed to make it through all those dangerous missions in JTF2 without a scar, but I always had good backup in JTF2."

"Not as a bodyguard?" she asked.

"No. Not so much," he said with a wry smile. "Many bodyguards are hired because they're big and look tough. A lot aren't trained properly, if at all. Others just don't really give a shit. They're there to pass the time and collect a paycheck. Those do half-assed or sloppy jobs, and get themselves and others hurt or killed."

Elspeth frowned. It sounded dangerous to her. "Then why do it at all?"

"Because I'm good at it," he said solemnly. "I do care, I don't do a half-assed or sloppy job, and every once in a while I get to make a difference and save a life."

Elspeth nodded silently.

"Sit with me," he said softly, and held up his hand. When Elspeth took it and settled carefully on the side of the bed, he asked, "Why did you take criminology?"

Elspeth smiled faintly. "I didn't intend to. Originally I was taking accounting."

"You don't seem like the accountant type to me," he admitted with a slight smile.

"No," she agreed. "But it's what my mother wanted me to take. She wanted me to work for my father's company."

"Ah," he murmured, rubbing his thumb back and forth over the top of her hand. "So, how did you end up in criminology?"

"I had to take classes from the different fields to get my degree. I chose criminology as one of them my first term and . . . I liked it," she admitted with a grin. "I took a couple more criminology classes the second term to test the waters and . . ." She shrugged. "I changed my major after that."

"I bet your mother didn't like that," he said with amusement.

"I didn't tell her," Elspeth admitted, her grin widening. "She used to check my schedule at the beginning of each term to see the times and days I would have to be in class, but she never looked at the class names themselves, so didn't know until I told her . . . the day before I received my doctorate."

Wyatt chuckled softly. "I bet she didn't take that well."

"The understatement of the year," Elspeth said with amusement. "I thought she was going to kill me. I swear I saw steam coming out of her ears."

"So, you got your doctorate and decided to teach," he said thoughtfully.

"No. I got my doctorate and Mother insisted all it was good for was teaching. No daughter of hers was hanging out with mortal criminal trash." Elspeth grimaced. "The way she talked about it, you'd think I would be joining a gang or something if I did anything with my degree but teach."

"But you want to use it with the Enforcers," he suggested.

Elspeth nodded solemnly. "Of course. Although I might have done better to take psychology to do that. Most rogues are crazy."

"Is that the technical term?" he teased.

Elspeth smiled and opened her mouth to respond, but paused and glanced toward the door when it opened.

"Sorry I took so long," Rachel said, striding into the room, carrying a tray with several items on it. "Marguerite didn't have any antiseptic or antibiotics so I had to mix up my own using honey, tea tree oil, and—Oh! He's awake."

"Yes, I am," Wyatt said with a smile. "Nice to see you again, Dr. Rachel. Sorry to be the patient this time, though."

"I don't blame you," she admitted, carrying her tray to the foot of the bed and setting it down next to his feet. "You really did a number on yourself. How bad is the pain?"

"I'll survive," he said with a shrug.

"That's not an answer," she said in a dry voice, and then tried again, asking, "On a scale of one to ten, how bad is the pain?"

"Five, maybe," he said.

"Uh-huh," Rachel said with disbelief, and knelt at the end of the bed. She picked up a pair of tweezers off the tray, did something to his foot, and then asked, "And now?"

Elspeth turned her head quickly back to Wyatt when his body jerked stiff and he spat out a vile curse.

"That's what I thought," she said dryly. "We'll have to wait for Lissianna to get here. She can keep you from feeling the pain until the painkillers arrive."

"Go ahead and start," Wyatt said through gritted teeth. "I can take it."

"I'm sure you can," Rachel said with dry amusement. "But I don't think I could, so we'll wait for Lissianna."

"I'm here," Lissianna said, joining them now. "Bastien is sending a delivery over right away. The pain meds should be here soon."

"Great, thanks," Rachel said, and then glanced to Elspeth. "You might not want to be here for this."

"I put a couple of nightgowns and some clothes in the room next door for you," Lissianna said as she settled on the opposite side of the bed to sit next to Wyatt, with her back against the headboard. "And you might want to take a shower too, or at least wash your face."

Elspeth's eyebrows rose at the suggestion, and when she glanced down at Wyatt he grinned. "You look adorable to me."

Grimacing, she stood up at once and started toward the door to the connecting bathroom. "I'll go wash and change."

"Right," Rachel said, her tone all businesslike. "Put him under, Lissi."

Pausing abruptly, Elspeth turned back with a frown. "I thought Lissi was just supposed to help with the pain, not put him under altogether?"

"It's because of what Dr. Rachel has to do," Wyatt said solemnly when both women looked at each other and didn't answer at once.

"You know?" Rachel asked with surprise.

"Been through it before," he told her solemnly. "My back. Got caught too close to a car explosion, sustained second- and third-degree burns," he explained. "And my shirt and jacket were melted into my skin."

When Rachel winced and nodded, Elspeth asked, "What do you have to do?"

"Remove the pieces of glass and clean his feet and lower legs," Rachel said quietly.

"By *clean* she means peel away the burnt cloth, as well as the worst of the burnt skin," Wyatt explained, his voice resigned.

Elspeth's eyes widened with dismay as she recalled a conversation she'd once had with Rachel. She'd asked if she ever wished she worked with living patients rather than the dead she dealt with in her job at the morgue, and Rachel had smiled wryly and admitted, *"Every once in a while I do . . . but then I just pop up to the burn unit and listen to the agonized screams coming from the 'tub room' for a minute or two and I leave knowing I made the right choice. I'm too empathetic. I can't handle seeing or even hearing people suffer."*

"What is the tub room?" Elspeth had asked.

"It's where the nurses scrub the wounds of the burn victims and peel away their dead skin," she'd explained. *"And the screams from that room . . ."* She shook her head. *"It sounds like you've stepped through the gates of hell."*

"Or, you could turn him."

Pulled from the memory, Elspeth glanced to Rachel with wide eyes. "What?"

"Well, he *is* your life mate," she pointed out. "If you turn him now it would speed the healing, save him this pain at least, and I wouldn't have to spend hours torturing the man."

Elspeth frowned at the suggestion. Everything was moving so fast. She wasn't ready to claim a life mate. She wanted to enjoy some freedom first. But she didn't want Wyatt to suffer either. In fact, the very thought was unbearable to her. There really didn't seem to be a choice here, Elspeth decided, and started to nod.

"No," Wyatt said firmly, startling her. When Elspeth glanced to him with surprise, he shook his head. "I don't want you to turn me just to save me pain. If you do it, it will be for the right reason. Not because you feel sorry for me."

"Right." Rachel sighed and shook her head, obviously thinking them both idiots. "Go shower, Elspeth. You don't need to be here for this."

Elspeth hesitated and glanced to Wyatt, but his face was now blank while Lissianna's was concentrated. She'd put him under, Elspeth realized, and hesitated another moment, but then turned and headed into the connecting bathroom. Wyatt had taken the decision from her. She couldn't turn him against his wishes. She should have been relieved at not being forced into accepting him as her life mate and turning him. Instead, she was oddly disappointed.

Strange, Elspeth thought as she closed the door behind her, and then she turned and spotted her reflection in the mirror, and her eyes widened incredulously as she took in the circle of soot on her face and the way her hair was standing up in all directions.

"Adorable my foot," she muttered, swinging toward the tub and turning on the taps.

Elspeth was sleeping fitfully when a knock sounded at the door, waking her. Sitting up, she pushed the covers aside just as it opened and Lissianna poked her head in.

"Is it done?" Elspeth asked, slipping her feet off the bed and standing up.

"Yes." Lissianna smiled wearily. "Rachel managed to remove all the glass, peeled away a lot of the dead skin, and then bandaged him up. She's given him some pain-killers and antibiotics to prevent infection and now we're going to lie down for a bit."

Nodding, Elspeth walked toward her. She'd returned to the room after taking a bath and dressing in the white linen nightgown Lissianna had left on the bed for her. But Rachel had suggested she sleep so that she could sit with Wyatt once they'd finished tending him. As it turned out, tending him had taken all night, Elspeth noted, glancing back at the clock on the bedside table. It was now seven o'clock in the morning. Everyone would be sleeping by now. Except perhaps Meredith, she thought with a sudden frown.

"Meredith will sleep for a while. She woke up about three hours ago and Mother gave her a sleeping pill," Lissianna said, obviously having read her thoughts. Backing out of the doorway for her to leave the room, she added, "Wyatt is hungry. I was going to toast him a bagel or something, but thought I'd see if you wanted something too."

"Yes, actually," Elspeth said with a smile of relief. If he was hungry, he must be feeling all right, and she *was* hungry. "But I'll make it for both of us. You're exhausted. Why don't you go on to bed?"

"I am exhausted," Lissianna admitted on a sigh. "Keeping him under while not feeling his pain was a lot more exhausting than I expected."

"Then go to bed," she said sympathetically.

Lissianna shook her head. "I want a drink first."

"Oh." Elspeth frowned to herself as they walked up the hall to the stairs. She should have thought of that and taken the two women drinks and food after the first couple of hours.

"No, you shouldn't," Lissianna said as if she'd spoken aloud. "The idea was for you to sleep so you could sit with him when we were done. You couldn't sleep and fetch us snacks."

They fell silent as they descended the stairs, but as they started up the hall toward the kitchen, Lissianna said, "Rachel says G.G. told her that you aren't ready for a life mate, that you want to date and experience life before settling down."

"Yes," Elspeth murmured and grimaced. "I'm young yet to have to settle down with a life mate. I want to do things, go places, and experience stuff before that."

"Interesting," Lissianna murmured.

Elspeth arched an eyebrow. "What's interesting?"

"Well, you didn't seem to feel that way when I met Greg," she said solemnly. "In fact, you said you were jealous and couldn't wait to meet your life mate."

"Did I?" she asked with surprise, not recalling that.

"Yes. Right here in this kitchen, in fact," she said with a smile as they entered the room. "I was making a snack for Greg and me, and you came in to get a drink and said you thought I was very lucky, and only hoped you got so lucky soon."

Elspeth frowned as she moved to the coffeepot and started to make a fresh pot. She actually had a vague recollection of what Lissianna was talking about . . . now that she'd mentioned it.

"So, what changed your mind?"

Elspeth glanced to her uncertainly as she finished with

the coffee and opened the bread box to retrieve the mentioned bagels. "What do you mean?"

"Well, something must have happened to change your mind about wanting a life mate. What was it? And when did it happen?"

Elspeth frowned and took three bagels out of the bag as she admitted, "I'm not sure."

"Well, it must have been after Jeanne Louise met her Paul," Lissianna said now. "Because you said pretty much the same thing at the wedding shower we held for her. That you were jealous and eager to meet your own mate."

"Yes, I did, didn't I?" Elspeth murmured thoughtfully, as she pulled a steak knife from the knife block and sliced the bagels. She remembered that as well now that Lissianna mentioned it, she thought as she set the halves of the first two bagels in the four-slice toaster. Elspeth distinctly remembered saying she was jealous of Jeanne Louise finding her life mate so young, and she'd meant it.

"Anyway," Lissianna said, grabbing a glass and sticking it under the tap, "Rachel says Wyatt needs to stay off his feet for a good two or three weeks, maybe even four. She's going to have Bastien send a wheelchair for him so he doesn't have to stay in his room for that long. In the meantime, though, don't let him get out of bed."

"What if he has to go to the bathroom?" she asked with alarm.

"You'll have to carry him," Lissianna said with a shrug as she headed for the door with her water. "Or maybe take a bucket up for him to use as a makeshift bedpan. There should be one under the sink. Good luck," Lissianna added with a wry smile as she pushed through the door and left the room.

Grimacing, Elspeth walked to the sink and opened the cupboard under it to retrieve the bucket Lissianna had mentioned. Trying not to think about what it might be used for, she set it on the table, then fetched a tray and began gathering the items they might need—a glass of orange juice each, a coffee for Wyatt, cream and sugar because she wasn't sure how he took his coffee, the steak knife, a spoon, and two plates with toasted bagels: two bagels on one plate, one on the other, all toasted, buttered, and smothered with cream cheese.

Elspeth hung the bucket over her arm, picked up the tray, and headed out of the kitchen.

"Ah, you're a goddess," Wyatt said as she entered the bedroom moments later. "I'm dying of thirst. Starved too."

"I hope you like bagels, then," Elspeth said as she pushed the door closed with her foot.

"Love 'em," he assured her. "What kind?"

"Cheese and herb bagels with garlic and herb cream cheese," she said as she crossed the room.

"Sounds great. Especially if you're having one too," he added, sitting up and maneuvering himself backward to sit leaning against the headboard.

"Yes, I am," she admitted.

"Good. Then you won't mind my garlic breath if I breathe on you. You'll have it too," he said cheerfully as she stopped next to the bed.

Elspeth smiled faintly, her gaze sliding over his face. Wyatt's eyes were dilated, she noted, and his smile completely relaxed. Whatever the meds were that Bastien had sent appeared to be working. Wyatt was definitely feeling no pain at the moment.

"Mmm, smells good. I think my mouth is watering."

Blinking, Elspeth glanced down at the tray, and then

eyed the bedside table with a frown. There were a lamp, an alarm clock, rolls of gauze, tubes of ointment, and several bottles of pills on the table, leaving little room for a tray.

"Set it here." Wyatt patted his lap.

Elspeth hesitated, but there really wasn't anywhere else to put it, so she shifted the tray to balance on one hand so she could let the bucket slide down her arm to her other hand. She then set the bucket on the floor next to the bed on Wyatt's side and set the tray on his lap.

"Come. Sit with me." He patted the bed next to him and Elspeth caught her breath as the tray jiggled, sending the dishes clanking against each other. But the tray stayed in place and nothing spilled, so she moved quickly around the bed and climbed on to sit next to him. Elspeth then took one of the glasses of juice and set it on the bedside table next to her. When she turned back, Wyatt had taken the other glass of juice and was half-turned away, setting it on his bedside table too, so she quickly retrieved the knife she'd wrapped in the napkin and slid it under her pillow. By the time he turned back, she was reaching for the plate with one bagel on it.

"I didn't know how you take your coffee," she said as she watched him now spoon sugar into his cup and then add a dollop of cream.

"Regular," he said, setting the cream and sugar on the bedside table with the juice. The coffee quickly followed after he stirred it. That left only the spoon, his napkin, and the plate with two bagels on it on the tray, and she relaxed a little, knowing the risk of making a mess of the bed had just been reduced.

"Mmm," Wyatt moaned as he chewed his first bite. Swallowing, he glanced to her and smiled. "Thank you. This is good."

"My pleasure," Elspeth murmured, and then her gaze slid to his feet as she took a bite of her bagel. The blanket and sheet were covering him from his knees up to his chest, but his feet weren't under the covers. She supposed the weight of the cloth on his injured feet might have caused him pain, so Rachel had left it off there. Even so, the wounds weren't visible. Wyatt was bandaged up like a mummy from below his knees to the tips of his toes.

"The coffee smells good too," Wyatt commented and picked up his cup to take a tentative sip. He followed it with a second, much larger mouthful, and nodded happily as he swallowed. "Oh, yeah. That's good."

Elspeth smiled, relieved that he liked it. Making coffee wasn't something she normally had to do. She didn't usually drink the stuff herself, so wasn't expert at making it, but she was glad he liked it. Wyatt fell silent then, his concentration on eating. Elspeth turned her attention to her own food as well, but her mind was preoccupied with what Lissianna had said in the kitchen.

When *had* she changed her mind and decided that she wasn't ready for a life mate? Elspeth pondered that as she ate. While she now recalled being jealous of first Lissianna and then Jeanne Louise when they'd found their life mates, she couldn't remember when that had changed. Both Jeanne Louise and Lissianna had found their mates before the time period during which Wyatt claimed they'd met. She did know that.

"That was good."

Elspeth glanced to Wyatt and smiled faintly. He was leaning against the headboard, head back, eyes closed, one hand on his stomach, and looking completely satisfied.

He opened his eyes, turned his head to eye her, and said, "Thank you. That hit the spot."

"My pleasure," Elspeth murmured, slipping off the bed with her empty plate and walking around to set it on the tray with his. Then she took the tray away and set it on the dresser. She turned back then and headed for her side of the bed, stumbling and cursing when she stubbed her toe on the foot of the bed as she walked around the corner.

"Are you okay?" Wyatt asked, straightening with concern as she limped up the side of the bed.

"Yes," she said with exasperation, irritated with herself for the clumsiness.

"Hmm." He relaxed back against the headboard, but added with a grin, "Maybe you should be the one not allowed out of bed."

Elspeth scowled at him as she sat on the bed again and picked up her juice. "Are you suggesting I'm accident prone?"

"You? Nah," he assured her. "You've just been stabbed, been run over, stabbed yourself, hit your head falling out of the shower, and nearly been burned to a crisp since we met again."

Elspeth grunted with disgust at the litany of injuries she'd had of late, and then murmured, "Again," thoughtfully. It reminded her of their date and how it had ended. The promise she'd made to meet him the next day, and her never keeping the date. Setting her glass on the bedside table, she turned to him to offer solemnly, "I'm sorry I didn't show up the next day . . . after our date," she explained. "I'm sure I would have met you if I could have."

Wyatt peered at her silently for a minute, and then asked, "Would you?"

"Of course. If I said I'd meet you, I would have," she

assured him, and then frowned. "Why would you think otherwise? You don't believe that my mother—?"

"Yes," he interrupted her quickly. "I believe your mother prevented it at the time."

Elspeth relaxed a little, but frowned and asked, "But . . . ?"

"But maybe if she hadn't intervened you would have rethought and still not shown up . . . because you aren't ready for a life mate," he said gently. "You said so yourself, and G.G. said something about your probably fighting being life mates too."

"Oh." She shook her head and then muttered, "But is that true?"

"Isn't it?" Wyatt asked with interest.

"I don't know," she admitted unhappily. "When Lissianna met her Greg, I was jealous and wishing I'd met my life mate. That was more than a decade ago. A couple years after that I felt the same way when Jeanne Louise met her mate . . . and then I certainly didn't seem to have an issue with finding my life mate four years ago when I met you," she pointed out. "We went on a tour, out to dinner, to a play, slept together, and then I promised to meet you again the next day." She shrugged helplessly. "That doesn't sound like I was fighting it."

"No, it doesn't," he agreed.

"So, when did this *I'm not ready for a life mate* business start?" she asked. "What if it isn't my idea at all? What if my mother simply put that thought into my head over and over again for the last four years until I got so used to the idea that I started to take it on as my own?"

"Ah. I see." Wyatt nodded. "You don't trust your own thoughts anymore."

"No. I don't," Elspeth agreed with dismay as she realized it was true. She didn't trust her own mind and memories anymore. "I mean, I think I wanted to enjoy some autonomy and freedom, but . . . a life mate?" She shook her head. "Every immortal wants one, and apparently I wanted one too four years ago when we first met."

"So . . ." Wyatt raised his eyebrows. "Do you want one now?"

Elspeth peered at him silently, her gaze sliding over his perfect eyes and sexy lips before gliding to his short but incredibly soft hair, and she shook her head helplessly. "I don't know. I want you, but do I want a life mate? I just—"

"You want me?" Wyatt interrupted with a smug grin.

Elspeth scowled. "That should be pretty obvious from what happened in my bathroom."

He shrugged. "It could have been a one-off. A passing fancy."

Elspeth rolled her eyes. "Yes, because my first thought when I realized the bedroom was in flames wasn't that the sex was so hot between us we set the house on fire."

"No," he said, and then widened his eyes. "Really? You thought that?"

"In my defense, I was half-asleep at the time," she said with amusement, and then added, "but yes, I did, and of course I want you. You're gorgeous, smart, commanding, sexy . . . Who wouldn't want you?"

"Commanding, huh?" he asked with a grin. "I like that."

Elspeth rolled her eyes.

"Okay," he said, becoming more serious. "You want me . . . but?"

"But do I want a life mate?" she asked, and answered the question herself. "I don't know. I didn't think I did. I mean, I've spent more than a century under my mother's thumb and not allowed to go anywhere. She controlled what I could eat and drink and when. Sent me to bed when she thought I should go there, like I was a child." Chin lifting, she said, "I want to stay up all day if I want to, and I want to go to movies and eat popcorn, and go dancing, and see museums and eat what I want when I want. But . . ."

"But you want me too," he said with a smile tugging at the corner of his mouth.

Elspeth nodded solemnly. "I'm very confused, Wyatt." Grimacing suddenly, she added, "And I'm being very egotistical. I mean, maybe you don't want to *be* a life mate."

"Maybe I don't," he agreed, and for some reason that made Elspeth's heart stop in her chest. Then he added, "But we'll get to that. First, I think you're a little confused about what a life mate is."

Elspeth stared at him with amazement. She was the immortal, after all. He'd never even heard of life mates before meeting her. She knew what a life mate was.

"I think maybe you've been living with your mother as your jailer for so long you're confusing a partner with just another jailer. Someone who will tell you what to do and when."

Elspeth blinked and sat back slightly as she realized that was exactly what she'd been doing. Thinking that claiming a life mate would mean trading her mother for someone else who would tell her what she could and couldn't do all the time.

"But," Wyatt continued solemnly, "I wouldn't think that was a life mate. When I think of the term, I think of a partner, someone to stay up all night watching movies and eating popcorn with. Not someone who tells you what you can or can't do. I have no desire to be a parent to my partner. Or a jailer."

Elspeth breathed out slowly, her body relaxing as she considered his words. He was right. She'd been thinking of a life mate as a replacement for her mother, someone else who would try to tell her what to do. But he was saying he had no interest in doing that. That was good, she thought, and then frowned as she recalled his saying *"Maybe I don't"* to her suggestion that he might not want to be her life mate. Elspeth bit her lip briefly and then turned the subject to that by reminding him, "But you said you might not want to be my life mate."

"That's true," he agreed easily, and then grinned and added, "But we mortals have a certain tradition that might help us both sort out what we want."

His smile made her relax a little, and Elspeth raised her eyebrows. "A tradition?"

Wyatt nodded solemnly and raised a hand to run his fingers lightly down her cheek. "It's called dating."

"Ah," she murmured with a wry smile as she relaxed completely.

"Mmm-hmm," he said gently. "When dating, we mortals do things like go to movies and eat popcorn. With double butter."

"I like double butter," she told him solemnly.

"So do I," Wyatt admitted, taking her hand before continuing, "Dating couples also often go to museums, or flea markets, the beach, loads of places they're both interested in. But they also have friend nights, girls' nights for her, and buddy nights for him, and then they get back together and maybe go dancing." Squeezing her fingers, he tugged gently, drawing her against his chest as much as he could on the bed as he murmured, "I'd like to dance with you."

"I'd like to dance with you too," she admitted softly, leaning her head on his shoulder.

Urging her back slightly, he eyed her solemnly. "Then, Miss Elspeth Pimms, would you date me?"

"I think I'd like that," she admitted on a whisper.

"So would I," he assured her and then bent his head to kiss her lightly on the lips. At least, Elspeth thought he probably meant for it to be a light kiss. But that was impossible between life mates. The moment his mouth met hers, they were both lost.

Elspeth moaned as passion shot through her, and opened for him before he even requested entrance. Wyatt accepted the invitation at once, though, his hands drawing her tighter against him as he kissed her with a passion and need that paralleled her own.

Gasping when his hand found and squeezed one breast through the soft linen of her borrowed nightgown, Elspeth arched into the caress and stretched, her legs shifting restlessly and bumping against his leg. Breaking their kiss at once, she glanced down, relieved to see she'd hit him just above the knee rather than below. Then Wyatt tugged the neckline of the nightgown aside, freeing one breast. She groaned and closed her eyes as his lips closed over it, drawing the nipple into his warm, moist mouth and flicking it with his tongue as he suckled.

"Oh God," she gasped, clutching at his shoulders and arching and shifting. When her foot bumped against him again, Elspeth groaned and shook her head. "Your feet."

Wyatt didn't stop laving and suckling her nipple, he merely reached down with one hand to shove the blankets and sheets aside. Her attention caught by the motion,

Elspeth glanced down, her eyes widening when she saw that he had been naked under the coverings, and then he lifted and shifted her to straddle him. They both groaned as she came down on top of his growing hardness, their bodies rubbing together with only the thin linen of her nightgown caught between them.

Wyatt released her breast then, and raised his head to claim her lips. Caught up in that kiss, Elspeth slid her arms around his shoulders and shifted her hips, rubbing herself eagerly against him as he fussed with the buttons of the nightgown to get full access. When cool air suddenly slid across her shoulders and breasts, she knew he'd got the nightgown undone. Still she gasped into his mouth when his warm, calloused hands closed over first one breast and then the other.

"Elspeth Argeneau Pimms! Get off that man and come here now!"

Caught up in what was happening, Elspeth couldn't at first make sense of hearing her name from the door, but when Wyatt broke their kiss and turned his head to look that way, she did as well and blinked in confusion when she saw her mother standing there. Recognizing the concentration on the woman's face, Elspeth knew she was trying to take control of her. However, it seemed passion was as much of a deterrent to her mother being able to control her as pain was, and she couldn't make her do what she wanted. Elspeth could tell that by the frustration creeping over her mother's expression.

Unfortunately, the passion was waning now that they'd been interrupted and she could already feel the ruffling inside her head as her mother sought to gain control. Panic assaulting her, Elspeth rolled off Wyatt, reaching under her pillow for the steak knife as she did. Her hand came out with the knife as her back hit the mattress, but she kept going, rolling right off the bed as she brought the knife around. By the time Elspeth landed on her knees on the floor, the knife was imbedded in her upper leg.

Thirteen

"Elspeth!"

Gritting her teeth against the pain shooting through her from the wound in her leg, Elspeth pulled the knife out. She then had to bite back the gasp of pain that tried to slip out at the action.

"What have you done, you stupid girl!"

Elspeth ignored that furious growl from her mother, and took a moment to let the pain recede enough for her to catch her breath. She then grabbed the edge of the mattress next to her and used it to help pull, then push herself to her feet.

Clutching the bloody knife in her hand, Elspeth turned to face Martine and in a voice devoid of emotion, asked, "Did you want something, Mother?"

There was no mistaking the fury on Martine's face as she glared at her. Elspeth could actually hear her grinding her teeth. Then her expression set, and she said coldly, "I will speak to you later."

Her mother whirled away to storm out, but came up short, and snapped, "Get out of my way!"

It was only then that Elspeth saw Sam and Alex standing outside the open door. The two women parted for Martine to pass, then watched her walk up the hall before turning to look into the room.

"Damn!" Sam said at once when her gaze landed on Elspeth's leg, and then she rushed inside with Alex on her heels.

Grimacing, Elspeth set the steak knife on the bedside table, and then turned back with surprise when she felt something touch her leg. Wyatt had dragged himself across the bed and was now lifting her nightgown to examine her leg, she saw with a scowl.

"You're not supposed to—"

"Stand up," he finished for her tersely. "And I'm not."

Elspeth swallowed down the rest of her concern, and glanced at Sam and Alex as they paused beside her and bent to look at her leg as well.

"Why is there so little blood?" Wyatt asked with a frown, running one finger lightly down her leg next to the path of blood dribbling down toward her knee. Glancing up with an expression of realization, he said, "There wasn't a lot of blood the last time she stabbed herself either."

"The nanos close all wounds as quickly as possible," Sam told him solemnly. "They don't like their host to lose blood, so do whatever is necessary to hold on to as much as possible when something like this happens."

Wyatt's eyebrows rose at this news and then he lifted his gaze to Elspeth's face. "Then why was there blood all over your car seat the night we had dinner with Violet and Oscar? There was a lot of blood then."

"Oh," Elspeth said with surprise. She'd thought she'd sat on it quickly enough to keep him from seeing it the night he'd followed her to her car. "That was because the guy who stabbed me twisted the knife like he was coring an apple. He left a big hole rather than just a deep cut like this one. The nanos had to close the wound to stop the blood loss, but a lot got out before they could do that."

"We have to do something about Martine," Alex said suddenly, and when they all looked at her she met Elspeth's gaze and said, "This is ridiculous. You can't keep stabbing yourself, Ellie. Besides, I suspect next time she'll sneak up on you and take control before you even know she's there."

Elspeth nodded in agreement. Her mother had left without saying anything once there was no chance to control her. Obviously, taking control of her had been the whole point of her coming to the room. But why? What had she wanted to make her do?

"She wanted to make you leave with her," Alex said as if she'd asked the question aloud, and Elspeth grimaced as she remembered that new life mates had a tendency to lose control of their thoughts so that it seemed almost as if they were shouting them to any immortals nearby.

"Leave where?" Elspeth asked. "This room?"

"More likely Canada," Alex told her solemnly. "One of your father's planes has landed on the airstrip behind the Enforcer House."

"What?" Elspeth squawked with alarm.

"It's true," Sam said with a nod. "I gather Martine ordered it last night. It landed about half an hour ago. Mortimer and a couple of men went out to find out who they were and what they were doing there. The pilot said

Martine called the head office of Pimms International and ordered them to send a plane at once. He and the copilot were called in to fly here and back. They're expecting four passengers for the return flight—Martine, Julianna, Victoria, and you."

"The bitch," Elspeth breathed, thinking that if she hadn't stabbed herself, she'd probably be in a vehicle on the way to the plane even now. Victoria had been right—her mother did intend to take control and force her back under her thumb. Only instead of moving to Canada and making her live with her again here, Martine was going to force her back to England. If she could get control of her.

"So, last night's fire didn't make you decide to return to England where you would be safer?" Sam asked.

"What?" She blinked at her in surprise. "No!"

"That's what I thought," Sam said quietly. "But that's what she told Mortimer when he called her about the plane. He immediately called me and asked why I hadn't given him a heads-up about this."

"And then Sam woke me up," Alex announced, "and we came to find you and make sure Martine hadn't got control of you somehow."

She hadn't, but that was pure luck. If Elspeth and Wyatt hadn't finished eating when they had and started to . . . Well, Elspeth was sure that was the only reason her mother hadn't been able to take control of her the minute she walked in. Their shared passion must have prevented her mother taking control of her for just long enough for Elspeth to get to her knife and stab herself.

"You look pale," Sam said now. "I'm guessing you haven't had any blood since we arrived?"

Elspeth shook her head. "No. I wasn't hurt, and was so

distracted with worrying about Wyatt I didn't even think of feeding before I lay down to try to sleep," she admitted.

"And now you've stabbed yourself," Alex said dryly. "I'll go grab half a dozen bags. Sam and I could use some as well."

Elspeth let her go, but wasn't sure she should have any of the blood when Alex did bring it back. She had no doubt her mother would try to control her again, and it looked like hunger, pain, and passion were the only way to fight her off. Elspeth had no intention of ending up back in England under her mother's control after working so hard to escape.

"I wonder if she's already taken control of Julianna and Victoria," Sam said suddenly. "I'm pretty sure they don't want to go back to England with her. They didn't even want to ride in the same vehicle as her to come here."

Elspeth frowned at the words, wondering that herself. She knew her sisters didn't want to go back to England. And while she had initially been annoyed at their dragging their mother here to Canada, she had calmed enough since then to understand. Especially now that she knew the depth of the control her mother had kept over them all. How much of what they'd done and thought had been their own decisions, and how much had been their mother? She didn't know, and it wasn't fair. She, Julianna, and Victoria were all adults. They should be allowed to live their lives, and make their own choices as well as their own mistakes.

"Are Julianna and Victoria still up?" she asked Sam.

"No, they were pretty wiped last night when we got here. They went to bed right away just like us," Sam said, and then smiled wryly and admitted, "Though I wasn't wiped. I just didn't want to deal with your mother."

"I don't blame you," Elspeth said with a sigh, and then moved around the bed. "I'd better go wake up the twins and warn them, then."

"Do you think that's a good idea?" Sam asked, following her. "Your leg is already healing. If the pain eases enough and your mother is able to get control of you—" Her words died when Elspeth paused abruptly and swung back to return to where she'd been and grab the steak knife off the table.

"Why don't you let me get the twins," Sam said, grabbing her arm as she made to stab herself again. When Elspeth started to shake her head, Sam added, "I really can't stomach watching you stab yourself, Elspeth. You wait here with Wyatt and I'll go get Julianna and Victoria. You can tell them what your mother is planning and we can decide what to do from there."

"Let her do it," Wyatt said quietly. "Your leg has taken enough abuse for now."

Elspeth hesitated one more moment, but then gave in and set the knife back on the bedside table. She really didn't want to stab herself again anyway. It was freaking painful.

"I'll be right back," Sam said, heading for the door.

"Sam," Elspeth called after her. When the other woman paused and glanced back in question, she grimaced, but said, "Fair warning. Julianna can get pretty cranky when she first wakes up, especially if she hasn't had a lot of sleep."

Sam smiled crookedly and shrugged. "My sister Jo was the same way. I can deal."

Elspeth watched the other woman leave, thinking that she definitely could deal. Sam was extremely competent, a perfect mate for Mortimer in life as well as in dealing with the Enforcer House and the rogue hunters who worked out of it. When the door closed behind Sam, Elspeth sat down on the mattress next to Wyatt again as he shifted back to his side of the bed. She then carefully drew her legs up onto the mattress, moving slowly and carefully to cause herself as little pain as possible.

"Does it hurt very much?" Wyatt asked with a frown.

"Probably not as much as it seems to me it does," Elspeth admitted with a grimace, and then admitted apologetically, "Unfortunately, I'm a wussy when it comes to pain."

"No one would know it from the way you keep plunging knives into yourself," Wyatt said dryly.

Elspeth shook her head, but then peered at him solemnly and murmured, "I'm sorry about all of this."

"No, I'm sorry," Wyatt countered, and when she raised her eyebrows in question, he explained, "For losing you that first time four years ago. None of this would be necessary now if I hadn't lost you then."

"That was hardly your fault," she assured him with a frown.

"Yes, it was," he countered solemnly. "I realized afterward that while we'd talked and laughed and joked and teased as we toured the tower and had dinner, we didn't talk about anything useful. I knew that you liked tea, chocolate, puppies, and action movies, and that you disliked pears and cottage cheese, but I never asked for your address or your phone number or anything that would have helped me find you when you didn't show up the next day. If I'd asked more questions the first time we met, I would have known where you lived and could have gone there and—"

"Mother would have taken control of you and sent

you on your way," Elspeth interrupted firmly, and then added, "And probably minus any memory of our time together. Neither of us would have known just how far she would go to keep me under her control."

Wyatt's eyes widened as he recognized the truth of that, and then they both fell silent for a minute before he said, "My being in pain didn't stop Lissianna from taking control of me and making sure I didn't feel the pain. Does that only work for immortals?"

"I don't know," Elspeth admitted solemnly. "I discovered that it worked for me by accident the morning I arrived home to find they'd arrived for a visit," she admitted, and then considered the matter before saying, "It may be that I was growing resistant to her control, though."

"Resistant?" he asked.

"Yes. Like a mortal's body can become resistant to a drug with constant use, I might have been growing a resistance to Mother's control," she explained, and then told him, "Aunt Marguerite's husband wasn't a true life mate and used to control her, but she started to become resistant to his controlling her after a while. Actually, I think I heard once that in a situation like hers, the one being controlled usually begins to be able to resist being controlled after the first century or so. I guess I'm just a little slower than most. Or perhaps it took longer because Martine is so old and my mother," she added, paused briefly to consider that, and then went on, "But anyway, I think perhaps I'll eventually be able to resist her control even without the pain, and it's just helping me do now what I would have naturally been able to do soon enough anyway."

Wyatt nodded, and then asked, "Do you know when your mother is controlling you?"

"Not usually until afterward, and not always then," she admitted.

"The night we had dinner with Oscar and Violet, she was controlling you then, wasn't she?" he asked and when she appeared surprised, Wyatt said, "She was holding your wrist at first, and your expression was blank, but when she released it so that you could eat, that blank look was gone."

"Yes. The blank look is a sure sign someone is being controlled," she admitted, leaning back against the headboard. "Most immortals don't bother to give the person they're controlling a facial expression. I suspect they often just don't even think of it. Or perhaps it is distracting enough to be difficult to do while controlling their minds."

"So whenever I see someone with that blank expression, they're being controlled?" he asked.

"Yes, but the reverse isn't true."

"How's that?" he asked.

"If you see someone with a blank face, they're being controlled, but everyone being controlled won't have a blank expression," she explained. "Some immortals do control the expression along with the thoughts of the one they're controlling. Usually when they're trying to hide their control from others."

"I see." Leaning back as well, Wyatt was silent for a moment, his expression thoughtful as he peered at her, and then he asked, "How much do you hate her for controlling you?"

Elspeth hesitated, and then avoided his gaze as she said, "I try to remember that there is a reason for her behavior, and that she doesn't mean us harm."

"Right, a reason," Wyatt murmured. "Something to do with your brothers dying, you said?"

"Yes," Elspeth murmured. She peered down at her hands briefly and then said, "My father is Aloysius Pimms."

Wyatt nodded solemnly, obviously not understanding the subject change, but willing to go with it.

"But he's not Mother's first life mate."

His eyebrows rose at that. "I thought a life mate was a once in a lifetime thing?"

"It can be, but there have been cases where one life mate has died and the surviving life mate was lucky enough to meet another. It often takes a long time. My uncle Lucian's first life mate died in Atlantis. He waited thousands of years to find Leigh, his second life mate."

"And this happened for your mother too?" he asked.

Elspeth nodded. "Her first life mate was Darius Valens. They had eleven sons together, but eight of those sons, plus Darius himself, were ambushed and slaughtered."

"Ambushed and slaughtered?" he said slowly, and then guessed, "Trapped in a building that was set on fire?"

Elspeth shook her head. "Beheaded and left on the side of the road by a business competitor who wanted to be free of the competition. By the time they were found, it was too late to save them."

"Damn," Wyatt breathed, a frown forming on his face. "Eight sons and a husband . . . I can see how that could make her a little crazy when it comes to her remaining children."

"Yes," Elspeth sighed.

"When was this?"

"They were killed in 230 B.C."

Wyatt blinked, and then shook his head. "I'm sorry. I thought you said—"

"Two hundred thirty B.C.," she repeated.

"Right," he breathed, and then pointed out, "That's over two thousand years ago, Elspeth."

"Yes," she agreed.

"Nearly two thousand two hundred fifty years ago, really," he added.

Elspeth nodded, and then tilted her head and asked, "Is there a time limit on grief?"

"I don't know," Wyatt admitted. "But do you really think it stands as a good excuse for her to ruin the lives of her daughters all this time later? Don't you think it's well past time she got over it?"

Elspeth struggled briefly with her answer. She wanted to say no, it wasn't past time, and yes, Martine's grief was a good excuse for her behavior, because Elspeth didn't want to hate her mother. But the truth was, she didn't think it was a good excuse. She understood that her mother had suffered a great loss. Losing eight children and a life mate in one afternoon must have been crushing. She didn't know how Martine had survived it. But the way her mother hovered over and controlled her living children was just . . . Well, frankly, it was a nightmare to be her daughter. It felt more like their mother was punishing them for being alive when those sons weren't than that Martine was trying to protect them, as she claimed.

"Yes," Elspeth said on an expelled breath. "It is well past time she got over it. For her sake as well as ours. And I *am* beginning to hate her," she added with regret. "Perhaps I already do."

Wyatt nodded solemnly, not seeming at all surprised. Reaching out, he took her hand and said, "I'm sorry."

Elspeth smiled and shrugged. "It's not your fault."

"No, but—" He paused as the door opened, and they

both glanced over in time to see Julianna and Victoria rush in with Sam. Alex followed behind, several bags of blood gathered in her arms.

"I can't believe she's going to try to force us to leave," Julianna cried, rushing around the bed and throwing herself at Elspeth. Hugging her tightly, she said, "Thank you for the warning. After the way I've been acting, I'm surprised you didn't just let her take us away."

Elspeth smiled faintly, and hugged Julianna with one arm while opening the other for Victoria to join the pile as she followed her twin. "Yeah, well, I'm sorry I didn't confront her about all of this years ago and save you guys suffering the same crap I did growing up."

"How could you?" Victoria asked solemnly. "She can control all of us, including you. Or at least she could, until now, and you have to hurt yourself to keep her from controlling you."

"Yeah," Elspeth said with a grimace.

"What are we going to do?" Julianna asked, pulling back to look at her anxiously. "I really don't want to go home and be controlled for another hundred years. This is no way to live, Elspeth."

"No, it's not," she agreed.

"It's not really living at all," Victoria said solemnly. "It's more like being a marionette in someone's puppet show. She pulls the strings and makes us do what she wants, regardless of what *we* want or how we feel."

"I know," Elspeth said quietly, hugging them both tightly.

Wyatt watched Elspeth with her sisters and felt a pang of envy slip through him. As a kid, he'd always wanted a brother or sister, or both. Hell, a couple of each would have made him happy. Most of his friends had at least a couple of siblings and, being an only child, he'd always envied them that. Wyatt had actually put *a baby brother or sister* on his Christmas list several years in a row before he'd learned that there really wasn't a Santa Claus. Once he had found out, he'd given it up, though. Even at that age he'd known his parents were too busy with their careers to even consider having another child, and since one wasn't going to be dropped on their doorstep, or down the chimney, he was out of luck.

"What are we going to do?" Julianna repeated, drawing his attention back to Elspeth and her sisters.

"I think Mortimer should report her to the Council," Sam said when Elspeth stared at her sisters helplessly. "Then they could . . . do something," she finished weakly, apparently not sure what the Council could or would do in a situation like this.

"I don't think the Council has laws against controlling your own children. In fact, I'm pretty sure most immortal parents do it to some degree," Elspeth said solemnly. "Just not to the extent that Mother has, and certainly not for as long."

"Well then, he could call Lucian and tell him," Sam suggested, apparently not willing to let it go. "Surely he could do something? Talk to her and make her see what she's doing is wrong, or just order her not to?"

Wyatt frowned slightly at the name Lucian. He felt sure someone had mentioned it to him before, but he couldn't place whom the name belonged to when it came to people in Elspeth's life. Then she said, "Uncle Lucian is in Venezuela. I can't bother him with this when he's trying to save all those missing immortals. I'm sure he has enough on his plate at the moment."

"Yeah," Sam said on a deflated sigh. "He's probably super stressed out."

"Especially now that some of his hunters have gone missing," Alex commented unhappily, offering Elspeth one of the bags of blood she'd gone to fetch.

Wyatt watched Elspeth reach automatically for the bag of blood, but then she froze before her hand was fully extended and asked sharply, "What? Hunters have gone missing?"

"You weren't supposed to tell her!" Sam snapped, turning on her sister furiously.

Alex's eyes widened with dismay. "I know. I'm sorry. I forgot. I mean, not *forgot* exactly. I just didn't mean to say it. It just slid out."

"Who's gone missing?" Elspeth asked impatiently, and Wyatt frowned at the worry in her voice. Of course, she must know some of the hunters, but the depth of her concern made him wonder how well.

"Tell us, Sam," Julianna demanded.

"All right, I'll tell you," she said unhappily. "But you can't tell anyone else, and you absolutely cannot let Mortimer know I told you. He'd be upset with me for blabbing."

She waited until each of the three sisters promised to abide by her rules, and then turned to him, one eyebrow arched. "You too. Promise."

"I promise," he said at once, rather surprised she'd bother to make him. Who could he tell? If he started blabbing about vampires who weren't vampires but immortals, his fellow mortals would think him nuts.

"Mortimer wouldn't," Sam pointed out, obviously reading his mind.

"Ah." Wyatt nodded. "Yeah, okay. Like I said, I promise not to tell anyone, even Mortimer. But I can't stop him from reading it from my thoughts," he pointed out.

Sam frowned at that, but then sighed in resignation and simply got to the telling. "Okay, you know they've been having a difficult time of it finding that Dressler guy down in Venezuela."

Elspeth, Julianna, and Victoria nodded, but Wyatt shook his head and admitted, "I'm afraid I haven't a clue what you're talking about. Mortimer mentioned that a lot of his hunters were down in South America on some sort of special case, but he didn't say what the case was."

"The CliffsNotes version," Alex said, "is that a lot of immortals have been going missing in North America. A trap was set to track down who was behind it. It turned out to be some guy named Dr. Dressler down in Venezuela. So, most of our rogue hunters—"

"Their proper name is Enforcers," Elspeth interrupted to tell him. "But everyone pretty much calls them rogue hunters."

"Right," Alex allowed, and continued, "Most of them went down to South America to look for this guy and the immortals he's taken. That's why Mortimer is so shorthanded that he had to enlist the three of us and Lissianna and Rachel to help guard Elspeth," she explained.

Wyatt nodded slowly, but commented, "From what Mortimer said, it sounded like he's been shorthanded for a while."

"Yeah," Elspeth agreed. "They've been there for—what?" She glanced at Sam in question. "Three weeks?"

"Almost four," Sam corrected her.

"Okay, so almost four," Elspeth said, and then turned to Wyatt and explained, "It's all got a bit messy. I mean, the only clues they had were that one of his men had mentioned a Dr. Dressler and some unknown island in Venezuela in front of a new turn while she was in their custody."

"And that the plane one of the kidnapped immortals escaped from was supposed to land in Caracas," Sam put in.

"Right," Elspeth nodded. "But there are tons of islands off the coast of Venezuela, so they started out looking for Dressler himself. After nearly two weeks of searching everything from hospitals to land records, Lucian decided enough was enough and they were going to do it the hard way and physically look for the island where he had his compound instead. So he rented a bunch of boats and sent the hunters and volunteers out in pairs to search the islands in different areas for Dressler and his base of operations. That was—what? A week ago?" she asked Sam.

"Eight days," Sam said quietly.

"Right. Eight days. And that's the last I heard," Elspeth admitted, and then peered at Sam solemnly. "So? What's going on? How is the search going? Who's gone missing and how did it happen?"

"They don't know how it happened exactly," Sam said reluctantly. "They sent the hunters out in pairs to search different areas each day, and they'd been doing it for a week when two of the boats just didn't come back. They tried contacting them both on the boat radios and by phone, but got no response."

"Who?" Elspeth asked, dread in her voice.

"I'm sorry," Sam said quietly.

Wyatt could feel the way Elspeth tensed next to him, but she demanded, "Who was it?"

"Mirabeau and Eshe were in one of the boats that went missing, and Decker and Nicholas were in the other."

Elspeth dropped back against the headboard, dismay plain on her face as Julianna and Victoria both gasped and blanched. Wyatt watched the trio with concern. It seemed obvious they all knew at least one of the people Sam had named. And well. Reaching over to touch Elspeth's arm, he asked with concern, "Are you okay?"

When she didn't respond, but stared silently at her hands now resting in her lap, he frowned and glanced to Sam. "Who are these people who have gone missing? At least one of them is obviously important to Elspeth and her sisters. Who—?"

"They all are," Sam said, eyeing the sisters with pity. "Mirabeau is a friend to them all. Eshe is their aunt, and Nicholas a cousin, but Decker . . ."

"Decker is their brother," Alex finished quietly, when Sam couldn't seem to do it.

"Shit," Wyatt breathed with dismay, his hand sliding down to cover Elspeth's now. He squeezed gently and when he got no response, glanced to Sam and scowled. "How long ago did they go missing?"

"The day before yesterday," Sam admitted solemnly.

"And you weren't going to tell her? It's her family, for God's sake," he said, anger churning in his stomach.

"Lucian didn't want anyone told. He felt it would be detrimental to the morale of the people filling in as hunters, and—"

"Who the hell is Lucian?" Wyatt interrupted impatiently. There was no excuse for keeping something like this from her.

"He's Elspeth's uncle," Alex said solemnly.

"He's also the head of the Council, and basically Mortimer's boss," Sam said quietly, and then reminded him, "I did tell you that earlier."

Wyatt shrugged the reminder away impatiently, and continued to watch Elspeth with concern. She wasn't crying. She was just silent and still. All three sisters were. They were also incredibly pale. Shock would have been his diagnosis.

"I'm sure Decker and the others are fine, El," Alex said, peering anxiously at her. "Lucian and the others will find them and bring them back."

"Yes, of course," Elspeth whispered.

Wyatt frowned at the lack of conviction in her voice and rubbed his thumb gently over her knuckles, feeling helpless. In the JTF2, his job had been to ride to the rescue in situations like this, but that wasn't an option here. All he could do was keep Elspeth safe, offer her what comfort she would accept, and hope this Lucian fellow found her brother and the other relatives who had gone missing.

"El?" Sam said tentatively.

"What?" Elspeth asked wearily.

Sam hesitated, but then said, "Your mother doesn't know about Decker . . . and Lucian said specifically not to tell her."

A humorless laugh slipped from Elspeth's lips, and she shook her head. "I'm not surprised. She'd go ballistic," she predicted, her tone dry.

"Yeah," Sam muttered, shaking her head. "That's exactly what she'll do when she reads it from your minds. Or Alex's." Closing her eyes, she shook her head. "I so wish Mortimer hadn't told me. He knows I can't keep secrets well."

"I'm surprised she hasn't read it from the two of you already," Elspeth said with a frown, and then added, "Or maybe she has."

Sam shook her head. "I didn't tell Alex until this morning when we got up, and I've gotten pretty good at keeping older immortals out of my head."

"Right," Elspeth said on a sigh.

"Here," Alex said, holding out a bag of blood again.

"Thanks." Elspeth accepted the bag and slapped it absently to her fangs, as her mind worked busily over what she'd learned. Her friend, aunt, and a cousin were all missing, as was her brother. It was inconceivable. Crushing. And would be doubly so for her mother. She would literally go a little crazy, and her thumb would come down like a hammer. She'd lock her, Julianna, and Victoria in the house and not let any of them out for a decade or more. And that was only if Decker was found alive and well. If not . . .

Elspeth couldn't even imagine what her mother's reaction would be then. But it didn't matter anyway. She had no intention of allowing herself to be locked away. It was well past time she confronted her mother on this issue and let her know she wasn't going to be controlled anymore, and wouldn't allow her to control the twins anymore either. She had to if she wanted a life, and dammit, Elspeth wanted a life!

"I can't believe she'd try to force you back to England like this," Sam muttered with a scowl, obviously trying to change the subject from the missing loved ones. "Aside from the fact that you're over a hundred forty years old and shouldn't be forced to do anything you don't want to do, Martine knows Wyatt is your life mate, and yet she was willing to split the two of you up."

She shook her head with disgust. "Hell, I can't believe she wiped finding him from your memory the first time. What if he'd got hit by a car, or reenlisted in the army and got shot or, hell, just had a heart attack or something during these past four years? It could have been a millennium before you found another life mate."

Elspeth stilled, her stomach turning at the thought of Wyatt dying. That had never occurred to her, but Wyatt was mortal and while he seemed strong and commanding, he was really quite vulnerable. At least compared to immortals. Well, not when it came to fire, she acknowledged to herself. She would have burst into flames if she'd run through the fire like he had. Still, just look at him now. It would take weeks for him to heal, weeks during which time he could get a life-threatening infection, or—

She didn't even want to think of all the ways this man could die. While Elspeth wasn't sure she was ready for a life mate, she *was* sure she didn't even want to consider continuing on without Wyatt. Besides, they were dating now, a step toward becoming life mates, but a slow step, allowing her to adjust to the idea. And him too. But if her mother got control of her again and dragged her back to England . . .

Ripping the empty bag from her mouth, Elspeth grabbed the steak knife from the table and slid her feet off the bed. "I need to speak to Mother."

Fourteen

Elspeth crept down the hall anxiously, glancing first ahead and then behind, her knife at the ready in case her mother popped up suddenly. She hadn't wanted to stab herself again in the bedroom with the others watching, but the pain had eased and Elspeth knew she would have to do it again before she encountered her mother if she was going to avoid being controlled again. This time, though, she'd have to do a lot of damage. No quick stick it in and pull it out was going to work this time thanks to the bag of blood she'd consumed. She was going to have to really mess herself up, and that was something Elspeth wasn't looking forward to. In fact, she was really wishing she hadn't had that bag of blood now.

"Ellie, dear. I thought you would be asleep by now."

Elspeth froze halfway through the kitchen door, her eyes widening as she stared at her aunt Marguerite standing by the blood refrigerator with a bag of the dark red liquid in hand.

"Ellie? Is there something wrong?" her aunt asked, closing the refrigerator door and moving toward her with concern.

"No. Of course not," she said quickly, forcing a smile and managing not to back out of the room and make a run for it. "I was just . . ." She shrugged helplessly, and then asked, "What are you doing up?"

Marguerite hesitated, looking like she really wanted to press Elspeth on the issue of why she was there, but then simply said, "I have to get up every two hours in the day to have blood."

"Oh." Elspeth shifted her feet and glanced back up the hall, muttering, "Mom had to do that while she was pregnant with the twins to be sure the nanos didn't abort the pregnancy." The nanos tended to see the fetus as an invading body, a drain on their host that needed to be removed if the host didn't consume enough blood to combat that. Blinking, she turned abruptly back to Marguerite, her eyes growing wide when she saw her aunt's face. "You're pregnant?"

Marguerite smiled widely and nodded. Then, her expression becoming serious, she said, "Julius and I don't want to tell anyone until at least the second trimester. In case . . ."

In case she lost the baby, Elspeth thought. Managing a smile, she nodded in understanding. "Of course. I'll keep it to myself, and I'll try not to think of it so no one can read it from my thoughts."

Marguerite relaxed and beamed at her. "Thank you." Lifting the bag of blood in her hand, she raised her eyebrows. "Did you need blood? There's plenty here. I had Bastien send a shipment over at once when I found out about the fire and suggested you all come here."

"No, thank you, I'm good. I—" Elspeth's words died abruptly, her mind going blank. She was vaguely aware of the sudden concern on Marguerite's face, and then her aunt reached her and moved her out of the doorway to take her place. Elspeth was immediately free to think again. Blinking, she backed quickly away from the door, her fingers tightening around the knife she held.

"Martine," Marguerite said with surprise. "For a minute I thought whoever has been attacking Elspeth had broken in and taken control of her. I—"

"Move, Marguerite. I can't see her."

"But—*Elspeth!*"

She heard that shocked cry from her aunt as the woman turned and saw her plunge the knife in, but Elspeth ignored it and ground her teeth as she then twisted the blade, causing as much damage as possible.

"Dammit, Marguerite," Martine snapped, pushing her way past the woman and entering the kitchen to see what Elspeth was doing. Mouth tightening when she saw the injury to her leg, she turned on the woman with frustration, and bit out, "This was what I was trying to prevent. If you hadn't intervened I'd have control of her and she couldn't have done this."

"Which is what *I'm* trying to prevent," Elspeth gasped, drawing her mother's attention back to her. Leaving the knife in her leg so the wound couldn't heal, she straightened and, in a voice high and strained, said, "I know about the plane. Did you really think I'd just let you take control of me and force me back to England to be your prisoner again?"

"Oh, stop being so melodramatic," Martine said with disgust, moving determinedly toward her. "I'm your mother, not some kidnapper. England is your home."

"My home is here now," Elspeth argued, and tugged the knife from her leg to point it at her mother instead. "Stay back."

Martine paused, her eyes widening in surprise at the unspoken threat, but then impatience flashed across her face. "Stop being ridiculous and put that knife down, Elspeth. You will not hurt me," she added with confidence. "I'm your mother, and I'm just doing what's best for you. You know that."

"Really?" Elspeth asked with disbelief, her fingers tightening on the knife. "Taking me away from my life mate is what's best for me?"

Marguerite gasped in horror and Martine's mouth tightened before she growled, "You're too young for a life mate. You want to have a life and experience some things before you settle down."

"Experience what, Mother? Doing what you make me do, eating what you order me to, going to bed when I'm told?" She snorted. "That's not a life. It's incarceration."

"I'm your *mother*," Martine growled furiously.

"Then start acting like it," Elspeth snapped. "Be my mother instead of my jailer."

"Elspeth Argeneau Pimms," Martine said sternly. "I *am* your mother. I know what's best for you, and you *will* listen to me or I'll *make* you listen."

"You'll try," Elspeth agreed dryly. "But I'll just keep stabbing myself so you can't."

"Wow," Marguerite breathed as Elspeth and her mother fell into a war of glares. "I never expected this."

"That's because you have good, *dutiful* children who listen to their mother," Martine growled, glowering at Elspeth.

"Actually, my children ignore my advice all the time," Marguerite said quietly. "And I'm glad they do. It means I did my job, which was to teach them to be independent and take care of, as well as *think for*, themselves." When her sister-in-law frowned at her, she added, "What I meant was that I never expected this from you, Martine. I never imagined for a minute that you'd turn out to be just like Jean Claude."

"What?" Martine's jaw dropped with amazement, and then snapped closed. She ground out, "Don't be ridiculous. I'm nothing like my brother."

"Aren't you?" Marguerite asked solemnly. "Controlling Elspeth and making her eat what you think is right, and go to bed when you think it's best is bad enough but—Do you really do that?" she asked with disbelief.

"She does it to all three of us, myself and the twins," Elspeth put in when her mother merely scowled.

"Children will eat junk food and stay up all day if it is left up to them," Martine said coldly. "I am just looking out for their health."

"Elspeth is one hundred forty-two years old, Martine. Well past the age where you should be interfering like this," Marguerite said firmly. "And the twins are adults too. You have no more right to take control of them and make them do your bidding than Jean Claude had the right to do it to me."

"I'm their *mother*," Martine began again.

"And Jean Claude was my husband," Marguerite interrupted. "And I hated him. I *loathed* him with all my heart and soul for controlling me like that. What do you think your children feel for you? What do you think Elspeth feels? For God's sake, she's butchering herself just to maintain control of her own life, Martine. You can't really think she'll ever thank you for that?"

"One day she'll understand," Martine said stubbornly. "And then she'll—"

"Understand what? That you're doing this for *her* good?" Marguerite interrupted, and gave a short laugh. "Preventing her from being with her life mate is *not* good for her, and you know that. The only person it might benefit is you, if it makes it easier for you to control her."

"She needs to stay with me where I can keep her safe," Martine said stubbornly. "I won't lose her or the twins like I did Darius and the boys."

"Oh, Martine," Marguerite sighed the words, sadness wreathing her face. "Honey, I know how hard that must have been. But—"

"You don't know," Martine snapped. "You have no idea what it was like."

"No, I don't," she admitted. "But I have children. I can imagine, and it's still no excuse for abusing your daughters."

"I would never abuse my daughters," Martine said with outrage.

"Taking control of them and every part of their lives as you've been doing is as good as locking them in a cage and keeping them prisoner. The only difference is that the bars are invisible," Marguerite said firmly, and then straightened her shoulders and said, "And while I love you like a true sister, I won't let you do that anymore, Martine. Not now that I know it's happening. Either you back off and let your daughters live their lives, or I will call both Lucian and the UK and North American Councils, tell them what you have been doing, and demand they do something about it."

Martine stiffened. "You've got no right to interfere like that!"

"And you've got no right to control them the way you have been doing. Elspeth and the twins have a right to lead their lives," Marguerite countered, and then sighed and said pleadingly, "Surely you can see this isn't right, Martine? You are making your daughters miserable with your paranoid fears for their well-being and your helicopter parenting."

"Paranoid?" Martine straightened abruptly, any uncertainty leaving her at once. "Elspeth moved here and now has someone trying to kill her. That's the truth, not paranoia."

"Actually," Elspeth said dryly, "no one started trying to kill me until you and the twins got here. In fact, Mortimer's looking into the possibility that it might be someone trying to get at you by harming me."

"*What?*" Her mother turned on her with amazement.

Elspeth shrugged. "Well, no one would want to kill me for something I've done. *I'm* likeable."

"Are you suggesting I'm not?" her mother asked, narrowing her eyes.

"Well, as he put it, you're old and difficult enough to have made enemies," she said, and then felt guilty when her mother flinched at the words.

"I think perhaps you need some counseling," Marguerite said quietly. "Martine, you need someone like Greg to help you deal with your fears and worries about your daughters' well-being. And," she added, glancing from Martine to Elspeth, "I think perhaps some family counseling to help deal with the anger the girls have with you would be good too."

Martine snorted at the suggestion, and opened her

mouth, no doubt to tell Marguerite where she could stick that idea, but Elspeth's aunt spoke first.

"But whether you get counseling or not, Martine, I'm not going to just stand back and allow you to take control of Elspeth and the twins and force them back to England against their will."

Martine narrowed her eyes, and asked coldly, "And how do you think you can stop me, Marguerite?"

"She won't have to."

All three of them turned to peer at the man in the doorway at those words. Dressed in pajama bottoms and nothing else, Julius Notte had a serious case of bedhead that looked just adorable on him, and a scowl on his face that was incredibly intimidating, at least to Elspeth.

"Husband," Marguerite said with relief, and moved to his side, leaning into him when he slid his arm around her.

"So, you would interfere too, would you?" Martine asked unpleasantly.

"Me?" Julius asked with amusement, and then shook his head and gestured over his shoulder as he ushered Marguerite out of the way for Mortimer to enter the room. "I was coming to see where Marguerite had got to and there was a knock on the door as I came down the stairs. Mortimer wanted to talk to you."

Martine *tsk*ed with disgust, obviously not thinking Mortimer much of a threat, at least not until Mortimer said, "I spoke to Lucian after talking to first you and then my wife this morning."

Elspeth noted the way her mother stiffened, and waited to see what was coming.

"He asked me to convey to you that now that Elspeth and the twins are in Canada, they are under the purview of the North American Council, and the protection of the North American Enforcers, and cannot be forced to leave for any reason, by anyone," he announced, his voice firm. "Should anyone try to force them out of the country, or even try to make them do anything they do not wish, that individual will be considered rogue and treated accordingly."

Mortimer allowed a moment for that to sink in and then added, "Lucian also asked me to remind you that it is considered rogue behavior to interfere with a rogue hunter in any way, and Wyatt is a deputized rogue hunter, so controlling him at all is not allowed. He also ordered me to ensure Wyatt, Elspeth, and the twins are not on the plane when and if you decide to leave. If they are not directly in front of my eyes, then I am to search the plane to ensure they are not on it before your plane is allowed to take off."

Elspeth had at first wondered why he'd mentioned Wyatt, but suddenly realized that her uncle Lucian had thought of something she hadn't. Unable to take control of her and make her leave, her mother might have taken control of Wyatt and forced him to leave with her so that Elspeth would follow. And she would have, too, if for no other reason than that he would be a prisoner because of her. Martine couldn't use him that way now, though.

"Lucian also asked me to have you call him," Mortimer added solemnly. "He wishes to speak to you."

"He does, does he?" Martine asked coldly as she headed out of the room. It was all that she said, but Elspeth was quite sure her mother would not be calling Uncle Lucian.

Silence briefly fell over the room once her mother was gone, and they all stood around for at least the count of ten. But when that ten-count passed and Martine didn't return, they all seemed to release a breath as one and begin to move.

"Ellie, dear, come sit down and I'll get you blood," Marguerite murmured, moving to her side to take her arm and usher her to a chair at the kitchen table.

"I'll get the blood," Julius said gruffly, moving to the refrigerator.

"You should have told me the extent of your mother's actions the first time you came out to the Enforcer House on arriving in Canada," Mortimer growled, taking her other arm to help get her to the table. "I could have run interference when she arrived in the country."

"I didn't know the extent then," Elspeth said wearily as she sank gratefully into a chair. "I mean, I knew she was controlling, but I had no idea she was wiping my memories and managing my life as she has. I certainly had no clue she'd got between Wyatt and me. I didn't even recall that we'd met before."

"Yes, Sam told me," he said on a sigh and shook his head. "This is the last thing I needed."

"I know. You have enough on your plate right now. I'm sorry," Elspeth murmured.

"It's not your fault," Mortimer sighed as Julius joined them at the table with several bags of blood.

"Did Lucian have any suggestions on how to deal with her?" Julius asked as he handed out bags of blood to each of them.

"He's going to call Aloysius, brief him on what's going on, and tell him to get Martine some help pronto," Mortimer said quietly and then shifted his gaze to Elspeth and added, "In the meantime, your bodyguards are now doing double duty. In future, they'll be guarding you from your attacker, as well as protecting you and the twins from your mother." Shaking his head with disbelief, he muttered, "It never rains but it pours."

"So she can't make us leave?"

Wyatt smiled faintly at that question from Julianna. It was the third time she'd asked it since Elspeth had returned to the room with Mortimer and told them what had happened in the kitchen. Wyatt had been glad to hear that Elspeth was safe, but had been quite upset to know how close she'd come to being controlled and, no doubt, dragged off by her mother.

"No, Julianna, she can't make you leave," Elspeth said again patiently, a faint smile curving her lips. "We're free."

"Well, you are so long as you are here in North America," Mortimer pointed out solemnly. "If she catches you in another Council's area, though . . ."

He didn't have to say the sisters might not be safe elsewhere. There were probably some Councils who wouldn't care what Martine did to, or with, her own daughters. So while they were free, they weren't totally free. They were only free here.

"Well, I have to get back to the house," Mortimer said now, and smiled at Wyatt. "I just wanted to see how you were doing before I go."

"I'm good," Wyatt assured him. "Dr. Rachel does great work, and the pain meds she gave me are top-notch."

"Glad to hear it," Mortimer said with a smile. "I brought some clothes for you, your grandmother, and

Elspeth from the stock room at the house. I was guessing at sizes, but hopefully they'll do for now."

"I'm sure they'll be fine," Wyatt said solemnly.

Mortimer grunted, and then continued, "Unfortunately, I didn't think of clothes for Julianna and Victoria." He cast an apologetic glance at the twins, and then turned back to Wyatt again. "And Sam didn't mention that you lost your weapons in the fire until I got here. She's going to follow me back to the house to change her clothes, pick up some clothing from the stock room for the twins, and collect some replacement weapons for you. Once she gets back, Alex can go home and change too."

"I thought Lissianna and Rachel were going to take over watching Elspeth at dawn?" Julianna commented with curiosity.

"Rachel was working on Wyatt's feet all night, and Lissianna was controlling him to keep him from feeling pain while she did. They're both wiped out and resting," Elspeth explained.

"Oh," Julianna murmured, and then said, "I can't believe Mother can't force us back to England with her."

"Me either," Victoria said quietly. "She's controlled us for so long . . . I really didn't think she'd ever stop."

"Well, she has to now," Sam said firmly.

"We should celebrate with shakes from that diner you took us to yesterday," Alex suggested.

"The diner?" Mortimer asked. Eyes narrowing, he turned on his wife. "You feed us grass soup at home and then go to the diner for burgers and shakes?"

"It isn't grass soup," Sam said, sounding outraged.

"Well, it's green and tastes like boiled grass," Mortimer said with disgruntlement.

"I thought you liked it? You said you liked it," she said accusingly.

"Of course I said I like it. I love you. But now that I know you've been eating real food and sticking me with nasty grass soup . . ." Scowling, he pointed out, "You were the one who insisted we had to go on that cleanse."

"Cleanse?" Wyatt asked, his eyebrows rising.

"Yeah," Mortimer said with disgust. "All veggie, no meat, and no taste."

Wyatt winced in sympathy.

"It's supposed to be good for us," Sam said with a scowl.

"The nanos keep us in our peak condition, Sam," Mortimer said dryly. "We don't need to eat nasty, tasteless stuff that's good for us."

"I know, but I thought maybe if we ate healthier, we could reduce the amount of blood we have to consume," she said unhappily.

Mortimer sighed, the irritation leaving his expression. Slipping his arm around her, he drew her to his side and said, "I understand, and we can eat more healthily, but I want meat . . . and potatoes . . . and pie. At least on occasion. Okay?"

"Okay," she agreed quietly.

"So, no more grass soup?" Mortimer asked.

"No more," she agreed solemnly.

"Good." Bending, he pressed a kiss to her forehead and then turned toward the door. "I have to get back."

"I'll be right behind you," Sam promised, and walked him to the door. He paused to give her a more proper kiss goodbye, and then left. Sam watched him walk up the hall, then closed the door and sighed. "Okay, so if you guys will call in an order, I'll head back to the house, get the clothes and guns, and then pick up the food on the way back."

"I'll call," Alex assured her. "What do you want?"

Sam rattled off what she wanted and then left the room, her expression distracted as if she were making a mental list of everything she had to get. Alex took Wyatt and Elspeth's orders next. When she moved on to the twins, Wyatt turned to Elspeth. She'd settled on the bed next to him when she'd returned with Mortimer earlier, and he now took her hand and squeezed gently, drawing her gaze to him. Smiling, he said, "You confronted your mother. Well done."

Elspeth snorted at the praise. "Aunt Marguerite and Mortimer did most of the confronting, or at least the successful confronting. I don't think anything I said held any sway."

Wyatt shrugged. "That doesn't matter. You still confronted her, and I know how hard that must have been for you. She's been like a jailer to you for more than a century, yet you stood up to her. You should be proud," he said solemnly, and then grimaced and added, "And please don't ever do anything like that again. I think I aged twenty years or so sitting here worrying about her taking control of you and stealing you away again."

"Yeah?" she asked, her expression softening and her body swaying toward his.

"Yeah," he assured her softly, his own body swaying her way until he heard Julianna say, "I'll ask Sam before she goes," in a slightly raised voice as she rushed from the room.

Reminded that they weren't alone, he eased back and said lightly, "In fact, I wouldn't be surprised if you told me my hair was now as white as Gran's. Speaking of which," he added with a frown, "I wonder if Grandmother is up. Maybe we should order something for her too."

"Oh! Merry!" Elspeth sat up straight beside him, and then was rolling off the bed and hurrying for the door. "I'll go see."

Wyatt opened his mouth to suggest she take Alex with her, but was too slow. She was already out of the room. Apparently, his concern showed though.

"She'll be fine," Alex assured him. "Martine can't take her away again. Mortimer saw to that. Well, Lucian did, I guess," she admitted with a frown. "But Mortimer called him."

Wyatt nodded, but said, "Now we just have to worry about whoever pushed her in front of the car and threw the firebombs into the house."

"Oh damn!" Alex muttered and rushed from the room.

"The prospect of food made her forget she was supposed to be guarding Elspeth," Victoria said with amusement.

"And it made them both forget to take the clothes Mortimer brought for my grandmother," Wyatt pointed out.

Victoria's eyebrows flew up her forehead. "Oh wow! You're right. I'll take them down."

"Thanks," he murmured.

"No problem," she assured him as she gathered the clothes and headed for the door. "I like your grandmother. Merry's a sweetheart."

"That she is," he agreed with a smile and watched her slip out of the room. The moment the door closed, Wyatt's smile slipped and he was moving. If he was very lucky, he might be able to drag himself to the bathroom and back before any of the women returned. His bladder had been screaming at him since Elspeth had left the first time, but he hadn't wanted to have to be carried to the bathroom by one of the women. He'd rather crawl on his belly than allow that.

Fifteen

Elspeth could hear voices in the kitchen as she approached. She'd checked the room Aunt Marguerite had put Meredith in, and on finding it empty had started going through the house in search of her, all the while hoping she wouldn't run into her mother along the way. That would just be awkward, she thought as she paused at the kitchen door to listen to the voices coming from inside. When the only voices she heard were Merry's and Julianna's, she pushed through the door, smiling at the two women when she saw they were alone.

"Good morning, Merry," Elspeth said with a smile as she let the door swing shut behind her.

"Oh, good morning, Ellie dear." Meredith smiled at her a little wearily.

"How did you sleep?" Elspeth asked with concern, noting her pallor and the bags under her eyes.

"Oh, well enough, I suppose," she said quietly, and when Elspeth gave her a dubious look, Meredith admitted,

"I was fretting a little . . . about Wyatt and the house . . . and insurance."

"Wyatt is going to be all right," Elspeth assured her solemnly. "He'll be off his feet for a while, but he will recover just fine."

"Yes, Julianna said that too, and I'm sure he will," Merry said, managing a smile.

"As for the house, we'll have some coffee and something to eat and then call the insurance people. Or we can call them while we're waiting for the food," she decided, and then said, "Speaking of which, Alex is calling in an order to a diner and Sam's picking up the food on the way back. What would you like for breakfast?"

"Oh," Meredith hesitated, and shook her head. "I'm not really hungry, dear. Maybe I'll just have one of the doughnuts today, if that's okay."

"Doughnuts?" Elspeth asked, glancing around. The word had barely left her lips when she spotted the box on the counter next to the back door. It had a popular doughnut shop logo on it. "Oh."

"Doughnuts!" Julianna groaned, lunging out of her seat and rushing to the box.

Elspeth shook her head with amusement, but then arched an eyebrow at Meredith. "Merry, you need more than a doughnut if you're going to deal with the insurance people. Those guys can be such a pain." She considered her briefly, and then said, "I ordered a cheese omelet for myself, and know you like them as well. I'll ask Alex to order you one with sausage too. If you don't eat it all, I'm sure Wyatt will help."

"Why is it you so often sound like the adult of the two of us?" Merry asked with affectionate amusement, and when Elspeth blinked in surprise, Meredith shrugged.

"Very well, order the omelet. I'm sure I'll have room by the time it arrives."

Elspeth patted her hand, and turned back toward the door. "I'll just run up and tell Alex, and then I'll come back and we can start with those calls."

"I can tell Alex for you," Julianna offered as she grabbed plates out of the cupboard. She pulled out two, presumably one for her and one for Victoria, and then asked, "Do you think Wyatt would like a doughnut too while he waits?"

"Oh, I'm sure he would, dear," Merry said, shifting as if to stand up.

"Don't get up, Merry. I'm already up. I'll get you a doughnut," Elspeth said, moving toward the counter.

"I've got it," Julianna said quickly, grabbing another plate.

Pausing, Elspeth glanced back to the older woman. "Tea or coffee?"

"Tea, please, dear," Meredith murmured.

Nodding, Elspeth turned on the pot, and then walked to the cupboard by the sink and pulled out three glasses. "I'm pouring Wyatt some milk to go with the doughnut. What do you want Juli?"

"Milk is good, and one for Victoria, please?"

"Of course," Elspeth said, and quickly poured three glasses of milk and added them to the tray Julianna found for everything.

"Don't forget to tell Alex what Merry wants for breakfast, Juli," she said as the girl headed for the door. She'd nearly reached it when Victoria entered, her eyes wide. Alex was on her heels, looking solemn.

"You forgot the clothes Mortimer brought for Merry," Victoria explained, clutching the clothes.

Elspeth raised her eyebrows, and moved to take them with a murmured, "Thank you," but then eyed her sister before glancing to Alex and back and asking, "Is everything okay?"

"I—Yes." Victoria grimaced, and then admitted, "I was coming down when Alex suddenly grabbed me from behind and dragged me into Merry's room."

"Martine came out into the hall, and Merry's door was right there and open. I thought it best to avoid her," Alex explained and then offered Meredith a solemn, "Sorry we used your room, but we only stayed in there a minute and didn't touch anything."

"Oh, goodness, that's fine," Meredith said with a laugh. "Nothing in there is mine anyway, and I know your mother can be difficult."

Elspeth barely heard the exchange. She was suddenly worrying that her mother might come in at any moment and cause some sort of upset.

"She left," Victoria said in a hushed voice.

"What?" Elspeth asked with surprise. "What do you mean, left?"

"We heard her pass the room and when we heard her on the stairs, we crept out to follow," Alex explained.

"She went straight out the front door," Victoria told them. "We hurried downstairs and . . ." Her sister shook her head with something like bewilderment.

"When we looked out the window, she was getting into a taxi." Alex said what Victoria seemed incapable of putting into words.

"Yes," the girl said now, a slightly stunned look on her face. "She just left."

"Oh." Elspeth hesitated and then shrugged. "Well,

perhaps she went shopping. She doesn't have any clothes here now either, thanks to the fire."

"We heard her give the address to the Enforcer House as she got in," Alex told them solemnly.

"Do you think she's going to the plane?" Victoria asked with a frown. "To go home?"

Elspeth considered that for a moment, and decided that must be exactly what was happening. Their mother had no other reason to go to the Enforcer House except to leave.

"Dear God, she's leaving us," Julianna said, obviously picking up on her thoughts.

Elspeth noted the lost look on Julianna's face, and—as much as she hated to admit it—totally understood what she was feeling in that moment. Their mother was leaving them. They'd been struggling for freedom and independence for what seemed like forever, but she had just left, without a word or comment . . . not even a note that they knew of. They had no idea where they stood with her, or if they even had a mother anymore. It felt like she was abandoning them.

Which is ridiculous, Elspeth told herself firmly. They were free. Martine was still their mother and, after a little time had passed, no doubt they would all get past this and have a relationship again. Maybe in a year . . . or a century. Grimacing, she straightened her shoulders, and slid an arm around each sister, hugging them briefly.

"We're okay," she told them firmly. "It's all going to be just fine. Now go on and take the doughnuts and milk upstairs. We're just going to make some phone calls, and then we'll come up too."

Relaxing, both twins nodded and even managed smiles as they moved toward the door again, but at the threshold, Julianna turned back and said, "Oh, Alex, Meredith would like a cheese omelet and sausage too, and I did catch Sam before she left and she said the diner does have French toast, so I'll have that."

"Got it," Alex said, whipping out her phone.

Nodding, Julianna turned and continued out with Victoria on her heels. Elspeth watched them go, and then turned back to the room.

"They're going to need you," Meredith said solemnly as Elspeth noted the kettle was boiling, and crossed to the cupboard to get down cups for the tea.

"They looked like lost orphans at the thought of your mother leaving," Alex commented. "So did you."

Elspeth grimaced and set down the cups, then moved to get the tea bags as she admitted, "I felt like one for a minute."

"I'm not surprised," Merry said solemnly. "You were right, though. It will be fine. Your mother will come around."

Elspeth glanced at her with curiosity. "Did Julianna tell you what happened with Mother?"

Meredith nodded. "She was very proud of you. She said you 'were the bomb' and confronted her," Merry announced with a grin. "She also said that your aunt Marguerite tried to help, but that it was someone named Mortimer with a message from 'the big dog, Uncle Lucian,' who really 'came down on her hard,' and now she can't force you all back to England."

A surprised laugh slipped from Elspeth's mouth. "'The big dog, Uncle Lucian'?"

"Her words," Meredith said with a grin.

Grinning back, Elspeth nodded and then stopped suddenly and glanced to Alex. "Did you want tea, Alex?"

"No, I'm good, thanks," Alex said, moving to join Merry at the table.

Nodding, Elspeth fetched spoons and cream and sugar, and then dropped tea bags in each cup and poured the boiling water in. Carrying the cups to the table, she said apologetically to Merry, "I'm not sure Aunt Marguerite has a teapot so this will have to do."

"It's fine," Meredith assured her as Elspeth returned for the spoons, cream, and sugar. She then grabbed the doughnut as well as another plate for the tea bags to be put on once taken from the cup and carried it all to the table.

"Aren't you going to have a doughnut?" Merry asked as Elspeth set the pastry in front of her.

Elspeth shook her head. "I don't want to ruin my appetite. I'm looking forward to the omelet." Glancing to Alex, she raised an eyebrow. "Can I get you a doughnut?"

"No, thanks. I—"

"Doughnuts!"

Elspeth blinked and glanced toward the door at that excited gasp. She grinned when she saw a sleepy-eyed Rachel entering, her eyes zeroing in on Merry's doughnut. Raising her eyebrows, Elspeth said, "You're supposed to be sleeping."

"I was, but then I heard giggling and half woke up as Julianna and Victoria walked past our room. One of them was saying the doughnuts looked good and they loved Boston cream doughnuts, and . . ." She shrugged helplessly. "I love Boston cream doughnuts too."

Elspeth chuckled at the claim, and started to stand. "I'll get you one."

"Sit," Rachel said firmly, urging her back into her seat with a hand on her shoulder as she passed. "I can get my own. Enjoy your tea."

Shrugging, Elspeth sank back in her seat and picked up a spoon to remove the tea bag from her cup. She squeezed it against the side of the cup with the spoon, then pulled it out and set it on the plate even as Merry did.

Elspeth then mixed cream and sugar into her cup as Merry picked up her doughnut. She started to take a sip of tea, but paused and started to glance around when she heard Rachel make an odd sound. She then gasped in surprise when Rachel was suddenly standing next to her, slapping the doughnut out of Merry's hand as the woman raised it to her lips.

Eyes widening incredulously, Elspeth gasped, "Rachel, what—"

"Poison," Rachel growled.

"Poison?" Alex gasped, standing abruptly.

Elspeth turned a blank gaze to the inoffensive-looking doughnut lying on the table, and then took in Merry's wide eyes and pale face. Turning back to Rachel, she asked, "Are you sure?"

"I smelled bitter almonds as I was about to take a bite," Rachel said grimly.

"Bitter almonds?" Elspeth asked uncertainly as Rachel grabbed a paper towel and used it to pick up the doughnut.

"Cyanide," Rachel explained as she carried the doughnut back to the box and dropped it in with the others. Frowning, at the contents, she said, "Three are missing. Did the twins take all three?"

"Yes, one each, and one for—" Elspeth paused abruptly, and could actually feel the blood draining out of her face.

"Wyatt," Merry finished for her with alarm.

Her heart leaping in her chest, Elspeth lunged to her feet and rushed for the door.

"**I** can walk," Wyatt growled.

"No, you can't," Julianna said with amusement. "Your feet are burned. You aren't *supposed* to walk, and you know it."

"That's why you were dragging yourself across the floor on your belly," Victoria pointed out sympathetically as she set him back in the bed.

Unable to argue the point, Wyatt merely snatched up the sheet and duvet and dragged them over to cover himself. He'd known there was a chance he'd get caught before he could finish with his business in the bathroom and get back to bed, and he'd meant to grab a towel to cover himself for just such a possibility, but had forgotten until he was out of the bathroom. He was debating dragging himself back to grab one or continue on to the bed when the door had opened and the twins had rushed in, chattering away about doughnuts, of all things.

Both girls had stopped abruptly on spotting him on the floor, and then the pair had exchanged a glance. Without a word, Julianna had continued forward with the tray she was carrying, while Victoria had crossed to him. She hadn't said a word. She'd merely turned him over, scooped him up, and carried him to the bed like he was little more than a child.

Wyatt tucked the duvet around his waist with a little sigh, and then jerked his head back with surprise when something appeared quite suddenly in front of his eyes.

"Doughnut?" Julianna asked just as his eyes focused on the pastry. A Boston cream doughnut, he saw.

"Thank you," he said, relaxing and taking the offered plate with the doughnut on it.

"We brought you a milk too," Victoria announced, setting a tall glass of the white liquid on the bedside table.

"Thank you," Wyatt said again, his body unclenching a little. So, the twins had seen his bare butt and naked family jewels. Oh well. Such was life. Still, it was humiliating that he had to be carried around by a woman.

"Is the big bad soldier embarrassed at being carried by a woman?" Julianna teased with amusement as she and Victoria gathered their own doughnuts and milk and settled near the foot of the bed.

Wyatt merely grimaced and set the plate in his lap as he took a bite of his doughnut.

"Mother left," Julianna announced abruptly.

Wyatt stilled midchew and eyed the pair briefly, and then swallowed and asked, "Permanently?"

"We don't know," Victoria admitted, watching him eat his doughnut. "She gave the address for the Enforcer House as she got into a taxi out front, so we're kind of thinking she might be flying home." She paused and watched him eat for another moment, and then asked, "Do you think she's giving up and leaving?"

Wyatt's head was starting to hurt . . . rather badly. And he found the question a little more complicated than one would expect, so he took another bite of doughnut to give himself the opportunity to consider the question as he chewed. Finally, he swallowed and said, "Probably. She's kind of stitched up here. She can't control you, and can't force you to leave for home where she *could* control you," he said, and frowned at the breathy sound to his voice. He felt winded, as if he couldn't catch his breath, he realized with concern. Then he glanced to the door as it suddenly crashed open and Elspeth burst into the room with Alex and Rachel on her heels.

"Oh God!" she cried, her eyes widening in horror as they landed on his last bite of doughnut.

"El? What—" Wyatt gasped the question with concern as she rushed forward. She was yelling something he couldn't quite understand. He thought he heard the word *poison*, and he saw Julianna and Victoria's eyes go wide. Then both girls dropped their doughnuts on their plates as if they were . . . poisoned, he thought with a frown, and then Elspeth reached him and snatched the remainder of his doughnut out of his hand.

She was still yelling, but Wyatt couldn't grasp what she was saying. He was gasping in great gusts of air, but felt like he was suffocating, and his heart was pounding so fast.

"Ellie, put him down!"

Elspeth shook her head frantically, and headed for the bathroom with Wyatt in her arms. "We have to make him throw up."

"It's too late for that! Look at him. He's hyperventilating. Next comes seizure, and then coma or cardiac arrest or both," Rachel predicted.

"But he just ate it," she cried with dismay.

"Cyanide is fast-acting. If the dosage is high enough, it's almost instantaneous and—" Rachel cut herself off and stepped in front of her. "He's going to die."

An anguished cry drew Elspeth's gaze to the doorway

where Meredith stood, her face pale and horrified, one hand over her mouth, and the other over her heart. Turning back to Rachel, Elspeth growled, "Get her out of here."

Rachel met her gaze briefly, and then nodded and turned to walk to the woman.

Elspeth carried Wyatt back to the bed, laid him down and peered at his face. He was unconscious. Her mouth tightened briefly.

"We need chains, blood, an IV, and whatever drugs they use to make the turn easier," she snapped, and tugged up one sleeve of the borrowed nightgown she wore. "And someone has to hold his mouth open."

"I've got his mouth," Julianna said at once, moving up the other side of the bed and crawling forward to kneel next to his head.

"I'll get everything else. You girls help hold him down until I get back with chains," Alex said, pulling her phone out and heading for the door.

Elspeth waited until Julianna got Wyatt's mouth open, and then forced her fangs out and tore into her wrist. Man! No one had warned her about how much *that* hurt. She'd thought the knife was bad, but this was brutal!

Wyatt started to convulse on the bed then, and Elspeth quickly placed her wrist over his open mouth. Julianna was having a bit of a struggle to hold it open. The man was having a violent seizure.

Movement out of the corner of her eye drew Elspeth's attention to the fact that Victoria was climbing onto the bed. When the twin was situated on Wyatt's legs, Elspeth quickly climbed onto the bed as well, and settled herself on the arm on her side, careful to keep her wrist over his mouth as she did. When Julianna noted what they'd both done, she raised her eyebrows and nodded toward Wyatt's arm on her side of the bed. Knowing she was asking if she should do the same with that arm, Elspeth said tensely, "Yes. You can let go of his mouth and sit on that arm. My wrist will keep his mouth open."

Julianna immediately released her hold on Wyatt's face and quickly shifted to kneel on his arm. Once he was secured, Elspeth turned her attention back to his still face, worrying over whether she'd done sufficient damage to her wrist to ensure Wyatt got enough nanos to start the turn. She had no idea how you could tell, but knew if she hadn't, Wyatt would die.

With that thought uppermost in her mind, when the blood from her wound slowed to a mere trickle, Elspeth didn't hesitate. She immediately tore into her other wrist, and placed it in his still-open mouth. Wyatt's eyes immediately popped open. Elspeth had barely taken note of the silver filling his eyes when he suddenly released a roar of pain and then chomped down on her wrist and began to thrash.

Gasping in pain, Elspeth tried to pull free of Wyatt, but he had her good.

"Elspeth!" Julianna cried and tried to pull Wyatt's jaws open, but the man had a firm hold and wasn't letting go. Not that Elspeth thought he knew what he was doing. His grunts and growling suggested he wasn't even aware he was human at this point.

A scream from Victoria drew her head around and she watched wide-eyed as the twin flew off Wyatt's legs, landing on the floor with a sickening crack that suggested something had been broken, and then Julianna crashed into Elspeth, their foreheads slamming together so that stars exploded behind Elspeth's eyes.

"What the hell is happening here!"

Elspeth didn't bother to look around. She was pretty sure that bellow came from Marguerite's husband, Julius, but she was too busy trying to free her wrist while avoiding being slammed into her sister again as Wyatt thrashed under them.

"He was poisoned! Elspeth had to turn him."

Elspeth almost sagged with relief at the sound of Alex's voice. Risking a quick glance over her shoulder, she asked, "Did you find a chain?"

"Yes." Alex was beside her at once, chain in one hand and phone in the other, but she froze, her eyes widening with horror as she saw what was happening. "Oh my God, Elspeth!"

Elspeth grimaced. Wyatt was so strong in his pain that his teeth were cutting through skin, bone, and tendon. Her wrist was now broken, his teeth sunk so deep in her flesh that they would soon meet, taking part of her ulna with it. Or maybe it was her radius. She had no idea which bone he was chewing through, but it sure hurt.

Julius appeared at her other side. She heard the air leave him on a shocked breath, and then he cursed in Italian and turned to rush back to the door, bellowing, "Greg! Etienne! Oh thank God! Come, come."

Elspeth glanced over her shoulder again to see Lissianna's husband, Greg, and Rachel's husband, Etienne, rushing into the room, obviously fresh from their beds, but concerned and ready to help.

"He is eating her arm. We have to get his jaws open," Julius growled, leading them back to the bed.

Etienne turned a little green when he saw what Wyatt was doing to her, but Greg, she noted, was surprisingly calm.

"Maybe if you grab his chin and I grab his head, we can . . ." Etienne's words died and they all stared with amazement when Greg leaned around Elspeth and simply pinched Wyatt's nose closed. It wasn't even a two-count after that before Wyatt's mouth popped open on a wet gasp for air.

Elspeth struggled backward off the bed at once, automatically reaching to cover the damaged wrist as she gained her feet and stumbled back a couple of steps. The men immediately closed in, taking over the spot where she'd been and blocking her view, but Elspeth was distracted by Rachel suddenly appearing beside her.

"You need blood," she said gently, slipping an arm around her waist to usher her away.

"But Wyatt," Elspeth said weakly, surprised to find herself weaving a bit and wobbly on her feet.

"Chain, Alex! Give me the chain," Julius barked and Elspeth tried to look back, but her muscles didn't seem to want to obey her and her head only turned halfway.

"The men will help Wyatt," Rachel said soothingly. "He'll be fine now, honey. Now you need looking after."

"Oh," Elspeth breathed, and lost consciousness.

Sixteen

"So, no one in the house bought or brought in the doughnuts?" Mortimer asked, pacing across the kitchen.

It was a rhetorical question, but Elspeth shook her head anyway as she rubbed her sore wrist. The wound had mostly healed in the twenty-four hours since she'd turned Wyatt. At least her shattered wrist looked normal once more on the outside. It was down to a scar that was fading fast. But there was obviously a lot of healing still going on inside, because it ached something fierce. Sighing, she glanced back to watch Mortimer take another circuit around the kitchen table and the people seated at it.

Marguerite, Julius, Lissianna, Greg, Caro, Sam, Alex, and the twins were all seated there, some with food, some with drink, some with both, but all looking exhausted and grim. Rachel was upstairs watching over Wyatt, and Etienne was keeping her company, but the rest had all made their way to the kitchen when Mortimer was finally able to get away from the Enforcer House and come to look into the situation here. It spoke to just how busy he was that it had taken him so long to get here.

Meredith was the only other person in the house who was not in the kitchen. Rachel had given her a sedative to get her to sleep, and then had put her on an IV drip of both fluids and another sedative to keep her asleep and out of the way while Wyatt suffered through the turn. It had been necessary. There was just no way to explain his pain-filled shrieks and his having to be chained down. Elspeth wasn't sure what they would say to her when they finally allowed her to wake up, though. How were they going to explain why she'd slept so long? Or how Wyatt had survived cyanide poisoning? She had no idea, but that was a worry for later. Right now they were trying to figure out how the poisoned doughnuts had got in the house.

"And they weren't here during the confrontation with Martine," Mortimer muttered now, and Elspeth murmured an agreement. The doughnuts hadn't been there the first time she'd entered the kitchen, or at least, no one recalled the box being there while they'd all faced off against her mother. But then, they'd all been distracted at the time and no one had been looking for anything out of place in the kitchen.

"So, someone had to bring it in and put it on the counter in the time between the confrontation and when Meredith got up and came down to the kitchen," Mortimer continued grimly.

After questioning everyone, and reading Meredith's mind, they'd concluded that she was the first to notice the doughnuts. She'd spotted them as she'd entered the kitchen that morning and had opened the box to peer at the contents, but finding twelve seemingly untouched doughnuts, she hadn't wanted to take one before checking that it was all right with her host.

Thank God, Elspeth thought, or Julianna would have entered the room a few minutes later to find the old woman dead on the kitchen floor.

"So someone on the outside, presumably the same someone who pushed Elspeth into traffic and threw the firebombs into the house, bought a box of doughnuts, injected them with cyanide, and put them in the kitchen, intending to hopefully kill Elspeth," Mortimer concluded.

"But it wouldn't have killed her," Alex pointed out. "It wouldn't have killed any of the immortals in the house. Only Wyatt and Meredith were truly under threat from this attempt."

"But a mortal wouldn't know that," Sam said quietly.

"So, we're back to it being a mortal behind the attempts," Mortimer said thoughtfully.

"A mortal who doesn't care how many people he takes out to get at Elspeth," Julius said his voice grim.

"But who is it?" Mortimer muttered, his brow furrowing. "Who would want Elspeth dead? And how did they get the doughnuts in the house when the kitchen door was locked?" Turning to peer at the counter where the box of tainted doughnuts still sat, Mortimer scowled and peered at the door next to it. "You're sure the door was locked, and the dog door as well?"

"Yes, Mortimer, I locked it myself after letting Julius out last night," Julius said patiently, reaching down to pet the big dog lying on the floor between him and Marguerite. "And the dog flap locks automatically. It only opens to Julius's collar."

"Right," Mortimer muttered, but scowled at the door.

"It could have been Mother," Julianna said unhappily, and when Elspeth glanced at her with shock, she shrugged and said, "She's probably pretty upset at you. Maybe she wanted to kill Wyatt and Meredith so you'd go back to England willingly."

Elspeth frowned at the suggestion and shook her head. She couldn't believe their mother would go that far. "No, but it's kind of weird that the doughnuts were all Boston cream. I would have expected a variety of doughnuts in the box."

"She's right," Sam said sitting forward with surprise. "No one ever buys one variety for a large group of people. In fact, doughnut shops don't usually keep enough of each type on hand to make a dozen. At least, not when I've stopped in. They'll have six of one, a couple of another, sometimes none of some varieties."

Alex nodded solemnly. "Either they got very lucky, or they ordered ahead of time to get a dozen of the Boston creams."

"Why?" Elspeth asked, troubled.

"Probably because it was easier to hide the cyanide," Rachel put in. "Injecting it into the custard inside the doughnut made it less likely to be noticed than if it had been put in a dry doughnut like a chocolate dip."

"Yes, but they could have used jelly-filled or something like that," Elspeth pointed out.

"Which suggests they picked the Boston cream on purpose," Mortimer said with a frown.

"Because they knew those are the only doughnuts you like," Sam said quietly, and when Elspeth glanced at her with surprise, she shrugged. "You mentioned it in Walmart the other day when we were replacing your purse and stuff. They had jelly-filled doughnuts on sale by the checkout. You saw them and grimaced with disgust, saying you hated jelly-filled, that you really didn't care for any variety of doughnut except Boston cream, but if there were any of those around, look out, you'd gobble them up."

"Yes, you did," Alex recalled with surprise. "In fact, I was just thinking of picking up a pack of the jellies when you said that, so I didn't bother."

"Why?" Elspeth asked with surprise. "Just because I don't like them doesn't mean you guys couldn't have enjoyed them."

"So anyone could have overheard you say you only like Boston cream doughnuts," Mortimer said, getting them back on topic.

Elspeth turned to him, her eyes widening. "Yes, I suppose anyone near us could have heard."

"Do you recall anyone nearby that you might have known or recognized?" he asked at once.

Elspeth frowned, and glanced to the others in question. When they all stared back blankly, she shook her head and said, "It was Walmart, Mortimer. Walmart is always busy. There were a lot of people around, but I don't remember anyone being there that I know. I don't know many mortals. I've only been here a little over six weeks now, and most of that time has been spent getting my apartment settled, working at the Enforcer House, or visiting with Meredith."

"Well, it wasn't Meredith," Alex said solemnly.

"Of course it wasn't Meredith," Elspeth said on a laugh, and then a frown claimed her lips. "You read Meredith to see if it was her? I thought you were just checking her memory to find out when she noticed the doughnuts."

"We did both," Sam said solemnly, and when Elspeth

scowled, offended on her friend's behalf, she added, "We had to, honey. We had to be sure."

"Not that we thought it was her," Alex put in quickly. "I mean, she couldn't have got out to get the doughnuts without a car, could she? We were just eliminating her from the suspect list like they do when they take everyone's fingerprints."

"I still say it is Mother," Julianna said mulishly. "She's trying to scare us back to England."

Elspeth smiled at her sister sympathetically, understanding her reasoning, but shook her head. "If it was just the car and this poisoning, I might agree with you, Juli. But firebombing the house could have killed us . . . and her as well. She was also in the house when it was set on fire," Elspeth pointed out.

"Was she?" Victoria asked with a frown.

Elspeth raised her eyebrows. "Is there a reason you think she wasn't?"

"When the Molotov cocktail came through the living room window, Sam and Alex pushed us out the door and told us to make sure Meredith and Mother were out and they'd go get you and Wyatt," Julianna told them.

Nodding, Victoria said, "We went down to Meredith's first. We broke down her door to go in, but her living room was on fire. We couldn't get through it to her bedroom, so we ran around the house and went in through her bedroom window on the side of the house."

"Then we ran around the front of the house, intending to break down the door to the basement apartment to get Mother, but we didn't have to," Julianna announced, picking up the thread of the story. "By the time we got around front, she was standing on the front lawn with her suitcase."

"She said she hadn't bothered to unpack, and that she'd grabbed it on the way out," Victoria added solemnly.

"But maybe she didn't unpack because she planned to set the house on fire," Julianna growled, her eyes narrowed. "She probably wanted to scare us home. She certainly didn't plan on leaving alone when she sent for the plane."

Elspeth frowned at the suggestion. Was her mother really that desperate to keep control of them? Would she really risk their lives that way? The fire could have killed one or all of her daughters.

Mortimer sighed, drawing Elspeth's gaze as he shook his head. "If it was your mother, then there won't be any more attempts. I watched her get on the plane and leave."

"I thought you weren't supposed to let the plane take off unless we were standing in front of you?" Victoria commented.

"Unless I could see you, was the point," Mortimer said with a shrug. "I didn't want to delay Martine leaving, so I called Alex when Martine got to the house right behind Sam."

"I had just found the chain when he called," Alex said dryly. "I put the phone on Facetime, told him what was happening, and rushed back upstairs to show him the three of you."

"Julianna and Elspeth were at the bed. You," he said to Victoria, "were just getting up off the floor."

Victoria grimaced. "Trying to hold down Wyatt's legs alone was like riding a bucking bronco."

Nodding, Mortimer ran a hand around the back of his neck. "It may have been Martine, but it may not have been. We can't know for sure with the little we have to go on. Marguerite, I suggest you throw out any food, beverages, and blood you have in the house. The Council will pay to replace it all."

"The blood should be fine," Julius said with a frown. "We had a special refrigerator installed several months back. It won't open to any but an immortal hand."

"Really?" Mortimer asked with interest.

"Yes." Julius stood and moved to a section of cupboard that looked like all the rest, and opened the door to reveal the shelves stacked with blood inside. "It's something Bastien's people have come up with. Added security to ensure mortals don't stumble onto an immortal's blood supply. It somehow recognizes nanos in the hand of the person opening it and will only open if those nanos are present. We're beta-testing it for him. It works well too. Marguerite's had a different service in once a week to help her housekeeper, Maria, with the cleaning, and we've asked them to clean the cupboards and then watched them try to open the door and fail. It works rather well."

"Hmm." Mortimer nodded as Julius closed the door. "I still think you should throw out the blood and have fresh sent over. We don't know for sure that the person behind all these issues is mortal. The blood could be poisoned too." He allowed a moment for that to sink in and then headed for the door. "I need to get back to the house. Keep me apprised of the situation here, and—" he turned to Lissianna, Sam, and Alex "—do not let Elspeth out of your sight until this is resolved, and tell Rachel the same thing."

The three women nodded, but then so did everyone else at the table, Elspeth noted, and suspected she'd picked up extra bodyguards here. Sighing, she stood and asked, "Aunt Marguerite, where do you keep your garbage bags?"

"In the end cupboard, dear. Why?" she asked with surprise.

"Because I'm going to start getting rid of the food," she said as she opened the cupboard she'd directed her to and found the bags.

"Oh, sweetheart, you don't have to—"

"Someone has to," Elspeth interrupted quietly as she pulled out a bag and shook it out. "And this is all because of me. Besides," she added wryly as she moved to the food refrigerator, "you'll be too busy shopping to do it yourself."

"Shopping?" she said blankly.

"You'll need to buy everything from milk to . . . well, just everything," she pointed out quietly, unsure what all the woman had in the refrigerator and cupboards yet.

"Oh," Marguerite said, nonplussed, and then she watched Elspeth begin to take salad dressings off the door shelves and drop them in the garbage bag. "Surely we don't have to get rid of the dressings and such. Do we?"

"Better safe than sorry, love," Julius said quietly. "We don't know what may have been tampered with. Mortimer said all food and drink," he pointed out. "That means everything, from the spices on the spice rack to the canned pop in the garage."

Marguerite's eyes went wide as she recognized the magnitude of the shopping trip she was going to have to take. Sounding a little dismayed, she admitted, "I don't even know what to buy. There is so much . . ."

"I'll go with you, Mom," Caro said softly.

Elspeth glanced around to see Caro, her cousin Christian's wife, reach out to squeeze her mother-in-law's hand reassuringly. She also noted the yearning on Lissianna's face and knew she wanted to offer to go too, but held back because she was supposed to help guard her. She was glad when Julius said, "I suggest Lissianna and Caro go with Marguerite to replace everything, and the rest of us will help with the removal of all the food, and keep an eye on Elspeth."

"Great!" Lissianna popped to her feet at once, and rushed over to kiss Julius on the cheek. "Thank you, Papa." Then she turned to give Greg a kiss too. "I'll see you when I get back."

"I'll look forward to it," he assured her, slipping his arms around her waist and kissing her on the forehead before releasing her.

Elspeth watched the three women leave, and then glanced to Greg and asked, "Where is Lucy? I haven't seen her since we got here."

"Oh." He looked surprised and then said, "Lissianna was going to tell you . . ." He glanced toward the door, as if considering calling his wife back to explain, but then shrugged, and said, "Elvi was kind enough to drive up and pick her up the night you all came to stay here after the fire. She took her back to Port Henry with her. Elvi and Mabel are going to keep an eye on Lucy until this is all over. It just seemed safer," he explained solemnly.

Elspeth frowned. "I'm sorry. I—"

"Don't be sorry. I could have taken her home and kept her away from here," he pointed out.

"But then you'd just worry about Lissianna and the danger she might be in while guarding me," Elspeth said quietly and when he nodded, asked, "Why didn't you just ask Lissianna not to accept the job of watching me when Mortimer asked her?"

Greg snorted at the suggestion. "Yeah, right. She'd have told me to go to hell. She'd have said you were family, she loves you, and you need her. Besides," he added, grabbing a fresh garbage bag and shaking it out as he joined her at the refrigerator, "you *are* family, we love you, and you need us."

Elspeth swallowed a sudden lump in her throat and gave up her almost full bag to take the empty one when he instigated the switch. "Thank you."

Greg shook his head as he tied the full bag closed. "You helped Lissianna and me when we met, Ellie. Didn't you know we'd be there for you too?"

The words made her smile as she recalled her first meeting with this man. He'd been tied to Lissianna's bed. Turning back to the fridge, she simply said, "Thanks for making Wyatt stop gnawing on my arm."

"My pleasure." He set the full bag by the back door, then returned to help retrieve items from the refrigerator, and commented, "I'm sorry about your mother. She seemed a bit overbearing when I met her all those years ago, but I didn't realize she was controlling you as she was."

Elspeth smiled wryly. "Neither did I, really."

Greg nodded, but asked, "Does your father know what she's been doing to you and your sisters all these years?"

"I don't think so," she said quietly. "At least, I don't think he knew just how far she'd gone. He must have known about some of it, though, don't you think?" she added with a frown, wondering now what he did know.

"Perhaps not," Greg said gently and when she glanced to him dubiously, he shrugged. "Life mates are very interdependent. They *need* each other, and when a person is dependent on another, they tend to blind themselves to the other's faults or misdeeds. They almost have to in order to ensure the continuation of the relationship. It's why spouses are often blindsided by a spouse being unfaithful, despite there having been all sorts of evidence and clues ahead of time. They can't see it, or they might have to do something about it. It's called Betrayal Blindness in some circles."

"And you think my father had this Betrayal Blindness?" she asked.

"I don't think it. I'm pretty sure he must," Greg said solemnly, and then pointed out, "If your father had allowed himself to see what your mother was doing to you girls, he might have had to do something about it and risk their relationship. For an immortal, even the thought of losing a life mate is unbearable." Greg shook his head. "Aloysius wouldn't have been able to accept what she was doing, no matter the evidence before him, and so he was no doubt blind to it to ensure the survival of their relationship."

Wyatt started to shift sleepily, and then stilled when he felt a heavy weight on his chest. Opening his eyes, he blinked down at the head nestled there and then smiled when he recognized Elspeth. She was curled up against him, one leg and one arm thrown over him, her head nestled just below his shoulder, but curled down so that he couldn't tell if she was awake or asleep. Turning his head, he glanced around the room, his eyebrows rising when he saw that all four of their guards were there; Sam, Alex, Lissianna, and Rachel, and all four women were asleep, he noted with amusement. Two curled up in the overstuffed chairs that were in the room when they'd brought him here, and two curled up in new overstuffed chairs that had been brought in at some point while he was asleep. The room was pretty crowded at the moment.

"Sam was the last to fall asleep, and that was just a few minutes ago."

Wyatt glanced down in surprise at that whispered comment, and smiled when he saw that Elspeth was awake and had tilted her head up on his chest to peer at him.

"What time is it?"

"Nearly seven P.M.," she said.

"And they're all passed out?" he asked with surprise. Night was when immortals were most active, from what he could tell. This was like early morning for them.

Elspeth grimaced. "They'd all been up for something like twenty-four hours."

"What?" Wyatt asked, and in his surprise, forgot to keep his voice down.

Elspeth pushed herself up on one arm to peer toward the women anxiously. When she saw they were all still asleep, she sighed with relief and then glanced back to him briefly, before pinching his arm and then slipping out of bed. Wyatt was just glancing down toward his arm, when she caught his hand to urge him up with her.

Forgetting about his arm, he tossed the duvet and sheet aside, and slid out of bed to follow her silently to the bathroom. His gaze moved with interest over the baby-doll nightgown she wore. Sheer red, with two red bows holding the back closed, and black lace along the hem, it was short enough to reveal the red lace panties curving lovingly over her behind. Not that the nightgown itself really hid them anyway. He could see the rest of the panties and the black lace trim along their waistband quite clearly through the sheer cloth.

Damn, Elspeth had some fine nightwear and a killer body, he thought and then nearly trampled her when she stopped abruptly in the bathroom.

"Sorry," he whispered, catching her arms to steady her. But when she breathed out a little sigh and leaned back into him, Wyatt's burst of chivalry faded under another response. Releasing her arms, his hands slid around her waist and then up to cup her breasts through the soft cloth, squeezing eagerly.

"Oh," Elspeth moaned, pressing her bottom back into him as her hands covered his and squeezed encouragingly. But when Wyatt growled in response and ground himself against her soft bottom, she suddenly slapped at his hands and then broke away from him when he was startled into releasing her.

He was all set to apologize when Elspeth turned, but she didn't give him the chance. She slipped around him and he turned to see her closing the door to the bedroom. When she turned back to face him then, he couldn't have apologized if his life depended on it. His tongue was stuck to the roof of his mouth as he took in the front of the short nightgown. It was as sheer as the back. He could see the panties, her belly button, and half her nipples before the black lace trim along the top of the cups covered the rest of them.

He wasn't the only one staring, Wyatt noticed when he was finally able to tear his gaze away from her luscious body and up to her face. Elspeth was staring at him as well, her eyes roving over his chest, before dropping to settle on the erection that had suddenly sprouted between his legs. When she unconsciously licked her lips, though, he couldn't take it anymore and caught her hand to tug her against his chest as his mouth dropped to claim hers.

Elspeth was ready for him. Her mouth opened before he'd even got his tongue out to request entrance, and her arms went around his shoulders, pulling tightly as she arched her back, lifting her breasts up to rub against his chest.

Growling deep in his throat with excitement, Wyatt thrust his tongue into her mouth and planted his hands firmly on her behind, one on each ass cheek. He squeezed the soft flesh eagerly, and then used his hold to lift her up off the floor until their faces were on the same level so he didn't have to bend his neck so far. When Elspeth responded by wrapping her legs around his hips to help him hold her up, Wyatt let his fingers shift closer together until he could run them along the thin cloth between her legs.

The little mewls of excitement Elspeth gasped into his mouth, and the way she shifted her hips into the caress, sent a shot of stark pleasure through him, making him harden to an almost painful degree, and Wyatt went a little wild as those shots kept coming. They were waves and echoes of waves of pleasure, washing through his body and egging him on, and Wyatt found himself tugging her panties aside so that he could touch her without the cloth between them as his mouth slanted over hers one way and the other.

Wyatt felt the first brush of his fingers along her damp skin as if she had her hand on his cock and was drawing it down his length. It was incredible, impossible, but this was what it had been like that first time in her bathroom at the apartment. As Tybo had said, he'd experienced her pleasure, he was experiencing it now along with his own, and it was damned heady stuff.

Turning, Wyatt set her on the bathroom counter, and broke their kiss to growl, "Spread your—"

His words died abruptly, and he stared at Elspeth in

surprise over the hand she'd suddenly slapped to his mouth. He understood, though, when she glanced anxiously to the closed door beside them. Frowning, Wyatt glanced toward it as well. They had to be quiet or risk waking up her guards.

Elspeth tugged on his hand, and Wyatt glanced back to see that she'd slid off the counter and was moving toward the second door, trying to pull him behind her. Smiling as he saw that the other door was open and another bedroom lay beyond, he followed quickly. Elspeth urged him into the room, paused to silently close that door as well, and then spun away and led him to the bed. She turned to him then, and he thought she was going to kiss him again, but instead she suddenly caught his arms, swung him around, and pushed him onto the bed.

Wyatt landed with a surprised grunt that ended on a startled gasp as Elspeth quickly took him into her mouth. He'd landed with his legs hanging off the bed, and she was now kneeling on the floor between them, her head bent as she lowered her mouth on him, and then drew it back. For the first stroke, or two, Wyatt would have sworn she'd never done this before. But he knew she had at least once on that night four years ago. She'd been the same then, unsure and unskilled at first and then amazing. She was the same now, going from unsure and unskilled to freaking awesome. It was the shared pleasure, he realized. Elspeth could feel when she got it right, and she was quickly applying just the right pressure, using just the right speed, allowing her tongue to rasp around his shaft and tip in just the right way.

The shared pleasure made her so damned good, Wyatt nearly blew his load after a mere half a dozen strokes. But he didn't want to go this way. If they were going to pass out, he wanted her in his arms, and his cock in her rather than him spread eagle on the bed, and her a crumpled heap on the floor. Besides, he was no five-minute wonder. He needed to slow this train down.

Elspeth gasped in surprise when Wyatt suddenly sat up, caught her by the arms and lifted her up until his erection fell from her mouth. Raising her head to look at him, she saw the determination on his face, and then he dragged her up next to him on the bed, rolled half on top of her, and kissed her again.

Startled she might be, but she kissed him back at once, her fingers roving over his chest and then skating lower until he caught her hands in his and pressed them to the bed on either side of her head.

Breaking their kiss, Wyatt smiled and growled, "My turn."

Elspeth's eyes widened and then she closed her eyes and bit her lip, her body arching as he began to explore her with his mouth. He nuzzled one breast and then the other through the cloth of her babydoll before catching the cloth with his teeth and dragging it down on the one side until the first breast popped free. Wyatt immediately released the cloth to suck that nipple between his lips.

Elspeth gasped when he claimed it, and then moaned when he alternately suckled and rasped his tongue over it. She was so caught up in what he was doing there, she didn't notice him shifting his leg until it pressed tight between both of hers, rubbing firmly against her.

"Wyatt!" she gasped, arching her back and closing her legs around his. He released her breast at once and covered her mouth instead, his tongue silencing her as he drew her hands over her head, and shifted both of hers to one of his so that he could slide the other one down over her body. It grazed the bared nipple, paused to tweak it lightly, and then continued down across her stomach, before gliding under her panties and between her legs to replace his knee. Elspeth gasped into his mouth at the first touch, and then groaned deep as he found the center of her excitement and paid it serious attention. His fingers danced firmly around it, and then lightly over, and then firmly around it again until she was as taut as a bow and ready to blow. The moment Elspeth was sure she would, Wyatt's fingers danced away and became almost soothing until she calmed a bit, but then they'd just glide back to excite her again. He was making her crazy, but Elspeth knew he was making himself crazy too, and that's the only reason she didn't bite his tongue to get it out of her mouth, and bark at him to stop mucking about and give her what she needed, what they both needed.

Still, Elspeth was pretty close to doing just that when he'd apparently *finally* had enough and removed his hand from between her legs. She groaned at the loss and then quickly lifted her bottom when he caught the top of the panties and started to tug them down. They were off and flying across the room in no time, and Wyatt immediately released her hands and shifted over her. Everything seemed to stop then. Her thinking, her breathing, her very heart seemed to stop in anticipation until he finally lined himself up and pushed into her.

Elspeth screamed into his mouth as he did, her body

spasming at once as the pleasure he'd been building finally exploded inside her. She was vaguely aware that he had stiffened and released a muffled shout into her mouth as well, but the pleasure was already overwhelming her and pulling her under its mammoth waves.

Seventeen

Elspeth was the first to wake up, probably because she was suffocating under Wyatt. The man was a dead weight on top of her, crushing her chest. Moving slowly and carefully so as not to wake him, she lifted Wyatt slightly and slid out from under him, and then turned on her side to peer at him. His eyes were open.

"Sorry, I should have put you on top," he mumbled sleepily, wrapping one arm around her waist and drawing her closer so that he could latch onto the nearest nipple.

Elspeth gasped in surprise, and then groaned and slid her hand into his hair, cupping his head as her so recently sated body began to fill with need again.

"Damn," he mumbled against her breast suddenly.

Elspeth blinked her eyes open and peered at him uncertainly as he lifted his head.

"I have to use the latrine," Wyatt admitted on a sigh, and then eyed the erect and now wet nipple he'd been suckling. Reaching out, he brushed his fingers over it.

Elspeth bit her lip and shuddered as her body responded.

"But we'll revisit this in a moment," he promised in a growl as he tweaked her nipple, and then he released it with a little groan and leapt off the bed to hurry to the bathroom.

She watched him go with amusement and then rolled onto her back and stretched happily. Life mate sex was amazing, and Wyatt was "lit," as her students would say. Seriously, the man was amazing. He was smart, funny, commanding, and sexy, and he knew his way around a bed, that was for sure. It wasn't just skill—that was a given when it came to life mate sex. Even she, who had no experience at all—well, that she remembered—could be awesome in bed with the shared pleasure leading the way. But Wyatt had control. He'd dragged the pleasure out to an almost painful degree before giving in to it and blowing both their minds. She suspected not a lot of immortal males could manage that.

She'd really won the life mate lotto with Wyatt, Elspeth decided with a grin.

"My feet."

Blinking her eyes open, Elspeth lifted her head to peer at Wyatt at those words. He was standing just inside the bedroom door, and she watched him stare at his feet with confusion.

"What happened?" he asked with amazement, lifting one to look it over and then setting it down to look at the other. "Just how long was I asleep?"

"Er . . . a day and a half, I guess," she said, trying to work it out. So much had happened, Elspeth wasn't sure, but she thought she'd turned him just yesterday morning. Yes, she had. They'd emptied the kitchen of every last bit of food and drink and restocked it with the new stuff when Marguerite and the girls had returned from shopping just that day. It was now—she glanced at the bedside clock—eight o'clock at night the day after she'd turned him. Wyatt had turned quickly, but then, he'd been in great shape before the turn—well, other than the cyanide poisoning and the burns, anyway. Elspeth supposed she shouldn't be surprised he'd turned so quickly. Not that the turn was probably done. The nanos would still be working on stuff inside him for the next little while and he'd need extra blood while that continued. But the worst of it was over.

"A day and a half and my feet are completely healed?" Wyatt asked with disbelief.

"Oh," Elspeth said with sudden understanding. "You don't remember."

Wyatt stared at Elspeth for a moment, his gaze sliding over her in that damned barely there nightgown and almost let his concerns go and jumped her again. She looked way too sexy for him to think clearly, but his feet were completely healed. Not only that, they were unscarred despite the burns they'd received, and he needed to know what the hell was going on.

"I remember the twins," he said finally on a sigh. "Your sisters caught me dragging myself back to the bed after a bathroom crawl, and Victoria carried me the rest of the way to bed." Grimacing, he added, "I was naked at the time. Most embarrassing."

Elspeth nodded. "What happened after that?"

"The girls gave me milk and a doughnut and started telling me your mother left the house, headed for the

Enforcer House, and they thought she might be flying home," he recalled slowly, and then raised an eyebrow and asked, "Did she?"

Elspeth nodded. "She did."

"Huh," Wyatt muttered.

"What happened next?" Elspeth asked.

Frowning, he searched his mind briefly and then said with surprise, "Oh yeah, you came rushing in . . ." Wyatt furrowed his brow and tried to grab on to that memory more firmly. It seemed a bit foggy to him. He had a vague recollection of Elspeth being in a panic, and shouting something about . . .

"Poison?" he asked uncertainly. "I think you were shouting something about poison, but it's pretty vague and the memory stops there."

Sighing, Elspeth sat up on the bed and nodded her head. "The doughnuts were filled with cyanide."

"Jesus," he muttered, moving to the bed to sit down on the end of it because his legs were suddenly weak. "Did anyone else eat—Is Gran all right?" he asked with alarm.

"She's fine. Rachel smelled the cyanide and stopped her from eating it," Elspeth assured him quickly.

"Oh, good, good," Wyatt nodded, and then bowed his head. He stared at his feet blindly for a moment, and then frowned and focused on them. They were perfect. Unscarred. And he'd been poisoned . . . He'd eaten a doughnut full of cyanide. He could have died. He should have died. Jerking his head up, he stared at her. "You turned me."

Elspeth bit her lip and nodded, but then blurted, "I'm sorry. I had no choice. You were dying in my arms. I—"

"I'm not mad," he said quickly, and her words died at once.

"You're not?" she asked uncertainly. "But I thought

you weren't sure you wanted to be a life mate? You said you didn't know, that dating would help you decide."

"I didn't say I didn't know," he corrected her gently. "You said that perhaps you were being very egotistical, and maybe I didn't want to be a life mate, and I said, 'Maybe I don't.'"

Elspeth frowned slightly, and then tilted her head. "I don't see a difference. You weren't sure you wanted to be one, and I took the choice away and turned you."

"To save my life," he said gently. "And if you had been able to ask me, I would have said yes, because when I said 'Maybe I don't,' that was just . . ." He hesitated, and then said, "You were upset, and I wanted to convince you to give us a chance. I wanted you to agree to date me so that I could woo you as you deserve and convince you that you could be happy with me. That I wouldn't stop you from doing the things you wanted to like going out with the girls, and staying up all night."

"You did?" she asked, appearing uncertain.

"Yes, El, I did," he said solemnly.

"Why?" she asked with bewilderment.

Wyatt smiled crookedly. "I wish you could remember our first date. It was . . ." He shook his head, unable to find the words to express what that day had meant to him. "I'd never met anyone I jibed so well with. We talked and laughed and held hands, and it was so perfect, the perfect day. I fell in love with you by dinner, and just sat and stared at you through the first three quarters of the play afterward, until I just couldn't resist any longer, and then I kissed you and . . ." He shook his head. "That was the best twenty-four hours of my life."

"It's the life mate sex," she said quietly. "A mortal couldn't compare."

"No, honey," he assured her solemnly. "It wasn't the sex."

"Yes. It's—"

"Elspeth," he interrupted firmly. "I dated a lot of women before you. It was a different girl in every port kind of a deal. But none of them even touched my heart, while you flat-out owned it before I even kissed you," he assured her, some of his own amazement at that showing in his voice. "You were a goddess, my soul mate, perfection made woman. I never wanted to leave your side, and I was stunned when you were suddenly leaving. But I was crushed when you didn't show up the next day."

Eyeing her solemnly, he admitted, "I've been looking for you ever since. I hired countless private detective companies, as well as computer geeks to search for just your name, and I've spent more time in England over the last four years than I have in Canada or anywhere else. That's why I haven't visited Gran these last four years. Because every spare moment I've had off, I was in London, looking for you."

He smiled wryly, and said, "And then my father insisted I had to check on Gran. I mean, he *insisted*. We had a terrible fight over it. As much as I love my grandmother, I had planned another trip to England to scour London for you, and didn't want to cancel it. My father freaked. He started ranting about how he and Mom have hardly seen me these last four years, how I no longer spend time with them, and I didn't visit Grandmother anymore. He didn't know what the hell was the matter with me, but if I no longer cared about any of them, and didn't want to be a part of this family, and would rather waste my time searching for a woman who obviously didn't want to be found, then I should just get the hell out of the family."

Wyatt shrugged. "It was the biggest favor he's ever

done me. I felt I had to come to check on Gran or lose my family too. Then I wouldn't have you or them. So I reluctantly came to check on Grandmother, and in doing so, I finally found you. Here, of all places," he said with a smile that faded as he added, "Only you don't remember me . . . I wish you did."

"I wish I did too," she said softly, and then they both glanced toward the connecting door to the bathroom when a knock sounded on it.

"I guess they're awake," Elspeth murmured with what sounded like regret, and then called, "Yes?"

The door opened and Lissianna arched her eyebrows and scowled at them. "You aren't supposed to be out of our sight."

"Sorry. We didn't want to wake you up with our talking," Elspeth said at once.

"Talking, huh?" Lissianna asked dryly, her gaze sliding from Elspeth obviously bottomless in the babydoll, to him completely nude, reminding them both of their present state of undress.

Wyatt didn't mind so much. There wasn't a lot of privacy in an army barracks. Besides, the twins had already seen him this way. What was one more family member getting an eyeful? But it was obvious Elspeth didn't feel the same way. Squawking with alarm, she scrambled to the top of the bed to grab the pillows and tossed one to him, even as she covered herself up with the other.

Shaking her head, Lissianna moved forward, scooped up Elspeth's missing panties off the floor, and tossed them to her. "Your father called and wanted to talk to you."

Wyatt stiffened in surprise at the news, but Elspeth paled and looked horrified.

"Mother told him you and the twins were sleeping and she'd pass the message on," Lissianna continued gently, her expression sympathetic. "That way you can call back or not as you like. She said she'll continue to give him that message unless you tell her otherwise."

"Thank you," Elspeth breathed.

Lissianna nodded, and then said more sternly, "Now get your panties on and get back in the other room. We can't guard you if we can't see you."

"Yes, of course," Elspeth murmured, shifting toward the side of the bed with her pillow.

Glancing to Wyatt, Lissianna added, "I'll grab you the pants Sam brought back for you, so you don't have to parade that monster in front of the other girls."

Wyatt grinned as she left the room, and then turned to watch Elspeth pull her panties on. He didn't know why she bothered. They were as see-through as the rest of the outfit. But she seemed to feel better once they were on. At least, she dropped the pillow and appeared much more relaxed, Wyatt noted, and shook his head. He really did not understand women.

"What do you think your mother told your father?"

Elspeth glanced at Wyatt when he asked that question, and then peered at her guards. Every one of them was asleep again. Which was fine. They'd wake up at once, and be on hand if anything happened. Besides, she knew they were all as exhausted as she.

"El?" Wyatt prompted quietly, keeping his voice low to avoid disturbing the others.

Sighing, she considered the question and then whispered, "Probably that we are horrible, disobedient children. That the twins refused to return with her and it was all my fault."

"And he'll buy that?" he asked dubiously.

"He loves her," she said simply.

Wyatt nodded solemnly, and then asked, "Do you think he knows what she's done? How she's controlled you all?"

Elspeth peered down at her feet. She was sitting cross-legged on the bed next to him. The women had all been awake when they'd first returned to the room, and they'd all chatted for a few minutes, mostly about Wyatt and how he was feeling, and the fact that he'd need more blood. Rachel had set up his IV again. Elspeth had tugged it out of his arm when she'd lured him to the bathroom. He apparently hadn't noticed at the time. Now he was receiving blood again, through the IV.

Rachel had glanced to her in question as she'd said she'd hook him up to the IV again. Showing him after some rest would be better for both of them.

"El?" Wyatt prompted quietly.

Sighing, she grimaced and said, "I think if he doesn't know, it's only because he doesn't want to, or can't allow himself to."

"How do you mean?" he asked quietly.

Elspeth searched briefly for a way to explain, and then said, "My uncle Jean Claude was a drunk. Worse than that, though, he was rogue with it. He drank Wino Reds at The Night Club, but he also—"

"I'm sorry," Wyatt interrupted. "What are Wino Reds?"

"Blood taken from individuals who are drunk," she explained quietly.

"Right," he nodded. "Okay, go ahead."

"Aside from the Wino Reds, he also bit mortals who were drunk or on drugs to get that high, no matter how temporarily."

"You're not talking alcoholic lovers, are you?" he asked.

Elspeth shook her head. "Unknowing and unwilling donors. That's against our laws."

Wyatt nodded.

"Uncle Lucian suspected he was doing it, but it was his twin brother," she said sadly.

"That would be a hard one," Wyatt said quietly.

Elspeth nodded. "So, he didn't look into it . . . because if he didn't know for sure, he didn't have to do anything about it."

"Ah." Wyatt nodded again. "And you think it's the same thing with your father. That he probably suspects, saw some things that would make him suspect, but didn't acknowledge it because then he'd have to do something about it."

"Yes," she said quietly. "Greg calls it Betrayal Blindness."

Wyatt nodded solemnly and then asked, "And how do you feel about that?"

"I understand," she said slowly, and then added, "But it doesn't make it hurt any less that he wouldn't protect us from her. Just as knowing that her behavior is caused by her past doesn't make it any easier to bear."

"I'm sorry," Wyatt said sincerely. "I wish I could make it all better for you."

Elspeth smiled faintly. "Thank you. That actually makes me feel better."

Leaning forward, she kissed him lightly on the cheek, and then slid down on the bed and lay next to him.

Wyatt peered down at her for a minute, and then did

the same, sliding forward so that he could lie flat. After a moment, he said, "I know you're tired. I am too, but how is my grandmother?"

"Oh," Elspeth said softly, forcing her droopy eyes open wider. "I'm sorry. She's fine. Rachel's been keeping her sedated so she wouldn't know what was going on with you. Your screaming and thrashing would have terrified her, especially since we couldn't tell her the truth to explain what was happening," she pointed out. "But I've checked on her several times, and Rachel checks on her regularly and assured me Merry would be okay," she told him, and then added, "She'll probably stop the sedative in the morning and let her wake up now that the worst of the turn is over."

When Wyatt grunted, she added, "And there's good news."

"What's that?"

"Sam met the insurance guys at the house today and took care of everything for Merry and me. They're willing to pay up and will get the money to us as quickly as possible."

"Really?" Wyatt asked with surprise. "But it was arson, and I thought in arson cases it took thirty days for the arson investigator to—"

"As far as they're concerned, it wasn't arson," Elspeth interrupted quietly.

"Huh?" he asked with surprise. "Of course, it was. Someone threw Molotov cocktails into the house. They—"

Something in her expression must have caught his attention, because he stopped talking and narrowed his eyes.

"What?" he asked.

"You remember the two immortals who arrived to handle things just before we left? Well, they handled things." When Wyatt narrowed his eyes, she sighed, and said, "Wyatt, we can't let mortals investigate events like this. If the perpetrator is immortal, their investigation could get them killed by a rogue immortal, or reveal our presence. We can't allow that."

"So, those guys 'handled things' by . . . ?"

"Putting it into the arson investigator's head that it was a result of natural causes—faulty wiring or something," she said. "And then they put it into their head to make their reports quickly and forget about it."

"And I'm guessing Sam did the same with the insurance people?" he asked dryly. "Put it into their head that as it was natural causes, they shouldn't hold up payment, but should make their reports, pay up, and forget it?"

Elspeth nodded.

"Okay. I can understand why that would be necessary," he said, and slowly relaxed. After a moment, he asked, "So, how bad was the damage?"

"Not as much as I expected," Elspeth admitted. She'd been rather shocked at the news herself, so wasn't surprised when he appeared startled.

"Really?"

"Really," she assured him, and admitted, "I was afraid the whole place would have to be demolished and a new house built, but the fire department was there pretty quickly and was fast about putting out the fire. Julius said most of the damage was to the floors and a few walls, although there'd be a little more work thanks to water and smoke damage."

"Julius?" he asked with surprise. "Marguerite's husband? Our host?"

Elspeth nodded. "Sam called him for advice on whom she should have look at it to tell her how much work has to be done, and he drove out there himself. He owns a construction company that takes on jobs all over the world. Big-type jobs, like building resorts and malls and stuff," she explained. "But he's been thinking about opening a branch office over here too since he spends so much time here with Marguerite. He's offered to do the work for Merry if she'd like."

"Wow, that's nice of him," Wyatt murmured.

Elspeth nodded. "He had to go through the house to inspect it. Sam said he found some items in a storage area in the basement that survived the fire intact. Some boxes of pictures and stuff, I think."

"Gran'll be glad to hear that," he said solemnly.

Elspeth murmured agreement, but her eyes drifted closed. She knew Merry had been upset at losing all of her photographic memories of her husband. Hopefully there would be some good pictures in the boxes for her.

"Speaking of Gran," Wyatt said with a frown.

"Yes?" she asked, forcing her eyes back open.

"I suppose I can't tell her about immortals and everything, can I?"

"No," Elspeth agreed.

"But then, what do I tell her? How do I explain my feet being healed?"

Elspeth considered the question seriously, before sighing and saying, "There is no way to explain your feet."

"Then what—"

"You might have to wrap up your feet again and stay off of them for a while," she interrupted apologetically and grimaced when Wyatt groaned at the thought.

"Three weeks in bed," he said with disgust.

"I'll keep you company," she promised.

"Great," he muttered, and before she could be too hurt,

added, "I'll have you right where I want you, and won't be able to do a damned thing about it because your four guards will be with us too."

"Ah," Elspeth bit her lip. That *was* going to be painful. He wasn't the only one with needs.

Eighteen

"You're looking pretty damned good for a guy who supposedly got burned to a crisp in a fire a couple of nights ago!"

Elspeth glanced up with surprise from the playing cards in her hands, and then launched herself off the bed and rushed across the room to hug the giant who had just appeared in the open door.

"G.G.!" she cried, giving him a good squeeze made up mostly of relief. It was just the afternoon after Wyatt had woken up, and being confined to the bedroom when he felt fine and healthy was already making him crazy. She, Alex, and Sam were playing poker with him to help pass the time, while Lissianna and Rachel helped Meredith with a jigsaw puzzle at the table by the window. Some distraction by a visitor could only be a good thing, to her mind. Releasing the giant, she grabbed his arm and urged him toward the bed. "Come. Say hi. I know Wyatt will be glad for the company."

G.G. snorted at the suggestion. "Looks like he has more than enough company as it is. Ladies," he added the greeting, nodding at Lissianna, Rachel, Alex, and Sam. "Nice to see you all."

Every one of them was already on their feet and moving forward to greet him. G.G. was popular with female immortals. He was easy to talk to and obviously loved women. It was easily read from his mind, a deep-seated respect and love for them, gained from having a pretty amazing mother. When he finished hugging and greeting each of the immortals, he crossed the room to Meredith.

"Hello, ma'am. You must be Wyatt's grandmother and Elspeth's dear friend, Meredith. They both spoke well of you the other night when I met your grandson."

"Oh, my," Merry said, staring up at his green Mohawk as he took her hand gently in his much larger one. "His hair really is green, Ellie. I thought you were pulling my leg."

"I may have mentioned her to you a time or two over the last six weeks," Elspeth admitted with a grin.

"She did," Meredith told him. "She said you were a dear man who used to listen to her whine about her mother when she went to your nightclub while at university. And she said she thought I'd like you. And I think she's right," Meredith decided, and said, "Please, call me Merry. All my friends do."

G.G. beamed at the words and nodded. "It would be my pleasure, Merry. And you can call me G.G. or Joshua, whichever you're happier with."

"Oh, I think you're definitely a G.G.," Merry assured him. "Joshua is a lovely name, but G.G. has a certain flare."

G.G. chuckled at the words, and opened his mouth to

say something, but was forestalled when Wyatt asked, "Is that Tahiti Treat?"

"Tahitian Treat," G.G. corrected with amusement.

Elspeth glanced at the bag in his hand. She'd noticed it, but hadn't paid it much attention, and had no idea what was in it, except that whatever it held looked pink through the white plastic bag.

"You'd best go see, Wyatt," Merry said now with amusement. "He never could stand being stuck in bed when sick. Used to drive his mother crazy. Hopefully a little visit with you will cheer him up some. Meanwhile," she added, getting to her feet, "I think I'll go get us all some refreshments. I made chocolate chip cookies this morning. I'll fetch some back for everyone."

"I'll help," Lissianna and Rachel said together. They glanced at each other, shrugged, and then both followed Meredith to the door, and Elspeth couldn't blame them. Wyatt wasn't the only one getting sick of the room. There was no television or radio for noise, and with so many people in the room, it seemed to get hot in a hurry, which was why they'd left the door open.

"For me?"

Elspeth glanced toward the bed at Wyatt's gleeful question, to see G.G. handing the white bag to him.

"Yes," G.G. said with a grin. "I'd have wrapped it, but that just seemed silly."

Wyatt chuckled at the claim, and pulled out a bottle of red liquid.

"It was cold when I left The Night Club, but you might need ice cubes if you want some right away," G.G. commented, settling in one of the chairs next to the bed.

"I'll get a glass and ice cubes," Elspeth offered, turning toward the door.

"You'll sit down and stay here where Sam can watch you," Alex countered. "I'll get the glass and ice cubes."

"Can you make it three please, Alex? Or . . ." Wyatt hesitated and then sighed, and said reluctantly, "I guess you should get glasses for everyone."

Alex snorted at the suggestion. "I know how hard that stuff is to get up here. Three glasses will do. Besides, as I recall, it was just okay to me as a kid."

"Same here," Sam said.

"Sacrilege!" G.G. said teasingly.

"Just get two glasses," Elspeth said before Alex slipped from the room. "I'm good."

"Okay," she said before disappearing into the hall.

"Tahitian Treat," Wyatt murmured, turning the bottle in his hand. "G.G., I think you're my new best bud."

"Good," he said with amusement. "It will be nice to be able to talk to a mortal who knows about immortals, but can still hang out in the daytime when I'm not working."

"Oh dear," Elspeth murmured, her gaze sliding to Wyatt.

G.G. narrowed his eyes and glanced from her to Wyatt. "What?"

Wyatt hesitated, and then raised his eyebrows at her. "Can I tell him?"

Elspeth nodded. There was no reason not to. G.G. was in the know already when it came to immortals, and Meredith wasn't there to hear.

Sam immediately stood and moved toward the door. "I'll watch the hall and warn you if Merry returns sooner than expected."

"Thanks, Sam," Elspeth murmured.

"Tell me what?" G.G. asked.

"I'm not mortal anymore," Wyatt admitted apologetically.

G.G. glanced down to his feet and then back to his face. "But you're all bandaged up," he pointed out. "And I was told you wouldn't be walking for three or four weeks, if then."

"Yeah." Wyatt grimaced. "Well, that was before a dozen Boston cream doughnuts were shot full of cyanide poison and somehow slipped into the house. The twins and I ate them and while they were okay, I was nearly killed. Elspeth was forced to turn me to save me."

"Poisoned doughnuts?" G.G. asked with dismay. "Cyanide?"

Wyatt nodded solemnly.

"Damn," G.G. breathed, and then frowned and shook his head. "Then why are you in bed with your feet still bandaged up?"

"Because Gran doesn't know about immortals and we can't tell her, but there's no way to explain my feet healing so quickly without explaining about immortals." Wyatt grimaced. "I'm stuck in bed for three weeks, healed or not."

"Right," G.G. shook his head. "You guys sure lead an exciting life. Stabbed, pushed into traffic, firebombed, and then cyanide poisoning. What's next? An elephant stampede, or getting shot with a bazooka?"

"Neither, I hope," Wyatt said with disgust, and then frowned at the bottle he held. Heaving a sigh, he held it out to the giant. "I suppose I should give this back. You thought I was still sick when you decided to give it to me."

G.G. waved the bottle away. "It's all good. You were burned, and you're still suffering, so . . ." He shrugged. "You earned it. Especially if you've gone through the turn," he added solemnly. "I was there when my mother went through it. Nasty business. Looked excruciating."

"I don't remember any of it," Wyatt admitted. "Not the pain anyway. I do remember some pretty horrible nightmares though."

"Yeah, my mom had those too," G.G. said, and then frowned and glanced around. "Is it me, or is it hot in here?"

"Stifling," Elspeth assured him. "I think it's because we've had so many people in here all day."

"Lissianna and your other bodyguards?" he asked with amusement.

"Heard about that too, did you?" she asked wryly.

"Customers talk," he said with a shrug, and then turned to Wyatt and said, "Why don't I carry you downstairs? You can get out of this room and get some fresh air for a bit. I'll bring you back up before I leave."

"Why don't I walk down and we can tell Gran you carried me when she asks," Wyatt countered.

"Deal," G.G. said with a chuckle.

Wyatt was out of the bed so fast, Elspeth was surprised he didn't give himself whiplash.

"Here we are!"

Elspeth glanced toward the door at Meredith's caroled words to see the woman leading Lissianna and Rachel into the living room. Both women carried trays—one with cookies and plates, the other with a carafe of coffee, a pot of tea, milk, sugar, and cups.

Merry beamed at them all as she entered. Elspeth smiled back from where she sat beside Wyatt. He was settled on the couch with his bandaged feet up on the coffee table, a smile on his face, and a cold glass of that Tahiti drink in his hands. He'd offered her a sip, and Elspeth had thought it quite nice, but had refrained from accepting a glass herself. He obviously loved the stuff, and it was apparently hard to get. She wasn't going to drink it on him.

"Thank you, G.G., for carrying Wyatt down here," Merry said as she settled into the chair opposite his. "I'm sure it will perk him up. In fact, he already has more color in his cheeks."

"I feel better," Wyatt announced with a grin, and Elspeth bit her lip to keep from laughing. The color was from his literally running out of the bedroom, up the hall, down the stairs, and straight into the living room. He'd made the dash the minute G.G. had got to the stairs and gave him the sign that it was clear and he should move now.

"Good," Merry said firmly as Lissianna and Rachel set the trays on the coffee table. "Now, who wants what? We brought both tea and coffee to go with my chocolate chip cookies."

Everyone but Wyatt converged on the trays, taking a plate and grabbing one or two cookies, and then choosing their drink. Elspeth got Wyatt two cookies, as well as one for herself, but he shook his head when it came to a drink. He had his Tahitian Treat.

Elspeth had just settled next to him again when they heard a vehicle coming up the driveway. She started to get up again, to see who it was, but Sam waved her back down.

"Stay put and definitely stay away from the windows," Wyatt said quietly next to her, and she noticed the sudden tension in his body as he kicked into bodyguard mode.

"A problem?" G.G. asked Sam, his own body tensing. Sam was silent for a minute as she swished the curtain aside and looked out, but then smiled and shook her head. "It's Donny with those boxes I mentioned."

"Boxes?" Merry asked, perking up. "The ones from the house?"

"Yes." Sam turned to smile at her. "Mortimer sent Donny out to gather them and anything else salvageable and bring them to you here so you could go through it."

"Oh." Meredith smiled. "That was nice of your Mortimer. You've got a good man there, Sam. I know how busy he is and how much he needs every man. It was kind of him to do without Donny for this."

"Yeah. He's a good guy." Sam smiled softly, and then headed out of the room. "I'll be right back."

"I think I'll see if I can help them unload," G.G. said, getting up.

"Me too." Alex followed him. The pair had barely seemed to leave the room before Sam was returning with Donny on her heels, each of them carrying three boxes stacked on one another. Sam led him to the coffee table and set her boxes down on the floor beside it.

"Cookies." Donny's eyes lit up as he set his own boxes next to Sam's and noticed the plate of goodies on the table.

"After we finish unloading," Sam said firmly, heading out of the room even as Alex and G.G. entered with boxes of their own.

"My goodness, I didn't know I had so much in the basement," Merry said, her wide eyes on the boxes as they began to stack up.

"Some of the boxes are stuff I found on the main floor and upstairs that was still good," Donny announced as he returned with another load. "All your dishes and pots and pans were fine, but Julius said I should remove them so they didn't get broken during the renovations. And there were some pictures on the walls that survived, although a lot didn't. I labeled the boxes I packed."

"Oh, thank you, Donald," Merry said. "That was so kind of you."

Donny flushed at the compliment as he set down his boxes, and then hurried back out for more.

"Maybe we should move the boxes with dishes and pots and pans down to the basement. They can be stored there until the house is ready," Lissianna said, standing up. "We're getting quite a collection here."

"Good idea." Elspeth stood even as Rachel did and they began to separate the boxes. Alex, G.G., Sam, and Donny all helped once they'd finished bringing the boxes in, and they soon had most of the boxes moved downstairs. That still left ten unlabeled boxes by the table though.

"Well, let's all take a box and see what's in them," Wyatt suggested, sitting up on the couch.

Elspeth grabbed one and carried it to him, and then grabbed Merry one too before settling back on the couch with a third one and opening the box.

"It looks like I have bills here," Elspeth said as she pulled the lid off her box, and rifled through the hydro bills, gas bills, and whatnot inside. Noting the date April 1995 on one, she added, "Really old bills."

"Oh, yes, Barry—my husband," Meredith explained with a smile. "He used to keep the bills for . . . well, I'm not sure why. In case of an audit or something. We had boxes and boxes of them in the storage area when he died. I thought I'd got rid of them all, but I guess I missed one."

"So . . . to the dump?" Elspeth asked gently.

"Yes, dear," Merry murmured, pulling the lid off of the box she'd given her.

Elspeth set her box by the door and picked up the last box that had remained after they'd each picked one.

"I'm not sure what I have," Alex said, and Elspeth glanced over to see her frowning down into the large box she held. As she watched, the woman reached in with both hands and lifted out a plastic-wrapped and obviously vacuum-sealed white something or other.

"My wedding dress," Meredith breathed, tears filling her eyes.

"The basement for storage until the house is ready?" Alex suggested gently, and Merry nodded, a smile trembling on her lips.

"All I have here are books," Lissianna announced, rifling through her box.

"Oh, probably just novels I read and boxed up, intending to put in the yard sale I never had," Meredith said with a smile.

"Actually, they look like university text books on . . . chemistry and . . . pharmacology," Lissianna said, reading the titles on a couple of the books.

"Really?" Meredith asked with surprise. "Why I can't imagine where—Oh!" she said suddenly. "Those must be Madeleine's books."

"Madeleine's?" Elspeth asked with surprise.

"Yes, her son went to university for a while. He wanted to be a pharmacologist. Apparently, he quit after a couple of years though," Meredith told them. "I imagine those were down in her storage area in the basement. I must have forgotten to mention that area to her son."

"Madeleine has a son?" Elspeth asked with surprise.

She'd not read anything about a son from the woman's mind.

"Yes, dear. He's the one who came to gather her furniture and other things from the apartment after Madeleine left."

Elspeth stared at her blankly. She'd never even thought to wonder who had collected Madeleine's things.

Meredith clucked her tongue. "I should have remembered to tell him about the storage area. I can't believe I forgot." She shook her head. "I guess I'll have to find his number again and call to have him come get his mother's boxes . . . if he wants them."

"El?"

Elspeth glanced toward G.G. in surprise. It seemed everyone was going to call her El now. "Yes?"

"I've got pictures in my box," G.G. announced.

"Oh, lovely!" Meredith said at once, and stood to move to his side.

Elspeth watched with concern as the woman began to maneuver her way around the boxes, but then glanced back to G.G. when he began to whistle. She'd never heard him whistle before, but then, she hadn't spent all that much time with him, she acknowledged. The tune sounded familiar, but she couldn't place it.

"That's 'If You Could Read My Mind,'" Meredith cried suddenly as she reached him. "Oh, G.G., you have lovely taste in music. I adore Gordon Lightfoot."

Elspeth's eyes widened, and she immediately concentrated on the man, searching for his thoughts. G.G. was thinking one thing over and over again. *"This is the man who pushed you into traffic. This is the man who pushed you into traffic."*

"Oh my God," Sam gasped, jumping to her feet, obviously reading G.G.'s mind as well.

"Did you find something exciting, dear?" Meredith asked, turning to her with interest.

"No. I—"

"El? What did he find?" Wyatt growled beside her, obviously having caught G.G.'s message in the tune, but unable to read his mind yet. It would take him time and practice to gain that skill.

"An important picture," she said, standing up to move to G.G.'s side.

"Oh," Merry said with disappointment as she peered back at the picture G.G. was holding. "Those are Madeleine's pictures, not mine. That's her son there in that one. Now, what was his name? Peter? No."

Elspeth peered down at the picture G.G. held as everyone but Wyatt got up to gather around them and try to get a look at it. The man was the same height as his mother, about five-foot-seven. He also had the same dark hair, angular face, and slim build. He easily could have fit through Julius's doggy door . . . if it hadn't been locked.

"Bring it here, El. I want to see too," Wyatt said, his voice tense.

"George?" Meredith murmured, but shook her head. "Maybe John. No, not John. But I'm sure it was the same as that singer from that band with that dingo fellow."

"Ringo?" G.G. asked. "The Beatles?"

"Yes, that's it. Madeleine's son has the same name as their fourth fellow. She told me she had a big crush on him as a girl and so named him after him," Meredith told them, and then grimaced. "I didn't think that said much for her feelings for her husband to name their son after—"

"Paul," G.G. said.

"Yes, Paul." Meredith nodded with satisfaction. "She named him Paul."

"El," Wyatt growled, shifting impatiently on the couch.

"Paul Albrecht," Elspeth murmured, staring at the face in the picture.

"Why yes, I guess so. I always forget that Madeleine wasn't her real name," Meredith said now. "She was Nina Albrecht, wasn't she?"

"Yes," Elspeth murmured, and took the picture from G.G. to carry it to Wyatt before he blew their pretense and lunged off the couch to get to the picture.

"Thank you," he said apologetically as he took the picture. "Sorry for snapping."

Elspeth just smiled slightly. He hadn't really snapped, but she appreciated the apology anyway.

Wyatt stared at the picture for a moment, and then glanced to G.G. "You're sure this is him?"

Elspeth knew he was asking if this was the one who had pushed her in front of the car, and wasn't at all surprised Wyatt knew this was the culprit behind the attacks. Why else would a picture of Madeleine's son be important?

"Yes, dear," Meredith said with surprise, obviously thinking he was talking to her. "That's Madeleine's son, Paul."

G.G. didn't speak. He merely nodded his head while Meredith was staring at her grandson.

Wyatt blew out his breath and peered back at the picture, murmuring, "Bastard."

Elspeth squeezed his shoulder and then glanced to Meredith. "Merry, did you say you have his phone number?"

"Yes, I do." She nodded. "Do you think I should call him right away and let him know we found some more of his mother's things? He lives in Alberta and had to drive all the way out here just to get her furnishings and things. He was quite angry about it I think. At least, he was angry about something. I don't know if he'll want them. But maybe we could mail them to him. I'll offer to do that when I call him."

"Meredith, why don't you give me the phone number and let me take care of that for you?" Sam suggested.

"Oh, I wouldn't want to trouble you with it. You've done so much already, Sam," Meredith protested.

Elspeth expected Sam to take control of Merry then and change her mind for her, but she simply said, "Don't be silly. We're happy to help. Besides, we have a contract with a local shipper and can send the boxes out for practically nothing."

"Really?" Meredith asked. "Oh, that would be lovely, then. I'll just get you the number and—Oh," she said with a sudden frown.

"What's wrong, Gran?" Wyatt asked quietly.

"I put his phone number on the refrigerator," she said on a sigh. "I suppose it was destroyed in the fire."

Every single person in the room deflated at that news, except Donny, who straightened slightly and asked, "The refrigerator?"

"Yes, dear," Meredith said, dropping back into her seat.

Donny turned to Sam at once. "There were a lot of bits of paper stuck to the refrigerator by magnets. They were unburned."

"We need to get it," Sam said at once. "We'll take the

phone number and this picture to Mortimer. Hopefully between the two he can track him down."

"Oh, I'm sure that's not necessary," Meredith said with surprise. "Just call Paul, dear. He's probably still driving back to Alberta. Or maybe he's there already. How long does it take to drive that far?"

Elspeth bit her lip, and then glanced to Alex and raised her eyebrows as she nodded toward Merry. Fortunately, Alex got the message and turned to concentrate on the woman briefly. Elspeth relaxed when the lovely lady's face went blank. Alex had taken control of her. They could talk freely now.

Wyatt seemed to recognize that as well, because he asked G.G., "Just to be sure I'm not misunderstanding things, this is the guy who pushed Elspeth in front of that car?"

"Yes," G.G. growled. "The little weasel. I nearly shouted it out when I saw the picture. His face was the last thing I expected to see when I realized I had pictures. Yet there he was, right on top."

"But who is this guy?" Lissianna asked with a frown, moving over to look at the picture Wyatt still held. "And why would he want to kill Elspeth? It sounds like she's never even met him."

"He's the son of Merry's old tenant in the downstairs apartment," Elspeth explained, and then admitted, "No, I haven't met him."

"Madeleine was still a tenant when Elspeth moved in," Wyatt explained. "But she read the woman's mind, realized she was robbing Gran, got her to confess to her and return the money, and then took her to the police and got her to confess to them too."

"She's been in jail ever since," Sam added, and when

Elspeth glanced her way, explained, "Mortimer looked into it."

"Oh," she murmured.

"Okay, but why would her son want to kill you?" Lissianna asked with exasperation. "I mean, it's not like he could know you controlled his mother and made her confess."

Elspeth shrugged helplessly. "I have no idea."

"I guess we'll have to ask him when we find him," Wyatt said grimly as he began unwrapping his feet.

"What are you doing?" Elspeth asked with surprise.

"I'm going to get the number off Gran's fridge, and take it and the picture to Mortimer. Paul's obviously still in Ontario. I'm thinking we call and lure him in with the boxes and—"

"You're not going alone. I'm coming with you," G.G. announced, standing up.

"Thanks," Wyatt said with a smile.

"No need for thanks. I want to have a word with the little bastard," he assured him. "I still have nightmares about Elspeth going under that car, and the shape she was in when she came out."

"All right," Sam relented. "The three of us will go to the house to get the phone number, and then take the information to Mortimer."

"But what about Merry?" Elspeth asked with a frown, and zeroed in on Wyatt as she said, "How do we explain your leaving? You're not supposed to be on your feet."

Wyatt paused and frowned briefly, but then smiled and started wrapping his foot back up. "We'll tell her that since G.G. is here to carry me, Rachel wants to take me to her office to treat my feet."

"My office is in the morgue," Rachel said with amusement.

"She doesn't know that," Wyatt said with a shrug.

Elspeth nodded. "Okay. But I'm going too."

"Elspeth," Sam began.

"I'm safer at the Enforcer House than here. Half my bodyguards will be gone and he *knows* I'm here," she pointed out. "Besides, I want to know why this guy has been trying to kill me. And," she added as Sam opened her mouth, probably on a protest, "I might know something useful that will help Mortimer find Paul. I read his mother's mind. She had friends here he might be staying with."

"Fine," Sam gave in on a sigh. "The four of us will go to the house, get the phone number, and take it and the picture to Mortimer."

"The five of us," Rachel corrected her. "He's supposed to be going to *my* office."

"Right," Sam said, and shook her head. "Okay then, everyone sit down. Alex will release Meredith, and Rachel will ask G.G. if he'd mind carrying Wyatt to the car, because if so, she'd like to examine him properly in her office . . . and then we'll go from there."

"**Y**ou can't take those off," Elspeth murmured, putting a restraining hand on Wyatt's arm as he leaned forward in his car seat to start unraveling his bandages. They were sitting on the back bench seat of the SUV. Wyatt was on one side, G.G. on the other, and Elspeth was in the middle.

"What?" Wyatt asked with surprise. "Why?"

"You don't have any shoes," she pointed out apologetically.

"Damn," he muttered with disgust. "I didn't think of shoes, and I was looking forward to getting these bandages off. Besides, if I walk on them, they'll get dirty and Gran will know I've been on my feet."

"You're right. You'll have to take them off," Sam said from the driver's seat in front of him, and then added, "We have shoes in the stock room at the Enforcer House. I'll get you a pair when we get there."

"Oh good. Thanks," he muttered and went back to work on the wrapping.

"Speaking of the house," Sam muttered, passing her phone back to Elspeth. "Can you text Mortimer and let him know what we're doing and that we'll head to the house right after we get the phone number from Meredith's fridge?"

"Sure." Elspeth took the phone, noting as she did that Rachel was busy tapping away on her phone in the front passenger seat. Probably texting Etienne to let him know she'd left the house, Elspeth supposed as she quickly opened Sam's messages, found Mortimer's name, and opened that string of texts. But then she paused and asked, "Wouldn't it be easier to call him?"

"Yes, but then he'd insist we leave it to hunters to get the number and chase this guy. He'd send us back to the house where we'll all be safe," Sam said dryly. "I think after all we've been through, we deserve to be in on catching this creep."

"Text," Wyatt and G.G. said at the same time.

Chuckling, Elspeth quickly texted the message and hit Send. She then held the phone out next to Sam, but she shook her head. "Hold on to it for me until we stop. In fact, put it in your pocket so we can't hear if he texts back to tell us not to go to the house. This way I can say I didn't have the phone and not be lying."

Elspeth raised her eyebrows, and slid the phone into the back pocket of the jeans Sam had fetched for her from the Enforcer House. "I'm learning all sorts of little tricks from you, Sam. You lawyers are tricky."

"We have to be. We deal with criminals," she said dryly.

A startled laugh slipped from Elspeth, and then something made her glance to her right. She peered out the window past G.G. and her heart seemed to stutter to a halt. A semi was barreling down on them from a side street. They wouldn't get past the road in time to avoid the collision.

Elspeth didn't hesitate. Her only thought that G.G. was mortal and was seated on the side that would take the impact, she unsnapped her seat belt and threw herself on the man, doing her best to cover as much of him as she could in the split second she had to do it.

"El! What—?" Wyatt began in a shocked voice, and then the truck hit them.

The sound was like nothing Elspeth had ever experienced before. It was like an explosion went off beside her. There was a crash and the scream of metal tearing and she felt the door driven into her legs, side, and arm, thrusting her and G.G. toward Wyatt even as her head flew in the opposite direction, toward the shattering window as the glass flew into the car. Some of the shards of glass imbedded in her shoulder, neck, and head like multiple darts. Others merely sliced her skin in passing, sending blood spraying around them as the truck plowed forward. It forced the SUV sideways across the road, until the tires hit the sloping grass, and then they were rolling.

Elspeth heard Wyatt shout, and Sam and Rachel scream, but her attention was on the moan G.G. released when their heads slammed into the ceiling of the car as it came down hard on its roof. She realized then that she hadn't covered the top of his head, just the sides, but it was too late to do anything about it. The SUV had stopped moving finally, and she was lying in a crumpled heap on the ceiling of the car around G.G.'s dangling head and arms.

Dazed and in pain, Elspeth tried to catch her breath, but couldn't seem to. She wanted to ask if everyone was all right, but couldn't do that either. No one was moving or saying anything, though, she noted with concern, and G.G. at least was unconscious. She hoped he was just unconscious. He looked terribly pale and there was blood dripping from the top of his head and the corner of his mouth. There were also a couple of cuts on his face and arms from glass that she hadn't managed to block.

Tilting her head, Elspeth looked for Wyatt and found him dangling from his seat belt above and almost right next to her. He was much closer than he should have been, almost directly beside them. That told her just how far G.G.'s side of the car had been forced in. But other than being unconscious, with blood dripping from a wound to the side of his head where he'd apparently hit his window, Wyatt seemed okay.

Elspeth wanted to check the others then, but she was woozy and felt like she was suffocating. She was on the verge of losing consciousness when she thought she heard a car door slam.

Help, Elspeth thought with relief, and held on desperately to consciousness. She heard footsteps and the crunch of glass, and then her foot was grabbed and yanked. Elspeth's body screamed in agony as she was dragged over the glass littering the roof, and then through the window hole on the crushed side of the car and out onto cool, soothing grass.

"Are you alive?"

Elspeth opened her eyes and turned her head toward her raised leg to find herself staring up at the man from the picture. Paul Albrecht, the man who had been trying to kill her.

"Yeah. You'll survive," he said, and started dragging her across the cold, damp ground by her foot, sending shafts of fiery pain through her body. That's when Elspeth finally lost consciousness.

Nineteen

"You're some kind of mutant. That's what you are."

Those were the first words Elspeth heard as she woke up. Or at least the first words she registered. For one moment, she stayed completely still, trying to sort out where she was. All she could tell was that she was sitting on a hard chair, her chin resting on her chest, and there was light beyond her closed eyes.

Gritting her teeth against the pain assaulting her body, she forced her head up on her stiff neck, and opened her eyes, wincing as shockingly bright light assailed her pupils. Dear God, it was like the sun was dangling directly in front of her, shining straight into her face, blinding her to anything else around her.

"Yeah, I knew you were awake," that same voice growled.

Elspeth closed her eyes for some relief from the light, and found herself staring at pink screens as the light poured through her eyelids. Ignoring it, she tried to figure out where she was and what had happened. It actually took her a moment, and then Elspeth remembered the crash, being dragged from the car, and the man standing over her.

"Paul Albrecht," she muttered as his name came to her.

"Yeah. So . . . what? Did you read my name from my mind?" he asked with disgust.

Elspeth started to shake her head, but stopped at once when pain crashed through her skull.

"I know you can do that shit," he told her, his voice half triumphant, and half hate-filled. "I know you can read people's thoughts and control their minds. You're some kind of freak of nature with weird-ass special skills like that scary-ass kid in *Firestarter*."

"*Firestarter*?" Elspeth murmured with bewilderment. She thought it was an old movie, but couldn't seem to recall what it was about. Well, a firestarter, she presumed, but didn't remember anything about the plot, or the scary-ass kid he referred to.

"Don't play dumb with me. I know. *I know!*"

"Know what?" she asked wearily, trying to move her arms to ease some of the ache in her shoulders, only to find she was unable to. Her hands were restrained somehow behind her back. Rope, she realized, feeling her bindings.

"Everything," he assured her. "I know the government keeps all kinds of little mutants like you around to do their dirty work. And I know where your secret ops building is. I followed you there one day. It's all gated, lots of dogs, and men with guns. I knew what it was right away."

Elspeth stilled. He was describing the Enforcer House. He'd followed her there?

"Yeah, that got your attention, huh?" he said snidely.

She instinctively opened her eyes, and then quickly closed them again as the light sent pain shooting through her head once more. Elspeth waited a moment to allow the pain to recede, and then said, "That's not a government building. There is no—"

"Fine, don't admit it," he cut her off. "That's okay. I know what I know."

"Of course you do," Elspeth said wearily, wishing he'd just shut up and go away. Her head was killing her, along with the whole left side of her body . . . and her gut was starting to burn as if acid was eating away at her. She was obviously desperately in need of blood, and he was standing there, somewhere beyond the lights, smelling pretty juicy to her at the moment. She needed him to leave so she could have a minute to think and figure out what to do.

"For instance," he dribbled on, "I know that instead of minding your own business, you read Nina's mind."

"Your mother," she muttered, recalling that Madeleine's real name was Nina Albrecht. Apparently, he didn't call her Mom, or even Mother.

"Yeah, you found that out by reading her mind too, didn't you?" he suggested. "And that's how you figured out what she was doing. But that wasn't enough, was it? Then you just had to control her, make her return the old lady's money, and then make her confess. *Confess!*" he roared suddenly with rage, making her start. "She told me you did. She told me she felt like she'd been hijacked, that she didn't want to do any of it, give back the old bitch's money, or go confess to the police. She said it was like you were making her do that shit and say that stuff."

Elspeth was silent for a moment, but finally said, "Don't be ridiculous. She was pulling your leg. No one can read and control people's minds. She was probably just too embarrassed to admit that her conscience got the better of her and she turned herself in to feel better about herself."

"Nina doesn't have a *conscience*," Paul said on a laugh of disbelief that seemed to say that was the stupidest suggestion ever. "No. You made her do it. And now she's locked up, probably for the rest of her life, and it's *your* fault."

"Of course," Elspeth sighed, tired of his rambling. "Her being locked up has nothing to do with her criminal activities, does it?"

"She's done that shit for years and never got caught," he snapped. "At least she's always been able to weasel away and start again somewhere else until now. Until you came along and wrecked everything with your mutant ways!"

Something slammed into the side of the chair with a loud clang, and Elspeth jumped in surprise. She sat completely still for a moment, but when he didn't speak or do anything more, she began working at the rope around her wrists, and tried to distract him by saying, "So you're going to kill me because you think I made your mother turn herself in?"

"That was the plan, but you just wouldn't die," he said, his tone accusing. "You should have died. I saw you after they dragged you out from under that car."

"I wasn't really hurt badly," she lied, working at the rope, but wishing the light wasn't there and she could see and control him. "The blood was mostly show and made it look like I was hurt worse than I was."

He laughed at the lie. "You were hamburger! But there wasn't much blood. At least, not as much as there should have been."

Right, Elspeth thought on a sigh. The nanos would have held in as much as they could. There was probably a smear, or several smears, from where she'd been dragged over the pavement, but much less blood loss than there would have been were she mortal.

"And then the next time I saw you, you were perfectly fine. Not a mark, a scab, a scar, nothing. That's when I figured out you're a female Wolverine," he informed her.

Elspeth blinked her eyes open, and then quickly closed them again against the light. A female Wolverine? She didn't get out to the movies much, but did buy the occasional film on iTunes. She knew who Wolverine was.

"You don't seem to have the blades like him. At least, not that I've seen so far, but you heal real quick like him. And you read minds and control people or manipulate them like that guy in the wheelchair."

Charles Xavier or Professor X, Elspeth thought. First he was comparing her to some firestarter, and now he thought she was a mutant. Both of which were fictional references. But then, she supposed vampires were too, and a lot of people would call her kind by that name.

"The car didn't kill you, the fire didn't kill you . . ."

"The cyanide in the doughnuts didn't kill me," she added dryly, and then asked what she'd wanted to know since it had happened. "How did you get the doughnuts in the house after you injected them with cyanide?"

"The doggy door," he said at once.

"It's a locking doggy door," she said with a frown, recalling what Julius had said. "It only opens to their dog's collar."

"It a magnetic lock," he said dryly. "I recognized that while walking around the house when you went there after the fire . . . and I recognized it because I worked in a pet shop during my brief stint in university. We sold a lot of those. Of course, we didn't tell the customers that all you need is another collar with the magnetic collar key in it to open them." She could hear the smile in his voice as he added, "I hit the pet store the minute it opened. I had to buy a doggy door to get the collar, but it got me in."

She had to tell Marguerite and Julius that, Elspeth thought. They believed they were secure, but they weren't. Wanting to keep him talking until she could get her hands free, she said, "You studied to be a pharmacist. You made the poison yourself?"

"Yes, back in Alberta. I had it with me when I came. It was for Nina, but I can make more."

"Nina wanted poison?" Elspeth asked with dismay. Had she planned to murder Meredith and manufacture a fake will leaving everything to her or something like that? Elspeth wondered and wished again that she could see him to read him.

"No," Paul said. "She didn't want it. I planned to slip it into her coffee."

The words shocked her into blinking her eyes open again, but the light made her quickly close them once more. "You planned to *kill* your mother?"

"Yes," he said easily, completely unashamed.

"Well then, why the heck have you been trying to kill me?" she asked with exasperation. "Dead or in jail, she's out of your life," she pointed out, and thought she'd done Nina a huge favor by getting her to confess. If she hadn't, the woman would be dead now.

"Because so long as she's in jail I can't kill her and get the insurance," he growled furiously. "With her record and all she's confessed to, she could be in there until she dies. She's only forty-seven. That could be another damned thirty years. Forty, even."

"Oh, for cripes sake," Elspeth said, dropping back in her chair with disgust, and realizing only then that she'd been sitting up tensely. Relaxing eased the rope somewhat, and she set back to work almost feverishly at it.

"Which made me think," he continued suddenly. "If I can't kill you, maybe I can use you."

Elspeth stiffened at the words. "Use me?"

"Well, you got her in there. Now you can just control the police, or the judge, or whoever you have to, to get her out," he said with cold satisfaction.

Elspeth raised her eyebrows, but remembered to keep her eyes closed this time. "So that you can kill her."

"Exactly," he said on a happy sigh.

"And you think I would do that because . . . ?" she asked dryly.

"Because if you don't, I'll kill the old lady, the twins, that fella who was going down on you in your bathroom before I threw the Molotov cocktails in, and everyone else in that house."

Elspeth's mouth tightened. He'd obviously stood out on the balcony watching them through the bathroom window that night. How long had he stood out there before finally throwing the firebombs in? Had he watched until they passed out? Beyond that even? Just standing there looking at them naked and vulnerable? Well, she'd been naked. Wyatt had still had his pants on.

"Chemistry isn't my only skill," he added, sounding much closer. "I took that to learn how to make drugs I could sell. But I also know how to make some pretty nifty bombs. In fact, I was making one when it suddenly occurred to me to use you instead of kill you."

Elspeth jerked as a finger ran down her cheek. His face was so close to hers, she could feel his breath on her nose and mouth. It smelled like blood to her.

His finger drifted down her neck, and to one breast. "I could just finish the bomb, though, and kill every last person you care about."

Furious, Elspeth stopped trying to untie the rope, grabbed one strand, and tugged viciously. Much to her surprise, it snapped like licorice. She really needed to take the time to find out just how strong she was once this was over, Elspeth thought grimly. As well as find out what she could and couldn't do as an immortal. She'd never thought it was necessary before this, but was learning differently, because if she'd known she could break the damned rope, she—

"So, what do you say?" Paul Albrecht asked, interrupting her thoughts and squeezing the breast he'd just been touching. "Death or friends?"

Elspeth didn't have to open her eyes. She could still feel his breath on her face and knew exactly where his head was. Whipping her hand around, she grabbed just below it, her fingers closing around his throat and lifting as she jerked to her feet, growling, "Death."

Elspeth never saw the gun. She hadn't realized he had one. But she certainly heard it go off . . . and felt the impact as it tore through her heart.

"Elspeth!"

Paul's voice sounded a lot like Wyatt's, she thought as she began to fall.

"Sometimes, Marguerite, I feel like you're older than me, rather than younger. You must have an old soul."

Merry, Elspeth thought as she swam toward consciousness. That was Merry talking. She also recognized her aunt's laugh as she responded, "A very old soul indeed, Merry."

Pushing her eyes open, Elspeth stared at the ceiling overhead, and then it was suddenly displaced by Wyatt's anxious face.

"You're awake."

Elspeth blinked, and smiled faintly. "Yes. Shouldn't I be?" she asked, and frowned as her voice came out a rough, dry whisper.

"Oh, Ellie, dear! You had us all so worried!"

When Wyatt turned his head to the right, she did the same and watched Meredith rush across the room with Aunt Marguerite on her heels.

"I can't believe the bad luck we've been having. First the fire, and then the doughnuts, and now a car accident!" Merry shook her head with dismay as she reached Elspeth and took her hand in both of hers. "I nearly fainted when G.G. carried you in all covered with blood. Thank goodness it was mostly show and you just suffered a knock on the head. But you did take your time waking up."

Elspeth turned her head back to Wyatt, who grimaced so that only she could see it.

"G.G. had to carry you because of my feet, of course," he said in a growl that showed his displeasure at not being able to carry her in himself. Wyatt probably also wasn't pleased because then G.G. would have had to carry him in to keep up the pretense that his feet were still recovering from the burns he received in the fire.

"G.G.'s okay, then?" she asked in a whisper to avoid the pain she'd suffered the first time she'd spoken.

"Yes, I am," a voice as deep as Wyatt's announced, and Elspeth looked to the left side of the bed to find the giant man seated in a chair. He smiled at her solemnly, and added, "Thanks to you."

"Yes, G.G. told us how he forgot to do up his seat belt and you reminded him to buckle up just before the accident," Meredith announced with a sigh. "He was so lucky you were there to remind him. He could have died."

Elspeth supposed they couldn't have told the woman that she'd jumped on him and played human airbag for the man during the crash.

"Thank you," G.G. said sincerely. "I got knocked out, and had a small bump after the accident, but that's all."

Elspeth nodded, relieved to find the action didn't cause pain to scream through her head as it had when she'd last woken up. Her eyes widened abruptly, and she turned her head back to Wyatt. "Paul?"

"Yes, we managed to get him the boxes after the accident," he said reassuringly, his eyes darting to his grandmother and back, and then he added meaningfully, "He's all taken care of. *Three* of Mortimer's men helped him in *one* little exercise."

Elspeth frowned slightly, wondering if he was saying what she thought he was. Had they performed a three-on-one on the man? Wiping his mind clean and leaving him a blank slate? Or possibly a drooling idiot? It could go either way with mortals. But no one deserved it more than Paul Albrecht, the homicidal psycho . . . wanting to kill his mother, kill her, kill everyone in the house. Honestly, she should have taken a bite out of his neck, a big one.

"I'm very glad you are all right, Elspeth," Aunt Marguerite said, drawing her gaze. "We've all been very worried."

Elspeth smiled faintly.

"But now I think I'm going to drag Meredith downstairs and ply her with dinner. It must be ready by now, Merry, and you did say you were hungry just a moment ago," Marguerite added.

"Oh yes." Meredith frowned, looking torn. She obviously didn't want to leave Elspeth so soon after her waking, but then her stomach growled, and loudly.

Smiling, Elspeth squeezed Meredith's hands. "Go on and eat. I'll still be here when you're done."

Smiling, Meredith bent and kissed her cheek affectionately. "Very well, then. But I'll be quick . . . and I'll bring you something when I return. Do you think you could manage to keep down food?"

"I'm sure I could," Elspeth told her solemnly.

"Good. You just rest, then, and I'll return soon," Meredith said, setting her hand down and patting it before turning to start making her way to the door.

Marguerite bent then to kiss her forehead and whispered, "I'm glad you're recovered and awake. I love you."

"I love you too, Aunt Marguerite," Elspeth murmured as the woman straightened.

Nodding, Marguerite turned and quickly caught up to Meredith. The two walked out of the room together.

"I'm afraid I'm going to have to leave you too," G.G. announced, standing up and smiling at her when Elspeth turned to him. "I have to get to The Night Club and prep for opening. I just wanted to make sure you were good before I did."

"Thank you, G.G.," Elspeth murmured. "I'm very glad you're okay. I was worried about the head knock on the roof as we rolled over. I hadn't thought to cover the top of your head."

"It's all good. I'm hardheaded, as my mother would tell you," he assured her.

Elspeth snorted at the claim. "Your mother would tell me no such thing. She thinks you're an angel."

"Yeah, she does," he agreed with a chuckle. "I've got her fooled, huh?"

Elspeth just shook her head with amusement.

"I'll come see you again tomorrow," he said, walking around the bed. "Or you could come see me at The Night Club, even. Your drinks are on the house there for life. At least, my life."

He was out the door before she could reply.

"How do you feel?"

Elspeth turned to peer at Wyatt and smiled. "Good. My throat's a little sore, and my mouth dry, but I'm much better than I felt the last time I woke up."

Wyatt was off the bed at once and pouring her a glass of water from a pitcher on the bedside table. There were two glasses, she noted, and he poured himself some water too, but left it there for now. Settling on the bed next to her, he slid an arm under her shoulders and urged her up as he placed the rim of the glass against her lip.

Elspeth wanted to tell him she could do this herself, but the moment she opened her mouth, he tipped water in. She gulped it down, and closed her eyes with relief as it soothed her mouth and throat.

"I love you."

Elspeth blinked her eyes open and peered at him wide-eyed. "I—"

"I nearly died when I came through the door and saw that bastard shoot you through the heart."

That made her frown, and she asked, "Where was I? How did you find me? What happened after he shot me? No, wait," she said suddenly. "First tell me if everyone was all right after the accident. What happened there?"

Wyatt hesitated, and then said, "Sam woke up before the rest of us and used Rachel's phone to call Mortimer. I was the second to wake, and when I saw you were missing, and the blood trail through the grass . . ." He shook his head, his mouth tightening, but then took a deep breath and continued, "We were all awake by the time Mortimer's men reached us. G.G. had the bump on the head and a headache, but seemed all right otherwise. Sam and I had a few bruises and banged our heads a bit in the roll, but were fine too." He paused then before finishing, "Rachel was in a bad way though."

Elspeth stiffened. Rachel had been in the front passenger seat, right in front of G.G. She'd been on the side that took the impact too. "How bad?"

"Her arm was nearly severed at the shoulder, and her right leg crushed. Mortimer's men had to cut her out of the car." He shook his head. "They were surprisingly quick at it."

Elspeth nodded, not surprised. "Is she all right now?"

"Yes. She woke up this morning," he assured her. "She's already up and about and went home with Etienne, who made her promise never to work for Mortimer again in any other capacity except as a doctor."

Elspeth smiled faintly at that.

"Two of Mortimer's men brought Rachel straight back here. Fortunately, Grandmother was apparently in the kitchen and didn't see. The rest of us went to the Enforcer House. I thought Mortimer would still have to track Paul's phone, but then Sam remembered that you had her phone. They were able to pull up your exact location on a map on the computer."

Elspeth nodded. "I know the program. I've seen him use it for other hunters. It's awesome."

"Yeah," Wyatt agreed, and then grimaced and said, "You were in an abandoned building on the edge of the city. Albrecht had rigged up some kind of battery and a desk lamp for light."

"That was a desk lamp?" she asked with disbelief. "I thought it was going to burn my eyeballs out."

"It looked like a desk lamp, but I think he had a spotlight bulb in it. Not sure how he rigged it up though. It was actually pretty impressive. The guy was brilliant I think. It's just too bad he . . ."

". . . was a homicidal psycho with matricide on the mind?" she suggested.

"Yeah," Wyatt said with a grin, and then sighed and continued, "Anyway, I wanted to charge in, but Mortimer insisted on a plan. Surrounding the place, yada yada," he said with disgust. "If we'd just rushed in we would have got to you before he shot you," he added sharply, and then cleared his throat and said, "Fair warning. I might have said some pretty choice words to Mortimer about that and . . . stuff, after I got you safely back here."

"Stuff?" she asked with interest.

"I might have maybe punched him . . . a time or two," he admitted with a grimace. "I was a bit upset."

Elspeth bit her lip to keep from grinning at the words. Wyatt had always seemed so in control of himself since she'd met him. He'd seemed steady and commanding to her as he'd acted as bodyguard. And the way he'd pushed them both to the limit over and over while making love, and then pulled back, just to do it over again . . . She really didn't think most new life mates could have maintained the control to do that. But while he seemed in control of himself and the situation, he never tried to control her, or make her do anything she didn't want. That was part of the reason she loved him, Elspeth thought, and then blinked as she realized what she was thinking.

Loved him? Did she? Elspeth bit her lip. Yes, she did. He was polite, kind, gentle, yet strong and commanding, and she suspected would handle any situation thrown at him with calm reason . . . well, everything except Mortimer making him wait long enough for her to get shot, she thought with a smile.

"I'll have to apologize to him, I suppose," Wyatt muttered now. "Planning was the smart move. We had no idea what kind of situation we were running in to." Sighing, he nodded. "Yeah, I'll apologize."

Elspeth liked that about him too. He apologized when he thought he was wrong. And she'd also been impressed when he'd had no problem acknowledging that she, Alex, and Sam, as immortals, were stronger than him. He hadn't even seemed to mind. Most men would have been uncomfortable with that, she was sure, but Wyatt was confident enough to accept it without issue. He was a man well worth loving.

"Anyway, we rushed in just as he shot you. Mortimer and some hunter named Rickart got to Paul first, and I rushed to you."

"And they performed a three-on-one on Paul?" she asked.

"You did understand what I was trying to tell you," he said with amusement. "Anyway, Mortimer had the men take him back to the cells behind the Enforcer House.

The Council was called in last night, and apparently ordered a three-on-one done on him. Of course, I didn't know what that was until Marguerite explained."

Elspeth nodded and they both fell silent for a moment, and then Wyatt lifted her glass and asked, "More water?"

She nodded, but took it from him this time and handled the glass on her own, so Wyatt took the other glass, walked around the bed and slid in next to her.

"You're lucky it was me and not Meredith who walked in and caught you on your feet, Wyatt."

Elspeth glanced over at that comment and smiled at Lissianna as she entered the room.

"Mom wanted me to ask if you two are interested in food now, or . . ."

"I can wait for Merry to come back," Elspeth assured her when her voice trailed off.

"Me too," Wyatt agreed.

Lissianna nodded, but didn't leave right away. Instead, she dithered briefly, and then heaved a sigh and said, "And I'm to ask you if you feel up to speaking to your father?"

Elspeth stiffened in the bed. "Dad?"

Lissianna nodded. "Uncle Aloysius arrived just before they brought you back after you were shot. He was quite upset when he saw the shape you were in when G.G. carried you into the house," she added gently. "He wants to see you, but if you don't feel up to it . . ."

Elspeth delayed answering by drinking her water. She was worrying about why he was there. Was he going to try to guilt her into returning to England to please her mother? Her father had always done what he could to make her mother happy, and had almost always been on her mother's side. Would he be this time too? The only way to find out was to speak to him, she supposed, and finished her water before saying, "I'll see him."

Nodding, Lissianna turned and slid from the room.

"Do you want me to stay or go?" Wyatt asked solemnly.

"Stay," Elspeth said at once, alarmed at the mere thought of his leaving.

"Thank God," he muttered, squeezing her hand gently. "I would have tried to go if you wanted me to, but don't think I could have brought myself to leave you alone with him."

"Afraid he's here to drag me home?" she asked with a crooked smile.

"I won't let him," Wyatt said grimly.

"Neither will I," she assured him solemnly.

"And I will not try."

Elspeth glanced sharply to the door at that solemn comment, her eyes widening on her father. She'd thought he was downstairs and Lissianna had gone to get him, but he must have been in the hall to have arrived so quickly. And he'd obviously heard everything they'd said, Elspeth thought as she watched him approach the bed.

Aloysius Pimms had always seemed bigger than life to her. He was a beautiful man—dark hair, chiseled features, a generous mouth, and large silver-blue eyes with lashes so long and thick, any woman would have killed to have them. Aside from that, he'd always walked with an air of confidence that said there was nothing he feared. That confidence was lacking right now, however, she noted with surprise. Instead he appeared almost tentative.

Pausing at the side of the bed, he peered at her silently for a moment, several emotions crossing his face in succession and so swiftly she couldn't really track them, and then he shifted his gaze to Wyatt. Giving a nod, he murmured, "You must be my daughter's life mate, Wyatt. I didn't see you come in when you all returned to the house, but Marguerite has spoken well of you."

"You were busy calming Julianna and Victoria by the time G.G. carried me in," Wyatt said quietly.

"Ah, yes," her father said quietly. "Your grandmother doesn't know about us, or that my daughter turned you."

"No," Wyatt murmured.

Elspeth's father nodded, and then shifted his gaze almost reluctantly back to her. For a moment, he just stared at her, conflict on his face. Just when she thought he wasn't going to saying anything at all, he blurted, "Ellie, I'm sorry. I'm so sorry. I knew your mother had some issues, but I didn't realize how bad it had gotten."

Elspeth opened her mouth when he paused, but then closed it again, not sure what to say. He should have known. There had been enough evidence of it, she was sure, but as Greg had suggested, she suspected he'd been blind to it to avoid having to do something about it.

"Yes, perhaps that's true," her father said on a weary sigh as if she'd spoken aloud. "Looking back I can see the clues and evidence of what she was doing, and I probably should have realized that she was more than just a little overprotective and a touch too controlling. But I promise you, I certainly had no idea you'd met your life mate on your birthday when you went missing four years ago, and that she'd taken the memory from you. I never would have stood by for that."

Elspeth relaxed a little, and nodded solemnly before asking, "And now that you know?"

"I'll ensure nothing of the sort ever happens again. To you or your sisters," he vowed quietly.

Elspeth couldn't help the doubt that slid across her face. It wasn't that she doubted *him* so much as his *ability* to keep her mother from trying to control them again. It was so ingrained in Martine's personality now that Elspeth found it hard to believe anyone could rein her in. So she was rather shocked when her father added, "Your mother has agreed to see someone about her . . . issues."

"What?" she gasped with amazement.

Aloysius nodded solemnly. "It took some doing, but she's agreed to speak to a professional."

Elspeth figured the part about it taking some doing was the understatement of the century. By her guess it had probably taken a battle royal to get her mother to agree to such a concession. Possibly even the threat of his leaving her.

"Yes. That's what it took," he agreed solemnly, obviously reading her thoughts again. "But she agreed, so I don't have to give her up, and all is well."

"Thank you, Daddy," Elspeth whispered, knowing how hard making that ultimatum must have been for him. Her father didn't make idle threats. Had Martine not agreed to counseling, he would have left. Which was probably the only reason her mother had agreed to seek counseling. Elspeth didn't know what that meant. Whether the counseling would do her mother any good or not when she was only going to appease her husband, but it was better than nothing, she supposed.

"I think it might be best if you sought counseling too," he added now, and when she stiffened, he added quickly, "To deal with any damage your mother's behavior and my lack of action may have caused. I don't want the rest of your life affected by it. I'll pay, of course. There's no need for you to cash in one of your bonds or—" He paused abruptly, his gaze narrowing on her forehead as confusion covered her face. "You didn't know about the bonds that were signed over to you at twenty-five," he said slowly with a frown and then sagged slightly and shook his head, muttering almost to himself, "Your mother said she'd told you, but of course she didn't. You might have used them to gain your independence."

He ran a weary hand around the back of his neck, and then let it drop and said, "We can talk about that later. In fact, we can talk about everything later. I don't want to wear you out while you are still healing. If you are willing to speak again later?" he added quickly.

"Yes, of course," Elspeth said at once, and then, because he looked so uncertain, she added, "I love you, Daddy."

A smile lifted his lips and he bent to press a kiss to her forehead, murmuring, "I love you too, baby girl. Everything will work out," he added as he straightened. "This is the best thing for your mother. For all of us."

"Yes," she agreed solemnly, because he seemed to need the reassurance. Besides, while she wasn't sure it would help, it might, and certainly couldn't hurt.

Nodding as if in agreement with her thoughts, Elspeth's father squeezed her shoulder and then held his hand out to Wyatt. "Welcome to the family, son. I hope to speak to you later as well and get to know you better . . . if you are willing?"

"Of course . . . sir," Wyatt added the title of respect in a slightly bemused voice. Elspeth smiled faintly, knowing how odd it was speaking to a man you knew was your partner's father, but who looked younger than yourself. Or at least, younger than Wyatt had looked when she'd first met him. While she knew he was thirty-six, he'd come out of the turn looking younger, although Meredith didn't appear to have noticed yet.

"Until later, then," her father said quietly, and then kissed her forehead again before leaving the room.

"Well, that was encouraging," Wyatt breathed as her father pulled the bedroom door closed behind him.

"Yes," Elspeth agreed. It *was* encouraging. Her father had convinced her mother to go for counseling. That meant they at least had a chance at a future relationship.

"A little bizarre, but encouraging," Wyatt added.

Elspeth turned on him with surprise. "Bizarre?"

"The guy looks younger than you do," he pointed out with a shake of the head. "Or at least the same age."

"Ah," she murmured, relaxing.

"And he looks like a male model, or an actor, or something. I mean, he could play Bond. He has the accent and everything," Wyatt added.

"Yeah, he does," she said with a grin.

"Between him and your mother, it's no wonder you're so gorgeous."

"Sweet talker," Elspeth said on a chuckle that turned into a husky cough.

"You need more water," Wyatt said with concern and turned to grab the glass from the bedside table, only to frown when he saw it was empty. "Hang on."

He was up at once and hurrying to the table to refill the glass from the pitcher that rested there.

"Here," he said, hurrying back to offer her the glass.

"Thank you," Elspeth murmured, accepting the water and gulping half of it down as he slid into bed next to her again.

"Do you want more?" Wyatt asked, taking the empty

glass from her when she finished downing the second half.

Elspeth shook her head at once. "No, thank you. I'm good. Besides, you shouldn't be running around. What if Meredith came back in while you—?"

"Yeah, I know," he interrupted on a sigh and set the glass back on the bedside table. "I have to stay in bed for the next two weeks."

"Three," she corrected him apologetically.

Groaning, Wyatt flopped onto his back next to her. "Three weeks stuck in bed."

"It won't be so bad," she said reassuringly. "I'll keep you company."

"Yeah?" he asked, turning on his side and propping his head on one hand to peer at her.

"Yeah," she assured him. "And the good news is, Paul has been caught and is no longer a threat."

"That *is* good news," he agreed.

"Which means no more bodyguards," Elspeth pointed out.

Wyatt stilled at the words.

"We can spend three weeks in bed. Alone," she added.

"Alone in bed for three weeks," he said with a slow smile, and reached out to run his fingers lightly over her cheek. His smile then faded and his expression became serious and he said solemnly, "I love you, El. You may not be ready to hear that, or—"

Elspeth pressed her fingers to his lips to silence him, and when he raised his eyebrows, said, "I *am* ready. I love you too, Wyatt."

He stayed completely still for a heartbeat, and then asked, "Are you sure?"

"Oh yes," she assured him. "How could I not? You're a good man, Wyatt. A strong man, a smart man, a considerate one, and you're an amazing lover with loads of control and, as Lissianna put it, a monster between your legs. How could I not love you?"

Wyatt blinked. Then a laugh slipped from his lips and he pulled her into his arms, hugging her tightly. "Damn, I'm the luckiest man," he growled, and pulled back to assure her, "I'm still going to woo you. You deserve wooing, Elspeth. We'll go to the movies, eat popcorn, go to The Night Club and dance. And you have to go on girls' nights with Lissianna and the other gals too, 'cause I plan to hang out with G.G. once in a while," he announced almost apologetically. "But we'll visit museums and the science center, and—Oh! I'm going to take you camping."

"Camping?" she said uncertainly.

"Yeah, you'll love it," he assured her. "A little tent, a hibachi, sleeping bags, making love in the woods and the lake. I'm going to show you such a good time, we'll . . ."

Elspeth smiled at Wyatt's enthusiasm as he painted a future for them that was miles away from the life she'd had under her mother's control. Catching him by surprise, she rolled him onto his back and shifted to straddle him.

Wyatt fell silent at once, his eyes widening, and his hands reaching to clasp her hips as he began to harden under her.

"I think you need to start showing me a good time now, Wyatt," she whispered.

"Oh El," he breathed, running his hands up her back. "Didn't I tell you we just seemed to jibe that first time we met? We did," he assured her. "And we are now too, because there's nothing I'd like more in the world than to show you a good time."

Smiling, Elspeth bent to kiss him, already anticipating his showing her that control she loved so much. She was a lucky woman.

ABOUT GOLLANCZ

Gollancz is the oldest SF publishing imprint in the world. Since being founded in 1927 Gollancz has continued to publish a focused selection of bestselling and award-winning authors. The front-list includes **Ben Aaronovitch**, **Joe Abercrombie**, **Charlaine Harris**, **Joanne Harris**, **Joe Hill**, **Alastair Reynolds**, **Patrick Rothfuss**, **Nalini Singh** and **Brandon Sanderson**.

As one of the largest Science Fiction and Fantasy imprints in the UK it is no surprise we have one of the most extensive backlists in the world. Find high-quality SF on Gateway written by such authors as **Philip K. Dick**, **Ursula Le Guin**, **Connie Willis**, **Sir Arthur C. Clarke**, **Pat Cadigan**, **Michael Moorcock** and **George R.R. Martin**.

We also have a strand of publishing in translation, which includes French, Polish and Russian authors. Gollancz is home to more award-winning authors than any other imprint, with names including **Aliette de Bodard**, **M. John Harrison**, **Paul McAuley**, **Sarah Pinborough**, **Pierre Pevel**, **Justina Robson** and many more.

The SF Gateway
More than 3,000 classic, rare and previously out-of-print SF novels at your fingertips.
www.sfgateway.com

The Gollancz Blog
Bringing you news from our worlds to yours. Stories, interviews, articles and exclusive extracts just for you!
www.gollancz.co.uk

GOLLANCZ
LONDON

BRINGING NEWS FROM OUR WORLDS TO YOURS . . .

Want your news daily?

The Gollancz blog has instant updates on the hottest SF and Fantasy books.

Prefer your updates monthly?

Sign up for our in-depth newsletter.

www.gollancz.co.uk

Follow us 🐦 @gollancz

Find us 📘 facebook.com/GollanczPublishing

Classic SF as you've never read it before.

Visit the SF Gateway to find out more!

www.sfgateway.com